Antipodes Series / Book 5

SESSRÚMNIR

Antipodes Series / Book 5

SESSRÚMNIR

T.S. SIMONS

4 Horsemen Publications, Inc.
1497 Main St. Suite 169
Dunedin, FL 34698
4horsemenpublications.com
info@4horsemenpublications.com

Typeset by Valerie Willis
Cover Design by Jenn Kotick

Library of Congress Control Number: 2021951238

Print ISBN: 978-1-64450-383-6
Audio ISBN: 978-1-64450-381-2
EBook ISBN: 978-1-64450-382-9

To the special people in my life who are there when I need them most, support me through the tough times, and share in the celebrations, I appreciate you more than I can say. *Tha gaol agam ort.*

Lewis
Newgrange

Melbourne
Kerguelen Islands
August Island
Auckland Island
Bellcamp Island

Arnol
Carloway
LEWIS
Callanish
Stornoway
Garrynahine
Leurbost
Balallan
Tarbert
HARRIS

CONTENTS

ACKNOWLEDGEMENTS:

WHO KNEW WRITING WAS a team sport? I would not have made it this far without the support of my fellow authors who celebrate the highs and share the challenges. Those who lift each other up and share opportunities—you are all wonderful, talented authors, and I am blessed to have you in my world. Debra, Stevie, Serafina, Chelle—you ladies are everything. I look forward to our banter and thank you for checking in and keeping me on track. I wish you every success in your own writing journey and thank you for sharing mine.

To my family, friends, and colleagues, thank you for the unwavering support. Knowing you have people in your circle who always have your back makes navigating life that little bit easier.

Jen–thank you for the wonderful editing support. I really appreciate all your guidance and apologize for perplexing you with my quirky Australianisms.

Caitlin–I hope you like this one, though I suspect you will like *The Latitude Series* even more. I can't wait to hear what you think.

If you enjoyed this book, it would mean a great deal to me if you could spare a few minutes to leave a quick review on GoodReads, Amazon, BookBub, or any other platform.

GoodReads: www.goodreads.com/author/show/20861749.T_S_Simons

Amazon: www.amazon.com/T-S-Simons/e/B08MT6YYDL

Bookbub: www.bookbub.com/profile/t-s-simons

CHAPTER 1

THE LONG, LOW WHISTLE from behind me signaled approval.

"Where are you off to, all tarted up?"

Putting the hairbrush down, I smoothed the flyaway strands near my face and checked the results. "Dinner."

"With?" Illy asked coyly.

"Stefan, if you must know."

"Well, haven't you come a long way. You said you couldn't stand him. Called him an arrogant twat. Now he is getting all this." A sweep of her hand illustrated this. My better clothes, to be sure. It wasn't like I had a lot of opportunities to wear them. But it was enjoyable to dress up occasionally, even if it was just my newer jeans and a heather gray cashmere sweater that set off my green eyes.

Ignoring Illy's taunts as I pulled on my cleanest boots and zipped up the sides, I had to admit she was right. Initially, Stefan had got on my nerves, been blatantly rude and arrogant, and he and I had more than one raging argument. I had come far too close on multiple occasions to throwing something solid at his head and storming out, telling him where to shove his traineeship. As the senior orthopedic surgeon on Clava, they had assigned me to him, and he took every opportunity to let me know his seniority and that he considered me underqualified. Despite my veterinary training and years of experience, shifting to orthopedic medicine had been a steep learning curve, but one I had enjoyed immensely, after I had overcome the weeks of sleeplessness and brain overload. Lewis had finally recognized that the community needed a specialist, broken bones being a common occurrence, and Clava had offered a six-month traineeship. The medical team had chosen me, despite my lack of medical training on humans. As head of the medical team, Sorcha had insisted I take the opportunity to train for six months on Clava after six years of working in that role in a de facto capacity on Lewis, especially now that the original population had more than tripled. The intention was that I would remain a full-time vet and only assist in a medical capacity when needed, and specifically on orthopedic cases. Despite this agreement, I found myself increasingly working on humans for more routine surgeries and felt guilty for Isla shouldering the veterinary load.

Illy was still watching as I checked my reflection one last time and turned. "You know he was one of the men they trotted out for me as a potential partner on Clava?"

I snorted. "He told me. You weren't interested. Why? Do you want him now?"

Illy neatly dodged the question. "What about Cam?"

"What about him?" I was not engaging in this line of questioning, especially not with my best friend.

"No chance then?"

"Why? Do you want him now?"

Illy raised her eyebrows at me derisively but said nothing.

"He is available, you know. You wanted him once before. You have been single for nearly seven years. If you want to go there, I won't stop you."

Illy raised her eyebrows at the insinuation. "I think we both know that will never happen."

"Not my business if you do. Is Summer feeling better?"

"She is okay." Illy's abrupt tone indicated she knew I was deflecting and didn't want to engage.

"She is a lucky girl. Whatever it was she ingested, it was pretty potent."

"Well, she can chew iron and spit rust, as Luca used to say. He always said she would turn into a keg on legs when she hit thirteen. I suspect her size may have helped."

"I wish he could see them now. All of them."

Illy smiled, but it didn't reach her eyes. Even after all these years, losing Luca was still foremost in her mind. How could it not be, with four children to raise? Two of whom he had never met.

Shrugging on my jacket, I placed my hand on the doorknob, still thinking of Luca. The love he and Illy had shared. The love I thought Cam and I had shared. But twenty years is a long time. *Maybe we have just grown apart,* I rationalized. *We were so young when we met.*

"Don't wait...." My last words were cut off by the harsh bleeping of the radio going off in the kitchen. Knowing it was likely for me, I lingered in the doorway. Maybe this was a stroke of luck. Kissing me goodnight two nights ago, Stefan had invited me to stay over, his intentions not disguised. I had struggled to make excuses and get away, still feeling awkward around him. While he was self-assured and confident, now that he treated me like an equal, he was also knowledgeable and easy to talk to. *Why am I so scared of this?* I berated myself. *I never had issues with shagging a stranger before. And it isn't like Stefan is even a stranger.*

Illy returned, radio in hand.

"No dinner for you, glamor puss. Mike has been thrown from a horse. They need you at the med center. Now."

Peeling off my cashmere sweater and heading into my room to change, I called back over my shoulder, "Did they say what injuries?"

Illy whistled after me. "Got the sexy stuff on. Planning to get lucky, were we?"

Ignoring her, I quickly changed into work clothes and looked at her expectantly.

Illy scanned my old t-shirt and jeans before responding, "Complicated fractures of the clavicle, arm, and several ribs."

Smiling, I nodded.

Illy grinned. "I know you enjoy your job, but you probably shouldn't smile at someone else's misfortune."

Quickly rearranging my face to something more appropriate, I saw Illy's nod of approval. "I'll make your excuses for you."

"Thanks, Ils. Appreciate it. Don't wait up for me."

"Try not to wake the kids when you get home."

"Sorry. I didn't mean it. I fell over one of the cats..."

"I know. Go."

Driving one of the uncomfortably tiny two-seater electric cars over to Garynahine, I pondered moving permanently into the main village. Caitlin, age six, was the only one of my children who couldn't drive one of the many cars gifted to us by Clava. Allegedly given as thanks for re-activating the portal, part of me firmly believed it was an apology for what they did to me. Shaking my head to dispel the awful memories, I thought again about the children. Aside from Cait, the rest could visit me. It wasn't like they woke from nightmares and needed me anymore. Cait, my biological daughter and one of the special ones who could live outside the domes, was a child I hadn't given birth to. Despite this, Cait was exactly like her sister Katrin, strong-willed, highly intelligent, independent, and carefree. So much so that I had often wondered who her father was. *No one needed me*, I thought with an unexpected twinge of pain. I loved living with Illy but wondered if I was cramping her style. If things continued to get serious with Stefan... well, perhaps it was best I was away from my former life. I was still angry at Cam, but I didn't need to rub his face in my fledgling relationship, especially when Illy's and Cam's houses were joined.

As I entered the small but modern clinic, Sorcha greeted me with a brisk nod. At least she and I were on cordial terms after our huge blow-up several weeks ago. She gave me a detailed handover, making it clear that she was handing Mike over to me to take the lead on his surgery. *Perhaps she is headed home?* I glanced out the window as the stars twinkled through the dome. Before she left, I quizzed her about the location and severity of the breaks and asked to see the scans. As I reviewed the images, making mental notes about the repairs required to tackle the complicated fractures, and the order in which to address them, I wondered if Sorcha and I would ever be close again. Even though we had both apologized for our part in the argument, and she had later admitted that I was right, she was still cool toward me. Then again, her loyalties would always be with her brother. It hadn't been until Stefan had arrived, and he had backed my methods, that she had thawed. But by that point, the damage was done.

As I prepped for surgery, Sorcha scrubbed in beside me. I scrubbed silently, running the procedure through my head. As I dried my hands, she held out the towel for me, her eyes meeting mine. *Am I ready?*

Several hours later as I slipped into my cool bed, I longed for the warmth of a body to share it with. After all these years, I was surprised to realize one of the things I missed most was the simple act of cuddling with someone, decompressing, chatting about my day. I should reschedule that dinner with Stefan in the morning. It was time to move on. Cam and I could continue to co-parent. The children all knew they were loved. They flitted between both homes daily, seemingly unaffected. Children here were raised by the village, anyway. Over the twenty years since these communities had been established, many couples had paired up and separated. Many had unusual living situations where the old partner and the new all lived together. Since we had reactivated the portal and rejoined the Nexus nearly seven years ago, migration to and from each community had increased. Learning people had friends or relatives in other communities, or even isolated communities, many people had arrived or moved away, often unexpectedly. Old partners sought to reconcile, causing a bit of angst in a new place. Even I had considered moving somewhere else, away from the memories.

Clattering in the kitchen woke me, and I staggered in without even checking my face in the mirror. Illy grinned at my disheveled state as I pushed the mass of hair out of my eyes.

"Morning. You came in late."

"Did I wake you? I tried to be quiet."

"It is fine, really. I don't sleep well knowing that you are traveling in the dark."

"Sorry, Mum." I smirked at her. Despite her diminutive stature, and being only a few years older than me, Illy managed all in her realm with a quiet ferocity. The twins were twelve and still attending the village school, along with my younger children, Xanthe, Thorsten, and Cait. Katrin was taking a week off and was due to start her apprenticeship, as all the children did when they reached the age of fifteen. With no formal exams and no colleges, they were all billeted out to professionals around Lewis aligned to their strengths and interests and passing whatever tests the professional set. Katrin, highly intelligent, and with a flair for maths and science, desperately wanted to become a doctor. She would be the first, the only candidate, who had met Sorcha's exacting standards and had passed every test Sorcha had set. As the medical center director, Sorcha was the boss, and she made sure everyone knew it. I suspected that she had been even harder on Kat when it came to assessments, not wanting to be seen to be playing favorite to her niece. But Kat passed with flying colors, and several of the other doctors had already told me how much they were looking forward to welcoming her to the team.

Louis was already apprenticed to Fraser and had proven a valuable addition to the agricultural team. Sorcha's eldest Sam had been apprenticed to Bridget for the past two years and would soon take over the teaching of the younger children himself, splitting the workload between them. A natural teacher, he was engaging, positive, but firm. Aroha, Jacinda's eldest, had been apprenticed to her mother as a natural healer for years. Builders, engineers, electricians all had assistants now, learning the role they would one day take responsibility for.

Illy's youngest two, Alasdair and Seraphine, were the same age as Cait, and couldn't be more different. Although Seraphine was Luca's biological child, she was also mine, and one of only two special children where we had been told the father's identity. Sera had been genetically engineered along with twenty-six others to be resistant to the Vienna virus and was immune to the protozoa's effects. While Luca and I had been the best of friends, our genes were not compatible in producing compliant children. Sera was sharp, witty, and had a wicked sense of humor. Many nights Illy and I had tried hard not to laugh over the things she had said and done during the day.

"Remember when we thought Summer and Ally were challenging?" she had groaned one day after she learned that Seraphine had used tree sap to stick the pages closed on the schoolbooks—Sera's payback after Bridget had forced her to read aloud for talking during class.

"She is so naughty, but I can't help but laugh at how creative she is! Between her and Caitlin, I am surprised poor Bridget hasn't had a breakdown by now. Do you remember the time they painted Bridget's chair with brown paint?"

"I do," Illy groaned. "I spent hours trying to get it out of Bridget's clothing! Why can't she be like Alasdair?"

Alasdair was calm and compliant. A dream child. So very different from his sisters and the second child that Luca had never met. But he looked like his father. Solid in stature, he was a big unit, but so quiet I often forgot he was there.

"You know Luca would have adored her. Egged her on."

"I know. It is bad enough that Ally and Summer encourage her. Imagine him too!"

"Between Sera and Cait, I'm not sure Lewis is ready for them to reach the teenage years. Can you imagine those two raging with hormones?"

"No boy will be safe."

"Darling, *we* won't be safe! Every parent here will hate us!"

"I've been thinking of moving to Garynahine," I announced between bites of toast. "Kat isn't used to the long hours she will need to work, including night shifts, and she will do better if she is living there and not commuting every day. She needs to study in the evenings, and it is best if she is near the medical resources and not distracted by the others. But I need to keep an eye on her. She can live with me and then you can have your home back. I feel like I arrived one day with a bag, and here I am, three months later."

Illy looked up from her bowl of porridge. "Frey, this is killing your 0ame man for nearly twenty years, it is bound to feel different.

Allegedly to be closer to his cousin, Aidan, Stefan moved here several weeks ago and joined the medical team. Numerous times he had invited me over for dinner, and I knew he liked me. We were both of an age where time wasn't worth wasting. I just wasn't convinced I was ready for a new relationship. With five children in my former home, and twenty-three others technically mine, but not raised by me, I wasn't sure any man would want to be part of my hot mess of a life. But he seemed to like me, despite our initial disagreements. While I didn't find him physically attractive, he challenged me and was intelligent and witty. His sons were in their late teens and had stayed with his former partner on Clava, although he spoke to them daily by radio. Maybe it was time to get my own place and move on? It would be nice to have conversations with someone about intellectual topics, not reverting to constantly talking about children and what they were up to.

It took me some time to locate the head builder who looked at me appraisingly when I asked him for a small vacant cottage in the village, something near the medical center. I could sense the question, "Why?" on the tip of his tongue, and quickly explained about Kat needing somewhere close to her new workplace, medical training being long and unsocial hours, and not wanting her to travel the road to Roseglen in the dark. Joel had teenage daughters of his own and nodded understanding. He had something coming up, but it needed a minor renovation.

"So, within a month, then?" I pushed gently, wanting a firm answer.

"Aye," he agreed. "That should do it. There is no bathroom, and there is dry rot in some of the walls. Everyone wants their own private bathroom now, and the communal ones are no longer in use. So it isn't habitable just now."

"Thank you." I tried to be charming but realized it was not my strong suit. I was far better at being direct. "I really appreciate it. I'm keen to start moving our things in as soon as we can. We don't mind a little mess. We can always shower at the medical center."

It was early, so I checked in on Mike, who was still asleep, before heading off on my rounds of the northern crofts. The day passed uneventfully, and after finishing my veterinary load, I was able to drop in and chat to Mike, assessing his recovery. It had been a nasty fall, and I was still concerned about the severity of his concussion and the potential for an acquired brain injury.

"No more riding until you are cleared," I ordered, and he grimaced.

"Can I deal with Sorcha instead?" he wheedled. "She understands."

"No, you may not. I'm the lead on your case, and I say no riding."

Sorcha was also horse-mad, and according to Cam, always had been. I was surprised she hadn't apprenticed her son Sam to Mike so that she could justify spending all of her non-working hours there. Perhaps she would send Kendra in a few years? Kendra also adored horses, although I hoped to apprentice her to Isla or one of the other vets. A calm, patient girl who loved animals, she would make a fabulous addition to the veterinary team.

I spent some time speaking with Mike, assessing his cognitive skills, but saw no cause for alarm. He was in pain, and recovery would be slow. But he was strong and willing to put in the time and effort for rehabilitation, so his prognosis was good.

Stefan arrived late in the afternoon, but with other staff around, it was hard to talk. That was probably just as well. I wasn't ready for other people to know my business, I realized, feeling the old me returning. I desperately wanted to keep my private life private, keeping my feelings safe and closed off. Life with Cam had been an open book. Everyone knew us and everything that happened in our lives. I enjoyed having something that was just mine. My stomach fluttered, making me nervous. I just wasn't sure if this was excitement or anxiety I was feeling.

We skirted around each other for the handover period, not able to slip in anything other than a furtive kiss goodbye in the hallway as I went to leave.

"Are we still on for dinner tomorrow?" I whispered.

"No," he oozed into my ear. "I can't wait. I have been dancing around the most brilliant, sexy woman for months, longing for you, and I don't want to wait anymore. I want you. I finish work in four hours. Come over and spend the night?"

My heart lurched, and I froze at his straightforward request. Knowing I needed to give him an answer and sensing the discomfort mounting, I nodded in agreement.

"Go," he oozed into my ear. "Grab something to eat at home. I'll grab a bite here. I don't want to waste any more time." He kissed me thoroughly, and I stepped through the door into the night, still feeling his mouth on mine. With a buzzing feeling in my belly, I drove home to Roseglen, wondering what it would be like to be with someone else after all these years. Feeling tingly with apprehension, I shivered into my jacket as I sped through the dark.

CHAPTER 2

"PACK A BAG."

Deep in thought, I jerked up from the sink at the sound of Illy's voice, splashing water onto my shoes. The bowl encrusted with pumpkin soup one of the kids had refused to eat the night before was still in my hand. Illyria, Summer, Ally, and I took turns, and this was my week to wash dishes, but being late home from surgery the previous night, they had piled up. Trust Illy not to let me get out of it.

"What? Later. Let me..."

"Pack. A. Bag."

I dropped the bowl I had been mindlessly scrubbing back into the water with a splash. "Now? I just..."

"Now, Freyja." Illy's steely tone made me turn to look at her. She thrust a tea towel at me to dry my hands.

"Where are we going?"

"No questions. Leave the dishes."

While ordinarily, I would have skipped away with glee at the thought of leaving the dishes, one of my most detested chores, there was something unreadable about Illy's face. She was fighting to maintain control.

Opening my mouth, she cut me off. "For once in your fucking life, don't fight me. Do what I ask. Now."

In the many years we had been friends, Illy had never spoken to me like that. Instinct made me want to argue, tell her to fuck off. But it was the tone. The harsh, emotionless tone. She was hiding something.

"Pack as much as you can, all seasons. Take your hiking boots and wet weather gear," she instructed as she stood in the doorway to my bedroom, confirming I was following orders.

Fuck. So we were going outside. Again.

As I changed in front of the mirror, I glanced down at my patchwork stomach, riddled with scars. Perhaps it was better than Stefan never saw them. He knew what Clava had done to me, but there is knowing something as an abstract thought, and there is seeing the evidence with your own eyes. I ran my finger over them. A cesarean scar for each of my three children, countless stretch marks, and scars from two keyhole surgeries. As I held out my arms to pull them through the sleeves of my top, I saw the faded cuts riddled along those as well. Cam had always described my scars as life marks and insisted he didn't see them. After all, he had several of his own. I wondered if Stefan would feel the same way. As I packed, a million scenarios flitted through my mind, but I couldn't process them. I felt like I was tipping letters down a well in a snowstorm, unable to grasp any of them.

I could hear Illy barking instructions somewhere else in the house, curt and sharp. Military mode. She only reverted to that when something was really wrong.

"When do you want to leave?" I called as I zipped up my backpack and glanced out the window to see the stars twinkling through the transparent fabric of the dome. "Morning?"

"Now." Illy reappeared in my doorway, looking grim, her own backpack on her back, swamping her tiny frame. "We go now."

"Where..."

"No questions. I will tell you everything. Not now."

Outside I could see several electric cars being started, the lights blinking through the windows, the chatter of children audible.

"Who..."

"*Not now!*" she snapped. "Move."

I gasped as I saw the light glint on Luca's gun in her belt, the ammunition clip fastened on the other side. Summer and Ally were standing in the doorway, watching. Fear etched into their beautiful, youthful faces. Summer looked so much like Luca, her large brown eyes looking up at her mother.

"You will be fine," Illy soothed. "I love you so very much. Take care of each other, and for goodness' sake, eat some vegetables while I am gone. I don't want to hear that you have contracted scurvy through stupidity."

"Mum..." Summer pleaded.

"I told you. I can't tell you anything. It is better this way. But promise me you will stay together. Always. You can sleep in my room. Stay away from boys. That is an order. And remember what I taught you."

"Hit first, ask questions later?"

Illy grinned. "That too. Take care of each other."

Nodding in unison, the girls stood shoulder to shoulder. Ally, small, calculating, and razor-sharp, like her mother. Summer was more solid in stature and effervescent in personality. Both dark-haired and with a character of steel.

"They aren't coming with us?" I asked, curiously. *So maybe we aren't going far. Clava maybe?*

"Only the little ones. Seraphine and Alasdair of mine. Caitlin of yours."

"Why...?"

"For fuck's sake, Freyja. Just get in, will you!"

Illy dropped her backpack into the footwell of the backseat as she helped Sera and Alasdair climb over it. I placed mine in the adjoining footwell and climbed into the passenger seat.

Without a glance back, she started heading up the track toward Garynahine. Two other vehicles were following, but I couldn't see who it was in the dark. Illy's grim-lipped silence scared me more than this late evening flight from our homes. Sera and Alasdair were clinging to each other in the back seat as Illy drove faster than she usually would in the dark.

It didn't take long for me to realize that Stornoway harbor was where we were headed. A place I had done my best to avoid for the past seven years. Aside from my recent travel to Clava, and my annual trip through the Nexus to visit my children, I rarely went anywhere. After spending years traveling or on rescue missions, I felt safe here. This was home.

Sorcha was already aboard the *Eurydice*, the lights shining on the dock, lighting our passage. She was issuing orders at Sam and Di. Her daughters, Mei and Kendra, were lurking in the shadows, trying to stay out of the way.

"Where are the others?" Sorcha barked at Illy, who responded in kind.

"Behind us."

Helping the kids and lifting my backpack from the footwell, I saw Cam pull up with Cait, Isla's daughter Rani, and Jacinda's youngest Arataki, plus Ruby and Scarlett. All special ones, immune to the protozoa. The vehicle behind, driven by Louis, contained the remaining six special children on Lewis, all piled in on top of each other, bags crammed into every spare space.

My stomach lurched at the sight of Cam, but I turned before he saw me. Bloody hell. I didn't get a chance to tell Stefan I was leaving. *How many dates can I cancel before he thinks I am a flake?* I wondered. He would be home from work soon and waiting for me. *Will he think I stood him up?* I didn't even have time to leave him a message. Something was obviously wrong with the girls, and Alasdair was only six, although it made no sense why Kendra and Sam were with us. Louis appeared to be unloading baggage but not boarding.

Following Sorcha onto the bridge, I opened my mouth to ask, but Sorcha cut me off as she started the engines.

"I know you have questions, and we will answer them. All of them. In private. But can we just get moving? We will have plenty of time later."

Grumbling, I agreed. "What do you want me to do?"

"Settle the kids into cabins. Try to keep them together. We have a long way to go tonight, and it is best if they get some sleep."

CHAPTER 3

SETTLING TEN EXCITED CHILDREN under ten into three bedrooms took hours, with lots of giggling, squabbling, and stealing of pillows and blankets. Inflatable mattresses were loads of fun apparently, and I lost count of how many times I threatened not to inflate it again if someone let it down. But the saddened face of the sleeper made me relent. Squeals of laughter echoed through the halls as they negotiated space, ran from room to room, whispered to keep each other awake, and cried when they realized they were away from their parents and not going to sleep in their own homes. Feeling the movement under my feet, it was nearly dawn before I resurfaced, exhausted. Sam and Alasdair were sharing a cabin with Cam. Kendra had agreed to stay with her sister, Mei. Scarlett and Ruby, being older, would bunk in with me when I made it to bed. All were terrified. Louis had looked especially fearful as he had waved us off. Given what had happened to his birth mother, that wasn't surprising. As desperately as I wanted to sleep, right now, I wanted answers.

"Right," I demanded, storming into the cabin where Sorcha was piloting the vessel at top speed. "Enough. I want to know why this ridiculous excursion, with a shitload of kids, at night and with no notice."

"Agreed. While you have been settling the kids, we have made great time. We need to make one quick stop at Mousa, and then we have all the time in the world for you to ask any questions you like. I assume you want all the story in one sitting?"

"Where are we going?" I growled, sleep deprivation making me less tolerant than usual.

Sorcha ignored my question, set the autopilot, and stepped into the main cabin. Cam was sitting at the table, a steaming mug of tea in hand. He looked terrible. Grey and haggard. Maybe he hadn't been sleeping? My attention was distracted by Illy, who started firing off directions in her no-nonsense tone.

"First thing. We urgently need to collect samples of the moss so we can transport it. Campbell, you've read the files we took from Auckland. We need you."

Cam looked up from his mug, his shoulders slumping from weariness, but nodded agreement. "How much?"

"As much as you can collect in an hour? But a lot, okay? We desperately need those samples. Take a bucket to keep them in. Two if you can. Take some bottles of uncontaminated water to rinse them and store the samples in. Wear gloves. We can't stop for long. We need to get going."

"Sorcha, can you salvage what building materials you can? Sam, can help you load it into the hold? Sheets of iron, especially. The building teams on Lewis are always running short. Frey, I need you to see what you can salvage from the huts on the island.

They must have had something of value—cooking pots, weapons, knives, anything that could be useful. Metal especially. We are running low, and it is a lot easier to repurpose than needing to go outside to smelt more."

"Di, I need you…"

Illy's crisp orders continued, and I zoned out. I had been functioning for thirty-six hours on very little sleep. No one would tell me why we were making this random trip, with children, no less. All of my genetically modified children living on Lewis were here, even the two older ones. A party, perhaps? It was three months until their birthdays. But why the moss samples? Exhaustion from the past few days made my eyes droop, and with Illy's voice droning in the background, I felt the warm blanket of sleep overtake me as my head rolled back on the sofa.

The stillness of mooring in shallow water woke me, along with the sound of chattering voices. Grumbling about wanting to sleep, I forced my eyes to open, blinking back the savage tears from waking in full light. Someone had placed a blanket over me as I slept, and I threw it aside, cranky at being taken on this ridiculous expedition, exhausted and now woken before I was ready.

Illy handed me an apple as I staggered ashore, following Cam and Sorcha, veering in the opposite direction as soon as we were off the pier. I did not want a conversation in this remote location and with no sleep. The sooner we got this bizarre and random mission finished, the better. Finishing my inadequate breakfast and tossing the core into the ocean, I headed into the closest house. Cautiously, I pushed open the sticky old door to see what I could salvage.

Why on earth did we need to raid this place? Surely the mainland was a better bet? This was a dump and stank like rancid public toilets. A filthy stained mattress lay on the floor, rubbish littering every corner. I cringed, both at the stench and envisioning what would have happened to Isla and the others here. What could have happened to me at the farm near Inverness, and likely not on a mattress.

Opening the single broken cupboard in the ramshackle kitchen, I poked around. A single chipped ceramic teacup. Two plates, browned and cracked from disuse. I opened the drawer and pulled out the single cast-iron pot, rusted, but salvageable. In the distance I heard the engines of the *Eurydice* start up, followed by a man yelling. Cam's voice.

Carrying the pot to the doorway, my jaw dropped as I watched the *Eurydice* pulling away, and Cam storming down the unstable and rickety jetty, yelling and waving his arms. A large wooden crate at his feet. He kicked it, and I grinned as he hobbled around the jetty on one foot. *Serves him right. Maybe he will do me a favor and fall in?*

I watched from the doorway as he plucked a single piece of paper from the top, read it, screwed it up, and threw it after the rapidly departing *Eurydice*. The paper fell weakly onto the timbers before the wind picked it up, rolling it back, and deposited it back at his feet.

"What?" I snapped, unable to remove the animosity from my voice.

"Fucking left us!" he raged.

"Can see that, genius. Why?"

Cam retrieved the piece of paper, unscrewed it, and held it up for me to see. Even at the distance I stood, I could read the words printed in large black lettering.

"Sort. It. Out."

Assholes. This had Illy and Sorcha written all over it. Pretending to be in a rush, only to ditch us here. But why bring the kids? Turning away, I escaped the reek of the cabin and headed over the dunes. I refused to be forced into something I no longer wanted. They would come back in a few days and see that it was over. We could go back to Lewis and start over. It was definitely time to move into town. I would need to harass Joel to renovate faster, bump the cottage up the works list. We didn't need a bathroom. Stefan was looking more attractive by the minute. Bloody Illy and her meddling.

Not wanting to stay here, to be near him, I craved space, solitude. The deep blue ocean surrounded the tiny atoll, extending as far as I could see. I set off down the beach, the wind fighting me as I walked, soothing my spirit. I found a protected cove and sat, gazing over the ocean.

As dusk fell, I returned to the pier, not wanting to navigate in the dark. Breaking my leg would top this off nicely. Checking the horizon in all directions, I saw no sign of life in the dim light. No lights other than the setting sun and the first few stars poking through the blackness. I felt my frustration rise again. Fuckers weren't messing around. They really had dumped us here. Checking the crate on the dock, I found a double sleeping bag, two blankets, a single butane-fired camping cooktop, and a large box of canned food and water. So they were planning to leave us here for some time then. Fine. I had patience in spades and could outlast them. All I needed was sleep.

Cam was sitting in the doorway to the broch, watching me. Ignoring him completely, I picked up the top two cans without even checking what they were, the blankets, and some matches. The cabin I had inspected first was mostly intact. I could sleep there.

The matches, old and brittle, took forever to light, and swearing profusely, I broke more than half the box in an attempt to light a fire in the small open fireplace within the cabin, not aided by the damp kindling. Using the pot I had salvaged, after wiping it out with the stained, threadbare sheet, I heated the can of baked beans as hot as I dared. It was freezing now that the sun had set. That bone-deep sense of wet cold when you fear you will never be warm again. My hands shook as I spooned the barely tolerable beans into my mouth. At least it was food. Wrapping myself like a cocoon in the blankets, I shivered through the night, fighting to keep the chill at bay as the wind howled between the houses, sounding like the screams of children in the dark.

My body was an ice block by morning, and I cursed my solid fingers as I struggled to relight the fire, making a mental note not to let it die out again. I should have taken the sleeping bag. Heating the remaining can, Irish Stew allegedly, I threw most of the vile slop away, unable to eat it without gagging. My stomach rumbled. Bastards. They had left us the stuff no one wanted, retrieved on our many raids on the mainland over the years, and kept in case we ever had a bad year of growing crops.

As the sun rose, I warmed slightly. No point in hanging around here. My hands trembled as I laced up my icy boots. I may as well get some exercise, warm-up, and ignore the rumbling in my stomach until I braved seeing what food he had left me. Mousa was a tiny island, nearly divided in two, and I walked the circumference of the island, feeling the sun on my face. It was a fine day, just bitterly cold with the blustering wind. As much as I wanted to gaze out over the ocean, I kept my face turned inland to avoid copping a face full of infected sea spray. As I roamed over the hills and sand dunes, memories filtered back. I recalled that single day we spent here, all those years ago. Luca. My heart lurched as I could see his ghost in the distance, helping the women we had rescued. Cam. His anguish. Exhaling forcefully, I banished that thought from my mind.

Her. It was always *her*.

Rounding the sizeable ancient broch, I saw him in the clearing directly ahead, head down in thought, his hands caressing the bark of a tree. *The* tree. He was standing in the exact spot he had been when Alize had told him about Laetitia. Of course, he was thinking about her. Here. Would that fucking woman ever be out of my life? Cam sensed me watching and whirled before I had the chance to slink away. I scowled at him, embarrassed I had been caught spying.

"What?" he snapped.

"I was always the rebound, wasn't I?" I growled, needing to raise my voice slightly to be heard over the whistling wind.

Cam took two steps toward me, his face as black as thunder.

"Says she who has moved on already. Bloody hell, Freyja. One fight. Months ago. You won't speak to me; let me explain. Apologize. You are killing me. Destroying our children. How long are you going to hold on to this? When it burns me to a crisp as well as you?"

"Why would you care who I see? You moved on years before I did."

"You can't possibly mean that."

Flames sparked before my eyes. "Oh, for fuck's sake. Don't pretend with me. I saw the way you reacted when you heard she had died. I was here, remember? I watched. The cries of anguish? Of torment? Your heart broke that day and never recovered. It tore my heart out just watching you. You never reacted like that about *me*."

"Are you fucking kidding?" Cam's booking voice echoed around the rocks in a menacing tone I had rarely heard. "I hunted for you for six fucking *months*! Day and night. I barely ate. Didn't sleep. After the first few days, I was searching for a body. *Your* body. Do you know what that did to me? I traveled through that vortex—twice. The second time knowing exactly what it would be like. For you. And you think I didn't *mourn* you?"

Cam's beast had risen with my words. His eyes flashed sparks of warning, and coolly I turned to storm away, not wanting to engage any further. There was no point in speaking to him when he was like this. Irrational. An arm grabbed mine from beside me, spinning me around, and threw me forcibly against the tree. Before I could protest, his mouth crushed mine, angrily.

No. I bit down on his lip, my knee rising at the same time. He blocked my knee with his thigh and ignored the swelling lip. With his much larger body surrounding mine, and my back squashed against the tree, I had nowhere to go. Writhing and squirming, I fought to get away. I would not give in. *It is over. Why can't he just accept it?*

He persisted, his kisses running down my neck before finding my mouth again. He was so warm, so demanding. *Yes,* his body said, and mine responded in kind. All the anger of the past months seeped out of me into a puddle on the ground as my mouth responded to his. Urgent, wanting. A churning chaos as he enshrouded me.

No! My final resolve rose as I squirmed and slipped under his arm, screaming in his face as I stayed beyond his reach. "Why do you have to be such a Neanderthal? Did *she* like it like that? You will always love her more. She gave you Louis when I couldn't. You would never have accused *her* of cheating. She was so… so… fucking *perfect!*"

"Is that what this is about?" he called after me. "Me apologizing, or you being jealous of a dead woman?"

The flight instinct vanished as I whirled. "I … am … not … jealous!" I raged, lunging and shoving him in the chest.

"Yes, you are. And you are being stupid."

I picked up a rock and hurled it at his head, missing by centimeters.

He advanced on me as I backed into a nearby tree. I flinched as he raised his hand and saw the look of pain cross his face, his eyes popping in shock as he paused mid-motion.

"Did you think I was going to hit you? Have I ever physically hurt you? My god Freyja, is that what you think of me?"

I watched apprehensively as he took a step back and lowered his cupped hand. "What were you going to do then?" I asked suspiciously.

"Touch you. Hold you. Apologize for the millionth time. I should never have sided with Sorcha. You were right, and she was wrong. I am so very sorry for that. As for accusing you of cheating, Frey, you misunderstood my words. I was jealous, exhausted, and my words came out wrong. Knowing you enjoyed your months on Clava, enjoying yourself with adults while I was home wrangling the kids. I never begrudged you that, ever. But you came home so full of life, and I was shattered. Dealing with daily fights and maintaining a home with five kids. Caitlin cried every night the entire time you were gone. The night before you came home, I had been up with her vomiting all night, comforting her and cleaning. Not once did you ask me how I was. I was weary and didn't choose my words carefully. But you never let me apologize. You just stormed out and moved into Illy's the same day. So, hear me now. I am sorry. I never want to lose you. I love you more than life itself."

The heat burning in my chest dissipated in a puff of smoke. "I'm sorry too," I muttered. "I never thought of how my absence would impact you."

"Can I touch you?"

My eyes met his, so clear and blue, with no anger or deception in their depths. I nodded, and he raised his hand to caress my cheek as his lips found mine. Soft and nurturing, I melted into his arms, unable to bear my weight any longer. His lips grew more demanding, his hands tore at my clothes, and I was in no mood to stop him.

I whispered, "These are my only clothes."

"Don't. Care," he growled as my body was exposed to the battering wind. His voice had dropped several octaves and made my stomach lurch unexpectedly. The months I was on Clava, I had hungered for him. The months I had been home, I had woken so many nights, cold and alone. He lifted me, and my legs found their place, my ankles locked around his waist, my arms holding onto him, fearful of losing him again. A universe containing the two of us engulfed me, blocking out the sights, sounds, and smells. I had spent my life chasing the elusive. But when it all came down to it, this is where I wanted to be—with him.

"Tell me what is going on," he murmured as he lay me on the soft moss being battered by the wind, his jacket barely covering us.

"Do you really love me?" I whispered, needing the answer more desperately than I thought possible.

"More than breathing," he replied without pause. "But in all the years I have known you, you have never needed validation before. What is going on in that head of yours?"

"Illy says I have never forgiven you for moving on … with her."

"Is she right?"

"Maybe. Probably. I guess."

"Honey, that was a very long time ago. Why is it an issue now?" Cam nuzzled my neck, kissing the spot where my neck joined my collarbone, making my eyes close in bliss. I steeled myself before speaking my next words.

"I know. But when I was on Clava…" I couldn't finish. The words stuck in my throat. I swallowed hard to dislodge the lump.

"What?" His hands started to caress my breasts, and I wanted to meld into him but was afraid to respond to his touch in case he pulled away with my words.

"I found her records."

Cam stirred slightly, lifting his head a fraction. "And?"

I closed my eyes and spoke the final words, ramming the steel blade into my heart. "She was your chosen partner."

His back stiffened as he hovered above me. His hand stopped cold on my chest, and my heart froze. I closed my eyes and swallowed hard, fighting back the tears. "Did you hear me?"

Cam exhaled slowly as his hands began to caress me again. "I heard. That means nothing. It was a scientific thing. After all, Angus was yours, and he was a lying fuckwit."

I desperately wanted to relax and enjoy the sensations he was arousing in me. But I couldn't. My heart chilled; he needed to understand.

"It was more than that. They chose couples who were compatible … to replicate genomes. But there was a significant personality component to the profiling. She was your perfect match. 97 percent compatibility. Among the highest of all the profiles I read. There was a very high rate of success. Once they could travel through the antipodes, more than a quarter of people ended up with their profiled match. Many ended relationships to be with their scientifically chosen partner. And you chose her." I was rambling, desperate to get it all out in one go so he could run, as I knew he would.

"I assume you and Angus had a high compatibility, but you never wanted him."

"Angus ranted at me that he and were highly compatible, and we were only 89 percent. Yours was near perfect."

"So what? It is just data. Numbers."

"It isn't just the profiling," I whispered, my face flaming.

"What then?"

"There were pictures. Surveillance footage images."

"Of me?"

"Of you... Together. Your wedding at the stones. Together at ... the broch. Dun Carloway, I mean."

"They spied on us?" Cam flushed, his face matching mine, and it wasn't from the cold.

I sniffed and pulled away from him, forcing the words out before I lost my nerve. "They gave me an iPad with access to everything. So, of course, I looked up the kids, my file, and your file at the first opportunity. That was when I saw it. The photos. I spent every night seeing you together. Haunted by how happy you looked. Feeling sick seeing the way you touched her. Those months away from you, I spent knowing she was the person you were supposed to be with, and Louis was the child that was destined."

Not Kat, or Xan, or Thorsten. Only Louis. That thought rammed home as the pain of reading that report, seeing those photos, again and again, resurfaced. Slightly out of focus, satellite vision, but I could see his joy, even at a distance. I punctured my lip, fighting to retain control as the images tortured me.

He froze, and I braced myself to tell him all of it. Best he heard it now and had all the facts. Then he could run. Justified.

"Do you remember when I gave you the letters about Amara, her grandmother? You disappeared all night, and I lay there awake, knowing that you would never be over her. Someone you had never met, but it brought back memories of her. So when I read those reports, saw those photos, I knew I would never be your first choice. A quarter of people chose their pro-filed match. I had flashbacks of that day when we told you about the other communities. You were gazing down at your baby, sitting beside her. And I knew."

"No, my love. It was always you."

"How can you say that?" I sat upright to look at him, my bare skin exposed to the battering wind, matching the chill inside me. "You chose her."

"Only when I thought I couldn't have you. Why on earth didn't you say something sooner?"

"I never got the chance. The day I came home you accused me of cheating on you."

"No, I didn't!"

"You did. I remember distinctly."

"So do I. Those words were burned into my brain, wondering what on earth I had said to make you go off at me and move in with Illy. I asked Di, and she set me straight. I said, 'There is my wayward, wandering wife'."

"Exactly. Unfaithful. Disloyal. Straying. You know, like she had a wandering eye?"

"No. Wandering meaning traveling. I realized how you interpreted it later when Di clarified it, but I couldn't work out why on earth you would take it that way. But now your response makes sense. You screamed at me, something about not being the meek and mild type, not being one to sit around and wait for you. I couldn't work it out at the time. You had Laetitia on your mind. When I went looking for you, and then for Sorcha, she waited for me."

"All I could see all the way home was her face, staring at me, disapproving. Louis' face. Knowing that she would never have left you to undergo training for six months. So when you accused me of cheating..."

"I did not accuse you of cheating. I was thrilled to have you home. Then you didn't even make it inside the house. Started swearing at me about how I never loved you and ran to Illy's. I have spent the past three months wondering what happened that day. I thought you were exhausted and just needed to rest. Sorcha had told me the workload on Clava was extreme and designed to break you. Then I tried to talk to you three days later and again, picked a bad time."

"It was about the worst moment possible. I was questioning Sorcha."

"I could see from a mile off that she was angry, and I was trying to help. Sorcha, in a temper, is something no one needs to endure alone. I should know. I have been the recipient of far too many bruises from her. Stitches on one memorable occasion."

"You took her side!"

"No, you didn't let me finish. What I had intended to say was that Sorcha had performed surgeries this way for years. Then you lost your shit, screamed at me, called me some rather choice names if I recall, and stormed off. But the second part of the sentence was going to be, 'But as Freyja has been training under an orthopedic surgeon for the past six months, perhaps Sorcha could consider a different perspective.'"

"Oh." My lungs deflated.

"But even when you worked it out with my sister, you were still furious at me. By that time, I heard…"

"About Stefan?" I guessed.

"He was on Clava when you were. Everyone was talking about it. You and him. Very friendly. I wondered if…"

"If I was with him on Clava, and I reacted that way because there was truth to it?"

Cam looked away, and silence thickened the air between us before he whispered. "Then he followed you here. I just wanted you to be happy. Truly. When I heard you were with him, I thought I should let you go. Be with someone who was your equal. Challenged you … intellectually."

"I've never slept with him," I whispered. "I promise. He was my teacher. I didn't know he was coming here until he arrived."

Cam's torso softened as I spoke. "Honestly?"

"Truly. I would never lie to you. I wasn't even that interested, to tell the truth. But when you didn't speak to me…"

"Honey, were you prepared to sacrifice us for some random words in a file? Words that mean absolutely nothing?"

"I thought it would be easier this way."

"But it wasn't?" he guessed.

"I saw the records in my second week there. I spent every day for the rest of my six-month placement torturing myself over it. I must have read that file, studied those photos a hundred times. I felt worthless, and there was the proof."

"And the last three months? Did being home and not telling me make it any easier?"

"No," I admitted, feeling foolish.

"So, in this churned-up rational brain of yours, what did you think was going to happen when you told me?"

"I thought you would tell me it was all a mistake," I whispered.

"The past *fourteen years*? Raising five children. Building two homes. Give me some credit. Why on earth didn't you tell me sooner?"

I paused, not wanting to answer that. Cam pushed. "What?"

"You process those things so deeply. I thought you would retreat into yourself, slink off, abandon me, and stew over it. Then, after disappearing and torturing me for days, you would return, rip my heart out, and tell me it was all a mistake. I could see it perfectly. Every word you spoke played out right before my eyes. Laetitia was your perfect match, and I was just … filler. So it was easier to get in first."

Cam shuddered, and I lifted my head to watch as he convulsed. With *laughter*.

"Filler? You tried to break us up based on something you read in a report? Some ancient photos of events you have always known about? That I never hid from you."

"Maybe," I mumbled, not looking at him. Cam tilted my chin to look into my eyes. I tried to avoid his gaze, but he wouldn't let me, forcing me to look at him.

"I loved Laetitia. You know that. But she has been gone for fifteen *years*. She and I were together for less than three years, compared to our fourteen in this marriage alone. So even if I had stewed over this, as you put it, what conclusion would I have come to?"

"That it was all a mistake. You and I getting back together. She was your selected partner. It was there in black and white. Undeniable proof. 97 percent. You were destined to be together. I was your second choice, and I couldn't deal with seeing the echoes of regret in your eyes every day."

"Did the past years mean nothing to you? Sure, we had tough times, but we had some wonderful times to balance it. Were we not important enough to fight for?"

"I just couldn't deal with having my heart broken. Again. I thought it would be easier if I left first," I whispered.

"Well, I will tell you what I think, since that is the basis of your ridiculous assumption. For once, science got it partly right. I chose Laetitia. She was an amazing woman. Louis is a wonderful young man, and he came from that partnership. But that was so many years ago. I chose you first and would never have left you, even for her. Here is a hot tip for the next time that overly logical brain of yours takes over: love is stronger than science. The heart wants what it wants. And mine wants you. With my dying breath, I will want you."

"Really?" I hated the feeling of being needy. I felt cold, weak, and shaky. But I needed to know the answer.

"Do you remember when you came to find me in Edinburgh? You asked me for a few days. If I wanted you to leave after that, you would. Do you remember?"

"I do."

"Well, I only ask for one day. Just a single day. If after twenty-four hours you don't want me, I will give you my blessing to move on with Stefan or whoever else you want."

"You don't need a timeframe," I choked.

"Prove it."

Our lips found each other, ravenous and craving. He stole every breath as we made up for nine lost months. Our limbs intertwined, our heartbeats pounding in unison. Contentment. The word floated into my head. I was content. I had found what I didn't know I was even looking for.

"Feeling better?" The honeyed voice in my ear made me aware of my surroundings.

"You are the only person in my life who can deal with me at my worst." I whispered into his ear, feeling like liquid chocolate despite the cold. At some point in the morning, Cam had lifted me like I was a feather and carried me to the broch, complaining about how much weight I had lost.

"I missed you so much." Despite the cold, the warmth of his words wrapped around me like a blanket. "I thought so many times about surprising you and turning up on Clava."

"Why didn't you?"

"Sorcha told me it was seriously hard work, and I would be a distraction. She said that you were the only real choice for that training, as she knew you were the only person strong enough to endure what they would put you through. Besides, you never ask for anything for yourself. After all you have been through over the years, I thought you needed it. Something just for you."

"Sorcha was likely right. I couldn't have split my attention. Goodness, it was arduous work."

"You are a born doctor. I am so glad you got that opportunity. I didn't want to mess it up for you. But then, when you got home … and the gossip started, I wondered if…"

"It wasn't true. None of it. I kissed him, I will admit. But only after you and I had broken up. Call me any name you want, but a cheater is not one of them."

"Any name?"

"Anything you like." I stretched and rolled toward him. "No one can hear you." As I languished, I caught Cam staring at my hip.

"What is that?"

"Oh, that. I got a tattoo when I was on Clava."

"You did *what*?"

"One of the anesthetists was very artistic. He put himself through med school by working as a freelance tattoo artist. I admired his ink one day, and he offered to do one for me. But I wanted it to be for me and no one else, so I got it somewhere private. Why? Don't you like it?"

Cam ran his finger over the snow-capped mountain range now permanently adorning my right hip. "I love it. It reminds me of home. Maybe you should take me there, and I can get one too."

"No!"

Cam jerked his hand away at my vehemence.

"I just meant, I am happy to be home. I don't want to go back there anytime soon. After he offered, I thought about a snowflake or a wave. All the things I have lost. Those simple things we will never get to enjoy again. Swimming in the ocean. The feel of snow falling on your face. But the more I thought about it, a mountain seemed right."

"My mum used to say that sometimes it takes an earthquake for a mountain to rise. We have faced so many and conquered so much. I love it. It is a testament to how strong you are, how resilient."

If only you knew the truth, maybe you wouldn't love me as much. Pain stabbed me in the heart, and I closed it off. Stopped feeling as Cam continued to trace the fine lines of my art.

Unable to be apart, we spent the next few days together, talking, walking, or enjoying companionable silence.

"Why do you think the moss that grows here is special?"

Cam shrugged. "I have no idea, but it works. You can see the patches where it doesn't grow, and that vegetation has perished. But it is widespread, and anything within a few square meters of a growing patch of the moss is alive."

"Will it be enough?" The bucket he had stored safely in the broch was overflowing with samples, keeping it from the infected rain and sea spray.

"I hope so. We don't have long to start re-greening before the effects are irreversible."

I tipped my head to the side, indicating he should continue. "Did you notice the air thinning as we left Lewis? I had wondered how long that would take."

"Thinning?" I quizzed.

"It is just that bit harder to breathe. Plants produce oxygen via photosynthesis."

"I remember that. I took biology as an undergrad. I'm not a complete numpty."

"Well, if there are no plants out in the open, or very few at least, the levels of carbon will build up and eventually reach toxic levels."

"How long will it take?"

"Scientists used to think a hundred years, but with all living creatures gone, it may happen sooner. Humans used to breathe very little of the earth's oxygen, comparatively. But when plants decay, they release their build-up of carbon, and the non-production of oxygen through photosynthesis will thin the ratio of oxygen to other gases in the atmosphere. It used to be around 20% oxygen, but that will lessen as the years pass and the earth can't produce more."

I stretched my arms around his neck and pressed against him. "As much as I love it when you talk science to me, could you use that luscious mouth for something that isn't talking?"

When the unfamiliar large white yacht approached the island just after dawn six days later, we greeted them standing on the beach. Cam held me in front of him, his arms wrapped around me, trying to keep my torn top together as the gusts exposed my stomach.

I could hear Di squealing from the lower deck as Sorcha cautiously approached the tiny dock in a smaller motorized boat lowered from the stern, avoiding generating spray. Illy's hair was gusting behind her as she stood beside Di, clutching Seraphine's hand.

"Bitch," I mouthed at her as Sorcha maneuvered the small craft alongside the larger one, and we clambered aboard.

"I love you too," she replied as she blew me a kiss.

"Where is the *Eurydice*?" Cam asked.

"We needed something bigger," Sorcha admitted. "We dropped you, raced to Edinburgh, and chose something larger. We were a little limited in choice and what we could start after all these years. We have a long trip ahead of us and quite a few people to accommodate."

"You left the *Eurydice* in Edinburgh?" Cam's face fell. He and I had spent many wonderful days and nights on that yacht.

"No. After we started this vessel, Illy took her back to Lewis while I supervised the loading of this one, and then we picked Illy up on our way here. We will always need something smaller, and she has been well maintained. Why? Didn't you wonder why we took so long to get back?"

"Not really," I confessed.

"How many days did it take?" Illy asked cheekily as she helped us unload, carefully carrying Cam's buckets of moss.

"Day two," I admitted.

"Well, six days of bliss explains your face and the state of your clothes. Let's go. Unless you want to remain here on your second honeymoon?"

My green eyes met Cam's blue for confirmation. I whispered, "Maybe just a few more days?"

Sorcha's cutting tone interjected. "We go. Now. You two can shag around the clock later. We have a long way to go and a few more stops along the way. Move it."

"Mummy, what's a shag?" Seraphine asked, her shrill six-year-old girl voice piercing the air, making everyone turn to look at her. Illy's face flushed.

"It is like a kiss, darling," she responded without missing a beat. "Now, have you got your lifejacket on?"

CHAPTER 4

THE DAMARA WAS ENORMOUS with more than fifteen bedrooms across four levels. Desperate for a shower, Cam and I were shown to our private room, one of the few with a king bed.

Raising my eyebrows at Illy at the luxurious space, she smirked. "We needed you to reconcile just for ease of accommodation. You would need to bunk in with the kids otherwise!"

"Thank you." I leaned in to hold her close. "Truly."

"Sometimes friends know what you need better than you do yourself." She cackled. "Hurry up and shower. We scrubbed and refilled the water tanks on Lewis, so the water is safe. The kids will be up soon. It's your turn to serve breakfast."

As Cam and I dressed, we heard doors opening and closing and the sounds of children chattering as they staggered out of bedrooms. Greeting them in the hallway as they rubbed sleepy eyes, I could see that they slept on bunks and floors; camping mattresses were scattered across every flat surface. I watched them emerge in twos and threes, looking full of energy and seeking breakfast. Cait emitted an ear-piercing shriek seeing Cam and me holding hands, and we hugged her tight as her smile lit the room. As we headed toward the main living space on the upper deck, the electric bread maker set up on the bench was releasing the most amazing aroma, making my stomach grumble audibly. Cam and I helped serve toast and porridge to all the children and then shooed them off to the lower living area, which had been set up as a learning space. Illy told us every child had moaned upon learning that school would resume, making Di laugh. She had missed teaching, and Sam and Kendra were happy to assist. *Maybe that is why Sam and Kendra accompanied us,* I wondered, the frustration of secrets being kept from me squeezing my tightening chest.

Once all the children were safely downstairs and the solid door closed, I sat at the table and demanded answers. On Mousa, when I had asked, Cam had told me it wasn't entirely his story to tell, and he only knew pieces. Busy catching up on the last nine months, I hadn't pursued it. I could have forced him to tell me, but it didn't seem important at the time.

Sorcha, Illy, and Cam looked at each other, deciding who would start. Clearly, it was quite the story, and the mounting frustration at being kept in the dark was making my head throb. Finally, Cam placed a second cup of coffee in front of me and sighed as he sat beside me, close enough for his leg to lie alongside mine.

"For me, it all happened the day we left. I had popped home for some lunch, my mind filled with all the work I needed to do, so I wasn't focused. Everyone was out working. The kids were all at school. I wasn't thinking about anything, only how much I could achieve that day. The orchard desperately needs work; it is harvest time. The nights are getting cold. We can't lose all the fruit because we didn't have time to pick it. So, I made a sandwich, wrapped it in a beeswax wrap, planning to eat on the way. As I went to leave, I pulled on my boots and was leaning on the hallway table. I remember thinking I was glad Kat hadn't seen me wearing them into the house. She would have blown her stack at me. She took taking over your role very seriously." Cam grinned at me. "I pulled myself upright, picked up the sandwich, turned to the door, and my heart froze."

"What happened?" I asked.

Cam looked over at Illy and Sorcha, and then away.

"Tell her," Sorcha said softly. "She needs to know Cam."

"I picked up my sandwich and then looked up at the door. That was when I saw it."

"Saw what?" Frustration at Cam's inability to tell a straight story was bubbling to the surface.

"That photo of you and your sister as teenagers. You know the one of you in bikinis standing on your parents' yacht?" The strangled tone made my stomach lurch, and I felt the bread I had just eaten for breakfast move up into my gullet and swallowed hard. "It was pinned to the back of the front door."

"Pinned?" I asked cautiously, his tone impacting me more than the words.

Cam's eyes filled with pain as his hand reached for mine and held it. "Your sister's face had been cut out. Haphazardly. There was a knife embedded in the middle of yours, holding it to the door."

I barely made it to the railing before the ocean claimed my breakfast. Hanging my head over the cold, white steel, I felt Illy on one side of me, Cam on the other.

"Tell her all of it, Campbell." Sorcha's voice came from behind me. "Now."

The wind whipped past as we moved through the waves at high speed, and I had to strain to hear, fighting to breathe as the steel band squeezed tighter around my chest.

"Someone had been there, in our home, after the kids and I had left for the day. I knew where the photo had been—in the boxes under our bed."

Unable to lift my head, I moved slightly, so he knew I was listening. Even in my current state, I could tell that there was more. "What?" I croaked. "What else did you find?"

A gurgling sound came from behind me.

After a pause, Illy spoke, calm and clear. "Every photo of you had been damaged. Slashed. Red crosses across your face. They were strewn all over your room."

"Someone was in our room?" I spoke, realizing as I said it that I hadn't slept in that room for nine months. Only most people likely didn't know it. Illy's house and ours had been joined for years, ever since we rebuilt following the fire. One large building connected by an enclosed corridor, doors at each end. Our promise to her when she had Alasdair.

"Yes."

Crashing down on the deck, I barely felt the impact shudder up my spine.

Illy, Cam, and Sorcha watched as I took in what Cam and Illy had said, then saw the wave of anger physically rise as it overtook the distress. I lifted my head from my chest and felt my skin flame to boiling point.

"How dare they? Some gutless asshole invades my home and threatens my family?"

Illy grinned. "There's my girl. That is what I love about you, Frey. You are a warrior. You might choose your battles, but when it is time to fight, you pick up your sword, you rise, and you conquer. Every time."

"What else did you find?" I growled.

"Not much," Cam admitted. "Clothes pulled out of drawers. Objects thrown around. But it was the photos that had been damaged."

"Only the ones of me?"

"Of you. And your sister."

"Kat? Why? Katrin has been gone for nearly seven years."

"Sit down," Illy instructed. It was her serious tone, making me look up.

"I'm about as sitting down as I can get." I looked up at her from my seated position on the deck. "Wha…"

"Sit." Sorcha unfolded some deck chairs, pulling them into a cluster. I felt Cam's powerful hands lifting me under the armpits, gently depositing me in one.

After checking that Di was in the lower-level living space and ensuring none of the children had come upstairs and could overhear us, Sorcha closed the glass door and pulled up a chair opposite me. Cam and Illy followed suit and huddled around in a circle.

Cam looked at Illy. By silent consent, she had now been appointed spokesperson. Perched on the edge of my seat, I listened.

"After you left Clava, there was an incident with Ceri."

That wasn't what I expected. "Ceridwen? Did she do something?" While my relationship with Ceridwen was strained, we had spent some time together in my few non-working hours on Clava and grown a little closer. She had visited me at the clinic some days. We had eaten meals together and taken the occasional walk. I finally found the time to tell her about her birth mother, my sister. She was still cold and robotic in nature but apologetic for the drama she had caused while living with us. Now nearly thirteen, she was scarily intelligent, and while she possessed no warmth, I had come to understand her. She was knowledgeable, full of interesting facts, and had come a long way from the scared little girl we had rescued from Angus.

Illy exhaled. "She is dead, Freyja."

"What?" I sat bolt upright, my eyes popping. "When? How?"

"She drowned. A few weeks ago."

"Couldn't she swim?" I wracked my brain, trying to remember whether we had ever tried to teach her to swim while she was living with us. A traumatized, destructive six-year-old who had burned down our home and shown no remorse—but one who had spent the first years of her life in a dormitory, raised with other children, shown no love, and who had no idea how to be part of a family.

"No. But she wouldn't have stood a chance. Her hands were bound behind her back, a pillowcase tied over her head, and she was held under."

"She was *murdered*?" I whispered, unable to believe it.

Illy nodded, and my blood turned to ice. My niece. Murdered.

"Do they know who did it?" I asked, unable to keep my voice from shaking. I had lived there for six months. *Had I known her killer?*

"No. But as you know, she is a tall girl. Slight, but tall. It had to have been someone older or at least physically bigger to hold her down."

I nodded, thinking of Ceri. "Kat was a centimeter or two shorter than me, but she never had the chance to grow to full height. Ceri was still shorter when I last saw her but tall for her age. Very slim, though. But she is only thirteen. Any adult is larger than she is."

"Frey, there is more."

I lifted my eyes wearily. Cam's arm tightened around my shoulder.

"Two more are gone. Both drowned."

I couldn't take that in immediately. "Which two?" I finally managed.

"Beth from Newgrange and little Solstice from Orkney."

"Accidents?" I squeaked, knowing the answer.

Illy couldn't respond as my body started to tremble, and I felt the familiar coldness threaten to pull me down. I fought the fog to listen.

"No," Sorcha responded coolly. "They were murdered. Only it took them a little longer to realize. Like our girls, they are only six, and both found fully clothed, which is of little comfort. Beth had been ... hit over the head with a rock before she was drowned. At first, both communities thought it was a tragic accident. It wasn't until we were told that we realized. Three of the twenty-seven drowned in the space of a month. Those odds are next to zero."

"Oh, my god." My head was spinning. *Three*? I forced myself to focus. *Not now*, I told myself angrily.

"Illy found out the same day I found the photos," Cam mumbled. "I went looking for her after I found them. It took me hours, chasing her on her market rounds. By the time I found her, and we exchanged news..."

Illy picked up the story. "I had only learned that day, from Bridget, about the other three. Aidan was backlogged with the milling, being fall, so she was operating the radio for a few months. She had heard about Ceri but was so distraught, Ceri being Ruby and Scarlett's sister, that she was waiting to tell us when she saw us. Not news to be passed on via the children like we normally would. She said she had dropped by three times but kept missing us. Then I missed a week because Summer was sick. So, by the time I saw her on my rounds that morning, and she told me of the three... I was planning to tell you that night. Then Cam found me and told me about the photos... Well, we knew we needed to get you and the children out of there. Immediately," Illy finished softly. "But I came home before you did. I checked your house. And I found... Writing. Graffiti, really. On the bathroom mirror."

"Graffiti? What did it say?"

"In red paint, E. 22:18."

"E.22:18?" I asked, puzzled. "What does that mean? East? Doesn't sound like coordinates."

"Did you go to a religious school?" Illy asked.

"Yes, but not really. I mean, we studied basic religion, ethics, I guess you would call it. But I didn't pay attention. My parents were atheists. They only chose an Anglican school as it was the best in the area. Why?"

"Well, I was raised Protestant. Lapsed, for the most part. But I attended Sunday School as a child. *E.22:18* is a biblical reference, although I admit I needed to go to the library and find a copy to check. Exodus chapter 22, verse 18. Thou shall not permit a witch to live."

"A witch?" I asked, perplexed. "Who is a witch?"

"You." Illy shrugged.

"Me? That makes no sense at all. I'm a vet, well, a doctor now. But so are you, Sorcha. Did your home get graffitied too?"

"But you are," Illy said gently. "You are the mother of the special children, the modified children. You created them. You are the witch that brought forth the plague if you like."

"But I didn't! They were stolen from me."

"That is probably a minor detail. Then I went to Bridget's, called Clava, told them what we had found, and asked them to check the location. That was why I was late getting home that night. They sent someone to check and found it in the dark. Marked on a rock near where Ceri drowned."

"What?"

"L. 20:27."

"Which is?"

"Leviticus Chapter 20, verse 27. A man or woman who is a medium or necromancer shall surely be put to death. Similar references were found at the other two sites. I don't need to bore you with which ones; only trust me when I say just as damning."

"It's a fucking witch hunt," I breathed. "Drownings. Stoning. Surprised they didn't burn them at the stake. What is this, the Dark Ages?"

"May as well be," Sorcha growled. "But for now, the safest place for all of you, the girls, and you, Freyja, is here. Together. Where we can protect you."

"You would do that for me?" I looked up at Sorcha, surprised at her vehemence.

"Freyja, you are opinionated, arrogant, and bossy. You piss me off and drive me mad. But you are also one tough bitch, and I love you. You are my sister, and yes, I would do anything to protect you."

"Takes one to know one." Cam smiled, despite the news that had just been laid at my feet.

"Are you sure they are best together?" I asked, panicked. "What if we are picked off? We are sitting ducks out here in the ocean. We have weapons on Lewis; so does Newgrange. But we have no idea who else does. What if they take us all out with one shot?"

"That is why we are on our way to get Tadhg after we stop and collect the girls from Orkney."

It all made sense. The mad rush to leave. The children being with us. All of them that couldn't be left, including Alasdair.

"I never did finish the dishes," I blurted as the random thought entered my mind.

Illy laughed. "You can make up for it here. But honestly, I am sorry for scaring you. We couldn't wait. We needed you away, quickly, and back with your man. Someone is targeting you and the girls."

"What about my other children? We left them! They could be in danger."

Illy was watching my face. "I left my girls too. Sorcha, Cam, and I talked before I came home to get you. We genuinely believe that none of the other children are at risk. But we couldn't leave the little ones, not when we don't know how long we will be gone. So we took those under ten and left the older ones. Jorja and Bridget will care for them all. After all, we have Ruby and Scarlett."

"Are they safe?" I asked, feeling sick at the thought of abandoning my children and hers.

"They are. I checked with Bridget when I returned the *Eurydice*. She still has the radio, so she was the only person who knew I was coming. We need to keep our mission a secret, not knowing who is behind the attacks and the invasion. Sam came, as we needed a teacher. Kendra too. They can help us look after the little ones, and it was important for them to come after we decided where we were going. We will have twenty-two of your children, plus Ruby and Scarlett, who are older. We will need some help."

"Where are we going?"

"Kiewa."

The *Damara* was significantly larger and faster than the *Eurydice* with the downside of using considerably more fuel.

"I would have suggested we take two smaller vessels," I murmured to Cam later that morning. "It would be far more economical." But there was no way I was questioning Sorcha publicly. Not after last time. It had taken long enough for her to acknowledge I was right and for me to recognize that directly challenging her surgical technique was not the best way of handling the situation. But leaving the *Eurydice* in Lewis may fool someone looking for us, not realizing we had left. Though, if the person who had invaded our home was looking for our children… it wouldn't take long for them to work out we were no longer there.

"Why Kiewa?" I asked Illy later when the maelstrom in my mind had slowed to a dull roar.

"It is isolated. Not connected by an antipode and no transportation. They are connected by radio, learning programs, and such, but there is no migration and no trade. Besides, Di has a cousin there, and Sorcha was part of the original settlement. She is known and trusted. Cam and Di have visited before, so they aren't strangers. We felt it was the safest place to take the children."

I recognized it as an excellent choice. Now that the Nexus connected all the antipodal communities, the safest place likely was a domed community that wasn't connected. People traveled fairly extensively now on each solstice and equinox. The heat suit technology had been further refined, making the process far smoother. Each year we traveled to one of the communities where my special children lived to gather and spend a week together before heading home. The transit was so smooth that even the children traveled with no issues. But it meant that anyone could travel anywhere and without notice.

"Why not one of the isolated communities in the UK?" I asked. We now knew there were quite a few, spread out, each with a safe water supply. I had even visited a few during my time at Clava, assisting with surgeries in the smaller communities with fewer resources. Stefan called it testing my skills in the field.

"We thought of that. But if someone targeted Ceri on Clava, they are already on the mainland and could easily find us. Australia is far safer."

"But so far away," I said watching Illy's pained expression, thinking of my older children.

"In this scenario, that is a good thing."

"Who knows? About the girls and me?"

Illy smiled, but it didn't reach her eyes. She looked exhausted. "Very few people, deliberately. Bridget and Jorja, mainly as Bridget received the messages. Fraser and Isla, as we need them to care for the older children, and I trust them both implicitly. They are old enough to stay home, yours and mine, but I feel better knowing someone is looking out for them. The other parents know we will keep the children safe, but we deliberately didn't tell them where we are taking them. It is always best that as few people know as possible."

"That is a lot of trust. They are only little girls."

"They trust *you,* Frey. They know you would do anything for these kids. Everyone knows that with you is the best place they can be."

"Only I am a target too?" I flopped onto the soft navy sofa, my stomach churning. Illy gently lowered her featherweight beside me, barely making a ripple. Her hand reached over to lightly rest on my arm.

"Sadly, yes. But Frey? We are a team. We will never let anything happen to you."

CHAPTER 5

WE STOPPED BRIEFLY ON Orkney later that afternoon, the residents still reeling from the loss of one of their children only a few days prior.

"I'm so sorry," Saba wept as she flung herself at me. "You trusted us with your baby, and we let you down."

Each year we held a birthday party for the girls. All the modified ones would come to one location, rotated between Orkney, Lewis, and Newgrange, for a week to catch up and socialize. Some of the medical team from Clava attended to check them over. Highly supervised initially, over the years, we had relaxed far more. The girls were all six now, and at the last gathering they had been weighed, measured, had a blood test, and sent on their way. Ten months ago, I had seen them all. Laughed and played with them. Just before I had traveled to Clava to start my orthopedic training. Ten months, and now three were gone.

"Saba," I said firmly, crouching down so I could see into her eyes. "You did not do this to Soli. Someone evil did this. I will find them, and I will make them pay."

Gerry, standing beside his wife, placed a hand on my shoulder. "I'm coming with you. I couldn't save my own daughter. Damned if I will let them take any more."

A glance at Saba confirmed she had consented to him accompanying us.

"Are you sure?" I asked her gently. "You have other children."

Saba and Gerry had five children, and I knew them all well. Three biological children. One from Saba's selected partnership pairing, and little Solstice, my child. Orkney was the only community we were still close with who had agreed to the selective partnerships, thus the acceptance of my children had been of little controversy.

"I'm sure," she sniffed, her dark eyes glistening. "We don't know who did this, and we need to get them to safety. Gerry knows them all. We have agreed. He should be the one to bring the other five. Keep them safe."

"Thank you," I said and meant it. Gerry had helped rescue the women kidnapped fifteen years ago, Saba being one of them, and had been a tremendous help. A trained police officer, now he was now a handyperson of sorts, but when we caught up each year at the gathering, had a drink together, and reconnected, he always admitted missing police work.

Back on the *Damara*, room shuffling, bed negotiations, and lots of hysteria kept us busy for hours. But we finally had the Orkney girls and Gerry settled.

"It's like a rave crossed with a sleepover," Sorcha groaned, listening to the squeals as the new girls ran up and down the stairwell, chasing each other with pillows.

"They are having a wonderful time," Di said. "Don't you remember the joy of being away from your parents and staying at a friend's house? It won't last, so enjoy the happiness while you can."

Our arrival on Newgrange the following morning was no less traumatic than Orkney. Eight scared-looking girls met us at the dock, all with parents we knew well. Faces were grim at the journey we were about to undertake. Callie threw herself at Cam and then at me, as was her annual routine. Tadhg stood back, looking more solemn than usual.

I took two steps over to him, catching his attention. "You okay?" I asked.

"Not really. I'm coming with you. Leaving the others behind will be hard. Especially as we don't know how long we will be gone."

"Are you sure? We will take care of them."

"We agreed one of us should come along to help with the girls. Someone who knows them. Who knows? I might be able to help in some small way."

"Your help has been invaluable so many times," I said kindly. It was true. Helping us find my sister, ensuring that we weren't spotted, allowing us to escape unfollowed from Inverness. So many times Tadhg had helped us.

"You could still help from here?" I tried again. "We could be gone for months."

"I know. I have been journeying before, remember? With your man here. No. It is hard to leave Cal and the kids. But they are older now, except little Fairlie. We all know it is for the best."

"I know how that feels. I didn't have time to say goodbye properly to my own children. I was just shoved onto a boat. But they are safe."

"I wish Jake could come," Tadhg muttered.

"Why can't he?"

"Makayla just had another bub, little Odhrán. He needs to care for her and the others."

"How many is that now?" I asked with a smirk.

"Seven. Including Lulu. So she will have one less."

"Bloody hell. Imagine giving birth to six children. And all singletons too. After her cancer scare, I was worried she would never have children."

"So were Cal and I, just quietly. But she is such a natural mother. Calm, patient. Nothing at all like Cal."

"Or me," I admitted. "I often feel like, 'have I parented today if I haven't lost my shit at someone?'"

Tadhg grinned at that. "Now I know why Cam likes you so much. You and Callie are very alike. My force of nature. Or is that all Australian women?"

"Just the special ones," Cam chipped in over my shoulder as he shook hands with Tadhg, and Callie reached to embrace me. "Another trip together?" Cam said.

"Looks like. Where are we off to this time?" Tadhg asked.

"Can't tell you yet but soon."

The sickening feeling deep in my stomach churned as I watched these people. All friends. People we had entrusted to care for these special children. Now one of them was dead, killed by someone they likely knew. But who and why?

Spotting Nadia standing at the edge of the group, I made my approach. She shrank away as soon as she saw me. I stopped several meters from her and held my arms out. She paused, looked into my eyes, then fell into them, sobbing. The loss of her daughter was so raw, she didn't need to say anything. Nor did I.

"We will keep them safe," I soothed in her ear. "I promise."

I could hear Sorcha rounding up children. Nadia pulled back and looked into my eyes, her own red-rimmed and wet. "Find whoever did this to my Beth and make them pay."

"Oh, I intend to," I assured her.

CHAPTER 6

BY THE END OF the second day, the girls were less excited about this impromptu vacation and became increasingly distraught as we traveled farther away from their families. A small number were fortunate, having a parent here. But most were homesick and desperately wanted to go home, terrified as they had been sent away, at night, with no explanation. Bedtimes were the worst. Tired little girls, crying for their parents as they fell asleep, setting off others. Soon it was all of them, sobbing their hearts out. We took it in turns to soothe them, talk to them. Tell them they were loved, and they would be home soon. But as the words passed my lips, I wasn't sure I believed it myself. *Would we be home soon?* Likely not. The truth was, I desperately wanted to be with my own children and feared for their safety. Unable to sleep with the ringing of cries in my ears, I went to sit on the deck and watch the dark waves surge past.

"It is time to tell them about their parentage. Why we are here." Illy spoke into my ear as I gazed over the ocean.

I was used to Illy's stealthy approaches by now and felt her lean into me. "I was thinking the same thing. Will you help me?"

"You know I will. I just spoke with Gerry and Tadhg, seeking their consent."

"And did they?"

"Of course."

I grinned into the darkness. No one refused Illy. "When?"

"Morning is best. They are too tired in the evening to be reasonable. We only need to give them the basics. Why they are special and why we are all together. Most of the girls know parts of the story, so it won't be as difficult as you think."

The following day after breakfast, and delaying schooling, we sat all the children down in the largest living room. Most of them were seated on the floor, some squashed together on the couches. The adults were standing warily, watching for an adverse reaction. Most were excited that they were missing some learning time. Illy had suggested that Di speak first, as the person they all recognized as an authority.

"We know you want to know why you are here, and you are all old enough for us to tell you. But you need to keep your questions to the end and put up your hand. You know how noisy it gets when you all talk at once? The grown-ups need to speak, and then you can ask any questions you like, but at the end."

The girls nodded, intrigued.

"You have always known that you are linked in some way. Every year, when we meet, you see each other. Some of you look alike. Some of you might already know. But you are all sisters. Half-sisters. You are all so very lucky, luckier than most children as each of you has four parents. Those you have at home, the ones who live with you. But for each one of you, Freyja is one of your mothers, and that is what makes you special. What makes you really special, and is kind of like a superpower, is that you can live outside the domes. You can drink, swim in the water, or be exposed to rain and not get sick. You are the only people in the entire world who are so special."

There was a collection of gasps from many of the audience and a look of pride at the term superpower. It was a clever choice of wording, I had to admit.

"Some people might be jealous that you are special and can do something that they can't," Illy said, looking around the room, making eye contact with each girl. "That you have this superpower. And that is why you are here. We need to keep you safe from people who might want to hurt you. We don't want to scare you. You are safe here. We are all here to protect you."

Several began to cry, the stress of the news taking a toll. Illy opened her mouth to speak again but paused as Ruby stood and moved to the front of the group.

"Even though we are older, my sister Scarlett and I are just like you," she said calmly, making them all look at her in astonishment. "We have known for a while now that we were a little bit different from other girls. We have two mothers, well, three in our case." She grinned. "Our birth mother was Freyja's sister, Katrin, so we are your cousins. She died a long time ago, and like you, we also have parents who raised us and love us. But we know many people are relying on us. We have been given a very important job. One day, we can live out here, safely with our own children. What kills other people can't touch us. We are very lucky. We were chosen for this job. And you were too. You are special, all of you. There is nothing different about you, except this one little thing. Our superpower. All of us can stand out on the deck and get the water in our faces, and it won't hurt us. But for all of these grown-ups, it will make them very sick. If you have questions, please come and ask Scarlett and me. We are a family. We will always look out for each other."

Illy placed an arm around Ruby's shoulder. "Ruby is right. We are a family. We look after each other. It is okay to be lonely or sad. It is okay to need to cry. But we are a big family. A team will always achieve what an individual cannot. If you are feeling alone, please talk to someone. We will help you. Now, putting up your hand, what would you like to know?"

When the girls had finished asking questions, Di ushered them down the stairs into the schoolroom, the clatter of feet drowned out by a chorus of whines.

"How do you think that went?" Sorcha asked Illy as the room fell into silence, and we slumped on the couches.

"As well as can be expected. They know the important bits without scaring them about what happened to the three who are no longer with us. They now understand why they are special, that they are related, and that someone wants to hurt them. We had no complete meltdowns, so I call that a win."

"Some knew, at least; that made it a bit easier. I am grateful that Sera knows. Cait and Mei, too."

"How unexpected was Cait's reaction?" Cam asked, grinning.

Caitlin had sat up in the back as Di and Illy spoke, wedged between Sera and Mei. There had been lots of giggling and whispering as we would expect from a group of six-year-olds. Cait had always known she was special and that she had lots of half-sisters, although we had never explicitly told her that Cam wasn't her biological father. But tears had started falling, and I couldn't work out why. Cam and I had looked at each other across the room, perplexed. None of this was news to her, except for why we were here. But she had both parents with her, which most of them didn't. Her reaction didn't make sense.

When it came to question time, Illy and Di had taken questions from around the room. Mostly simple questions, confirming what we had told them. Finally, Di had asked her if she was okay. With tears streaming down her face, she blubbered that it wasn't fair, as she had fewer parents than the other girls. Where all the others had four, two biological, and two actual parents, Caitlin had howled that she wasn't as special. She only had Cam and me and felt ripped off. No matter how much Cam tried to soothe her, she worked herself up to the point where he needed to take her outside to settle her.

"I'd lay money Seraphine whispered something in her ear," Illy muttered. "Little minx. She has a knack for knowing how to upset people."

"Especially siblings?" I asked.

"Most definitely. She is awful to Summer and Ally too, but she and Cait are so close. She uses that bond to stick the knife in sometimes."

"Because *my* sister would never have done *that*," Cam smirked.

Sorcha punched him in the arm.

"I'm going to check on her," I announced. "It is my teaching session today. Hadn't you better head off to bed? You are on the night shift tonight."

"On my way."

CHAPTER 7

STANDING IN THE DOORWAY, I scanned the room, looking for Cait over the heads of children sprawled randomly across the room. Unlike my classrooms at school, this room wasn't ordered. Some children were at tables, others in beanbags or lying on their stomachs on the floor reading or drawing. I over-heard Kendra ask one of the new arrivals, "What's your name?"

I knew all the girls. The girl in front of her was Tadhg and Callie's daughter. I was just about to speak when the girl responded.

"Fairlie," she announced proudly.

"Fairy?" Kendra asked, surprised, making me smile. She looked like a dainty fairy, the smallest of the group. She could have been Illy's, she was so petite.

"No!" The tiny brunette fairy stomped her foot impatiently at Kendra and spoke in a lilting Irish accent. "Fair-lie. F-a-i-r-l-i.e. No one can spell my name, and it makes me so cross!"

Di, hearing the conversation and recognizing this could end badly after the news we had just dropped on them, crossed the room, crouched down, and spoke calmly at Fairlie's height.

"I used to have a friend from school named Fairlie. Everyone used to get her name wrong, too. Do you know what she did?"

"No." The bottom lip was still protruding but receding.

"She used to treat it like a game. Every time she went to a shop, and they asked her name, she would wait to see how they spelled it."

"Why would a shop ask your name?" Fairlie asked suspiciously. "My mam says I should never tell strangers my name."

Di sighed. That was a complicated question, under the circumstances. "You see, back home, before we moved here, people used to buy lots of things at shops. Things that we make for ourselves now."

"Were people really lazy then?"

Di giggled. "No, not really. But to buy something meant that those people had a job, and everyone having a job was important."

Fairlie nodded wisely. I tried not to grin. Her mannerisms were so much like Callie's.

"So one of the things you could buy from a shop was a drink. Coffee, tea, or maybe even juice."

"Juice? Why would you buy juice? You just eat the fruit or squeeze it yourself."

"Well, yes. But sometimes people liked to mix their juices."

The wide-eyed look on Fairlie's face was priceless, and it was all I could do not to interrupt. "Mix juices?" she breathed like it was the most horrifying thing in the world.

Di laughed. "Oh yes. Orange and pineapple and passionfruit all mixed together."

"What's a passionfruit?"

"It is a small purple fruit with little black seeds that grow on a vine. They are delicious. Maybe I will grow some for you when we get home. But what I was saying was that my friend used to tell people in shops that her name was Fairlie, and she would wait to see how they spelled it on the cup. She used to take photos and share them so we could all laugh too."

"I've seen photos. My Mam and Dad have some. They are very old."

"They are. But do you see—you have a choice. You can be cross about it, or you can think it is funny that some people can't spell your name. It is a unique name."

"Did your friend like it?"

"She did. It is very unusual. I'll bet you are the only Fairlie in your school at home."

Fairlie thought about that for a moment before nodding cautiously.

"Now, Miss Fairlie, which book are you going to choose?"

Fairlie pointed at a book on the table.

"Ahh, that is one of my favorites. Let's read it together."

I smiled at Di. She was a natural with children. Knowing instinctively how to engage with them, not to be overbearing or demeaning, it was quite a gift. Even three days at sea with so many children was exhausting, and I often wondered how teachers did it. Cait was sitting calmly beside Sera, drawing. At least she had calmed down.

Closing my bedroom door with a sigh, I leaned against it and closed my eyes. This morning had been my turn to teach basic science, and I had been smothered with questions thrown at me by twenty-two six-year-old girls as I tried to teach them about chemical reactions by making a volcano out of bicarbonate of soda and vinegar. Thank goodness Di had used her time in Edinburgh to collect as many textbooks and reading and writing materials as she could. Months with so many girls, plus poor Alasdair, would have been hell without them. But we weren't even past continental Europe yet, traveling as conservatively as we could to stretch out the requirement to refuel.

"How were the mini-me's?" Cam's voice reached me from the bed, the room darkened by curtains and blinds. He was on night piloting duty, and I was due to be assisting. But teaching had taken precedence today, and now I was shattered and looking forward to a nap.

"Freaking exhausting, apart from Alasdair, who didn't get a word in. I don't know how Di does it," I admitted. "Remind me to look after her. I'd hate for her to get sick and leave teaching to us."

"Well, they are all half you," Cam teased. "Intelligent, stubborn, opinionated."

"Caitlin and Seraphine are the worst. Sharp and with cutting tongues. Poor Alasdair. He is belittled, ridiculed, and generally beaten into submission by those girls."

"As I said, they are all half you."

Crossing the room, I opened the curtains a crack and stared out to sea, watching the glistening blue waves surge past, white caps on the tips. I wished more than anything that Luca was here. Not only for his wife and family but for his friendship and support. This expedition would be so much safer with Luca along. *I miss you, my friend.* I sent the message silently across the ocean. So many nights, he and I had sat on the deck of the *Selkie*, talking and laughing. He had been my rock in the years I had lost Cam. How close I had come to losing Cam through my own stupidity. Hugging my arms around myself, I knew I was blessed. Even though I couldn't quite shake the feeling of insecurity, I was so fortunate to have spent all these years with a man I adored and to have friends and family who would pull up roots to accompany me and these children across the ocean.

"Come to bed," Cam soothed. "I'll make you forget about everything."

CHAPTER 8

"TELL ME EVERYTHING," ILLY gushed with a cheeky grin as she collapsed onto my bed as I closed the door firmly behind us and sat down beside her. With so many people aboard, it was impossible to get more than two minutes of peace. Cam barely left my side, which meant speaking about him was a little tricky.

"You said day two? Why did you hold out that long?"

"Because I didn't want to be near him. I was angry. I was angry at you, angry at him. I feel like I'm angry all the time."

"I'd noticed. Mousa is tiny with little shelter. Where did you go?"

"I stupidly took the blankets and tried to sleep in one of the cottages. It was barely waterproof, stank like nothing I can describe, worse than any male public toilet block. After the stench had seared my nasal passages to the point of no longer being able to smell, I froze my butt off is what happened. I was an icicle by morning. Everything hurt as it thawed. I cursed you something fierce that night. Good thing I didn't have the materials, or I seriously would have made a voodoo doll."

"So you went and snuggled in his double sleeping bag?"

"Hardly. I went for a walk at dawn to thaw and ignore my hunger pangs because you left us the most disgusting food you could find. Deliberately, I have no doubt. After a few hours, I hated you ever so slightly less but would still have happily rammed a fork into your eyeball had you been near me."

"We needed to. You just needed a push. Traveling all this way without someone by your side wasn't going to happen. Besides, you are meant to be together. But tell me all about the reunion part."

I sighed, realizing she would never let it go. "I walked a lap of the island. It isn't that big, so it was only mid-morning by the time I got back to where you dropped us near the broch. My hands and feet finally had feeling return to them. The sun was shining directly in my eyes as I came around the side of the broch, so I was farther around than I realized. Then I saw him."

"Waiting for you with open arms?"

"No. I found him in the spot he had been standing when Alize told him what happened to … *her.*"

Illy nodded excitedly, indicating for me to continue.

"I was in the open before I realized. The broch was close, so I tried to creep away, but he sensed me there, despite the howling wind and roaring waves. He spun around and caught me watching. So we fought … and it ended not in a fight."

Illy flopped back on my pillow dramatically. "Oh, come *on*! I have been widowed for seven fucking *years,* Freyja! You need to give me more than that!"

Sighing and avoiding eye contact, I told her. All of it.

"Phwoar! That is hotter than any of my romance novels! What was it like? To be together again after nine months?"

"It was like finding the missing piece of myself," I admitted. "Only I didn't realize I was incomplete."

"That is so romantic!" she squealed.

I shook my head. I still couldn't get over Illy loving romance novels. But she had read them ever since I had known her. The happily ever after. The alpha male. The friends-to-lovers tropes. She adored it all. "Her escape," she called them. Many times, she had tried to push them on me—shirtless men on the covers, heavily tattooed bikers—but I repeatedly told her it wasn't my thing.

"Did Luca know you read romance novels?" I asked suspiciously.

"Of course! We had a running list of the worst adjectives used to describe male anatomy."

My mouth dropped. "Like what?"

"Oh, meat stick, steel rod, sword. I think my favorite was rumple foreskin. I couldn't even finish that book."

I gasped. "Luca read these, too?"

"Oh no! He just got me to read him the smutty parts."

I wasn't sure how to respond to that. "Too much information," I finally managed.

"I had to hide them before I left. I don't want to be providing that type of education to my daughters."

"I learned from magazines the girls handed around at school. Didn't you?"

"Well, yes. But they are twelve. I am not ready for that." Illy propped herself up on an elbow, turning to look at me. "Just so I understand, you spent six months away, then you broke up with him, treated him like shit for three whole months, tortured your kids because you thought he and Laetitia were … what? Soulmates?"

"They were. The science proved it."

Illy threw back her head and roared. "For someone so smart, you can be so dense. Soulmates, my ass. You can't possibly believe that, can you?"

"You are the psychologist. You know, touchy-feely emotional shit. How can you not believe? Like you didn't think you and Luca were soulmates?"

"I don't believe in such a thing. Compatible—yes. In love, absolutely. The only one in the world for me—hell no. Even now, with the far reduced offerings, I could still find someone I was happy with, if I chose to. I choose not to, but I could. As for Luca, that wasn't love at first sight. I made an educated decision to jump him that day. If I hadn't, likely both of us would have met someone else. Luca and I made a conscious effort every day to make our relationship work. There is no such thing as the Hollywood movie romance, Frey. That isn't real life."

"What was Laetitia then?" I whispered. "I saw those photos. He was madly, deeply in love with her."

"He loved her. He loves *you*. Love isn't sunshine and rainbows all the time, Freyja. It is dirty floors, sick kids, changing nappies, and washing dishes. But doing it together. With your equal, a partner. Getting up each day with your friend, coping with the challenges life throws at you, and falling into bed, still laughing. That is love. You've built up his relationship with her as something more than what he has with you, but it isn't true."

"I saw them," I whispered.

"What did you see? A blissfully happy moment? Sure. He had those; of course he did. You don't spend three years with someone and not have some. I have seen plenty of happy moments between the two of you. At my wedding, he gazed at you with such devotion. When you were pregnant with Xanthe, and he couldn't keep his eyes off you. I saw the look on his face when he held Thorsten in his arms for the first time. He was bursting with love—for you. Just watching you buzz around the kitchen, I see him watching you with love in his eyes. Besides, I think you are forgetting one rather important detail in this utterly ridiculous story you have concocted to convince yourself."

"What?"

"She is *dead,* Freyja. Dead and gone for a long time now. So really, what happened, if we are to be completely honest about it, is that you are jealous of a dead woman."

Cam had thrown those words at me too, and I had vehemently denied it. But this time, they hit me like a freight train.

"I am." I wheezed, all the air seeping from my lungs. "I ... am ... jealous. I wanted him to love me and love me only. Then I found the records, proving that he was meant to be with her. I saw the photos of their wedding. Their ... honeymoon. I know that was when Louis was conceived. It killed me. My heart froze, and I couldn't feel. Everywhere I turned, I was haunted. I could see him with her, lying out on the grass. That night I saw them together in the hall. She was holding their baby, and he was gazing down at Louis in a way that felt like ice shards impaling my heart. I waited for him, but he didn't wait for me. I couldn't deal with feeling like that again."

"So instead, you blamed him for something that wasn't his fault."

"I did. I really did."

Illy brought her arm over my stomach as I lay beside her. "That's more like it. Only when you accept it can you heal. He is only who he is because of you. You are such a control freak, and this situation made you felt out of control. You reverted to type and did what has served you well in the past, and you walked away. From him. From your children. And can I just say: you are a bit of an angry bitch without him."

"Hey!" I protested as she laughed.

"Have I ever sugar-coated it?"

"No," I admitted begrudgingly. "I was so full of rage at him. I told myself it was because of what he said."

"But now?"

"I was angry because he loved her," I whispered, shame flooding my face. "And I saw it. I always knew. But when I saw it with my own eyes, I couldn't erase the memories. Those photos. The file. It all compounded my isolation. I had nightmares when I first arrived in Clava. Of that room. The operating theater. And I was alone. I couldn't tell anyone. Then I saw those photos, and all I could do was focus on the work. Work myself to exhaustion until I dropped into bed and could no longer think. Stopped feeling."

"I wondered how you would cope with that. When you came home, you were so bitter. You wouldn't talk to me. You were a cow to Cam, to Sorcha, to me. Everyone. Except for Stefan, it appears."

"I would have scared him off soon enough," I admitted. "Boys always told me I was too intense."

"Because you are."

"Thanks for the support. But that raises a question. How do I tell Stefan? Hi honey, I'm home. Reconciled with hubby. Thanks for the dinners. Sorry you didn't make it to second base."

"He didn't make..."

"No!" I cut that comment off. "Nothing like that happened. I swear. Although I admit, the timing was close. I was planning to visit him the night we left."

"You know..." Illy said, then stopped.

"Know what?"

Illy thought, choosing her words carefully, "I have been wondering for a while if there is a chance he is behind it."

"Stefan? Behind what?"

"You. The girls."

"Come on. Why?"

"Motives are often only ever known by the perpetrator. You have to admit the timeframes are suspicious. You leave Clava. Ceri is murdered. He arrives on Lewis. Your home is ransacked. No one else has been in both places during those times."

"Was he on Clava when Ceri died?"

"I'm uncertain," Illy admitted, "but the timeframes would be close."

"Okay, but children were killed on Newgrange and Orkney too."

"True. We are looking for more than one person. We know that."

"Why would he ransack my home? Cut up all my photos?"

Illy raised her eyebrows as she lay on my pillow, watching me, assessing my reaction.

"The oldest trick in the book. Place the woman in danger. Terrify her until she comes flying into his arms. The white knight on his trusty steed, ready to save her. Protect her from evil, when all the time he is the evil."

"Hang on, that makes no sense. Why target my old house? He knew I lived with you."

"The houses are joined. Maybe he was confirming you were telling the truth. Or it could simply be that the photos were still there. He knew Cam would tell you, and you would run. Did you tell him you were planning to move?"

"No. I didn't get the chance. Or rather, I did. I saw him that morning, but I wanted something just for Kat and me. Not the three of us."

"So you weren't that interested?"

I sighed. "Physically, no. Logically, I knew I should have been interested."

"Ah, logic. Hello Freyja! But back to the important bit, you saw him that morning?"

"I did. After I left you at breakfast, I saw him on my way to Garynahine."

"Where was he going?"

"He didn't say. I didn't ask. It was a little awkward. He had me up against the car, kissing me. We were in public, and I wanted to get away before anyone saw."

"Did he ask where you were going?"

"I'm fairly certain I told him I was headed to the northern crofts and would meet him back at the clinic in the afternoon. He was on an afternoon shift, and I wanted to check in on Mike."

"He knew you were out, and he had an opportunity? Everyone knows Cam would have been at work with the fall harvest. My schedule is well publicized. He knows the house would have been empty."

"I guess so. But don't you think it is a bit extreme?"

"Maybe. But you are one tough chick. It would need to be extreme for you to fall into someone's arms. Was threatening your life enough?"

But I am not tough, I wanted to say but couldn't. "It would have been. If I had seen the photos, I would have felt the need to run."

"Everyone has a fight-or-flight instinct, Frey. Yours is fight … usually. But when your life is on the line or your children? Most people run. Look at us now. We could have gathered all the girls and guarded them on one of the communities."

"Why didn't we then?"

"We thought about it. But we had no idea who was responsible or why. It could be someone we know and trust. It was also obvious that there is more than one perpetrator. The religious references are the strange part. There has been no organized religion, as far as I am aware, for twenty years. But the original settlers may have hung onto this. I mean, Tadhg is certainly still Catholic. I was raised Protestant. When people get sick, or old, or something else changes in their lives, people often turn to religion. Faith helps people."

"Does that mean we are looking for older people?"

"I don't know. All I know is that there were Biblical references at each of the murder sites."

"Unless he hid it from me, Stefan isn't religious. He is a scientist. A doctor. I can't see it."

"I didn't know him well on Clava, I admit. We had one date, and he was too arrogant for my liking. Kept trying to tell me about the important scientific work he was doing and demeaning the soft skills of my work. Like surgeons were more important than psychologists. I couldn't get home fast enough."

"You have been giving this a lot of thought."

"It is you. It is Sera. Cait. Mei. All of them. Even Ruby and Scarlett aren't safe. We need to work this out. We can't stay out here in the middle of the ocean. We have limited supplies. Taking them to the one place we know they will be safe while we work this out made the most sense. Sorcha is known there. Di's cousin is there. If there is someone on Clava willing to … kill," she said softly, "then we are limited in places to go. Auckland, even August or Bellcamp likely aren't safe. Except Kiewa."

"I wish Luca were here," I whispered to the ceiling. "He always knew what to do. He always made me feel it was under control. That it would all work out. Even getting to Kat, I never felt anything other than the plan would be a success."

"He was freaking out about that mission," Illy admitted.

I turned back to face her sapphire blue eyes. "You never told me that! Really?"

"It was *you*. The person in the world he loved most after the girls and me. He would have done anything for you. He and I ran the variables so many times. He kept me up at night working through contingencies."

"I would have done anything for him, too."

"You did. You gave him a fourth child. A special one. He would adore her."

"Seraphine is one tough cookie," I admitted. "She would have walked all over him. Damn, that kid can take a split-second pause and exploit it."

"She is a born lawyer," Illy sniggered. "Only she will never know what a lawyer is with any luck."

"She might be mine biologically, and Luca's, but bloody hell, she is you personified," I teased. A brilliant young lady who constantly pushed against boundaries, much like her sisters, Sera was no pushover. While Luca had always asserted that the twins' stubborn personalities were inherited from Illy, Sera had proven more than once that she was her father's daughter. I had long suspected that Sera was a gift to Illy from Ashton. An apology, perhaps, for keeping her hostage along with me. He had attended all the birthday gatherings, and more than once I had seen him watch Illy with a look of longing. But he had never made a move, and she seemed oblivious. Not wanting to recall memories of that time, I had said nothing, even to Cam. But I wondered all the same if Seraphine's father was a deliberate choice.

"Why on earth did I name that little demon after angels?" Illy had groaned on more than one occasion as she had despaired of Seraphine's resistance to anything she didn't want to do.

The second child with a known father was little Fairlie, adopted by Callie and Tadhg. Fairlie was biologically mine and Tadhg's, and a lovely, sweet girl she was. Always caring for the others, she was smaller but appeared far older than the other girls. When she was an infant, she had needed a blood transfusion after an accident. Unable to get me to Newgrange fast enough, the scientific team had admitted that Tadhg was her biological father. His blood had been tested and was compatible so that he could act as a blood donor.

"Well, Sera is enjoying being here. She told me she sees it as an adventure."

"She threw one of Di's textbooks overboard yesterday, did you hear?"

I sniggered. "That poor kid. Cam always says being a mix of you, me, and Luca, she has no hope."

"I hate to admit it, but I think he is right. And with four, I am too tired to parent her."

"I don't think Sera will ever be parented. If Ally and Summer can't get her to do anything, then it can't be done. Our Cait gives her a run for her money, though. I never thought I would raise a child more stubborn than Katrin. But holy hell, Caitlin is so bloody determined. And so intelligent it scares me."

"Do you still wonder who her father is?" Illy asked softly.

I stared at her. "I've never told you that."

Illy's eyebrows raised. "Oh, come on. I have watched you assessing her a million times. Analyzing her. Wondering who on Clava her father could be."

"I'm just scared it could have been *him*," I exhaled.

"I doubt they would have done that."

"But if she was in the first collection, then it was before he tried to assault me," I whispered, my fingers touching the cheekbone he had broken that night.

"You've been thinking about this far too much. What are the odds, really? They had samples from all the Edinburgh processed residents, so thousands of samples. They had Tadhg's and Luca's. What are the chances, really?"

"Too bloody high."

"Would it change how you feel about her?"

I considered that. I wanted to say, "No, of course not. She is an innocent little girl." *But would I? Would I see her differently if I knew she was Dale's child?* The truth was that Cam was her father in every way that counted. Like Louis was mine, Cait was his. Nevertheless, I would catch sight of her in the distance, the sun shining off her glossy dark hair. A look would cross her face, making me wonder who she looked like.

"I don't know. I love her. That isn't in question. But if I knew, would I see *him* in her? At least with the others, there is no doubt."

"Louis isn't yours," she pointed out gently. "Yet you risked everything for him."

I sighed deeply. "And I would do it again. Even knowing what I sacrificed. I hope they are okay. Yours, too. They are so young to be left alone."

"The girls drive me insane, but I miss them more than I thought possible," Illy admitted. "I know they will be fine. Better than fine—they will thrive. It will force them to step up and be responsible. But I worry all the same."

"Isla won't take any nonsense from yours or mine. Bridget and Jorja, too. But Jacinda likely will. Do you think they will try to move in with them?"

Illy snorted. "Not as long as they are vegan! My two are their father's daughters. Although, I wouldn't put it past Summer to try to convert them back to eating meat. She loves a challenge, that girl."

"My money is on Summer if it was a battle between your girls and Jacinda. I often think the universe sent them to you as you were the only one who could handle them!"

"The same could be said of you. Katrin and Caitlin are no walk in the park. Cait would have sent Jacinda to an early grave with her determinedness by now."

"I couldn't handle Ceridwen," I admitted, sadness creeping in. "And now I will never get the chance."

"That is not your fault."

"I still feel guilty. She is my niece. Was my niece. We spent time together when I was training. She was still cold and awkward, but I understood her more. She just wanted to learn, to belong somewhere. She never got to be part of a family, and now she never will. I just can't believe she is gone. She is younger than Kat. A child. Who would do something like that? And despite what you think, I can't believe Stefan would hurt a young girl."

"How well do you know him, really?" Illy's dark brows raised enquiringly.

I shrugged, thinking about it. "He was my supervisor. It was his job to teach me everything I needed to know in a limited timeframe. We worked together for twelve to sixteen hours a day, seven days a week. Or, rather, I did. He set me tasks late at night and disappeared off to bed while I worked. I hated him at first, found him condescending and egotistical. But he grew on me. Slowly. Many late nights were spent in the training labs, working closely. But nothing had happened. No sparks. Not until Lewis. But even then, it was a slow burn. It didn't progress to more than kissing. Hot steamy kisses, to be fair..." I sighed, realizing how close I had come to leaving Cam. One more night on Lewis and my relationship with Stefan would have progressed into something more.

I sensed Illy watching me, reading me.

"He had no reason to harm her. I can't see it," I admitted.

"You are an excellent judge of character, Frey. If you think it wasn't him, then it likely wasn't."

"You don't sound convinced."

"I just can't think who else it could possibly be. No one else is new, and to think that someone we know, and likely know well, is capable of killing a child? Invaded your home?"

A thought struck me, and I watched her. Illy's face was only a few inches from my own. "Summer. Do you think...?"

"I do. I have been thinking about that for a while. When I questioned her as I waited for you to come home, she finally confessed that the cupcake was for Seraphine, but she had forced Sera not to tell. Summer managed to convince Sera that it wasn't very nice. Sera only had a small bite. Summer ate most of it. But she is a big girl, so a poison wouldn't have the same effect on her."

"Poison?" I choked. "Sera is only six!"

"But what easier way than to get her to water and drown her if the same pattern was followed? That was why I genuinely think there is a potential murderer on Lewis too."

"Who gave Sera the cupcake?" I choked.

"She doesn't know. She said it was left in her schoolbag in the outer room. There are no windows between the classroom and the coatroom. Everyone knows they attend school there. We have all been there a hundred times. Her bag had her name on it and her hook. It could have been anyone."

"How long before my photos? About a week?"

"Eight days. Summer vomited and was seriously ill for nearly a week. She could barely get out of bed. But she is more than twice Sera's size. It would have killed Sera or at least incapacitated her."

"I can see why you rushed to get us all away."

"Stefan wasn't working that day," Illy whispered, not looking at me. "Sorcha checked."

"Fuck. So the timelines fit. Hang on, how long have you suspected him?"

"I haven't trusted him since he moved to Lewis and started showing an interest in you, especially when he hadn't made a move on Clava. Had he been truly besotted with you, he would have hit on you there when there was no husband and children around to complicate the fledgling relationship. But of this, only since the day Cam found the photos. As much as people think they are original, the truth is, most violent crimes follow a profile. Perpetrators are rarely complete strangers. I mean, it happens, but more often than not, it is someone close to the victim. In your case, Cam isn't a suspect. That leaves Stefan. I agree it makes no sense, but we don't have any better theories. And if Stefan is involved, then we can't trust anyone on Auckland Island either. Of course, it could just be heuristics."

"Now you are just showing off. What are heuristics?"

"Heuristics is the name given to the natural biases in the way people think. Heuristics are like intelligent guesses derived from experience and intuition."

"You know Luca would roll his eyes and say, bloody psychologist. So you are saying that we are naturally biased because we had unpleasant experiences with Auckland and Clava in the past?"

"We are, aren't we? Especially you and me. Everyone has bias. It isn't possible not to. The key is to recognize your own and not let them decide for you. Like if you had a bias against people with tattoos, you need to find other ways to assess someone, not just judge them for artwork on their skin. Set fair criteria and don't let your bias come into play."

"That makes sense. So you are saying we may be biased against Stefan because of his allegiances?"

"I don't see how you expect me not to be. I was one of them, but only Magali and I actively chose not to support the project. She, Nasir, and I were the only ones who left once we had an inkling of their true plans. Then there was the situation with you and me. We won't forget that as long as we live. While the relationship has improved since the girls were born, I can never entirely trust them. Any of them. The medical team likely all knew, and that means Stefan too. If he isn't behind this situation with the girls, then I am sorry I suspected him. But he will never know. If I am right, and he is responsible, well, then moving the girls far away is in their best interest. If it saves one more life, then it is worth it, isn't it?"

"Saving a life is always worth it," I muttered, thinking of the two we took. She and I.

Illy saw the storm crossing my face. "What would you have had me do? Leave him there? Nate would have warned Angus, and he could have taken Louis and Ceri and been well gone by the time we arrived. As for Angus, if we left him, he would have tried again. With Clava's backing likely."

"I know. I have replayed all the variables a million times. Same with Mousa. It had to be done. I just didn't want to be the one who did it."

"Despite what you might think, every single returned serviceman or woman I have counseled has said the same thing. The instruction needed to be followed. They just wish that they weren't the ones who carried it out. Luca still had nightmares about some things he saw and did under orders many years before."

"He did? He never told me that. So how did you help those people?"

"You listen, make suggestions. Often they come to a conclusion on their own. It was their job, their responsibility. Would they have wanted a friend to do it? Usually not. Most people would spare others that pain."

"You tried to spare me that pain. But I still feel it like I did it myself. And I would have done it to spare you."

"I know, and that is the part I wasn't expecting. Witnessing it, and doing it, feels the same."

After I ordered the kidnappers to be killed on Mousa, I struggled with the most jumbled mix of emotions. Guilt, shame, but also relief. We killed a former friend in Angus, but I was relieved knowing he would never come after Louis again. Or Ceri.

"Do you think Ceri was targeted because of Angus?" I asked.

"No, I considered that. But why Soli and Beth? They weren't Angus' children, as far as we know. And why target you? If Angus was the motive, then why not target Louis, Ruby, or Scarlett?"

"Well, we have some time to work it out, although I don't know we will learn much out here in the middle of the ocean with no communications."

By agreement, we had disconnected the radio and anything that could track us. As distressed as the parents were letting their children go with us and not staying in contact, they all knew the risks of being traceable. Three girls killed in a month across three communities. No clues about who was responsible.

"They trust you," Illy whispered, her blue eyes flashing with concern. "Each one of those families knows you would lay down your life for those girls, despite their origins. That is why we faced no resistance in taking them. They don't even know where we are going, yet they let them go."

"They sent someone from their community too, and I am pleased to have them both here."

"True. But they trust *you* to keep them safe."

The burden of that responsibility hit me like slamming into a brick wall at high speed. "What if I can't keep them safe?" I gasped as all the air escaped my lungs.

"We will do this together. We are a team, Frey. All of us."

CHAPTER 9

"MERRY CHRISTMAS!"

My heart pounded out of my chest as I jolted awake at the unexpected noise. My eyes burst open, blinked, and cowered back under the quilt as I tried to soothe my frazzled nerves. The chattering continued, and I peeked to see Caitlin and her sisters crowded around the foot of the bed.

"Wha...uh?" I slurred, praying this was a dream. My heart, continuing to thump erratically, indicated otherwise.

"Mummy, it's Christmas!" Her tanned little face lit up like a sunbeam, making me feel like the grinch.

"Uh huh." I closed my eyes, praying Cam would take over. We both knew who was the better parent.

"Merry Christmas, sweetheart! Now, could you see if Auntie Sorcha is awake, and we will meet you in the kitchen in a few minutes?" Cam said, saving the moment.

"Okay, Daddy!" The racket made by twenty-some-thing pairs of feet stomping out of our room and associated chatter reverberating down the hallway made me bury my head under the pillow.

"Kill me now," I breathed. Before Sorcha did when she realized we had sent them.

"Oh, come on. It's Christmas!" He lifted the pillow, exposing my face in the dim morning light, smoothed back my bird's nest of hair, and kissed me on the cheek. "Merry Christmas, honey!"

"Urgh," I gurgled.

"You know, if you don't get up, they will drag you out of bed. It is Christmas, and they are away from home. We need to make this special."

"Special for whom?" I grumbled. The large, firm hand ran down my back, kneading along my spine, making me relax even more into the mattress. "As awesome as that feels," I muttered, face down into the pillow, "you'd better stop, or I will relax so much I won't be able to get out of bed."

Cam threw the quilt back. The rude gust of cool air striking my back made me tense instantly.

"Okay, that was mean!" I rolled over and slapped at him.

"But it works every time. Come on."

The squeals could be heard from a deck away, twenty-seven children of various ages. Sorcha emerged from her room down the corridor, looking every bit as unimpressed as I was.

"Sending the feral pack of Valkyries into my room was *your* idea, I hear?" she fired at Cam.

"Your three were among those who woke us," he shot back sweetly. "Just sharing the love."

Stuck on the main glass window between the living space and the deck, Di and the children had affixed a beautiful makeshift tree made of colored cardboard.

Each child had created a branch, and together they formed a spectacular artwork of differing greens, with hand-painted decorations. On the floor beneath lay an enormous pile of gifts, each wrapped in artwork, and with a handmade tag bearing the recipient's name.

"Who did that?" I whispered to Cam, feeling like the worst parent in the world.

"Di, Illy, and Sorcha. They knew we would likely still be at sea, and the kids wouldn't be home with their families. So after ditching us on Mousa, they made the sensible decision to source a Christmas and birthday gift for each child. Each child was assigned to paint the wrapping paper for one of her sisters or brothers."

"That is a lovely idea. Where did they get the gifts?"

"Edinburgh."

Sitting back and watching, I needed to block my ears from the squeals of joy after a while. I wished I could share their happiness but somehow couldn't find the energy. Cam's hand found mine on the couch.

"Wishing the others were here?" he whispered in my ear.

I nodded. "Why didn't we bring them?"

"Lack of space. Not wanting to interrupt Louis and Kat's work. A whole raft of reasons. But keeping them safe was the primary one. If we are the targets, they are safer there."

I understood the rationale but felt a pang of jealousy that Sorcha had all of her children surrounding her. Illy didn't and knew exactly how I felt, wondering if we had left them behind to keep them safe or had inadvertently placed them in greater danger. Not knowing who or why we were being targeted made it even more uncomfortable. Knowing someone despised you was one thing, and a feeling I was no stranger to. Even on Clava, I knew who my captors were. Their motives were never hidden. But a secret assassin invoked fear of a type I had rarely felt. Knowing that they could strike at any moment—just when you felt safe, in your own home, sleeping, traveling to work—the paralyzing fear that someone was intent on doing you harm, but no idea why or how to stop it.

I was glad I hadn't seen the cut-up photos. That would have made it even more real. Cam wasn't sleeping well, I knew, his restlessness often keeping me awake. But sometimes, I was grateful for the lack of sleep. Being awake meant fewer nights spent lurching awake in terror, my heart pounding, needing to get up and change my sweat-soaked pajamas before he realized. I knew he was fearful for the girls and me. But we were headed somewhere he was known. Sorcha, Di too. The residents on Kiewa owed me no loyalty, and I wondered what sort of reception I would receive.

"You know you aren't a target," I whispered, not wanting the girls to overhear. "I am. You could have stayed on Lewis and likely been safer than here. You could have looked after your children."

Cam's hand clenched mine tighter, his knuckles turning white with the pressure. "Caitlin is my daughter. Staying behind wasn't an option I even considered. Letting her, or you, head off into danger without me? That would never happen. You went after Louis, and even after everything that happened to you, you kept going. You could have come home, but you didn't. Why wouldn't I do this?"

"Because I was awful to you. I can't believe you would come, even when you thought I was with someone else."

"My heart will always love you. Even if you had left me and married him, I would never stop loving you."

"You really are a god among men." I nuzzled his neck, making his breath quicken and more audible as his arms came around me and lifted me onto his lap.

"Frey!" Illy hissed, and I turned to see Cait holding out a gift and the entire room watching.

"Oops," Cam whispered in my ear as he slid me back to the couch beside him.

Happiness pervaded the day. Di had done an excellent job of arranging gifts, Christmas carols, games, and some old DVDs for the lounge later in the afternoon. Most of the children had never seen a movie and were fascinated.

"Video sedation," Cam murmured in my ear. "Mum used to say it was always a winner."

"I'm surprised the player still works," I whispered back. "I hope it doesn't break down mid-movie."

While the children were fascinated by old Christmas family movies, Illy, Sorcha, and I arranged a dinner, the best we could with the long-life food we had aboard. Di had suggested we place lots of different dishes along the table and let the children help themselves. This had proven to be a fantastic idea, and each child thought it the best thing ever to serve themselves whatever they wanted and be allowed to sit out on the deck to eat it, watching the sunset over the water. We were finally relaxing slightly about them being outside. After all, they were immune to the protozoa that could kill us, but initially we had feared that one of them might slip and fall. But permitted to go outside in groups of three or more, they had proven to be sensible, and Di regularly made them run supervised laps around the deck when the level of silliness got out of hand.

"We just need lights, and it would be like the feasts in Harry Potter," Di told them, her eyes glittering as they came back for dessert.

I looked at her. "Harry Potter? How on earth would they know about that? They are six."

"Nearly seven, and I am reading it to them in class."

"You don't think the concept of witches, wizards, magic, and evil spells is a little farfetched for most of them? They live on an isolated rural island community."

It was the word witch that had stung, remembering the vandalism on our bathroom mirror and the sickening feeling of being hunted churned in the pit of my stomach.

Di didn't seem to notice my discomfort. "It is wonderful for them to use their imaginations. I took an enormous stash of books from a lovely bookshop in Edinburgh. We started with my favorites, Enid Blyton's Faraway Tree series. After we finished those books, they wanted something else magical. I have limited texts here, and they love it. Every afternoon they snuggle down on the floor with cushions and listen to me read. Sometimes they fall asleep!" Di giggled. "But I'd like to think that is because they are relaxed and not that I am so boring."

"Boring is never a word used to describe you," I assured her. "You are a wonderful teacher. I can see why you miss it."

As we rounded the southern coast of Africa, the fresh food we had taken from Lewis and donated by the communities on Orkney and Newgrange was nearly depleted.

"What do we have left?" I asked Cam as I got out the chopping boards and started preparing lunch.

"Carrots, potatoes, onions, pumpkin. Not much else, but those keep well, and we can space them out. Most of the children don't like turnips, but we can use them in soup. Garlic too. But there are plenty of cans of red kidney beans, chickpeas, and lentils. Just don't use too many, or they will grizzle and only eat the bread."

Sorcha was one of the few people on Lewis who had an electric bread maker and taking it with us had been a stroke of genius, as we needed to run it twenty-four hours a day. Illy had the foresight to take as much flour as she could from each community to make bread and pasta, plus oats to make porridge. The mill made me think of Aidan and Stefan and what she had told Aidan to get so many sacks of flour. I wondered once again how long he had waited up for me that night before realizing I wasn't coming. I flushed as Cam looked at me.

"You need to help me with quantities," I reminded him, trying to cover my discomfort. Each day, we made a pot of soup with bread for lunch. Fresh and canned vegetables, lentils, and other pulses. At least we knew Arataki, who was vegan, was getting enough protein. She was a quiet girl who never complained, and I was increasingly worried about her. She was withdrawing from the others and could often be seen sitting alone, staring off into space. I made a mental note to speak with Di. They were all homesick, but this was extreme, especially in a young girl.

All jobs were shared among the adults, except Di, who single-handedly carried the teaching load. It was a standing joke that when it was my turn to cook, I made enough food for all of us for several days. Never having cooked for so many, I had no idea about quantities to cook for thirty-four mouths and across a progressive sitting. There simply wasn't enough table space for everyone to eat together. Cooking for my own family was challenging enough. One night cooking pasta, there had been so much leftover that it had necessitated a menu shuffle, and we needed to add leftover pasta to soup for lunch and tuna bake for dinner the following day. Wastage simply wasn't an option. But we had sacks of rice and pasta for bulk, and Sorcha and I had carefully considered nutrition for each of the children. Personally, I would much rather have been allocated a set job but recognized that no one enjoyed cleaning up after twenty-seven children. The older four were helpful and helped with dishes, so I was eminently grateful for that. Daily cleaning of bedrooms, showers, and toilets for so many children was awful, so I was thrilled when it was my turn to pilot the vessel, a job that basically involved monitoring the equipment and reading a book. Overnight, there was a stint of taking the cooked bread out of the machine, cleaning the tin, and making a fresh loaf.

"How much longer?" Cam asked me, looking up from the pot.

"Faster vessel but uses more fuel. Hard to guess. We will need to slow down a lot after we refuel in Madagascar. Three, maybe four weeks?"

"I'm not sure we can stretch these veggies out that long."

"Then canned food it is. We don't have a lot of choices."

"How long until scurvy becomes an issue?" he asked, adding the chopped carrots to the pot.

Squinting, I tried to recall my learning. "Initial symptoms after four weeks of no vitamin C, but three months until it becomes severe. But that would mean no ascorbic acid at all. They get some, but I am concerned it isn't enough. The canning process and long-term storage removes a lot of Vitamin C as it dissolves in water."

"Shame we didn't think to bring supplements."

"That is an excellent idea. Any supplements we source will be old, and they lose efficacy, but surely it is better than nothing. Perhaps we can stop in Cape Town and find a health shop."

"No point," Sorcha said as she entered from the deck. "Nothing will have been produced for nearly twenty years. The shelf life of vitamin C is less than two years. Sure it loses potency after that, but by now, it is nigh on useless."

"Damn. What do you suggest then?"

"Of what we have left, tomatoes are an excellent source. Potatoes too. We just need to ensure that the kids get a serve every day."

"Did you see it a lot in your development work?"

"Strangely, no. Scurvy was more prevalent in developed countries where people ate fast food, very restricted diets, and food with low nutrition.

In developing countries, they didn't have access to processed foods. They ate what they grew or caught locally, and while often it wasn't enough in quantity, green leafy vegetables and berries are reasonably rich in most vitamins and nutrients. I saw a case, once, in a four-year-old girl in Melbourne. She only ate custard, and her mother allowed it, thinking she was doing the right thing. It was her kindergarten teacher in the end who acted. The teacher called child protection, and they sought medical advice. Poor kid—she had bruises that didn't heal, rashes, loose teeth, and was constantly fatigued. So while I am concerned about the girls, they will be okay for a while yet."

"That is a relief," Cam said as he added the final vegetables to the soup. "I would hate to think we placed them in more danger."

"I am so glad you came along," I said, as genuinely as I could manage. "Your medical training far surpasses mine, and it makes me feel more comfortable that you are here in case something goes wrong."

Sorcha tilted her head to the side and stared. "Are you okay? Did you bang your head? Feeling sick?" Cam snorted. "You have never once praised my medical skill. Besides, I thought you still hated me for leaving you on Mousa."

"I am happy to insult you if it makes you feel more comfortable."

"No. Let's hear more of this grateful Freyja, shall we? I like her."

CHAPTER 10

THE GRINDING OF METAL on metal pierced my skull. Burying my head under the pillow, I prayed I was dreaming. *Please, no.* I wasn't ready to wake up. As the noise jolted me into consciousness, I registered we weren't moving. Even under the muffled warmth of my pillow, I could hear Cam speaking to someone.

Feeling woolly-headed, I cracked open an eye. "What?" I grumbled.

"We've broken down."

"No shit. What is it? Surely we haven't run out of fuel?"

"They aren't sure. Tadhg and Gerry are looking now, but you have the most knowledge. They are asking for you."

"Fuck it." I rolled dazedly, not registering how close I was to the edge, and hit the floor with a thud. Cam bolted to my side.

"I'm fine," I snapped. "Just tired."

Cam's powerful arms lifted me onto the bed and lowered me gently. "I'm sure there is nothing so urgent that it can't wait twenty minutes. Sit there. I'll be back."

Swaying, I forced myself to sit upright on the side of the bed, desperate to lie down. A glance out the window indicated it was mid-morning. No wonder I was tired. We had piloted the vessel overnight and handed it over at dawn. A few hours of sleep might be enough for Illy and Cam, but it just made me feel nauseous, especially when my sleep was constantly disrupted. Like jetlag, I recalled, shocked that I could remember the woozy, lightheaded sensation of long-haul air travel after all these years.

Cam returned with a steaming mug, and I sighed.

"I love you," I mumbled as I reached for it, sighing contently as both hands cupped the smooth curvature of the porcelain, absorbing the heat as I sipped.

Cam disappeared, returning with a tray holding two mugs and a bowl of porridge drizzled with honey.

"Now you are just showing off." I smiled as I replaced the empty mug with a full one as he sat beside me. "Tell me what is going on."

"I have an update. Gerry and Tadhg are in the engine room. They know what it isn't. We have fuel. It isn't the spark plug."

"And?"

"Well, that is about it. It is making a grinding sound."

Between mouthfuls, I asked, "I assume we haven't run aground or hit anything? Doesn't sound like dirty fuel or a fuse." My eyes winced as I heard the grinding noise shudder through the room. "Have they checked the fuel filter? Drive belt? Prop shaft?"

Cam looked at me blankly. Sighing, I swilled the rest of my cup and dropped it on the tray as I stood, spooning a last bite of porridge with my other hand. "Go back to bed. This could take a while."

Several hours later, we convened to address the issue. The prop shaft was bent out of shape. We had no spare, and even if we did, we didn't have the tools to replace it.

"We are in about the worst spot imaginable." Illy sighed. After refueling in Mauritius, we had left Africa several days before and were headed toward the western coast of Australia.

"Where do you think we are?" Sorcha asked.

"Roughly half-way between Africa and Australia. At a guess, Australia is the closest sizeable landmass, but we are still hundreds of kilometers from Perth. What are our options?"

Everyone was looking at me. Great. Just a bit of pressure.

"Choices." I started listing them on my fingers. "Sit here and wait for someone to find us. Not a great option under the circumstances. Drift and hope we find our way somewhere. Possible. But running out of food and fresh water is a genuine risk as is drifting in the wrong direction. We also need to find somewhere with spare parts and tools. Radio for help, but that would alert absolutely everyone to where we are and where we are headed." I shrugged. "Not much else we can do. We are sitting ducks."

Illy pursed her lips, and I watched her. "What?"

"How far do you think we are from Auckland Island?"

I considered that. "A few days, maybe. A week. Why?"

"What if we sent someone in the rescue dinghy? It is motorized…"

"Yes, but who? We could rig up some shelter, but we couldn't stay out of the water for that long. We are past halfway, but even so, it could take several days to get to Fremantle. That is probably our best bet. We were only there a few years ago, know the layout and where the shops are. We also know they were fairly well stocked, so likely to have what we need."

"Ruby and Scarlett could go," Illy said in a low voice. "They are immune."

Sorcha's face lighted as I shook my head in negation. "No! They are twelve. We can't send them out there on their own. Their mothers would kill me."

"They would indeed," Cam added, "after prolonged torture. If it was Illy's girls, or even Kat, maybe. But not Ruby and Scarlett. They have led very sheltered lives. They wouldn't survive."

"What do we do then?" Sorcha asked. "Call Auckland? They would help if they knew we had the girls."

Tadhg responded in his Irish lilt, "Are you certain that there aren't any potential assassins on Auckland? What if the person who killed Ceridwen is now on Auckland Island and heard the radio transmission?"

Illy fell silent. "I have no idea of who is behind this, what their motive is, nor where they are. No one does. That's what makes this threat so dangerous. Aside from the biblical references, and someone targeting Freyja and the girls, we have nothing to go on. After Ceri… no. I think we can safely assume that Auckland isn't safe. Nor Kerguelen. We genuinely are on our own."

Di spoke, and I turned, hearing her sweet, gentle voice. I had forgotten she was even here. "I'll ask them," she said softly. "Explain how important it is. They are our only hope."

Two days later, after a full day of preparation, teaching Ruby and Scarlett how to use the GPS and setting a course for Fremantle, listing and showing them what parts we were seeking, and hours of relentless instruction on how to operate and refuel the boat, we lowered the dinghy, now equipped with a radio, GPS, and enough fuel and food for a week. We had rigged enough shelter to keep the girls out of the sun and ordered them never to take their life jackets off. We tied them together, so even if one was swept overboard, her sister could pull her in. Being sprayed with water scared me, even though we knew they were immune. Looking terrified but trying to hold it together, we farewelled Ruby and Scarlett, lining the deck and watching them until they disappeared out of sight.

"Have we just sent them to their death?" I murmured in Illy's ear.

"God, I hope not. But we can't just sit here waiting. If we run out of food or water, we are all gone. Besides, it only takes one satellite to spot us sitting here, and goodness knows who might show up."

Sitting stagnant and worrying about the mounting risks to the girls and ourselves, tempers frayed. With nothing to do and fretting constantly, people started snapping at each other. A few of the girls were visibly distressed, especially Arataki.

"Goodness, are you sure she is your child?" Illy asked one day as Taki grew increasingly agitated at being away from Ruby and Scarlett. Most had taken our lack of movement in their stride. While upset about being away from their families and home, the girls from Newgrange and Orkney were comfortable with Gerry and Tadhg. But Taki was distraught and ended up sleeping with Kendra as the only person she would relax with.

"I'm terrified of what she will tell Jacinda," I admitted to Illy one day as Taki sobbed in a corner, inconsolable.

"What can we say? We took her to keep her safe. Only they don't know that. I never told them what the risk was, just that there was one."

"Their families have demonstrated a lot of trust," I said again, meaning it. I wasn't sure I would let my six-year-old leave home with no parent for months. Potentially longer.

As the days passed, Di did her best to keep the children focused with the assistance of Kendra and Sam. But the rest of us were snappy. Guilt-ridden that we may have sent these girls to their death. How long did we wait before we enacted Plan B? Only there wasn't a feasible Plan B, other than radio Auckland and beg for help, dealing with whoever found us first.

Illy did her best to keep the tone light and casual. She and I had been through far worse together, and I knew her approach was to keep up a light level of banter. Chat about what would be going on at home, what we were missing. Stories from our past. I appreciated it as did Cam. Gerry and Tadhg were concerned, but they didn't know Ruby and Scarlett well. Gerry, in particular, was looking stressed, but I suspected it was more fear that we would be raided or shot at as we sat here, day after day.

With no piloting, we set ourselves other jobs. Cleaning, washing bedding, assisting Di with the teaching, cooking. But as the days passed, there was little to do but sit and wait.

"Do you want to make pasta with me?" Illy asked on the afternoon of the third day.

"Sure. I should warn you: I'm not very good at it. Luca tried to teach me, but I could never get the consistency right. He always teased me that I didn't have the patience."

"Well, we need a lot to feed everyone, so you can learn as we go. Crack open the bottle of Riesling I put in the fridge, would you? Luca always insisted that you couldn't cook without wine."

"Oh, I remember. I can't tell you how many liquor warehouses we had to raid to ensure Luca always had cooking wine. Did you ever notice that he put very little in the food and quite a lot in a glass as he worked?"

Illy giggled as she arranged the safe water, flour, and salt. I poured a glass for Illy and myself, then a third, and placed it quietly on the small table beside the couch where Sorcha was reading.

"The last time we did this on a yacht was with Luca on the way back from Auckland." I sighed. "He would have found a way to make me laugh, even about my current situation."

"What? Am I no substitute?"

"When you can throw me over your shoulder, we'll talk. That was always his solution if he couldn't win a disagreement. Manhandle me, or tickle me, until I relented. So no, you fall well *short* in that department!"

Illy's mouth dropped, and she threw a handful of flour at me playfully. The fine white cloud dispersed across the room as the light breeze coming through the open window caught it and blew most of it onto Sorcha, leaving a light dust layer across the navy couch. Sorcha leapt off the couch rounding on us.

"For fuck's sake! We are about to run out of food, and you think the best thing you can do is throw it around and waste it!"

"Hey!" I snapped at the unexpected outburst and Sorcha's hostile tone. "Leave her alone. We were only having a bit of fun."

"Fun? Let's talk about having fun then, shall we? Is that what you were doing, you unfaithful bitch? We trusted you. Sent you to Clava to learn skills for the team. Was that just having a bit of fun? Disappearing for months and then showing up with your new boyfriend, flaunting him in front of everyone? Do marriage vows mean nothing, you cheating whore? Just a joke?"

"Whoa!" Cam held his hands up and spoke more calmly than I would have had the situation been reversed. His dark hair appeared at the top of the stairwell and caught the last part of his sister's diatribe. "You are lucky the kids are all downstairs with Di and can't hear your venom. Not that it is any of your business, but Freyja never cheated on me."

"Really? That is not what half the town was saying. I saw you with your tongue down his throat, thinking no one could see you. How many nights did you spend at your boyfriend's house?" Sorcha sneered.

"None," Illy interjected firmly, stepping around the bench before I could flare. "And I am in a position to know. Freyja did nothing of the sort. You would do well to not listen to narrowminded gossip. Now lower your voice in case the kids hear."

"Don't you tell me what to do..." Sorcha jumped up from the sofa, bristling. *She is like a lion,* I thought. Her long red mane stood on end, ready to take on the pack of hyenas.

Glowering, I realized the best thing I could do was to say nothing. I scowled at Sorcha, who glared back. But I couldn't bite my tongue, let her insult me, and get away with it. But I remembered enough about what Cam had said. Keep it civil. If I got angry, that would set her off. The last thing I wanted was to have another long-term disagreement with her. Not here.

"I didn't, you know." I kept my voice low but audible enough. "I never cheated on Cam. Never. Not even in all those years we were apart after our first marriage. I was never with anyone else."

Sorcha's face went purple as she inhaled, ready to let fly. Cam jumped in, recognizing the blow-up about to happen, and bellowed at her. "This is over. Sorcha, keep your nasty and inaccurate remarks to yourself. I love Freyja. You are my family, but she is the family I chose. Say something nice or say nothing at all. This ends. *Now.*"

Sorcha stormed out of the room, slamming the door behind her.

"Well," Illy remarked once the echo had stopped ringing in our ears. "Who wants another drink?"

New Year's Eve came, and we tried to celebrate with the girls, to keep some sense of normality. But with limited supplies of food and water and no idea how long we could be stuck out here, we celebrated with a cake and not much else. Di, Sam, and Kendra helped the children make and hang colored paper streamers around the upper deck living space. Di had found some old sparklers in Edinburgh, and while only one in ten actually lit, the children thought they were magical and were fascinated by the sizzle and smoke released outside. Cam got the old stereo working and found some CDs to play for the party. Not exactly to my taste, but music. The girls and Alasdair were in heaven, dancing and running around the decks, squealing merrily. Oblivious to the danger we were all in.

We let them stay up until well past dark, none of us having any real idea of the precise time. We counted down from sixty to one and made a show of yelling *Happy New Year!* We hugged each of them and let them burn off some energy before chasing them to bed. Time was an arbitrary concept at the moment. With no one to communicate with, we had lost track of time. *Time is such a strange concept,* I thought as I encouraged stragglers to go downstairs. Yet, it was one we had maintained. Mainly so we could communicate with other communities at set hours. There was a tight schedule on the satellite radio. People catching up with family members. Clubs and groups covering all sorts of topics. Book clubs, foreign language learning, even learning groups were set up, so the children born here could communicate with others their own age in other communities, ensuring they were connected and so that they had a wider choice of potential partners in the future. Some people had met up using the Nexus, and a few relationships had occurred as a result. Cam had tried to set up an agriculture group, but it had been an abject failure, with only two people showing up.

"How come knitting gets twenty participants, and I get two?" he had grumbled.

Each day someone was allocated the role of lookout, watching for the girls returning with the tools and parts we needed. But as each day passed, the tension increased. Sorcha was the worst and rarely left her cabin. I felt the constant tightness in my chest and recognized that staying away from others was the most sensible choice.

We knew our way around Fremantle and had given detailed instructions on where to go to source the parts we needed but also where to find food and water for the return journey. Luca, Illy, Cam, and I had stopped there on our way to Auckland and had sourced parts for the *Eurydice. If only we had taken her instead of this beast,* I thought for the millionth time. I had an almost complete set of spares aboard, plus tools, and we had conducted regular maintenance. Few people understood the care required for a boat. So many times I had heard of people at my parents' yacht club complaining about the maintenance bill. Up to twenty percent of the purchase price per year was standard. Not that money was a factor anymore. Maintaining a vessel this size was an enormous expense, both in terms of time and parts, and this one hadn't been cared for in years. How they even got it started, and we managed to make it this far, was beyond me. But here we were, stranded in the middle of the Indian Ocean, miles from anywhere. Sitting ducks if whoever was after me had weapons.

How long would it take them to realize we had gone and taken all the children with us? Someone was on Lewis. Had been in our home. As I stared out over the still blue expanse, shame washed over me again for leaving Cam and exposing the children. I slumped over the rail. This was my fault. Yet again, we were on a bloody mission, miles from home, and it was my fault. Illy and I had been held captive for months on Clava. Cam and I captured near Inverness. Even the trip to find my sister. All. My. Fault.

"It's not, you know." The gentle, familiar voice sounded near my right ear, and I jumped.

"But it is," I responded. "They are after me, my children. I've put those girls in danger. They could drown, be captured. Anything could happen to them. You are all caught up in this, and it is my fault."

"No, it isn't." Sorcha's voice sounded from the doorway. I sighed. Could I not even wallow in peace?

"How is it not?" I asked, looking from one to the other. "These are my children these whack jobs are after. Mine and Katrin's. Calling me a witch. Three little girls are dead. Now the rest are all in danger. You are all here, away from your homes, because of me. So how is it not my fault?"

"Oh, for fuck's sake, Freyja," Sorcha snapped. "Stop being a bloody drama queen. It isn't your fault. I'm shitty and foul-tempered. I didn't mean what I said the other day, and you know it. You didn't ask for any of this, and no one blames you. I'm just worried sick about those poor girls and dreading what we will need to tell Jorja and Bridget. Either way."

"Look!" Illy pointed, and I squinted into the sun. A speck was moving on the horizon.

For what felt like an eternity, we stood at the railing and watched. It didn't take long to realize that this was not the small craft we had set them off in, and there was no way those girls would have the skills to bring back a larger vessel.

"Ahh shit," I muttered. "This can't be good."

"Fuck. Fuck. *Fuuuck!*" I heard Illy rant behind me but didn't have the mental capacity to respond. Illy snapped into military mode, barking orders.

"Di, get all the children downstairs, now! Keep them together, quiet, and away from windows. Draw the curtains. Sorcha, I need Gerry, Cam, and Tadhg up here, *now!*"

Sorcha disappeared in search of the men. Di hurriedly shooed all the children down to the lower level with her usual calm manner. I was envious of her disposition, always sweet and kind. How she wasn't screaming at them to get downstairs was beyond me. Cait hung to my leg, sensing that something wasn't right.

"It's okay, sweetheart," I soothed. "Auntie Di will take care of you."

"I want to stay with you, mummy!" she squealed, screwing up her face and attaching herself like a limpet. Di, seeing my difficulty, stepped in. "Caitlin. You know how important your learning is, and today I need a special helper. Everyone is waiting for us. Let's go together, shall we?" I smiled at her in gratitude.

The large blue and white vessel was approaching at high speed. My stomach dropped as I watched, knowing this was it. It was over. There was no way we could protect all of these children. We couldn't outrun them, and with limited weapons, we may be overpowered in minutes.

"Gerry?" Illy called as the last children disappeared down the stairwell, Cam behind them to ensure they were all together and safe. Gerry appeared silently at her side. "Get the weapons from the safe. Give Freyja one. Me too. One for yourself." She cocked an eye at Sorcha. "Ever used a gun?"

"No. But to protect my daughter and yours, I'll give it a red hot go."

"Good. One for Sorcha too. Take Tadhg and Cam. We will stay up here. Everyone knows we are with them, but they won't know you are with us with any luck. Promise me you will protect those girls."

"With my life," Gerry swore.

The vessel slowed as it neared, and Illy stood on the main deck, a pistol coolly aimed at the glass-fronted cockpit. She made no effort to hide. Sorcha and I stood close behind, each with weapons loaded and primed. There was a man there; I could see from his size. Our best bet was not to let them board. Once aboard, we could easily be outnumbered.

Waving arms caught my eye. "It's the girls!" I said breathlessly, seeing the long blonde hair fly in the wind, and I sensed Illy's shoulders relax slightly. "Who are they with?"

Illy tilted her head slightly and squinted in the bright sunshine reflecting off the waves. "It's Ashton!" she responded, amazed.

Relaxing her stance and lowering her weapon, she allowed the smaller vessel to pull alongside. "Who is there?" her tone was crisp.

"Carl, Ruby, and Scarlett," came back the male voice. "Anyone else?"

"No. Just the three of us."

Illy holstered her gun and threw the rope ladder down to assist them aboard. "How on earth did you find the girls?" she asked suspiciously.

Ruby and Scarlett boarded, looking tired, sunburned, but proud. "He isn't a stranger. We know him from all the birthday parties," they explained.

"Of course," Illy soothed. "You did wonderfully. Now Sorcha needs to check you over. You have had quite an adventure. Tell them to stand down," she called to Sorcha.

Sorcha nodded assent and took the girls into the cabin, leaving Ashton, Illy, and me on deck.

Ashton recognized the unanswered question. "I heard from Clava about Ceridwen. I am so sorry," he said, looking directly at me. "She should have been safe with us. I am so sorry."

"How did you know about the girls? Surely that wasn't luck."

"I have some surveillance equipment in my home," he confessed. "After I heard about Ceridwen, I was watching. I saw the satellite footage of you leaving Lewis. When I saw you heading north, I thought something must be wrong. I lost you for a bit, then found you again as you were rounding Africa. I thought you must have been bringing the girls to us at Auckland."

"You didn't tell anybody, did you?" Illy gripped his arm.

"No. After the news from Clava, I can't be certain that who killed Ceridwen isn't in touch with someone on Auckland Island. People moved between on the solstice, so I was doubly wary. We heard about the other two as well, so I watched. Then you stopped for several days. I wondered what was going on and saw the lifeboat being lowered. I gathered you needed help, so I took one of the vessels from Auckland and intercepted them. They were beside themselves when I pulled alongside, trying to hide, poor things. But I was alone, they remembered me, and I convinced them to come aboard, and we could tow the rescue boat behind us. They explained the problem, and we traveled to Fremantle together to source what you need. They remembered everything. We retraced their steps, and here we are."

"Thank you for helping them. For helping us," I said sincerely. "Are you sure no one knows where you are?"

"Fairly sure. Like you, we have satellites so anyone looking could spot us. But it is a lot of ocean to search for two boats."

"Why?" Illy was still standing back, assessing. "Why would you help us?"

"I know these girls. All of them and all of you. It broke my heart to hear what happened to Ceridwen, Solstice, and Bethany. No child deserves to die like that."

Illy nodded gravely.

As she took Ashton off to meet the others, I was left on the deck, staring down at the second smaller but likely more economical vessel. Judging by the enormous bank of solar panels glinting on the upper deck, she was solar-powered, or at least partially so.

Did we transfer everyone to that one and leave the *Damara* here?

Despite my reservations, Ruby and Scarlett had obtained everything I needed, and with Gerry's help, he and I fixed the *Damara*.. Not wanting to relocate so many of us, we took both vessels in case we had any further mechanical issues. Much to my surprise, while I was busy with repairs, Tadhg, Sorcha, and Sam moved across to the *Belisama*, leaving the rest of us on the *Damara*.

"Ashton doesn't want to pilot his own vessel?" I whispered to Cam as we held a party that night, once we were moving once more. The *Belisama* was following behind us, within visual sight.

Cam shrugged, but with so many people in the room congratulating the girls for their bravery, it was hard to talk.

"You know, you may have saved all our lives," I said to Ruby and Scarlett in one pause when the younger girls couldn't hear. They flushed.

"It is true," Cam spoke over my shoulder. "You are both heroes. Without you, we would all still be out there, stuck. You have done a wonderful job. Your mothers will be so proud."

"I'm dreading telling them," I whispered to Cam as they flushed and moved away. "I'm not sure who they will kill first when they come down from hitting the roof. Likely me."

"You watch," Illy added as we watched the girls return to the group, beaming with pride. "It will do those girls a world of good. Build their confidence. They will mature so much on this trip, and we need to keep building them up. Come on. We need to wrap this up and get the younger ones to bed."

"Trust your sister to escape parenting," I seethed as soon as we were in bed, realizing that there were now fewer people to assist with meals, schooling, and getting twenty-two bored stupid six-year-old girls ready for bed. Alasdair was a dream, compliant and trustworthy. But the girls ran around wildly, losing toothbrushes, swapping beds, having nightly pillow fights, and generally exhausting all of us. "Surely she took Mei?"

"She did not. Di and Kendra stayed too."

"She ditched her wife and two of her three children!"

"Jealous?"

"Absolutely."

CHAPTER 11

A WARM ARM SLID ACROSS my bottom and wrapped itself around my waist as I stared out to sea, watching the South Australian coastline drift past in the distance. I tipped my head back to be kissed.

"What would you have done if it was someone else?" he murmured in my hair.

"Thrown him overboard," I said without missing a beat as I found his lips, feeling the laughter playing there.

"I don't doubt it. Remind me never to upset you."

"I was angry at you for too long," I confessed. "And it wasn't your fault. Illy made me realize it was me, not you."

"She loves you. She just wants what is best for you."

"Your sister doesn't. I get she was stressed, but she spoke her truth. She genuinely thinks I cheated on you."

"I trust you implicitly, and I know you didn't. So it is done. But I need to ask, do you think I cheated on you?"

"What?"

"With Laetitia."

My heart stopped, and I tried not to let the reaction to his unexpected question show on my face. Too late. He knew me well and had been watching for my split-second unguarded reaction.

"Yes," I whispered.

"Frey, I love you more than life itself. But you need to understand that it is only you I want. How do we move past this?"

I shrugged and looked over his shoulder across the ocean. I was jealous of her, but I blamed him. He had left me alone and lonely. It may not be logical or rational, but there it was. I had been fine until I had seen those photos, and there had been far more than I had told him. So many of them. Slightly out of focus, taken through the dome, but detailed enough that I could see the expression of absolute joy on his face—and hers. Before seeing the photos, I had known about her but couldn't visualize them together, apart from that one night when I had seen them together. It was an abstract thing, aside from Louis. But he was a baby and accepted me. He never compared me to his birth mother or treated me like a stepmother. Now? Now I had irrefutable proof. It felt like I was a participant, a witness to their wedding and their honeymoon. And it made me feel sick. Unable to stop myself, I had looked at the photos again and again. Torturing myself over how happy he was with *her*. They had been saved on the file, as Clava loved knowing that their profiling had resulted in a match. It was a pat on the back to the profilers. But it ate me up like a rotten apple, disintegrating from the inside out.

"Do you want to talk to Illy?" he asked gently.

I snapped out of my trance. "I will. I can't keep blaming you for something that isn't your fault.

Nothing changed for you. But it changed within me. Something snapped that day, and I can't seem to fix it on my own."

"Can I kiss you?"

"Of course. It isn't that I don't love you. You know I do. I am just haunted by those pictures, that report, and I can't get past it. Every time I see you, I see you in those pictures, with someone else. I don't want it to destroy us, but I can't help how I feel. I've never felt like this in my life, and I don't know how to handle it."

"Talk to Illy. Promise me."

"I promise."

I could still feel his warmth on my lips when I opened my eyes. *No time like the present*, I thought, as I watched his dark hair turn the corner to the aft deck.

CHAPTER 12

"ILS," I CALLED AS I opened the door to her room and froze. In the split second between opening and stepping in the room, I had seen far more than anyone should of their best friend. Unsure what to do, I ran, forgetting to close the door behind me.

"Frey, we need to talk."

"Damn straight we do!" I seethed, the wind whipping past and blowing my hair into my face. "How could you?"

"What? You don't think I deserve to be happy too?"

"After what he did to us? To me?"

"Frey, I know how you feel."

"Do you?" I spat, fury raging within me.

"Betrayed."

I started to argue with her, but as usual, she had nailed it with that single word. That was precisely how I felt. "I can't... can't be around you," I muttered, pushing past her and storming away. *How could she?* The heat was burning me, my skin aflame with rage.

Not wanting to be around people, and despite the mechanical noise, I went and sat in the cold engine room, where at least I knew I could be alone. Finding a small corner, I sat on the silver checkered plate floor with my back to the wall, pulled my knees to my chest, dropping my head, and willed my brain to stop. Stop seeing! Stop feeling. Why couldn't I be that girl I was at university? Cold, distant. Always in control. No one hurt me then. Was that the downside of letting people into your heart? They inevitably let you down? My parents, my sister, Cam, now Illy. All of them I had let hurt me. I had allowed them in, and now they had torn my heart into tiny pieces and stomped on it like it was jelly.

A hand on my shoulder woke me with a start. I looked up into Cam's concerned face and realized that we weren't moving.

"Illy told me you walked in on her. We have been searching for you for hours. Everyone is frantic."

"I'm fine," I snapped, embarrassed and being seen down here. Hiding.

"Let me just tell them to stop searching. We were scared you had fallen overboard."

"Jumped, more like it," I huffed, making him turn to look back. He paused, then continued up the stairwell, and I heard muffled voices overhead. Another man's voice. But not Luca. Tears filled my eyes as I thought of my friend. If he hadn't died, then Illy and I wouldn't have ended up on Clava. I wouldn't have seen those photos, and Illy wouldn't be... ugh. I couldn't even think about her being with *him.*

But, the tiny logical spark in the back of my mind reminded me, *if it hadn't been for being held captive, you wouldn't have Cait, or Seraphine, or any of the others. Fuck, fuck, FUCK! Why is life so goddammed complicated?* I punched my clenched fist against the nearest surface and screamed in pain as the bones crashed into the steel pipes. *Fuck!* I seethed as I held it to my chest, throbbing. Vomit rose into my gullet, and I knew it was broken as I fought back the nausea.

"*Fuck!*" I bellowed, drawing Cam's attention as he descended the ladder.

"What is it?"

"Broke my fucking hand!" I raged, angrier at myself than him.

The look of puzzlement crossed Cam's face before sympathy took over. "Come on, let's get you upstairs."

Climbing a steep metal ladder out of the bowels of a ship with one hand is surprisingly tricky, especially when the pain is staggeringly intense, and you are constantly choking back vomit. I saw the *Belisama* tied up alongside. *Great. So everyone would know I am an idiot.*

Cam seated me at the table, and Sorcha hurriedly spread the contents of her medical kit across the table. I could see Illy lurking in the doorway, but I couldn't look at her. Thank goodness *he* wasn't here. I let Sorcha palpate my hand, roaring when she found the broken bone.

"Broken metacarpal," she said slowly. "Boxer's fracture. Who did you punch?"

"The metal engine casing," I muttered.

"You'd rather it was my face?" she asked with a cheeky grin.

"Something like that," I muttered, not wanting to discuss it. I watched as she drew the clear liquid from the refillable vial she had taken from Lewis. I gasped as she kept filling the syringe.

"I need to realign it, and that is going to hurt, morphine or not."

"Bloody hell!" I said, watching the syringe in horror. "That is enough to fell a horse!"

"That's the plan," she smirked. "If you are unconscious, then I don't need to listen to you complain about my substandard orthopedic technique."

"Sorcha, no!" Illy was across the room in a shot, realizing what was going on and seeing the terrified look on my face. "No!"

Sorcha froze, the plunger half emptied.

Horror had crossed Cam's face as he watched.

Sorcha's eyes widened. "I'm so sorry. I forgot. That is enough. You won't feel the realignment. But it shouldn't knock you out. I'll work quickly."

I nodded. "Will I ... be okay?"

"You should be fine in about six weeks. If you keep it mobile and do the rehabilitation vigilantly, it won't impact your surgical technique."

I nodded weakly, the injected morphine already taking effect, making me feel drowsy but numb on an empty stomach.

Sorcha worked quickly, pulling and pushing until my fingers were swollen but straight. I could still feel the discomfort, but the pain was muffled. I stared out the window and tried to remove myself from my body. She splinted the fingers, not speaking throughout the process. I found myself fighting the drowsiness, feeling stupid. These people wouldn't hurt me. But the last time I had been injected with a sedative, something precious had been stolen from me. My dignity and my children. Finishing off the bandaging, Sorcha sent me to my room to rest. Firmly but kindly. I was grateful for her intervention, and I felt Illy's eyes on my back as I left the room. I couldn't speak to her. Not yet.

CHAPTER 13

AS I LAY ON the bed, I heard the door open and close. I rolled over to look out the window, unable to meet his gaze. The morphine had taken the edge off the pain, and I felt lightheaded but instinctively fought against unconsciousness. The mattress sank slightly behind me, and I felt the impression on the pillow beside mine. I stared out the window at the monotonous waves drifting past for the longest time. We were moving again.

"What do you see in me?" I asked finally.

I felt the bed sink behind me as his heavier weight laid curled up behind me, one warm arm draped over my waist.

"Where do you want me to start?"

"The beginning."

Air left his lungs, and I felt the warm exhalation on my neck as he spoke with purpose. "When I saw you for the first time, as you walked off the helipad on August Island, I thought you were the most beautiful woman I had ever seen, but so far out of my league that I didn't even try to speak to you. Your hair looked like a halo glowing in the sunshine. You were wearing jeans and a fitted black top, and I remember thinking that maybe being there wasn't so bad. All the men on August thought you were the complete package— beautiful, self-assured, intelligent. I saw you at our dorm meeting that second night, but you didn't even glance in my direction. You held yourself with such grace, such confidence. The first time we spoke was a few months later. That night when you helped me with the tablets, when I had cut my hand open. I realized you were everything they had said, but also kind, with a razor-sharp wit and easy to talk to. But you didn't speak to me again after that night, so I assumed you didn't feel the same way, or just saw nothing attractive in me."

I wanted to interrupt, object, but couldn't lift myself out of the hole and form the words as I watched the waves roll past. The white caps broke at the tops of the sapphire blue waves.

"Then, on our first anniversary of arriving, August Day, I was in a rush to get away from the crowd and slammed into you, and you took me to the springs." He paused. "I had relationships before moving there, but I remember feeling, *this* is what people write poetry and songs about. I had never felt like that in my life. On the walk back, I was positive that you were the one, a feeling reinforced every time you stopped to kiss me. My heart lurched, and I couldn't stop touching you. The days and weeks that followed proved my initial reaction. I felt empty when you weren't around. You moved into my place and became as crucial a part of my life as oxygen. I couldn't imagine life without you. When you proposed, I had never been so happy. When I lost you, I was destroyed. I thought I was damaged beyond repair. It was like all the air had been sucked from the room, and I was suffocating. It took me a year of searching to feel like living again. But I never stopped loving you. In the years we were apart, I thought about you, pictured what you were doing. I could be doing the most mundane of tasks, and I would see you. On the deck of the *Selkie*, your beautiful hair blowing in the breeze. Laughing at something someone had said, the most wonderful sound in the world. I saw you exploring exotic communities, roaming through deserts, and trekking through rainforests. I never forgot you. Then life brought us back together, and I felt complete again. The past years have been the happiest of my life, having my partner, raising a family. So what do I see in you? I see a soul bonded to my own. We are a team, Frey. We have a common purpose. Not to mention a tribe of kids. I couldn't do it alone. Those months after being shot, and you were gone, I felt so lonely. When you were on Clava, and when you lived at Illy's, I had to fight each day to breathe in and out, put one foot in front of the other and keep going. And I only did it for the kids. You are part of me, and I never want to be away from you again."

"I love you," I whispered, wanting to roll over, but my head was spinning from the morphine. Even as I said the words, I wondered why I couldn't feel them.

"I don't think I have the words to describe what I feel for you. Love doesn't cut it. I loved pizza. I loved my parents. This is different, and so much more. It feels wrong, too simplistic to use the same four-letter word. Without you, I barely exist. I can't tell you how many times I turned to tell you something, and the knife stabbed me in the heart anew, knowing you had left me. That you chose someone else."

"I didn't." The pressure of Cam's arm pressing slightly into my side was reassuring. Calming.

"I know that, now. But in those months, I genuinely thought you had. I saw you together once, from a distance. You and Stefan. A few days before we left. You were talking and standing close. He touched your cheek. Even from where I stood, you leaned into him. You looked happy. So I was left alone, to rot, while you *lived*."

"That was how I felt when I saw you with Laetitia," I admitted. "That you had it all. A wife you loved, a child. And I had nothing. Just an empty shell trying to find the glimmer of happiness in each day. Luca got me through that time. Without his friendship to look forward to, I don't know what I would have done."

Cam's larger form stiffened behind me.. "Why didn't you hook up with Luca? It is clear he wanted to."

"I never knew that while he was alive. But he was my friend, my confidante. I think after finally letting someone into my life, and losing you, I couldn't do it again. Keeping him at arm's reach, as a friend, was safe. Maybe eventually I would have, but I doubt it."

"What do you think he would think about Illy and Ashton?"

"I want to be happy for her. Luca would want her to be happy. I don't want her to be alone. But *him*? He may not have personally inflicted those horrors on me, but he knew. And he did nothing to stop it for nearly two months."

"But he did stop it. You said yourself that if it weren't for him, you likely would never have made it out." Cam's voice was low and calm, always the mediator. He rolled me gently towards him and gazed into my eyes.

"That is true, and for that, I am grateful. But in the seven weeks and three days we were there, it was me they injected, tortured. It was me who was assaulted—twice. It was me that Dale attacked and smacked around. Maybe Illy isn't as angry, or maybe she is more forgiving. She knew Ashton beforehand, even dated him for a short time, a long time ago."

"Illy dated Ashton? I never knew that! They are nothing alike."

"The way she told it, it was a few dinners and nothing more. It was when they first arrived. They were both still living on Auckland Island. Each year when he comes to the girl's party, he is kind, and while I minimize contact, he always speaks to me with respect. But I see him watching her. He was on Auckland when I was training at Clava, so I didn't see him. Maybe if I had, I could have moved past that feeling of betrayal and accept this."

"She is your best friend. You can't shut her out."

"I know. But seeing them together, in bed? I can't unsee that."

"No one is asking you to. But you want her to be happy, don't you? Luca has been gone seven years. I know you miss him terribly, and your loyalties will always be to him. But she has been alone for a very long time. Raised those kids alone. She deserves to meet someone."

"She does. I don't dispute that. I just wish it wasn't *him*."

"But we don't choose who we fall in love with."

I grimaced. The pain relief was starting to wear off. Now I just felt sick. My hand was throbbing, the pain reverberating up my arm. Cam caught the look as I lay back on my pillow, fighting back the pain.

"Do you want more pain relief? Sorcha brought an enormous first aid kit, all the medications we had on Lewis, then sourced a hospital's worth of supplies from Edinburgh. She has enough to run a field hospital the way she tells it. While they didn't know how many of the girls would come, she suspected most would, and knew we could be away from civilization for months. She has no shortage of morphine or anything else you might need."

"No. Maybe later. Is she still here?" I could feel the engines rumbling and the gentle movement of the boat cutting through the waves.

"She is. She said she would stay as long as you need her."

As much as the pain was crippling, I didn't want to relinquish control. After that night... after Dale... No. I would never willingly let someone take control over me again.

"Sleep then."

"Will you stay?" I whispered. "At least until I fall asleep?"

"Of course."

CHAPTER 14

"JORGENSEN. THERE IS SOMETHING you should know."

I shot daggers at him as I sat, Cam closing the door firmly. After waking and a quick wash, Cam had insisted that we meet with Illy and Ashton in one of the small reading rooms.

"Ashton," I started.

"Call me Carl," he suggested. I couldn't. Calling him by his first name was too familiar. He may have helped us, but I still couldn't see him as anything other than the man who had orchestrated my capture. Aided my abuse.

"What?" I sat back and waited for the pathetic story about how he loved Illy, and it would all be okay.

"It is about your daughter, Caitlin." My eyelids lowered, and I tried not to growl at the mention of my daughter. The one he had created. Had they found something wrong with her? Was she not immune? As I opened my mouth and was about to fire off, he spoke quietly into the void. "I thought you might like to know who her father is."

All the air rushed out of me, and I was unable to speak for a moment. Since she had been placed in my arms when she was only a few days old, I had wondered. And he knew. In the space of three seconds, I could know.

Ashton waited, then asked, "Do you? Want to know?"

Cam's arm rested on mine. "She does. She has always wanted to know." I turned to look at him, my mouth open. "Oh, come on. Every time you see her walk into the room. Her eyes, dark eyes that aren't yours. Her ebony hair, muscular build. Her personality is like you, like Kat, but she doesn't look like any of us."

"But what if..." I gulped, stood, and took two steps toward the door, my hand throbbing in time with my pounding heart. "No. I can't."

Ashton watched me. "I understand...."

"You understand nothing!" I flared, turning back and taking two menacing steps toward him. "She wouldn't exist if it weren't for you. And while I love her dearly, the trauma you put me through so that these girls can live, I will never forgive you for! Do you know how many nights I wake in a cold sweat remembering being chained to that bed? Being drugged? Waking to that slimeball trying to rape me before breaking my face? It has been seven years, *Carl*. Now you come and want to tell me who her father is, thinking that will make it all okay?"

Ashton's face dropped, not expecting my outburst. Illy sat quietly in a curved lounge chair, clearly conflicted.

"Then tell *me*." Cam stepped forward, and Ashton whispered in his ear. I watched as Cam's eyes opened wide and his face blanched. I couldn't. I closed my eyes and counted to ten, exhaling forcefully. *What if it is Dale? Derek?*

"Truly?" he asked. The tone of his voice, choked, made me open my eyes.

Ashton nodded, the look of seriousness not leaving his face.

The mixed look on Cam's face perplexed me. She wasn't his. She looked nothing like him, nor me. Nothing like any of our children. My hands clenched into fists at my side.

"Luca," he mouthed. "She is Luca's biological daughter."

My mouth dropped. So did Illy's.

"You mean..."

"Caitlin and Seraphine are full siblings," Ashton interjected. "Not twins, exactly. They were born to different surrogates, eight days apart. But siblings."

I turned to look at Illy. I don't think I had ever seen her lost for words. Her mouth hung open like a goldfish. I wanted to hug her but couldn't. All I could see was her, naked, on top of *him*.

Cam's face moved fuzzily into my line of vision, trying to assess my reaction. My head was spinning with the news. It all made sense. Her forceful personality, so like Sera's. Her tanned skin and dark hair. I can't believe I never saw it. She looked like Luca. A six-year-old female Luca. She looked more like Luca than Seraphine did. Sera's hair was fair, like mine. Slimmer in build. Cait's physique was powerful, like Summer.

"But why?" I whispered.

"An apology, in part. We had a sample of yours," he nodded toward Cam, "and we would have done that, but..."

"It was destroyed?" he guessed.

"It was. So, we took the next best option. We knew from MacLeod how close you two were. He was mighty jealous that after Mr. Mackintosh, you enjoyed Mr. Cadman's company over his. Mr. Cadman also had a strong genotype that we wanted to be replicated, and as he had passed, we knew he wouldn't have any more children. Knowing that you were already pregnant, Illyria, and even when you agreed to take Seraphine, we thought it best not to tell you right away in case it caused issues between you. Then, well, it never seemed to be the right time. We also didn't know how *you* would react, Campbell."

"Thank you," I whispered, barely able to form the words. "Thank you."

Cam's cerulean blue eyes held mine in his gaze. "Do you want to tell her?"

I looked between him and Illy, seeking answers.

"No," Illy said, finally able to speak through her shock. "You can't. Not now. As crazy, stupid intelligent as she is, she is only six. You are her father, and it will only confuse her. But one day. I would like it very much if we told her about Luca one day. Our children are as close as twins. It won't make any difference to their relationship."

"I will tell her everything," I promised. "How wonderful he was. How much I loved him. All the amazing things he did. The adventures we had together. How blessed she is to have two phenomenal fathers."

"Thank you," Illy sniffed and held her arms out to me from where she sat, her lower lip caught between her teeth. I froze, stared at her, then dropped into her arms. Her tiny frame engulfed my taller one as the ice queen thawed. I heard the door close as we were left alone. Finally, I lifted my head and stared into her beautiful blue eyes framed with wet, dark lashes.

"I want you to be happy," I confessed. "I always did. I just never thought it would be with *him*."

"Nor did I," she admitted. "But we have always liked each other before the project got in the way. Life is too short, Frey. He is single, and I am desperately lonely raising four kids. It may not work out, but I don't want to play games. If the last years have taught me nothing, it is how precious life is. Losing Luca, nearly losing you after finding your sister. Summer being poisoned and those girls being taken far too young. I need to act on these feelings."

I understood. After all, that was why I had made my move on Cam all those years ago, why I had gone after him. Needing to know for sure, one way or the other.

"So that is why he let the others take the *Belisama?*"

"It is. We both felt it. Figured we had time, here, with nowhere to go. Work out if there is something there."

"I am pleased for you. Really." Illy leaned into me, and I slipped my arm around her shoulder.

"Now, what is going on with you, Miss Smashed-up Hand? It is more than just seeing my raunchy sexcapades!"

"I need your help," I confessed.

"Talk to me."

Settling in beside her, I opened up, telling her about the nightmares, the flashbacks, and the inability to feel. The feeling of being out of control, of falling into the well, unable to climb out. The anger. The numbness.

"Oh, Frey. I'm so sorry. I've let you down."

"You? This has nothing to do with you."

"I kept thinking you were exhausted, stressed. But Frey, the symptoms you are describing are indicative of post-traumatic stress disorder."

"I know what PTSD is. My mum was a psychiatrist, remember?"

"I should have seen it before, but when you came home, you shut me out. I was so caught up with Summer being sick, then getting away. When did the flashbacks start?"

"My second week at Clava."

Illy's mouth dropped. "And you didn't tell anyone?"

"Hell no. They would have deemed me unfit and sent me home."

"I am such an idiot. Now it all makes sense. Being irrationally angry with Cam, alienating him. Difficulty sleeping, nightmares."

"It was seven years ago. I thought I would be over it by now."

"You are in what is called the long-term recovery phase. Going back there has likely triggered it. I was fearful it might, but you wouldn't talk to me. Do you think that people who experience war or torture should be okay after a set period? There is no hard and fast timeframe, Frey. It tracks differently for everyone."

"Ils, what do I do? I don't want to feel like this."

"You talk to me, to Cam. You work through these feelings and accept that these feelings are valid. Cognitive behavior therapy. I am so sorry I didn't spot it sooner. I did this a lot back in the army. Nearly everyone who returns from a war zone is impacted in some way."

"But I didn't go to a war zone."

"Do you think your emotions aren't valid? Do you think PTSD is reserved for military personnel? What you experienced, in many ways, was far worse. Military personnel are a team, highly trained. They go in as a unit and have some idea of what they will face before they go. They are debriefed. What we went through was completely unexpected, and by people we trusted. Captivity, torture, attempted rape. I know you struggled when we first came home with Ceri and then with Caitlin. I was too, losing Luca, dealing with Alasdair and Seraphine. But as the years passed, I thought you were doing well. You were the old Freyja again. I should never have let you go back there alone. I should have gone with you." Illy rested her head on my shoulder. She really was like a tiny bird.

"I didn't give it a lot of thought. I just thought that it was terrible memories. I avoided that room, the one they kept us in, but I couldn't avoid the operating theater. Every time I walked in there, it was *me* I could see lying on that table, the one I used to heal people. It was like an out-of-body experience, watching on as someone cut into me. But they didn't heal me."

"Oh, Frey. I didn't think it through. It all happened so quickly, the offer and you going. You seemed so excited, and I thought it would be okay."

"It was okay. I learned so much, and I love the work I do."

"Was it worth sacrificing your marriage? Your relationship with your children?"

I paused, knowing she was spot on. "No."

"But that is what you have been doing. Sure, seeing those photos would have been traumatic, but you could have dealt with that if you were in a normal frame of mind. Accepted that it was a long time in the past and recognized that Cam loves you. But you are traumatized, and emotional detachment and mistrust are common symptoms." Illy slapped her forehead. "I should have seen this sooner. I've been dealing with trading eggs and pumpkins for too many years. I am out of practice."

"Please stop apologizing. But I need to ask, what is a panic attack like?"

Illy looked up at me, concerned. "They differ between people. Why? Describe them."

"Sometimes, without warning, my heart pounds, and I hear that door slam to the meeting room or the clang of the restraints against the bed frame. I am freezing and start shaking uncontrollably. That feeling of being out of control tries to burst out of my chest, and I know I am in danger, only I am not. Does that make sense?"

Illy exhaled, her tiny chest barely puffing against my side. "I think what you are describing is an anxiety attack. What triggers it?"

I considered that for a moment. "Anything. A sound, a smell."

"What helps?"

"Not much. But sometimes, if I can manage it, going for a long walk."

"Did you tell anyone?" Illy whispered.

"Goodness, no. I kept quiet, recognized the warning signs, and would hide in a toilet or storeroom until I came to my senses again."

Illy's eyes filled with concern. "Have you tried keeping a diary? Writing your thoughts down?"

"Where do I get a diary here? Kind of a shortage of paper in case you hadn't noticed."

"Fair call. How long do they last?"

"It varies, sometimes minutes. Other times, hours. I just lose sense of time and place. But it doesn't happen often," I rushed to say.

"The fact that it is happening at all, and you never thought to tell me, disturbs me."

"I didn't want you to know," I admitted, feeling foolish for telling her now

"Why?"

"Like you haven't been through enough! You don't need to take on my problems."

Illy slapped at my leg. "I love you, Frey, but you are a fool. Listening to someone, helping them, doesn't mean you take on their problems. If a psychologist took on everyone's challenges who sought support, they wouldn't survive a week. Did you ever feel that your mother took on other people's problems?"

"No. She compartmentalized them, I guess. Listened, offered support and advice. But they didn't become her problems."

"Exactly. So why did you think I couldn't do the same?"

My voice dropped. "Because you are my friend. I didn't want to burden you. Make you relive that time."

Illy snorted. "And you wouldn't do the same for me? Listen? Understand?"

"You know I would."

"And would it make your own experience worse?"

I considered for a moment. "No. My experience is what haunts me. Not yours."

Illy settled back against the sofa, turning to me. Her crystal blue eyes full of concern.. "Have you told Cam?"

"How do I, without him feeling responsible? He supported me in going there. How do I tell him it left me traumatized? Besides, he has been through far worse. He was shot. Hung up and tortured on a butcher's hook. His first wife was snatched away and the second brutally murdered. Son kidnapped. How do I burden him with my problems after all he has been through?"

"So you expect him to sit idly by while you destroy yourself and him? He wants to help you. But you need to let him in, Frey. You are strong, and I know you will overcome this, but even you can't do this alone."

"I will tell him, but not yet. It feels like we have only been back together for five minutes. Give me some time."

"It won't get easier the longer you leave it. You will keep feeling like this. Cold and alone. You are damaging your relationships and not just with your husband."

"Help me." I felt foolish, weak somehow. Asking for help was not something I was familiar with, and not a feeling I was at all comfortable with.

"You know I will always help you, but you need to do the work. There is no magic wand. And you need to tell him. Soon."

CHAPTER 15

ARRIVING IN MELBOURNE IN the late afternoon evoked a strange sensation. The city skyline was still visible from the pier, the once decadent luxury homes facing the bay from Beach Road obscured by filth and fallen trees. Despite the excited chatter of the girls to see land, it was quiet outside, still. Twenty years had passed, and very little was left intact. Everything was crumbling and decaying. Dead trees had fallen onto rooftops, never to be removed. Sand had blown everywhere, windows filthy and smashed. Most of the homes had roof tiles missing, exposing timber beams and battens. Paint was flaking from every surface, fences sagging, fallen onto the footpath in places. It looked like a ghost town. One of those places you visited as a tourist, only this had been my home. Once.

"Okay, what now?" Sorcha asked.

"We check the *Damara* first," Illy instructed. "Frey and I have learned the hard way that you always have the vessel fueled and ready to go. More than once we have needed to leave in a hurry. Did I ever thank you for that?" She shot her brilliant blue eyes over to Tadhg. "For Inverness, I mean. I keep meaning to, but then when I see you each year, it is so manic, and I forget."

"It was my pleasure." Tadhg bowed graciously. "But you know, most of it was Jake. For your husband, Jake would have blown up the entire continent."

"Why is that?" I asked as Gerry jumped out to tie up the *Belisama*. We had all been friends.

"Well, it was Luca that overheard Angus on the radio that night and woke Jake. Had he not worked out they were being used and jumped ship in Newgrange, Jake may never have met Makayla."

"Nor I him," Illy said wistfully, making Ashton shuffle around behind her uncomfortably. Only Cam and I knew about their fledgling relationship, and neither of us was happy about it. But her friendship meant more to me than holding onto hatred for him, so I tried to be happy for her.

"Well," I interjected, before the conversation became melancholy. "We need to refuel, restock, and we need tools and spare parts for the yacht."

"Refueling we can take care of," Sorcha said. "Where do we get parts?"

"I know a few places," I admitted, "but they are all some distance away. My father had an extensive tool collection at home, plus some manuals that would be useful as a starting point. We also had several cars, all garaged, which would help transport us all. I suggest perhaps I head home first, get the tools and another vehicle, then Cam and I can go raiding boating suppliers for spares."

Illy scratched her temple contemplatively. "I think a few smaller vehicles makes sense. Break the children up, just in case one car breaks down. How far was your place?"

"Too far to walk. But about a twenty-minute drive, I guess, now that there is no traffic. We might need a four-wheel drive. We could face some obstructions."

"Can you help us start a car?" I asked Tadhg, who grinned wickedly.

"Of course! How many would you like?"

"Six, maybe?"

Tadhg went below deck and returned a few minutes later with some batteries. "Do you know how to fit one?" he asked Cam.

Cam nodded. Tadhg and Cam set off to locate a suitable car to liberate and send us off on our way, while Illy and Sorcha made plans to restock and refuel the vessel. Illy, Cam, Sorcha, and I had lived in Melbourne and had a good idea of where to source supplies. Di had visited once on holiday, and again when Cam had found Sorcha, but couldn't find her way around. Tadhg had only been here once and had spent nearly all of his time in the government buildings where we had been assessed. Gerry had never been to Australia and was looking around, wide-eyed and enjoying the warmth of the summer sun.

Within fifteen minutes, I heard the familiar beep of a car horn. The girls jumped, some squealing in fright. Di quickly reassured them and explained that they were just slightly larger and noisier vehicles than what they had at home, but fundamentally the same.

"I'll drive," I offered. "I know the way."

"Are you sure? Can you drive with a splinted hand?"

"I have driven one-handed more times than I can count," I confessed. "Besides, who is going to arrest me?"

Cam raised his eyebrows at me. "Nothing dirty!" I exclaimed. "I meant drinking coffee or brushing my hair."

"Or putting on lipstick?" Sorcha teased as I climbed in.

"I rarely wore makeup. Only for a big event, or if I knew they were taking photos."

"Do you know," Cam grinned as I drove, "I don't think we have ever been in a real car together."

I looked over at him as our hair blew in the wind gusting in the open sunroof.

"That is true. Golf carts and tiny electric cars don't count, do they?"

I accelerated the large diesel BMW and deftly maneuvered the vehicle around a fallen power pole, recalling the exhilarating sensation of driving fast and changing gears after so many years, the sensitive feel of transitioning from accelerator to clutch. Once I regained my confidence, the feeling of driving fast was wonderful, dodging the road blockages, drifting onto the tram tracks and the opposite side of the road. Cars littered the streets, and buildings were crumbling around us.

"It is quite surreal, isn't it?" I said, mostly to break the silence. Cam was looking out of the windows, staring at places we once knew and took for granted.

"Twenty years. I've been back once. You too, I guess. But even then, it looked like home. Home without all the people, but the buildings were the same. I never thought I would see it looking like this."

Using my splinted hand to cradle the wheel, I slipped my left hand onto his knee, making him turn and smile at me.

"Where would you have taken me on a date?" he asked cheekily.

"Oh, somewhere waterfront," I admitted. "Fine dining at Southbank maybe, then a walk along the banks of the Yarra. A kiss in the dark. There was something so romantic about cities and rivers at night. Vienna. Paris. London. Prague. I loved them all, and even as a teenager, I longed to have someone to share it with. Walk along the river in the dark, seeing the city lit up, but lots of dark places to slip into with someone special."

"I always thought you were planning life solo," he teased gently.

"Not until she died," I confessed. "Before that, I wanted … this. What about you? Where would you have taken me?"

Cam paused. "A small traditional Italian trattoria, perhaps on Lygon Street and a walk through the Botanical Gardens."

"You and plants!"

"You have clearly never been there. The gardens were lit with fairy lights at night, laced through those majestic old trees. It was so beautiful. Lots of shadowy spots to stop and talk."

"Talk? Really. Is that what you would have done?"

"I would have been the perfect gentleman."

"Just like you were in the park in Edinburgh?"

"You came after me, remember?"

"How many girls did you take there then?" I asked curiously.

"None as special as you."

As we approached my street, I slowed, taking in the state of the neighbors' houses. Roofs were caving in, gutters barely hanging on. It was a wide boulevard with large houses along both sides. Previously a prestigious street with pools, manicured lawns, and expensive cars. As I rounded the corner, I gasped. The solid white fence obscuring the view of the house was filthy, the stucco render falling off in places, revealing deep cracks in the brickwork beneath. The beautiful, once enormous elm trees in the street were dead and bare. Many had fallen or had dropped large boughs. Filthy cars lined the road, abandoned, some crushed under fallen trees. It looked like a war zone. Sighing heavily, I exited the car, the slam of the car door echoing up the deserted street. My street. One I had walked up so many times, day and night, but had never really paid attention to the neighboring houses.

The wrought-iron gates were filthy but intact, barring entry to intruders. I jiggled them, but they were locked.

"How do we get in?" Cam asked, looking at the electronic keypad and solid barrier.

"Wait here."

Returning to the car, I started the engine and pulled the car up onto the nature strip, narrowly avoiding the dead tree, and pulled it alongside the fence. Shutting it off, I climbed awkwardly with my single usable hand onto the roof and up onto the wall, slipping down the other side. Unlatching the pedestrian gate, I opened it, letting Cam inside.

"And the house?"

"Key safe. I can't tell you how many times I slipped in after a party and used the spare keys. Something our kids will never get to experience."

I disappeared down the side, the beautiful tropical foliage my mother had once adored now gone, leaving dirt patches where the garden beds had been. Armed with the key, I opened half of the enormous double door, and it creaked deafeningly on its unused hinges, making me step back hurriedly, worried it would fall if the hinges were rusted through.

I paused in the doorway, the stench of two decades of dampness, dust, and locked up house making me flinch, but despite my former confidence, I couldn't enter. Cam paused the length of two heartbeats, then, with his arm around my waist, steered me inside, leaving the door open to ventilate the house.

"Scared of bringing your boyfriend home? We are over forty, you know."

"Yet I still feel like they would have disapproved," I muttered, slinking in beside him.

Despite the lack of lighting, the house was still large, open, and well-lit from the dirt-coated windows and skylights. I felt Cam tense as he took it all in. The carved timber staircase. The white marble floors across the expansive lower floor. The enormous kitchen with a wall of four ovens and once gleaming stainless benchtops, now coated in dust.

"Wow," I felt him breathe from beside me.

"Come on." Embarrassed, I veered into my father's study to the left of the main hallway. Cam was still standing in the atrium, looking around the living space, up into the sky-lit second story, split into two wings. Carefully curated artworks, now coated in dust, still hung along the stairwell. Fossicking around in my father's antique timber desk, surrounded by mahogany bookcases filled with old volumes, I pulled out the toolbox. Cam raised his eyebrows as he stood in the doorway, taking it all in.

"Seriously. Did the man not own a shed?"

"Darling," I teased. "One does not own something as common as a garden shed. Of course, we do. I just needed the spare keys to the garage. Dad hid them here."

Cam's eyebrows raised at the four luxury cars parked in the lightless garage, so I made the decision.

"That one," I suggested. We used Tadhg's second battery to get it started. Pulling the Cayenne into the driveway, I blinked like a startled owl at the sudden onslaught of light.

"I've never driven a Porsche." Cam looked like a naughty child.

"Well, you can drive this one. But I can't imagine the insurance is up to date, so take it easy."

"What else do you want to get?" Cam asked as he loaded the boating parts, manuals, and tools I had sourced into the boot.

I sighed. "Leave it running. There is a full tank. Let's see what else they had worth taking. It isn't like I am coming back."

"Sorcha and I said that last time," Cam teased. "Yet, a decade later, here we are."

I could sense Cam's rising anxiety as we trawled the house, and I selected a few small items of significance which I placed in my backpack. But this hadn't been home for a long time. It felt like visiting a place I knew but was no longer part of.

He followed me up the stairs and into the east wing, what had been Katrin and my space. A bedroom each, a shared study and bathroom. The bathroom. As I entered my bedroom, Cam raised his eyebrows but stood in uncomfortable silence just inside the doorway.

"You can come in, you know."

"I just feel... well... out of place." He glanced down at his t-shirt and jeans.

"You are just fine." I waved my uninjured hand at my similar attire. "My family were just people you know."

"You didn't take your furniture when you moved out?" he inquired.

I shrugged. "Fresh start. After all that happened, I just wanted to get out. Furniture meant nothing to me."

Cam picked up ornaments sourced on various family holidays. A small metal Eiffel Tower. A nautilus shell picked up on a beach. I watched as he poked around my bookcases. I wasn't entirely sure I was comfortable with this, being judged for choices I had made so many years ago.

Opening the wardrobe, I smiled, memories of ski trips and formals engulfing me.

Cam moved to stand beside me and pulled out a dusty pink strapless silk dress I had worn to a formal event, long forgotten.

"Pink?" he teased. "Not once have I ever seen you dressed in pink."

I rolled my eyes. "And you never will. I loathe pink. My mother bought that."

He gazed at it, still on its hanger. "I think it would still fit you," he remarked, a sly grin crossing his face.

"I was about sixteen when I wore that, all of once. I doubt that somehow."

"You haven't changed a day since I met you." Cam's arms gathered me in. "Did you ever bring boys here?"

"Never," I whispered. "To the house, yes. The pool, absolutely. But never up here. They wouldn't have approved."

"Can I be the first?"

Tucking the fingers of my free hand into the waist of his jeans, I drew him closer before I threw off the dust encrusted formerly white bedspread from my queen bed, revealing slightly yellowed sheets underneath. He lowered himself onto me, seeking my lips.

"It feels so naughty to have you in my parents' home," I whispered, pulling his top over his head.

Cam paused, hovering over me. "How naughty?"

"I feel like a teenager again," I whispered as he blocked my words with his lips.

"I'll feel you like a teenager." His voice held a whisper of wicked promises, and I felt my stomach drop through the floor. Both floors.

CHAPTER 16

"WHY IS YOUR MUM'S surname Jorgensen? After all you have told me about her, I would have thought she was the type not to change her name," Cam called, looking at the frames containing the many degrees and certificates in Norwegian and English lining the hallway as I made a final sweep of the downstairs. It was surprisingly hard to say goodbye, although I had emotionally left this place a long time ago. I wondered if we could even safely house the girls here for a time. It was big enough. But almost immediately, I dismissed the notion. Memories of that bathroom would haunt me until the day I died.

"Well, she was born a Jorgensen."

"Is it that a common Norwegian name?"

"I guess. But my parents are distantly related. Second cousins or something like that. Kat and I learned by accident when we were back visiting grandparents. One of Mum's aunts got drunk at a family dinner and fired off a nasty comment in Norwegian at my father, not realizing we understood. Kat and I spoke basic Norwegian, although we always spoke

English with family. We were made to go to language school on a Saturday for years."

"Good to see drunken outbursts aren't limited to Australian families. Or Scottish ones. I distinctly remember my uncle firing up one Christmas when we visited them in Scotland."

"Mum was from old money. We attended a family gathering at the ancestral home, a huge place, far grander than this. My great-aunt had been getting stuck into the wine over dinner, several courses, and over dessert made some cutting remark about Dad only marrying her for her inheritance."

"What did your aunt say?"

"I don't recall exactly. But the equivalent of gold-digger. Mum fired back something that I couldn't quite catch. I was maybe twelve, and I wasn't fluent. It is a difficult language. But it was something along the lines of 'mind your own business, you old cow.' But it fired up my great-aunt, and she threw the word 'incest' at them. Unfortunately, it is the same word in Norwegian, so Kat and I knew exactly what she had said. After that, Mum and Dad were forced to explain."

"Explain what?"

"They were barely acquaintances growing up, part of the extended family. They knew each other to say hello but only saw each other at big family celebrations, weddings, and funerals. The families weren't close. Certainly not birthdays and Yul, what we call Christmas. But then they had gone to university together. In Mum's second year and Dad's third, quite by accident, they ended up living in the same share house and fell in love. But the way they told it, they faced some resistance, especially from my mother's family. So after they graduated, they married and migrated to Australia.”

“Wow, love against the odds.”

“Maybe. The thing is, I never saw them be affectionate with each other. But they never divorced, and both earned enough that they could be self-sufficient, so they could have walked away. It was never a big thing, being distant relatives. Once they explained it was very distant, it was never brought up again. The truth is, I never thought about it after that.”

The strangest expression crossed Cam’s face. “Do you think that is why you and Kat’s genes could be modified? Because your parents shared common DNA?”

“Do you know I’ve never thought about it … but it is certainly possible. I always knew there was a story there, but they always brushed it off. A couple of times, I heard Mum joke that she was Miss Jorgensen, who married Mr. Jorgensen to become Mrs. Jorgensen. In Australia, it was simpler. They were just known as Mr. and Mrs. No one questioned it.”

“How close were they? Family-wise, I mean.” Cam’s face darkened, stewing on the possibilities.

“I have no idea. Second cousins, we were always told. But I am not inbred, if that is what you are thinking of. It wasn’t incest. I can’t imagine we would have been visiting family every second year if that was the case. Someone would have said something. As it was, it was only that one comment. My maternal grandparents were not that fond of my father. That was plain. He was not who they would have chosen for their daughter. But they never openly said anything against him either. They were civil, and they adored Kat and me. It was clear that they didn’t consider us the children of an inappropriate relationship.”

"Regardless, I think we should keep this to our-selves. Can you imagine if Clava learned that was potentially why your genes were modifiable?"

"They could try again." I swallowed. Hard. Though not with me. There were enough adolescents now, upper teens. Even Sam was eighteen, and he was by no means the youngest child I had met in my travels.

"Louis and Ceri," I gulped. "That was exactly what Angus wanted to do."

"Did he know? Did you ever tell him?"

"No. I haven't thought about it myself since well before I left Australia. Unless he knew some other way..."

"They may have done their homework on you. Especially when they worked out Katrin was the only surrogate with a genome they could adapt."

"Maybe. Do you think I should ask Ashton?"

"No. I don't trust that man. Illy said once before he put the project before her. I don't see why that would change, especially if we handed him a piece of useful information on a silver platter."

I returned my attention to the walls as Cam wandered off into the formal dining room, the one kept for guests and not family meals. As I looked at my parents' wall of pride, the professionally laid out gallery of qualifications and achievements, I was distracted by what Cam had said. *Could it be? How close were they? Should I look for evidence before I leve?*

"Honey. You need to see this."

Open on the long, now dull timber dining table was a stack of large black leather-bound books. I had ignored them walking past the room earlier, assuming them to be academic books belonging to my father. But on closer examination, they were far too large.

Cam had wiped the thick layer of dust off the top to reveal the contents.

Glancing over his shoulder, I came face to face with a photo of myself scowling in a school photo, wearing a navy pinafore dress with a matching blazer, my almost white-blonde hair plaited neatly down my back. Roughly upper primary school. Cam returned to the beginning of the book and flipped the pages slowly. Each page was filled with images of my life. Baby photos I had never seen. School photos. Family holidays. I gasped when I saw the artworks neatly pasted in. The clippings from school newsletters. Articles from the newspaper with the swimming events I had won, yachting regattas I had entered.

My hand covered my mouth.

"They loved you, honey. Really. This is a brag book if ever I saw one."

"What are the others?" I gestured to the other three, in part, to hide my embarrassment.

Cam flicked through them, pausing on the occasional page. Another volume filled with my achievements, the remaining two for Katrin.

"I had no idea! Why did they never tell me?" But as the words came out, I knew. They didn't want Kat or me to be conceited. My parents believed that people who achieved a goal would often stop trying to set and achieve new goals, stop striving to be better. But after Katrin overdosed, I would have loved to have known these existed.

"I am so pleased they left them here—for us. They can replace the ones you lost."

"There are so many!" I breathed as I thumbed through the photos. So many pictures I had never seen before. Me on the podium for winning the freestyle event at the State Secondary School Championships. Another of me accepting an award at school.

"Well, we have plenty of time to go through them all. Is there anything else you want to take? I remember once you wanted something of your parents to remember them by."

I nodded, feeling closer to my parents than I had in two decades. "Let me go upstairs to their wing. But they had an extraordinary wine collection. See that door there. I pointed to the back of the dusty kitchen. The glass door?"

Cam nodded.

"That is the wine storage. Take as much as you can, but mainly the reds. The white has likely deteriorated, but if you have room, take that too. It isn't like anyone here needs it, and we can always use it for cooking. There might be other useful items too. And grab a corkscrew or two."

"We will toast to them as we drink it," Cam promised, scooping up the albums in his arms.

An hour later, we had loaded cases of wine, bottled water, and boxes of dried lentils, rice, pasta, and other edible goods into the back of the two vehicles and were ready to return to the dock.

Cam, sensing my discomfort, asked, "Did you find something?"

I nodded, dropping my backpack on the passenger seat of the BMW, not wanting to speak.

Cam was sensitive enough not to press me as I handed him the keys to the Porsche, and he followed me back to the pier.

CHAPTER 17

"**HOW DO WE TRANSPORT** so many children?" Di asked as we watched twenty-seven children tear along the beach, their heads tipped back and screaming, arms outstretched in the wind. The younger ones were in heaven, finally being on solid land. Apart from the few short refueling stops on the way here where we had heavily supervised them, this was their first real taste of freedom. After an inspection of the beach and removal of any hazards, we let them run wild. Many had never been to a beach and kept stopping to kick the golden sand, laughing as the arc dissipated in the wind. I couldn't help but smile watching them. Even with the dead landscape running the length of the foreshore, between the beach and the road, the ocean and warm sand were still beautiful and evoked memories of my childhood.

"I mean, you can all drive, except me. I am assuming it is harder than a golf buggy?"

"Just a little," Sorcha teased. "You should have taken me up on my offer of driving lessons years ago."

Di smiled. "My darling, I love you with every beat of my heart. But there is no way in hell I would ever let you teach me to drive. Our marriage would be over by the end of the day."

Sorcha grinned. "It is all good. We will make do with the rest of us."

"How many batteries did you bring?" Cam asked Tadhg. "Anything here will surely be dead beyond redemption."

"Only six," he admitted. "And we are using two. It would take some time to make more."

"I can drive a Unimog," Illy offered. "Then we can transport all of them together."

We all turned to look at her.

"Seriously?" Cam asked. "How did I not know this?"

"I don't even know what a Unimog is!" I admitted.

"A couple of times I needed to drive one when no one else was available, to transport personnel. We could get one from Victoria Barracks and take them all together?"

"No." Sorcha piped up. "A Unimog is a good idea as a backup, and if we can get one, then we should take one. But I think it is best if we take several vehicles. Four-wheel-drives are best as the roads are littered with branches and potholes. It allows the Kiewa residents to conduct raids on city warehouses. According to Kendra, when she speaks with Di for their monthly chat, they have no vehicles. As it is so remote, no one has left the community in twenty years. They didn't even know they could until Cam arrived, and even then, he didn't teach them how to locate and open the access panels. None of the children have ever seen the world outside."

"Is it our place to show them? It isn't safe. Look around," Cam queried.

"There are a few older than Sam, some as old as nineteen. They need to see the world we left. What we gave up to give them a better life."

"As much as I want to stay with the girls," Tadhg interjected, "I know they are in safe hands. I think I am better utilized accessing the facility in Melbourne again. If we want to know who is behind this, I can do that from there. Track radio transmissions, access satellites, review files. I left the generator last time, so I could start it up again without too much effort. Not that I am looking forward to being alone. I nearly went mad the last time. But..."

"I will stay with you," Ashton spoke so softly I had to strain to hear him over the gusting wind. He was a quiet man and rarely interrupted group conversations. But when he did, it was considered and thoughtful.

"Why?" Sorcha asked, suspicion creeping into her voice. Sorcha had already confided in me that she didn't trust him, a feeling Cam and I endorsed wholeheartedly.

"I was head of that facility. I know where everything is, all the access codes, where the backup generators are, and where the data storage is. I can help."

Tadhg considered. "That would certainly make my work a lot easier. I assume you know where Kiewa is?"

"I do. I approved all the settlements. I can get you there when we have accessed what we need."

Of course you did. I seethed inwardly, watching him stand beside Illy, gently touching her, but spoke as calmly as I could. "That is a good idea. If Tadhg, the tech genius here, can start another car, you can come and meet us when you have news?"

"We will," Ashton promised.

"Do you need food stores?"

"Initially, yes. All the supplies remaining were sent to the last settlements. But I know where there is a supply. Warehouses we ran out of time to empty."

"Better than what I had to do last time I was here," Cam muttered. Di and Tadhg looked sympathetic. Cam had told me how much he had hated breaking into private homes, taking their remaining supplies. The risk of coming face to face with the now long deceased inhabitants. One resident from Bellcamp, an uptight bitch, by all accounts, accused him of being a thief. That insult had hurt him for years.

Throughout the afternoon, Cam and I helped Tadhg and Carl source several months' worth of supplies as well as raw materials for Tadhg to make more batteries, while Illy and Gerry raided the army barracks on St. Kilda Road. Illy returned in a monstrosity of a personnel carrier with camouflage canvas sides and an open back but capable of holding all the children, or as was currently the case, forty or so sleeping bags, tents, camping stoves, and a range of other equipment.

"Is *that* what a Unimog is!" I exclaimed. "I've seen them but didn't know what they were called."

"They are a Mercedes Benz," Illy teased as she slipped down from the high driver's seat. "I would have thought you would feel right at home."

Even in the long summer daylight hours, dusk was

falling before we had finished loading up all the vehicles. It was several hours to Kiewa, and we all recognized that driving in the dark with likely road blockages was not a sensible choice. We briefed the children on where we were going and explained that we would break them up into several vehicles. Twenty minutes of madness ensued as small groups were decided, resulting in tears when friendship groups were separated. A cry erupted over the others as Tadhg gently explained that he wouldn't be accompanying us immediately.

Fairlie's distress of the night before turned into hysteria by breakfast, refusing to eat and pleading with her father not to leave her. We gave them some space to take a walk along the beach as he explained to her what needed to be done. From the deck we could see him holding her hand, occasionally stopping to kneel in the sand and hug her.

"I'm so glad that isn't me," Cam spoke softly in my ear as I watched them. "I don't think I could leave Cait for weeks, potentially months."

"Me too. You are her father in every way that counts. But I am glad I finally know."

"I am too. There is a relief that comes with learning the truth, knowing it was someone we knew and trusted. But if I am honest, there is an enormous relief in knowing that it is someone who will never try to take her from me. She is mine, the same as the others."

"I never thought of that," I admitted but understood the weight that had been lifted from his shoulders. Even though I hadn't grown Caitlin, she was mine. "Do you think that could ever happen? The men that fathered those girls may want access to them? Custody?"

"It is one of the few aspects I think Carl handled well."

"You called him Carl. Does that mean you like him now?"

"I will never trust him. I can't. That might make me a bad person, but I could never trust any man who allowed a team of people to do what they did to you. But for Illy's sake, I can be civil."

"It wouldn't have been any easier if it was a woman who did that to me."

"Mum always said that women in positions of power were often worse than men. Women were awful to other women, demeaning their choices, clambering over them to achieve success. I remember once she had a regional manager who belittled everything Mum did. I never really saw Mum at work. She refused to let us go to the same schools where she was employed as principal, but I heard enough from other people to know she was a great boss. She was respected, and she cared. Knew everyone's name, their partners, and their children. Mum allowed working mothers to work part-time, to do work from home so they could care for their children, especially if they were sick. But this woman insisted that they weren't pulling their weight. Mum always went to bat for them, but it wore her down. That constant feeling of needing to watch her back."

"What bullshit. Do you honestly think Isla, Sorcha, Illy, or I worked any less just because we had children?"

"Not at all. But life is different on Lewis, isn't it? Flexible work was a thing before we left, but it wasn't commonplace. Certainly not in schools."

"I guess not. My mother employed a nanny to care for us. She barely popped us out before she handed the bottle and packet of nappies to someone else to deal with."

"Makes you wonder why they had you, doesn't it?"

Since visiting my family home, I sensed Cam viewed me slightly differently. Not that I had hidden my privileged upbringing, but there is a difference between being told something that happened in the past and seeing it with your own eyes. If anything, it had made him more understanding of me but less tolerant of my parents. Considering he never met them, this was a little awkward.

Frustration rose in me, feeling the need to defend my parents. "They loved us, you know."

Cam looked at me. "I'm sorry. That was rude. I didn't mean it like that."

"I know. And I know how it looks. That they outsourced parenting. Now that I have done it myself several times, maybe they did. But we rely on other people too. It takes a village, as they say."

"They paid a village."

"Maybe, but they both worked. It isn't like they went off on tropical holidays and left us with the nanny. We always went with them. They exposed us to wonderful places and experiences. My childhood may not have been the same as yours, or as our children, but it was no less wonderful."

"I know. But it didn't save them in the end, did it?"

"No, they perished, like everyone else. I am pleased though, to have closure."

"Do you think we will ever have closure?" he asked softly.

"Closure about what?"

"Learning who is behind this. I want to go home, Frey, back to our kids. It has been months already, and we are no closer to learning anything. I want to stop running and go back to our life. With you."

I reached for his hand with my unsplinted one, resting it over his as it lay on the rail. "We will. I want that too. But now, we go to Kiewa. What was it like?"

Cam sighed. "It was fifteen years ago, and I wasn't even there that long. Di could probably answer that best. She has never missed her monthly call to Kendra, but it hasn't changed much from what she says. It was the most like what we left behind. Here. In the old world. They started in dormitories but paired up and moved into houses. But people didn't live collectively. They allocated each person a vegetable patch and a plot of land for crop growing—wheat, oats, rice. But there wasn't the same sense of community. Sorcha saw it more than most, being on the med team. She was paid in food usually, but there wasn't the sense that everyone supported everyone else. They lived their own lives. Social, yes. But not a team."

"I'm not sure I am going to like it," I confessed. "One of the things that surprised me when I finally settled down was the sense of community on Lewis. Coming from a family where I could buy anything I wanted, goods or services, it was strange to be part of a team. To know that one person's success or failure could impact others. But I grew to love it. I'm worried about how I will adapt, especially if we end up there for months."

"Let's just hope Tadhg learns something soon."

"It surprised me he came, to be honest. He has a better set-up on Newgrange. He could have established surveillance from there."

"Callie told me he insisted. Kevin and Nadja are distraught at the loss of Bethany, and it terrified her

Fairlie would be next. They knew the girls needed to leave, to get them out of danger. Cal said that she felt better knowing he was with us, even if it meant him being away from her and their children."

"That is some commitment," I admitted. "Although Fairlie is his daughter."

"You keep saying this. Like we don't love those girls like they are our own. They were all only days or weeks old when they came to us. The moment I held Caitlin, I knew I would lay down my life to protect her. You have this bizarre notion that women can bond with babies and men can't. It isn't true."

"No, it isn't," I admitted. I had seen Cam with Louis, Katrin, Xanthe, and Thorsten enough times to know that he indeed would sacrifice anything for any of them. But Cait?

He was watching me. "I will say this one more time. You sacrificed everything to go after Louis, and he isn't your biological child. But he is your son. Caitlin may be Luca's child, but she is my daughter. Do you understand?"

"Caitlin is Luca's?"

We whirled to see Sorcha standing in the doorway behind us.

"Shut the fucking door," Cam growled.

"How long have you known?"

"Not long. Ashton told us after Frey walked in on him and Illy shagging."

Sorcha's eyebrows hit her hairline. "That fucking snake. And you believe him?"

"Look at her," I whispered. "Of course, it is true. She looks like a hybrid between Seraphine and Summer."

Sorcha nodded slowly. "Why did he tell you?"

"He thought I wanted to know."

"So nothing to do with the fact that he is shagging your bestie and needs to get you onside?"

"I'm sure that was part of the motivation. I'm not stupid."

"Well, now I know who you wanted to punch that day. What about Mei? Did he say anything about her?"

"None of the others. He just asked if I wanted to know."

"And you said yes?"

"Actually, *I* said yes," Cam interjected. "Frey was too worried about it being someone awful. Then she could never not know. So he told me."

"Does Caitlin know?"

"Absolutely not," I snapped. "And it isn't your place to tell her. She is Cam's daughter, and that is all there is to it."

"Good." Sorcha briskly turned to leave.

"Did you mean that?" Cam breathed in my ear as we watched Sorcha walk away.

"I did. I really did. That is how I see her, you know. I just worried for so long that you wouldn't see her the same way as your other children. That one day you would realize that you didn't have a connection with her. It is stupid, I know. But when blood parents can walk away from their own children, I was scared that one day you wouldn't feel the same about her as you do about the others."

"She is nearly seven. When were you planning to tell me this?"

"Likely never."

"What else is stewing away in that beautiful head of yours?"

"You don't want to know."

"Try me."

CHAPTER 18

THE LOW RHYTHMIC HUM of the tires on the freeway lulled the girls to sleep. I glanced back at the six of them across two rows and smiled. We had let them have a last run along the beach, hoping it would burn any silliness off before a long road trip. They had been fascinated with the size of the vehicles but scared of the sound. Before they came here, they had only ever seen the small electric vehicles we used, which ran almost silently.

"Do you ever miss university?" I asked Cam.

His lips quirked, not expecting the random question, but he answered readily enough. "Not really. I hated the crowds, the noisy lecture theaters, and especially the cafeteria. But I loved the learning, so I pushed through."

"How did you manage it?"

"As soon as the day finished, I would need to go somewhere quiet, just to be alone for an hour or so. A park, a walk along the beach in winter. Somewhere where I could sit and clear my head. Sometimes to meditate or do yoga. It wasn't always possible, of course. Some nights I had sports or plans with people. But it helped when I could.”

“You did yoga?”

“I did, for a while. It just helped me decompress after a manic day.”

“I’ve never seen you do yoga.”

“When I first moved to August, I did. But truthfully, since I left Australia and my old life, I have rarely felt the need to. Now I can just take off into the mountains and walk. Here, living in a city, it was so loud all the time. Finding a quiet sanctuary took planning. On August and Lewis, it was a few minutes’ walk.”

“What did you do when you were younger? Before you could drive?”

“Primary school was the worst. Mum and Dad both worked, so I went to after-school care. It was loud and chaotic, unstructured. I hated it. At least when I got to high school, I could ride my bike home. I loved riding. Just the peace of it. It was like skiing in many ways. You can’t be wrapped up in your problems when you are on a bike, or you come off. So it was good for me to focus on the ride and not be in my own head.”

“You can ride on Lewis anytime you like. Why don’t you?”

“Lack of time, for one. What little free time I have I want to spend with you and the kids. But I don’t have the same frenetic pace to my day now. I work with the team on some days, but on other days I am alone. If I don’t finish my work because someone needs me, the world won’t end over it. Remember what school was like when bells rang, announcements over the PA, the crush of kids in the hallways getting books from lockers, homework due dates? That constant state of pressure was my worst nightmare.”

"We didn't have the same feel at my school. It was a lot more orderly, but I have seen enough sitcoms to know what you are talking about."

"It is something our kids will never experience. A high school with hundreds of students. Different subjects taught by different teachers. Lockers and cafeterias. Uniforms." He paused and grinned. "What was your uniform like? Your primary school one was kind of cute."

"Horrid. A blazer and long skirt in winter. Summer dress in summer but always with awful black leather school shoes. I hated them. You?"

"Awful gray pants that scratched, no matter how many times they were washed. White shirt and tie that had to be ironed. Blazer in winter. I remember thinking that starting your day by tying a noose around your neck is a fairly apt description of high school. But it was a means to an end."

"What end?"

"I wanted to work in food security. Perhaps Sorcha rubbed off on me, talking about her work in developing countries. I thought I might try to get a job with the United Nations. Then the world imploded."

"You got your wish, but perhaps not in the way you thought it would work out."

"What about you? Was a vet all you ever wanted to be?"

"You know, I guess I thought I would start off being a vet. When you have money, nothing is an insurmountable problem. If I hated it, I could have returned to university and studied something else. There is a lot less pressure when you know that there is enough money to pay the rent and the bills. You can take your time to choose."

"Do you think you would have chosen medicine, eventually?"

Exhaling, I thought about that. "I really don't know. I am good at maths and science, but I wasn't great with people until I met you, Di, Illy, Luca. Even before Kat left me, I was known as the ice queen."

"I knew plenty of medical professionals who had no bedside manner! Most of whom worked with children."

"Yes, but they must have wanted to help people. Truthfully, I didn't like many people. My parents' friends were rich and entitled. Even then, I rebelled against it."

"What did you find at your parents' place? You came downstairs looking ... strange. I thought you needed time, but then you didn't bring it up, so I thought maybe it was something unpleasant."

"Them," I admitted, seeing the image before me as I stared out the windscreen at the desolate brown landscape. "Mum was lying in bed, wearing a navy silk robe. I remember thinking how much she liked navy. She must have been sick because Dad was sitting in one of their bedroom chairs, holding her hand. But he was dressed, casually, for him. All I could think about was how much Mum looked like Katrin. Her hair was longer and had more gray than the last time I had seen her. Dad just looked like Dad. They looked ... peaceful. Well, as much as you can tell from a decomposed twenty-year-old corpse."

"I'm glad."

"Me too. I stood in the doorway and looked at them. Their skeletons, really, but that didn't freak me out. I could see the love between them, if that makes sense. I never saw it before. But it made me feel... happy is the wrong word. Closure maybe. At peace even. They weren't alone, and I think that is all any of us can ask at the end. To be with someone who loves us. I know Ceri didn't get that, nor Laetitia. But somehow, it makes me happy, not that they died before their time, but that they were together at the end."

"I get it. I had that sense of closure when I found my parents. Not that they had passed. That was horrible, although knowing for certain was better than not knowing. It was the fact that Dad was there for Mum. I guess she was there for him, even though he went after. Does that make sense?"

"I've never believed in heaven or an afterlife, but sometimes I feel people who have passed. Not them. I have never sensed my parents. But my sister. Luca." And Laetitia too, I wanted to add, but couldn't.

Fortunately, he did.

"Do you know I felt Lae's presence for a long time after she passed? For a while, I wondered if she was trying to make amends for fighting on that last day. Even after Katrin's birth and you and I reuniting, I still felt her. In the first few weeks, I kept thinking she was still alive, and I sensed her as she was calling to me. Over time, I realized it wasn't her, but her spirit. Does that sound odd?"

"Only if you find it odd that I felt her, too. Not malevolent, and it was strange, as I never met her in life, but I just felt her there. In our home."

"You never told me that."

"I didn't want you to think I was a little cray-cray."

"Honey, I know you are cray-cray. You willingly married me. Twice. When did you last feel her?"

I sighed and told him all of it. Sensing Laetitia after we reunited in Edinburgh and returned to Roseglen.

The day I rode out to the broch to speak to her, promising that I would care for Cam and Louis. Invoking her help several times.

Cam's eyes popped. "You prayed to her for help?"

"Praying is probably the wrong word. But speak to her? I did. I knew that if there was an afterlife, and she had the power to do anything, she would help me find Louis."

"Do you think it helped?"

I shrugged. "I don't know, honestly. I'm not into psychics, seances, and tarot cards. All I can tell you is that I was dreaming about her when Ashton... Carl..." I corrected myself, "woke me. She was calling me, and I remember thinking it was strange as I never heard her voice."

Cam was speechless and looked at me, dumbfounded.

I shrugged. "I had asked her for help as we set out to find Louis. When I was being held, I dreamed about her once before that night, but it was like she ignored me. But that night, I heard her calling me. Pulling me back."

"She would have, you know. Helped. She would have overcome any feelings she had toward you and helped you to save Louis."

"It was the strangest thing. After that day at the broch, I truly felt that she had given me her blessing. I mean, I barged on in and took over the role of mother. But I never felt like the wicked stepmother. Louis asked me, and I accepted. That was it. But after that day, I felt like she accepted me in that role too."

"You are so logical. I have never known you to be so ... metaphysical," Cam admitted. "I can't believe I could love you more, asking her to help you, but I do.

I am thrilled that you could see past your own feelings toward her."

"Jealousy," I admitted. "I am horribly jealous of her."

"Why would you be jealous of her?"

"Because she gave you what I couldn't. A child."

"Really? Is that what all the drama of the last nine months has been about? Louis?"

"It is more than just him," I hurried to say. "Do you want to hear this?"

"If it helps you, I do."

"Illy says we need to talk about it."

"Then tell me. I'm here. The kids are asleep, and we aren't quite there yet."

"I was torn away from you. The reason I avoided coming home that night was because I was devastated I wasn't pregnant. I thought it was me. I was a failure, and I didn't want you to know. All my life, I had always succeeded in achieving anything I wanted—until then. I could have left Fred out overnight. I mean, where would he have gone on a domed island? But I stayed away so I could slip in after you were asleep, and you wouldn't know how gutted I was."

"Oh, Frey…" He reached a hand out, but I raised my injured hand, quietening him.

"Then I ended up on Lewis and spent months trying to get back to you. By the time I did, you were remarried and had a baby—with her. You had everything we wanted, but not with me. And it was all my fault. I was upset about not being pregnant, and you ended up with another woman because of my stupidity. That was why Luca insisted we leave again. He could see how much it tore me apart."

"You never told me you were avoiding me because you weren't pregnant. The rest I knew. Why would you avoid me? Didn't you know how much I loved you? Sure, I wanted a family, but I wanted you more."

"It felt like everyone was having babies, and every month that passed devastated me. I wasn't used to feeling like a failure. I had never failed at anything in my life until that point. I got whatever I wanted when I wanted it. Then she gave you what I couldn't."

"It wasn't like that."

"It was to me. There is something else. The photos."

"Photos?"

"The ones on your file. There were a lot of photos. Rather graphic photos of what I know was your honeymoon."

"Oh."

"No matter how hard I try to block it out, the images haunt me. I can't help but see you with her. How happy you were together. Even in the years after we reunited, logically I knew you were happy, but I only saw you together once so I could deal—until I saw those pictures. They were so vivid. It felt like your happiness was being rammed down my throat at a time when I was away from you. Learning that you were a chosen pair killed me. Soul mates, as I would describe it. Illy says there is no such thing, but…"

"She does? Why?"

"She laughed at me and said the concept of soul mates is bullshit."

"Well, I believe in finding my soul's partner. Don't you?"

"I did. I always thought it was you. But maybe you got two. After all, Sorcha got two."

"Three, actually. Sam, her fiancé from Melbourne. Then Tom, now Di."

"I know little about Sam, and Tom, to be honest. Sorcha keeps her private life private."

"I never met Tomori, her partner in Kiewa. Although I suspect now that her worlds are about to collide, we may learn more. But Sam was a good man. Gentle, kind, intelligent. But he struggled with his own demons. A drug addict mother, an alcoholic father. He spent some time in foster care as a child when she couldn't care for him, and his father was in jail. But he was intelligent, won a scholarship, and studied medicine in the year above Sorcha."

"Is that how they met?"

"No, actually. Sam met Sorcha through my mother. Every year Mum would volunteer at soup kitchens, prepare Christmas lunches for the homeless, and run charity drives collecting winter coats for people doing it tough. He was volunteering at one event, and I'm ashamed to say I can't remember which one. It was a charity that had helped him when he was a child, bought him schoolbooks, uniforms, and shoes. Mum, being Mum, dragged him along to our family Christmas lunch."

"Wow, so he wanted to give back?"

"He wanted to help other people out of the hole he had once been in. But you could see that his demons plagued him. He and I used to play golf sometimes."

I sniggered. "You? Played golf?"

"I wasn't very good. I have always liked the quote, 'golf is a good walk spoiled.' That is pretty much how I felt about it, but Sam loved it. One of his foster families taught him, and he was talented. I would go along, hit a few balls, usually into the lake, and we would talk. I think that was why he invited me. Someone to talk to. He called me and wanted to play. I put him off.

I had exams and was struggling to focus. Then when Sorcha couldn't get in touch with him, I drove her over to his place, and … we found him."

I knew this part and waited until Cam had recovered.

"They were due to be married in less than a fortnight. Sorcha had bought the dress, shoes, everything. Everything was booked and paid for. Instead, they used the church for his funeral."

"I know this isn't the point, but Sorcha wanted to marry in a *church*?"

"No, Sam wanted to marry in a church. It was the gardens, technically. She refused to have the service in the chapel itself but agreed to the rose garden."

"Did she change? After that?"

"Sorcha was always a bitch. Hard-headed and with no tolerance. But she adored him. He was her first love, and they were inseparable. She encouraged him to be the best he could be, and he softened her edges. But something in her died that day."

Glancing back into the back seat, the six children we had crammed in across the two rows were still asleep, unused to long, boring car trips.

"Do you think they will be happy to see her?"

"I would think so. They were unhappy at losing one of their med team. Now that I have seen her in action, I would suspect she was their best doctor. But they understood she wanted to come with me."

"And Di leaving with Sorcha?"

"The relationship was still secret when we left. I didn't learn myself until we were back in Melbourne about to depart. We were on the yacht, waiting for Tadhg. They just dropped it on me and walked away."

"Well, they are perfect for each other, although I would never have seen that coming when we were all friends on August. For a while, I thought you and Di were a couple."

"I never felt about Di that way, but I didn't know she was gay. Either of them. But Kendra must know now, so likely all of Kiewa does now. Di speaks to her every month."

"Do you think they will accept us? There are quite a lot of us."

Four carloads with six adults and twenty-seven children aged from six to seventeen, to be precise. It was a lot to take on. But it had been nearly twenty years since they moved here. All communities were established now. One of the isolated communities had struggled in the first few years, almost a quarter of the population dying of an unknown illness, and several had perished altogether, although Clava had a hand in that we later learned. But the rest had found their rhythm. Worked out how to get along and made a life.

As the anxiety knotted my stomach with the thought of entering a new community, I knew I needed to tell him, all of it. I opened my mouth to tell him, what Illy had said, but before I could speak, the car slowed.

"I don't know, but they had better batten down the hatches. We are here."

CHAPTER 19

WE WAITED FOR THE others to arrive. As the car was no longer moving, the girls woke, scared and confused, needing reassurance that it would all be alright. I silently prayed it would be. After some discussion, Illy, Sorcha, and I agreed to meet with Rafael, the most senior official on Kiewa. Sorcha was known to the community here, and Illy was a powerful communicator. Many times I had seen her steer a tricky conversation away from potential conflict. They were my children, so I was there to play the "parent needing help" card if needed. Sorcha advised us that Rafael may be sympathetic, being a parent himself, and suggested that three women were also less confrontational than six adults barging in with so many kids in tow.

"What is he like?" Illy asked, preparing herself as we walked along the main road toward Raf's home.

"Strong-willed, very controlling, and always gets his way, but I have always found him fair. He isn't unreasonable, although we would do well not to get on the wrong side of him. I warn you: we won't be considered guests for long. They will expect us to work."

"I have no issue with that. We aren't here to freeload."

"How did he get this gig?" Illy asked. "We didn't appoint leaders in any of the communities we established. Self-appointed?"

"Ever since we were settled here, he was a powerful figure. He just had a way of organizing people. He gave instructions, and they listened. He was recruited to be the principal teacher, though we didn't have children when we first arrived, so he was a kind of project manager, allocating resources and that type of thing. Once children were born, he set up the school, and goodness did he keep them under control. Nothing at all like Di." She smirked. "But according to Di, once they worked out how to connect with other communities via radio, after learning about them from Cam, he now controls the radio communications. All the radio scheduling goes through him."

"Did he respect you?"

I smiled at Illy's question, noting that she hadn't said "liked" as she researched her target.

"He did. I assisted his wife Yashira in giving birth twice, and not without complications. There was professional respect and personal gratitude."

"Not a bad place to start negotiations."

Fortunately, Rafael was home when we arrived, and visibly startled to see Sorcha. After a pleasant greeting, she introduced us. A tall man, he reached out to shake hands warmly enough and didn't seem unhappy to have unexpected visitors. Illy was in assessment mode, I noted, but smiling charmingly. Only someone who knew her very well could tell that her mind was ticking over, evaluating, and calculating the best approach.

"Sophie!" Raf called, and after a few minutes, a stunning, dark-haired girl appeared in the doorway. "Can you bring us some drinks and something to eat?"

He turned back to us. "I assume you have time?"

Sorcha smiled. "It has been a long journey. A cold drink would be wonderful." She looked up at the girl, who stood in the doorway looking bored, like we had interrupted something important.

"Hi Sophie," Sorcha smiled. "I assisted your mother when you were born. I think you were about four when I left. How you have grown!"

Like all teens when reminded they were once children, Sophie scowled and tossed her long sleek hair over her shoulder.

"Come in, Soph," her father wheedled as she leaned against the door frame. "Do you remember Sorcha? She was the best doctor Kiewa ever had. She saved your life when you were born."

Sophie flushed, a beautiful rose tint coloring her exotic Eurasian appearance. She was womanly in appearance, curvaceous but one of those women who held themselves with total confidence. Her eyes scanned us appraisingly, but she clearly didn't like what she saw, as her nose turned up as she looked back at her father.

"Drinks, Dad?" she reminded him, and disappeared.

Raf turned his attention back to us. "Have you come back to live?" So there was no beating around the bush. That was good.

Sorcha quickly filled him in on the situation. The children and I were being threatened and needed refuge.

Raf pursed his lips. "We have nothing available to house so many people..." I could see his brain whirring as he surveyed at Sorcha. Illy would have noticed, too. "What do you need?" he asked.

Sorcha was sharp and knew the game. "Just shelter. We have sleeping bags and cooking equipment. We are prepared to work, Raf. I would love to rejoin your medical team. Freyja here is an exceptional orthopedic surgeon. Cam and Di are with us, and as you may recall, they are both skilled horticulturists. Illy is a psychologist, not that you need one of those."

"You'd be surprised," he grumbled, but his eyes lit at Sorcha's offer. "I'm drowning in teen angst."

"I am more than happy to help in any way I can." Illy's lilting and charming manner made him smile at her. "I have a lot of experience with teens. I have two of my own." She laughed delightfully. "Truly, we don't need much. Just somewhere to stay. We are all willing to contribute."

I could see his brain weighing up the benefits, six skilled additions to his team. "Well, we have one of the old bunkhouses free, if that works? We have stripped it of furniture, but it still has a functional kitchen and bathroom. We were going to turn it into another school, but that never happened. I'll need to get the tanks hooked back up, but that won't take long. Does that suit?"

"Oh absolutely," Illy gushed, turning on her charm, and I watched as he gazed at her, almost drooling. "We appreciate your help. Truly. It is very kind of you to take us in. Please let us know what we can do to help."

"Well, let's get you settled, and we can talk work in a few days."

I saw what Sorcha had meant. Even as captivated as he was with Illy, there was no way we were getting away with freeloading.

Sophie returned with a jug of sangria, the red liquid glowing in the light with fragments of orange floating on top. She dutifully poured and served each of us a glass, taking the tongs to place an orange slice in each. As I reached out to take mine, I noticed her staring at my exposed forearms just a fraction of a second too long.

"Wow," I gushed, tasting it, drawing her eyes away from my arms to my face. "This is amazing. I haven't had sangria in years!"

Raf beamed proudly as he held his glass up to check the clarity, and Sophie slipped out, a scowl marring her beautiful face. "Well, we perfected the art of grape growing years ago, but people wanted an alternative to red wine all the time, especially in summer. You may recall that we also do well with citrus fruits, so one of the team suggested sangria. It took a while to finesse the recipe, but this is what we have."

"It is delicious!" Sorcha agreed, taking another sip. "How are your children?" Sorcha asked. "And Yashira? Is she well?"

Raf's face clouded and his eyebrows furrowed. We all saw the warning signs, but it was too late. The storm cloud settled, and after a long pause, he spoke gruffly, "Yashi passed a few years ago. During childbirth. The baby too."

"Oh, Raf, I am sorry to hear that," Sorcha said, clearly shocked. Childbirth was complicated at times, as we both knew, but we had never lost anyone.

"Wouldn't have happened if you were still here."

Ouch. Sorcha recoiled visibly.

"Family is so important, isn't it?" Illy quickly picked up the thread, making me pleased she had come along to this meeting. "I have four children myself, and my husband passed a few years ago. They can be so challenging. How many do you have?"

"Six. That was the seventh. We had agreed no more after that. But..."

"Sorcha has three herself," Illy kept the tone light and friendly. "Freyja, well, that is the complicated part, isn't it? Freyja has five of her own, but nearly all of these special children are hers genetically. Do you have boys and girls?"

"Goodness, he only had two when I was last here," Sorcha muttered under her breath as we walked back toward the dome where we had left the others. "Six!"

"Thank goodness you were here to turn that conversation around," I said to Illy. "I thought he was going to slap Sorcha for leaving. He blames her for losing his wife."

"If he rules his kids with the same iron fist he uses on everyone else, he will need a psychologist," Illy noted. "Force never really works on teenagers. Hormones, rebelliousness are just par for the course. Goodness, think of what we got up to!"

"I don't know what you are talking about. *I* was an angel," I announced haughtily, making them both laugh hysterically.

"Oh, who are you kidding!" Illy taunted as we headed down the road. "You've told me enough for me to know you had a jolly good run at it before you settled down with Cam."

"Bit of a tart, were we?" Sorcha's eyebrows raised.

"Come on. Who wasn't?" Illy retorted, seeing my face redden. "And if I hadn't been ragingly conspicuous in appearance, I would have had a lot more, too!"

"I was engaged by twenty-two," Sorcha admitted. "I feel like I missed out."

"More fool you," Illy teased. "I miss living in a big city and being anonymous. Kissing a boy in a club, going to the loo, and ducking out the back door."

"Or taking them home and kicking them out before sunrise," I added, making them both stare at me. "I don't do mornings. Never did."

Illy screeched with laughter. Sorcha recoiled, blinking.

"How did you meet Tom?" I asked coyly in an effort to turn this away from my misspent youth. "You must have had Sam fairly quickly."

"Go on, tell us," Illy urged. "Raf said the dorms are halfway back to the dome. It is a long walk."

Sorcha sighed. "It goes back before that, I guess. I met Sam at the end of my second year of medicine. We met through Mum, but we clicked and spent a lot of time together, studying, eating meals at his place, him staying over at ours. We kind of fell into it. I don't remember him not being part of my life. We were just Sorcha and Sam, and I never really questioned it. Then, he... he took his own life." Sorcha paused. "I didn't see it coming. It blindsided me for the longest time. I couldn't function. I went back to uni, focused on my work. But I didn't live. I couldn't breathe. I just put one foot in front of the other and kept going."

"I know how that feels," Illy said, putting her hand on Sorcha's arm.

"I started my postgrad, took international placements on my summer holidays, so I was always busy, didn't have time to dwell on it."

"Dwell on what?" I asked.

"What went wrong."

"What made you think something was wrong?" Illy asked.

"He didn't want to be with *me*. It is a fairly permanent way of breaking up with someone."

"Bullshit." The single word reverberated from Illy's mouth like a gunshot. "That was everything to do with Sam's mental health and nothing at all to do with you."

"How can you say that? He left me."

"There are a million ways to break up with someone. Leave the country. Send them an SMS. Go to a party and sleep with someone else in front of them. Trust me: suicide isn't one of them."

Sorcha shrugged, unconvinced.

"Did you not speak with someone at the time?"

"I did. But what got me through was putting my head down and just keep going. Then about six months later, Cam was accepted to go to August. I didn't make the cut, as you know, because I have asthma. I was torn. I wanted to go too, to escape all those memories. But I saw what his leaving did to our parents. In part thrilled that he was chosen, knowing he would survive, but devastated that they would never see him again. It was like knowing someone had died, only they hadn't. We knew we were the ones left to die, slowly and painfully. They needed to make up excuses, as people called looking for him. Every time Mum had to lie about where he was, I watched another tiny piece of her die."

"Your poor mother," I murmured, wondering for a moment if my own had gone through something similar, fielding calls and avoiding people asking where I was.

"Then, a few months later, after things were dire, I was told there was a place for me. But I had to go that day. I had only a few hours to pack and say goodbye. I think that was the worst day of my life. Worse than finding Sam. Worse than losing Tom. Those events I had no control over. But this was a choice, and one I regretted for a long time. Sure, I fought them. I didn't want to go, make them lose both of us. Mum insisted, of course. She wouldn't accept no. When I arrived here, I hated it and sought ways to get out. I knew Mum and Dad were heading to the block, and it was only a few hours away. I wanted to go with them, as we had planned. I wanted to help them. I had nearly finished my placements and was due to start as an intern at the Royal Melbourne Hospital in a few months. Get some more ED experience. Only the world imploded, and that never happened. I planned ways to escape and leave here so many times. Cut through the fabric, tunnel underneath. As long as I avoided water, I could walk it in a few days."

"Was it really so bad?" Illy asked gently as we trudged down the dirt road, houses and home gardens blending into each other as we focused on her story

"People didn't speak to you here. They housed me in a dormitory with nine other women. I've never enjoyed slumber parties or secretly wanted to go to boarding school with a group of girls. I absolutely loathed it. They were loud and giggly, and I used to lay awake at night, regretting my decision to come." Sorcha's voice was full of pain, and even my heart broke for her. The strongest woman I knew, other that Illyria, and she too had endured unspeakable hardships out here, alone.

Sorcha sighed but continued, "There wasn't a lot of work for the med team in the early days. People were healthy, and there were no children, so aside from a few accidents I was bored. I couldn't stay in the dorm, as there was this constant level of chatter, just pointless noise. Each day, after checking in at the clinic, I would go for long walks. That was how I met Tom. He had come to Australia to study for his Masters and then Ph.D. in biotechnologies, algae farming. His family was still in Japan. But Japan was affected before Australia, and they closed the borders. He couldn't get home and never got to say goodbye, and that ate at him. He was sitting down at the lake one day, in my spot. I wasn't focused on where I was walking. All I could see was Mum and Dad, needing me. He was sitting on my rock, his legs outstretched. I tripped over his legs and gave us both quite a shock. I was about to leave, and he asked me to stay. It was the first time in the weeks since I had moved here that someone had actually tried to engage me in conversation. So I sat, thinking we would make polite conversation, then I would leave."

"And did you?" I asked, desperate to learn more about the woman I thought I knew.

"We talked for six hours until it was dark. Tom was intelligent, funny, and so easy to talk to. We walked back together, starving. He was housed in one of the men's dorms. So we made plans for the next day, to take a walk. He showed me the algal tanks, and I spoke about medicine."

"Love at first sight?" Illy asked, gently teasing as we turned the corner in the road

"Not exactly. It was a slow burn, I guess. It was his brain I fell in love with. He was brilliant. But kind and gentle. He never spoke down to me. He treated me with the utmost respect."

"Because you are also brilliant," I noted, but Sorcha was deep in memory.

"We continued like this for a few months. Finding time to spend together each day until I didn't remember being alone. He was one of the first to get his own cottage. While his English was excellent, being in a dorm wasn't to his liking either, and he struggled with the noise. Raf was the project manager back then and in charge of allocating homes, and I suspect he realized that Tom's work was important for the long-term sustainability of Kiewa. So we spent a lot more time at his place, and we would talk until sunrise. This went on for a few weeks. I still remember the first day he kissed me. He had cooked me dinner. After dinner, we sat and talked for hours. He asked if he could kiss me, and I said yes. Then I nearly ruined it all by crying, thinking I was betraying Sam's memory. He wiped my tears and asked me about Sam. I told him everything, fully expecting he would push me away. He didn't. He listened and didn't judge. Instead, he told me about the Tanabata festival."

"Tanabata?" I questioned.

"It is a Japanese festival, the Star Festival, held on the seventh day of the seventh month. Two deities, lovers, were separated by the Milky Way. On that one day each year, they were reunited."

"That is lovely," I said, meaning it.

"Tom suggested I dedicate that day to my love for Sam. On that day, I was Sam's, but for all the rest, would I consider being his?"

I stopped dead in the road, shaded under an enormous eucalypt and gaped at her. "That is the most romantic thing I have ever heard. I wish he was here to teach your brother!"

"It really was. But he was genuine. It wasn't cheesy. He asked if there was enough room in my heart for both of them. What could I say to that? So we moved in together, and his son was born a year later. He insisted we name our baby Sam as, without my Sam, he would never have met me."

"How beautiful is that! Oh, I want that for both of you." I turned to Illy. "One day each year to be reunited with your lost loves."

"Only now I have two." Sorcha smiled wanly.

"So you pick different days. But you have Di."

"I do, and she is wonderful."

"Can I ask when you realized..." I broke off, feeling like I had overstepped the mark. Sorcha and I were friendly, but I had never dared ask about her private life lest she bite my head off. I dropped my head and sped up, hoping she would ignore my blurted comment.

"That I was gay?"

"Well, yes." I glanced up, wondering if I had offended her.

Sorcha laughed. A deep, genuine laugh. "You know, I never did. I never lusted after men or women in general. I just find particular personalities attractive. Sam, Tom, and now Di. They all had characters I was attracted to, traits and qualities I found myself wanting to be around. It was never about gender. That part didn't matter. So when I met Di, I fell in love with *her*. As soon as I met her, I knew she was the one, and it didn't matter what bits she had. It was that wholesome goodness about her that knocked me for six. That unwavering kindness and gentleness I knew I needed in my life."

"That is possibly the most wonderful thing I have ever heard," I admitted,

"Well, you know what I think is wonderful? You and my brother finally sorting your shit out. Took you long enough. He moped around for months, and you were an utter bitch to everyone."

"So I hear." I flashed a glance at Illy, who was grinning wickedly. Clearly, they had already spoken about this.

"What happened? Now that you know all of my dirty secrets. Spill."

As briefly as possible, I told her about finding Cam's file on Clava. The photos. The heartbreak.

"That would have hurt." Sorcha's tone had softened, but wasn't quite understanding.

"It did," I responded cautiously.

"You know, I knew Laetitia. And you are right: he loved her. But she wasn't you."

I desperately wanted to probe, to ask all the questions I had always harbored about Laetitia, but I didn't want to come across like I was obsessed. Sorcha smirked, reading the unspoken question. She paused and turned to me, standing in the middle of the road.

"She was sweet. Like Di, but softer, quieter. One of those people that everyone liked because she was lovely. But she didn't have your spark. I felt like I was always tiptoeing around her. I could never have told her exactly what I thought. She was ... fragile, I guess is a good word. You and Illy here are the only two women I have ever known I could challenge and know that you give as good as you get."

"And you don't think I am fragile?"

Sorcha roared at that as she kept walking. "You are as fragile as a brick, Freyja. Honestly!"

"You didn't like me when I reunited with your brother," I noted drily.

Sorcha paused in her laughter. "That wasn't because I didn't like you. It was because I saw the state Cam was in, and yes, I blamed you for that. I had been there when I lost Sam, and I knew how dark that road was. But now I look back, I can see that it was meant to play out this way. Had you not had Katrin, and he had her to focus on, I don't think he would have made it. As Tom told me once, when you are in the dark phases of your life, you can't see the road in front of you. You take one step after another, day after day, and then one day, you turn around and realize you have climbed the mountain. You don't even realize you are doing it. Cam needs you in his life. You, those kids, are the reason he gets up in the morning. But I am sorry if I wasn't exactly welcoming."

"Understatement," I quipped but kindly.

"When did you hook up with Stefan then?"

"What is that?" I gestured toward the fields in the distance. We were out of town now and surrounded by fields and paddocks. Sorcha snorted.

"As you well know, that is sugar cane. Now, about Stefan."

I relented. "We kissed a couple of times but not until he moved to Lewis. Nothing happened on Clava. It went no further. I swear."

"Good. I don't like him. There is something shifty about him."

I glared at Illy, who was walking quietly on the other side of Sorcha, feeling betrayed. "You've had this conversation."

"Yes, but we both feel the same way. Our concerns are for you. Stefan can't be trusted," Illy replied flippantly.

Exhaling forcefully as I stomped down the road, I had to admit that both of them had highly attuned bullshit meters. Usually, so did I. *Maybe mine is off? Could that be a symptom of PTSD? Goodness, I hope Illy didn't tell Sorcha about that. She might think I am unfit to work.*

"Well, I am here, and he isn't. I didn't even have time to say goodbye. He likely thinks I blew him off. Disappearing in the middle of the night is an impressive way of getting out of a date."

"And why do you think that was?" Sorcha's eyes flashed with mischief. "A midnight jaunt with a boarding house full of screeching girls. Do you think that is my idea of fun? We did it to save you, whisk you away while he was at work. A thank you would be nice."

"Thanks," I muttered, not feeling it. "And dumping Cam and me on Mousa? I suppose I should thank you for that,, too?"

"Oh, that was your bestie's idea. I take no credit for that. But it had the desired outcome. There was no bloody way I was going to watch you two scowl at each other across a dining table for months on end. My idea was to lock you in a room until you sorted it out. Illy is the creative one. Realized that you needed time away. Alone."

Illy's beautiful sapphire eyes sparkled behind her dark lashes, not even hiding her glee. I rounded on her. "I suppose you just wanted me out of your house?"

"I loved having you around. When you weren't a surly cow. But truthfully, it would have destroyed Luca knowing that you blamed Cam for something that wasn't his fault. You came home from Clava a different girl. We could all see it. I could hear you crying out in your sleep. I even tried to ask Stefan if something had happened, and he got huffy and couldn't get away from me fast enough. But it made no sense why Cam was the target of your wrath. I just kept waiting for it to come out so we could process it."

I bristled. "Process it. I'm not a bloody cake, Illyria."

"But how much easier would it have been if you were." Sorcha sighed dramatically. "We could have beaten it out of you. Come on, that is the dorm Raf has assigned us over there."

CHAPTER 20

SORCHA SHOWED US INTO the building Raf had referred us to. One of the original bunkhouses that had been used before the houses were renovated or built, but not the one Sorcha had lived in. They stood in a row, like military barracks. Long double-fronted buildings, they looked very much like extra-large school portables that could once be seen in every primary school across the country. Some others were being used as storage sheds; we could see the boxes and piles neatly stacked against the windows. They had evidently been brought in and placed here, rushing to establish another community, save more people. Like August, everyone here had arrived as a young single, although here, unlike other communities I had visited, they had allocated the housing based on gender. Bunkhouses with communal kitchens and living rooms had been quick to set up, and inexpensive accommodation in the early years. But unlike August Island, where they had been turned into duplexes, this one had been abandoned, likely because of its remoteness from the main village.

As we entered the dusty abandoned building at the edge of the cluster, we could see that the contents had been stripped, but it was still a functional space. It looked much like a large schoolroom, with ten bedrooms, five off each side, and a bathroom with three showers, toilets, and a simple laundry at the far end. Basic, but it would suit us fine.

Sorcha and Illy stayed to clean the dusty building, sending me off to fetch the others. Sorcha warned me not to expect to use the excuse of only one functioning hand for much longer. After a quick briefing, and every child moaning at being asked to carry a bag, we ferried our personal belongings from home, as well as the sleeping bags and supplies sourced from the barracks in Melbourne. We set up the bedrooms, six rooms for the children, and a room for each adult or couple. The children ran around happily, choosing a camp bed for their own, and orienting it to be close to their friends. Each child was allocated a sleeping bag and pillow and placed their bag from home underneath. Di dutifully made labels for each child's bed, which she promised they could decorate later.

As Cam and I set up our inflatable mattress and zipped together two sleeping bags to act as a doona, we closed the door for a moment and breathed a sigh of relief. For the first time in months, I felt like I could relax, really let go of the sense of fear that we could be attacked at any moment. We lay on the bed and looked out the window at the green forest that ran behind the dormitory. We were a long way out of town and closer to the dome edge. It was tranquil, and bird noises were radiating through the dense green foliage. I closed my eyes and let the serenity sink in. That sense of utter peace, deep-set reassurance came from knowing we were safe under the protection of the geodesic dome.

Throughout the afternoon, various people dropped by to undertake tasks Raf had directed or simply to say hello. Sorcha was greeted warmly, the rest of us welcomed and shown hospitality, but I couldn't help but get the feeling that most people were keen to keep their distance. Pleasant, but cool.

"Feel like we are intruding?" I murmured to Illy as another awkward interaction took place before us as Sorcha directed the plumber to the water tank that needed to be hooked up.

Cam was busy talking with someone who had met Cam and Di on their last visit and wanted to talk about crops. Listening to them catch up like old friends, I learned that Cam and Di had been instrumental in assisting the residents in maximizing greenhouse growing and teaching them about aquaponics and companion planting.

"Uh-huh," she said, smiling sweetly as yet another stranger appeared in the doorway.

In the late afternoon, a whirlwind arrived in the form of Kendra, who had been so thrilled to see Di that she had thrown herself squealing across the room. I saw what Cam meant. They were like twins facially, although Kendra was pleasantly rounded while Di was slight.

"Why didn't you tell me you were coming!" she shrieked, making everyone turn and watch. "When you didn't turn up for our radio chat for four months, I thought something must have happened to you!"

"Something did happen!" she exclaimed. They conversed in a strange mix of Chinese and English, using their hands both as part of their speech but also to communicate physically. They didn't keep their hands from each other, pausing periodically to hug or touch each other. It was fascinating to watch as they stroked each other's hair and patted arms. When finally introduced, Kendra said hello to Di and Sorcha's three children, but wasn't as enthusiastic as I would have thought, given her very tactile reunion with her cousin.

"How are you?" she asked Cam. "How is little Mack?"

"Goodness, he is sixteen! No one calls him that anymore!" Cam laughed, making my eyebrows lift in surprise. I vaguely recalled Cam calling him that, but mainly as Laetitia had. After she passed, his more formal name had been used, perhaps as it brought back sad memories. "You've met my partner, Freyja, and we have quite a few more now!"

"It is lovely to meet you finally," I spoke with as much warmth as I could. "Di has spoken about you for so many years. It is wonderful to put a face to all the stories."

Kendra smiled at me, but it wasn't a genuine smile. Maybe she was just shy. She knew Di and Sorcha and had met Cam before. I certainly understood being wary of strangers, especially those who turned up announced with a horde of children and a rather far-fetched story of being persecuted.

"Tell me you will come for dinner tonight?" she begged Di.

Di's face lit with pleasure. "Of course, I want to spend as much time with you as possible. Get to know Shalu and Sanjiv. Meet Arjun again. It has been too long!"

"Wonderful! I still make the most amazing satay. Do you remember? I still… What is it?" Kendra gripped Di's forearm. "Don't you like satay anymore?"

"Oh no, not that. It is just that peanuts trigger Sorcha's asthma. Not that they are easy to grow on Lewis. The climate just isn't right."

A series of expressions crossed Kendra's face, making it clear to those of us watching that Sorcha hadn't actually been invited. A moment later, Di flushed, comprehending her mistake.

"I can cook…" Kendra started to respond, but Di cut her off.

"Oh! That is fine. You know how much I love satay. It will be so hard for anyone else, with you and me in the room. No one would get a word in! Next time?"

"Next time," Kendra mumbled, a fake smile plastered on her face. "Give me some time to get home and prepare. You remember where we live?"

"Right. What are we preparing for dinner?" I asked to cover the awkwardness of Di's gaffe and Kendra's departure, which had left a sizable indentation in the previously joyous mood.

"What do we have?" Sorcha asked.

Cam grinned. "Anything you want in a can. But the ag team are keen to get me working. So they offered us anything we liked in the way of fresh foods as payment."

"We should take them up on that," I announced. "It has been weeks, and I am desperate for fresh broccoli and carrots. Besides, the kids need fresh vegetables. I am still worried about them contracting scurvy."

"Ooh, do you think they have peas?" Sorcha sighed, making Cam laugh.

"If only Mum could see you now. You used to pick peas out of soup when you were a kid."

"That was because they were the awful, mushy kind. Fresh peas in the pod are amazing. Crisp and flavorsome."

"I'll see what I can rustle up. Di, want to accompany me?"

Taking some reusable bags, Cam and Di headed to the greenhouses, leaving the rest of us to finish cleaning and setting up a living space while simultaneously dealing with kids running in and out, pouncing around doorways, and squealing. The kind of chasing game that left adults frazzled and exhausted.

"Ignore it." Illy laid a soothing hand on Sorcha's arm as she was about to bellow at the latest intrusion that had seen three girls run across the sleeping mats in one of the bedrooms, scattering them everywhere. "Let them exhaust themselves. They will sleep better. But are you both thinking that perhaps we shouldn't be in a hurry to hand over the car keys?"

Kendra's strange reaction to Sorcha was still reverberating in my ears. I nodded. "No rush. We might need more supplies, so better if we keep them for a bit longer."

"How about I move the cars?" Gerry said quietly from behind me. "Somewhere less conspicuous."

On day three, Raf called in the favor, and the holiday was over. Sorcha and I joined the medical team, dealing with the same injuries that we dealt with on Lewis. For Sorcha, the usual cuts and wounds requiring stitching, and for me, the occasional broken bone or soft tissue injury. I was still limited in what I could do as I still had only one functional hand. Gerry and Cam joined the tiny agricultural team and found their days long and exhausting.

"Why is the team so small?" I asked as he flopped onto the thin and entirely uncomfortable inflatable camp mattress. We had been here for two weeks, and Cam and Gerry's workload hadn't abated.

"When they set up the homes here, each household was established with their own vegetable patch, beehive, goat, chickens, and algal tank. They thought that each family would want to be self-sufficient."

"Crap, I would have starved!"

"And that is exactly what happened. There was a grim winter while Sorcha was here, but several years after Sorcha left, they had a terrible year. People died. Many more were quite ill."

"Seriously? They let people starve? To death?"

"Apparently. The community here was established to be every man for himself. It was Raf who called a meeting and convinced them that there needed to be a better way. I helped them set up a greenhouse or two when I was here fifteen years ago, but they have built a lot more since then and have a team. It is too small for people here, but Gerry and I can help them grow more productively with less intensive labor. The way we set up August and then Lewis."

"They are lucky to have you," I noted, knowing that Cam's skills were highly sought after. While I was training on Clava, I learned they had genuinely wanted Cam to assist all the communities in setting up highly productive, low-intensity farming, and teaching them about seasonal planting and all the things he rabbited on about.

"We are fortunate Raf agreed to take us all on. We are a lot more mouths to feed. But I think he would have done anything to get Sorcha back. One of the guys told me today that there was nearly a riot a few months after she left. The remaining medics didn't know how to treat serious injuries. They had always left anything complicated to her, and after she left, quite a few people died."

"Raf is quite a forceful man," I noted, now having seen him in action several times. "But you should have seen him ogling Illy."

"Perhaps we could set her up with him instead of Ashton?" Cam smirked.

"She doesn't think much of him. Thank goodness Di is teaching our kids."

Raf had flatly refused to take on so many more, instead suggesting that we use our living space as a schoolroom, as all the other adults would be out at work all day. While he had proposed that Illy act as teacher, he had said little when we appointed Di instead. Secretly, I was pleased. While active and challenging, they weren't bad kids. We had moved away from the teaching style Cam and I had experienced in our school days, prescriptive and taught to a prescribed curriculum. Di was warm and engaging, and the learning was child-led. Each child could choose a topic of interest as long as they learned the concepts. This had proven challenging on more than one occasion, most recently, when Cait had asked to study forensic science and medical procedures. But Di, ever the professional, had used her interest to teach her about spelling and grammar, getting Cait to write detailed autopsy and medical reports using correct punctuation.

"At least they are safe here," I murmured, rolling over to sleep. "You should have seen them after school today. Running around screaming like banshees. We will need to get them under control or someone will complain."

"Give them a few more days," he urged. "We have ripped them away from their families, kept them on a boat for weeks. Surely we can allow them to have a little freedom."

Smiling, I snuggled into his side. "It is a strange place, isn't it?"

"What do you mean?"

"Well, everyone is so independent. People don't seem to work toward common goals. Support each other, I mean." *Not like home*, I wanted to say but didn't want to sound elitist. Fortunately, Cam knew what I meant.

"It was like this the first time I was here, too. Everyone lives separate lives. I mean some jobs help people, teachers, doctors, and such. But there isn't the same feeling of..." Cam struggled for the word.

"Connectedness?" I suggested.

"It is more than that. I want to say co-dependence, but that isn't quite right either. We don't rely on each other in a needy way on Lewis, but we know, without asking, that absolutely anyone would do anything for someone else. Do you know what I mean?"

"I do. I can't believe they let others starve."

"Sorcha has never said anything explicitly, but I got the distinct impression that she struggled herself at times. People were supposed to pay for her services in food, but if there was a shortage, likely they couldn't pay. She would never have refused care, but it would have left her in a difficult position. When I found her here, she was painfully thin. But she had lost her husband, so at the time, I thought it was grief. But a few things she has said over the years has made me think they did not look after her. She was run ragged and worked constantly, so had little time to grow anything for herself."

"I suspect there are many layers to your sister that I am only beginning to see."

"Speaking of layers..." I felt his arms lifting the old t-shirt I wore over my head and pulled me against him, my breasts squashing against his chest as he kissed my neck, and I melted into his arms. Reaching my arms up, I ran the fingers of my unbound hand through his thick, dark hair, pulling it slightly, making him moan. His mouth caressed my collarbone and down between my breasts, my head rolling back against the pillow. He slid down my torso, planting kisses slowly and deliberately down my sternum, stomach, and hips. I pushed into him urgently, but he ignored me, taking his time to arouse me. My skin was aflame as he slipped two fingers into me. I gasped.

"Oh, so you do want me."

"I always want you," I whispered, grinding into his hand as he awakened the passion inside me. The tsunami came crashing over me as I convulsed, unable to focus on anything but my pleasure. Coming to my senses, I flipped him over and sat on his hips, pinning him down. Running my lips down the length of his chest and stomach wounds, I could feel his desire, but kept it at bay, slowly trailing my hair across his stomach.

"Oh god!" he moaned as I kissed his stomach, working my way down to the carved V above his hips, and paused, teasing. His head lolled backward, eyes closed, enjoying every instant.

Without warning, he tossed me on my back and was poised over me, tensed. I nipped his neck playfully, and he growled deep in his throat. I felt him pause.

What is he waiting for? I thought, desperate to have him inside me.

I pushed against him, but still, he waited, watching me.

"I love you," he whispered and paused, waiting to hear my response.

The words clogged up in my strangled throat. *Fuck!* My brain whirred. *It is just three little words. Say it!*

He saw the struggle in my face and pulled back, hurt. Tears filled my eyes and threatened to overflow.

"It isn't you!" I forced the words through my thickened throat as he backed away from me.

"Then what?" Pain dripped from his growled words, and I felt him turn away in the dark.

"I love *you*. I just... I don't like *me* very much," I whispered.

He didn't move, and I wondered if he had heard me as the tears spilled. Curled into the fetal position, I let a single sob break free from my chest. Without realizing he had moved, I felt his arms cradle me as I cried, unable to communicate the numbness piercing my heart.

"It's okay," his voice soothed. "I have enough love for both of us."

"I'm... so... sorry..." I sobbed. "I ruin everything."

"That is where you are wrong. You make everything brighter, my love. The day you walked into my life, you lit my world. I didn't even realize I had been living in darkness until I met you, and you shared your joy of life with me. The adventures we had together and the children you gifted me. Every day and night we have spent together has been wonderful. You spoil nothing. I just wish I knew how to help you."

I knew I needed to tell him, but I couldn't form the words as the tears flowed. He curled up behind me and stroked my hair.

"Sleep. I'll keep you safe."

CHAPTER 21

"WHY DID YOU TELL Raf I was a doctor and not a vet?" I asked the following morning as Sorcha and I walked toward the clinic. Clinic was a broad term for the small medical facility here, poorly resourced in terms of equipment and medication. I hoped I wouldn't need to perform any complicated surgeries. Even though we had been here for weeks, I still saw this place as temporary.

Better snap out of that idea, I berated myself. *We could be here for months. Longer.*

Sorcha paused before asking. "Several reasons. One, I see you as a doctor. I knew that the facilities here had likely not improved since I left, and truthfully, they were scratching the bottom of the barrel with the candidates then. I knew you would be an asset."

I tried hard not to grin. I hadn't been overly impressed myself with the few medical staff I had worked alongside but warned myself it was too early to judge.

"Second," she continued, "Illy and I agreed that someone should always be with you. The girls are safe with Di, Sam, and Kendra. Ruby and Scarlett stay with them, too. You are a target, and while we are safe here, it doesn't hurt to be cautious. Finally," she paused as I waited for the kicker, "I enjoy working with you, Freyja."

"Really?" The raging argument she and I had several months ago flashed to mind.

"I do. You anticipate need and act rapidly. You look for alternative solutions that are in the best interest of the patient, not interventions that make things easier for you as a practitioner. You are a team player, and I like that."

"I kind of like working with you," I admitted. As much as I missed Isla and veterinary work, I had acknowledged over the past year that medicine was my calling. The variable nature of the work, trying to help people in a way that minimized the impact on their life. I loved it.

"So, Doctor Mack, what are we doing this morning?" I asked.

"Well, Doctor Mack Two, this morning, I have called a maternal and pediatric clinic so we can check all the pregnant mothers and children under five. They are all coming to us, so it will be a busy day. First, I need to remove your splints and x-ray your hand."

"I don't know a great deal about obstetrics and children," I admitted as she unwrapped my hand and made me flex my fingers, testing my mobility.

"You know more than you think. You have great instincts. Besides, you have five of your own. Can you bend them back?"

"What are we looking for exactly?" I grimaced at the stiffness of my joints and was mildly embarrassed at the stench of my unwrapped hand.

"Anything out of the ordinary. Signs that might indicate illness, abnormal development, malnutrition, even neglect. Your fingers have healed well."

"Neglect?" I stopped stretching my hand and looked at her. "You can't be serious?"

"Life here is a little different than Lewis." She sighed. "When Cam came all those years ago, it was leaving these women and children in need that haunted me. I needed to go, mostly for Cam. It was new with Di, and Sam was only a toddler. But it wasn't a simple decision. They needed me here. It is why I got into medicine, to help those who needed it."

"Cam said you wanted to join *Medicin sans Frontieres*?"

"That was my dream. Get some emergency experience in a big city hospital and then work where I could make a real difference to people's lives."

"This isn't really close, is it?"

"Not at all. All I could think in those early months here was that all those people I wanted to help had died. And here I was, the chosen elite, something I had always detested."

A chill ran through me as she cleaned up the discarded wrappings from my hand. "The chosen elite." *Is that why she hated me for so long?*

"I'm sorry," I finally whispered. "I didn't choose my upbringing."

Sorcha whirled on me. "I am sorry. That was thoughtless. When I first met you, I admit, I saw you as the spoiled rich bitch who got everything her own way. It wasn't until you went after Laetitia that I saw you differently. You didn't need to go, but you did. For him, and not yourself."

"But you detested me when Kat was born!"

"No, I didn't want to get too close to you, in case it didn't work out with Cam. If he didn't want you, then I didn't want to be your friend, as that would put him in a difficult position. I had to choose him until the time came when he chose you. Di and I always knew he would."

"So, when you offered to look after Katrin when she was a baby...?"

"It was time. He had moped about enough. He needed you. We could see it. Di and I used to take bets on how long it would take. He was just too busy wallowing in his own self-pity to see what was right in front of him: an amazing woman who loved him."

"I wish I had known that at the time," I whispered.

"And I wish I had saved you some pain by telling you. Right, your hand is fine. Take it easy for a few days, and you know what exercises you need to do to strengthen it."

A steady stream of couples, women, and children flowed through the clinic before starting work or during their breaks. It was manic, and I loved every second. Sorcha and I divided the room, a curtain drawn between the two beds, and shared the load, occasionally consulting each other on an unusual rash or a deformity. Her extensive knowledge of pediatric medicine astounded me, and I said so during one quick break between patients.

"I've always loved obstetrics and pediatric work," she admitted. "I thought of specializing, but emergency medicine was more general. I was younger, and it was more exciting, I guess. I also thought emergency medicine would help more with fieldwork. Malnutrition, amputations after unexploded landmines, and that sort of thing. But helping pregnant women and children has always been my favorite work."

A woman entered, heavily pregnant, and I smiled at her. She looked much like I remembered Makayla, Jake's wife, on Newgrange when I first met her. She was exhausted, and I showed her to a chair. I remembered all too well what the last weeks of pregnancy felt like. I drew the curtain and heard Sorcha greet someone, an older woman, by the sound of her voice. Palpating the woman's stomach and keeping up a pleasant dialogue about her pregnancy and other children, I hoped she couldn't see my concern. I could tell the baby was breech, and while I had a lot of experience with animals, not so much in humans. I thought about calling Sorcha for advice, but something in her tone alerted me. I tried to listen, but the conversation was muffled and indistinct. Knowing other people were waiting, I asked the woman to wait outside for me, explaining that I wanted to speak with the other doctor. She agreed readily enough, and my next patient arrived, a young boy with a nasal obstruction.

Fifteen minutes later and he was good to go, with a warning not to stick things up his nose and a red-faced mother shooing him out. Sorcha was still speaking to the same patient. I stood beside the curtain and listened.

"Do you want me to talk to him?" Sorcha asked. "I can be quite persuasive."

"No!" The terrified response shot back, making me freeze for a moment. I strained to listen, but the volume had dropped again, and with the chatter outside, I could only hear that they were speaking, unable to make out the words. Recognizing that this was serious, I closed the main door between the waiting room and the consultation area, smiling and assuring the waiting patients I would only be a minute. Almost instantly, the words became intelligible.

"Are you sure?" Sorcha was asking. "I can do this, but you need to be positive."

"Only if Miles never knows," the woman was saying in a choked, tearful voice.

"I promise you. He will never hear it from me," Sorcha assured her.

"How can I be certain I will get you?" she asked, fear rising. "No one else will do it."

"Leave it with me. I will think of something."

I turned as I heard the curtain being drawn and watched the woman struggling to get off the bed, even with Sorcha's help. *She is older than me,* I thought as I watched her waddle out of the cubicle. Perhaps late forties and heavily pregnant. Ready to drop any day by the look of her. I wondered what on earth Sorcha had promised her. Sorcha's expression was grim as she looked for her next patient.

Softly I asked, "What was that about?"

"Later. How many more?"

"Quite a few. First, I need help with a breech presentation."

Sorcha nodded, and I returned to the waiting room, beckoning at the young woman to return.

Walking home several hours later, I asked, "Are you going to tell me?"

"Angie is pregnant with her thirteenth child. It is going to kill her."

"Why so many?"

"Asshole husband won't get a vasectomy."

"Okay, but there are other ways."

"You forget, there is no access to the pill here, no IUDs. Short of abstinence, and that isn't going to happen with her husband, tubal ligation is all there is. Only he won't let her have one, and the other doctors are terrified of him. I also strongly suspect none of them knows how. Too many women here have died in childbirth since I left, especially those needing cesarean deliveries. I have been reviewing the records. They should be mortified to lose so many."

"What did you promise?"

"I promised her a cesarean birth and a tubal ligation. Her husband will get told that she was damaged by the difficult labor and can't have more children. She is forty-three. This is going to kill her. It is also much higher risk having babies after forty." Sorcha paused. "Ever performed a cesarean?"

"Lots of them—on cows," I admitted.

"The principles are exactly the same. After all, I did yours."

"Why are you asking?"

"Miles, the asshole husband, doesn't trust me. I told him fifteen years ago that four was enough. It got quite heated. Tom had just passed, and I wasn't very tolerant back then. But he refused to let me touch her when the time came. One of the other doctors assisted, but it was luck, not judgment, that saw the baby survive."

"She has had another eight. She must know what she is doing."

"I trained one or two of the women to act as midwives. That helped. But what he is doing is driving her to an early grave. It is abuse."

"You don't know that."

"Not abuse as in rape. I mean, he won't allow her to take control of her body. He doesn't help with the kids. She is expected to do everything. It is controlling and abusive behavior. Abuse can come in many forms. Physical, sexual, but even financial or emotional."

"Financial?"

"Not so relevant here, but when I was volunteering at a medical clinic in Melbourne, I saw many women who had no money. Husband paid for her phone, clothes, train ticket and barely gave her enough to pay for the food. Everything was controlled. She couldn't pay for medical treatment or medicine. It prevents them from leaving, from paying for birth control. It is abuse."

"I had no idea such a thing existed," I admitted. For a moment, I realized how blessed I was to have Cam. He who had never forced me to do anything. Encouraged me to follow my dreams of becoming a doctor. Said yes whenever I wanted anything.

"What do you need me to do?"

"Nothing, except assist. I will do it. Miles can be angry at me. There is nothing he can do about it once it is over, anyway."

"You don't think that places our stay here in a precarious position?"

"I have to. My job is to help people—yours too."

"My children are my priority," I snapped back. "I will always help people, but not to the detriment of my family, and that includes your children."

"I'll take care of it," she promised. "You don't need
to be involved."

CHAPTER 22

AS I ROUNDED THE corner of the med center, I stopped dead.

"Scarlett!"

The blonde head popped out from behind the darker one, eyes popping wide in fear.

"Don't..."

"I am responsible for you, young lady!" I snapped, hearing my own mother's voice echoing those precise words in my ears.

Scarlett flushed and looked down at her feet.

"Go. Home. Now. I will deal with you later."

She fled, leaving me face to face with a defiant Sanjiv, Di's nephew. "Care to explain?" I growled.

"We were just talking," he mumbled. My eyes popped.

"Is that what you call it? Kissing is what I call it. She is *thirteen*! She is a child! You should be ashamed. How old are you?"

"Nineteen," he mumbled, barely audible.

"That is illegal where I come from!" I bellowed.

"Good thing we aren't where you came from," he muttered, not realizing I had exceptional hearing.

"What did you just say to me?" I advanced on him menacingly, and he turned and bolted into the forest.

"Where is she?" I thundered as I entered the dorm where Di was still teaching.

"Who?"

"Scarlett." Glancing around the room, I realized I had quite an audience and said to Di in a lower tone, "A word, please. In private. Now."

Di gave them all an instruction, but we all knew not one of them had any intention of complying. Something far more entertaining than school was happening, and they were dying to learn what. Closing the bedroom door behind her, Di looked at me expectantly.

"I just caught Scarlett kissing your nephew in the forest."

Di sank onto the nearest mattress, her hand clapped over her mouth. "Are you sure? Sanjiv is nineteen! He is far too old for her."

"I know what kissing looks like. He had his hands up her top, and she wasn't saying no, so we aren't talking a friendly peck on the cheek."

Di's face blanched. "She told me she had a headache and could she get some air. She looked flushed, so I agreed. She played me."

"How many times has she been out of your sight?"

Di looked mortified as her face turned from white to red. "A few," she admitted. "She is older. I thought she and Ruby could be trusted."

"Their mothers trusted us to care for them. I am not sure this is what she had in mind."

"What do you want to do?" Di looked at her feet, unable to make eye contact.

"Let me speak with Illy. She will know best. But if she were my daughter, I would lock her in her room for a month. The last thing we need is a pregnant thirteen-year-old."

"Do you want me to speak with Kendra?" She whispered.

"No. Leave it with me. Any idea where Illy is?" I asked.

"She went for a walk in the forest. She said teaching English was enough to make her want never to speak it again."

Standing I strode out of the bedroom to find Illy, hearing Di return to teaching as I closed the door.

"Ils! Wait up!" I called, seeing Ill's long dark ponytail swishing as she walked down the road toward the edge of the dome.

She turned and waited for me to catch up, and we set a cracking pace down the road. "Is your hand better?"

"It is," I said, flexing and stretching as I walked. Getting dexterity back as soon as possible would be essential if I were to operate again.

"How are the medical rounds going? Haven't killed Sorcha yet?"

"She genuinely is the best doctor here," I confessed. "And the others know it, although they won't admit it. It is like watching a bad first date, tap dancing around each other, but no one saying what they honestly think. The others get a challenging case, act like they know what is going on, and ask her for her opinion. She tells them, and after some waffling, they agree. Then they ask if she would mind assisting with the procedure. Of course, she runs the show, and we all know it. It is painful to watch."

"How on earth does Sorcha manage that? She isn't exactly subtle."

"She is diplomatic in those circumstances. It is others where I question her judgment."

Illy raised her eyebrows and indicated that I should elaborate.

Sighing, I told her of Angie visiting the maternal clinic several days before and her husband's refusal to prevent more children.

"Ah, I met Miles when I was visiting Raf's school. He was picking up his tribe. Not winning any awards for the greatest husband and father."

"I haven't met him, but she is terrified of him."

"I can see why. He is controlling and manipulative. So, will you help her?"

"Sorcha said she would take care of it, and Miles will never know."

"And you disagree?"

"It places us all in a great deal of danger, doesn't it? What if Angie regrets it, says something? Or he suspects Sorcha? They had a falling out years ago, and apparently, he has never forgiven her."

"What if she doesn't, and Sorcha hands her the greatest gift? I only have four and don't cope some days. Imagine having thirteen! Not to mention, I doubt I could come up with so many names!"

"Where does your name come from? I've never heard it before I met you, and I never thought to ask."

Illy smiled as we turned a corner in the path, the blue, mist-shrouded mountains looming in the distance. "Two places. My parents say I was conceived while they were on holiday in Croatia. That region in classical antiquity was known as Illyria, the people Illyrians. It comes from Greek mythology. He had six sons and three daughters, and their names were associated with the tribes of the region."

"Ha! Nine children," I scoffed. "Walk in the park, buddy! Triple it, and then we can talk."

Illyria grinned.

"What was the second?"

"It is kind of linked. Mum loved Shakespeare, and particularly Twelfth Night. Have you read it?"

"I think so. I took English Literature at school."

"Well, Illyria was the rather exotic setting for the play, and it was quite romantic. I was the child they never thought they would have. They were forty when I came along. So I suspect Mum had fluffy, idyllic ideas about motherhood. Instead, she got me."

"I love that. So we are both named after mythological figures."

"Are you going to tell me what is up? Ranting about Sorcha could have waited."

Briefly, I told her about finding Scarlett in a compromising position with Sanjiv. To my utter astonishment, Illy giggled.

"You can't possibly think this is okay?"

"Of course not. But I have been stressing for weeks about my girls left at home unsupervised, and here it is happening right under my nose, and I didn't see it."

"Well, I saw it alright. And let me tell you, it wasn't going to stop at kissing."

Illy sighed. "Part of me knows this is normal teenage behavior and remembers what I did at the same age. The other part of me wants to lock her in a cupboard in case Jorja and Bridget murder us both."

"The latter aligns with my thought. Bloody hell, when did we become the responsible ones? Shit, I was thirteen when I kissed my first. I was at a party."

"Same. I still remember it. Scott, his name was, he was a surfer, that typical beach type. Sandy blonde hair that flopped into his eyes. He walked me home from netball practice; he had been at footy practice, and we had shared clubrooms. On the way, he stopped, caressed my face, and kissed me against a fence. I thought I had died and gone to heaven. I floated home and dreamed about him for weeks. He never spoke to me again."

The sound of pounding footsteps thumping along the path made us turn. It was Di, her long black hair flying behind her.

"Sorcha needs you," she gasped. "Now!"

"The kids?" I asked as I jogged beside her, back along the path into town, Illy close behind.

"No, Angie is in labor."

"Does she need help?"

"Not exactly."

CHAPTER 23

"HONEY!" THE FAMILIAR VOICE sounded behind me as I stormed toward the dorm, kicking up dust and trying not to cough. I had no idea where I was headed. Being around people would be a disaster.

I slowed, unwilling to turn around. Instead, I waited for Cam to catch up, still levitating with fury. As soon as he was within arm's reach, he scanned my face, assessed the volcano, gripped my arm, and steered me down a side path, moving me away from residences and people.

"Fucking bitch! I can't believe she dropped me in it!" I seethed as soon as he slowed and rested under an enormous pine tree. "How dare she make me do that?"

"Whoa! Back up. Who did what?" Cam shook his head trying to catch up.

"Your fucking sister!" I spat. "Angie was in labor. Miles brought her in and refused to let Sorcha treat her, so she forced me to do it. Told him I was an experienced surgeon. Lying fucking bitch. She stayed out in the waiting room with him, all the while I am mutilating his wife." Unable to contain my fury, I grabbed at the tree, pulling down a handful of pine needles and crushed them in my hand.

"Isn't it what Angie wanted?" Cam asked gently as the scent wafted between us.

"So not the point!" I threw the pine needles against the tree, fuming.

"Ahh, what is the point?"

"I've never done that before. Tubal ligation. What if I mucked it up? What if I didn't? It is so permanent! What if she changes her mind? It can't be undone." I was babbling, barely coherent. The scent of the pine tree drifted into my nose again, reminding me of home.

Cam paused, and I felt the space of three heartbeats before he asked, "Is this about Angie or about you?"

"What do you mean?" I growled, narrowing my eyes in warning.

Cam lowered his voice, although there was no one around to hear us. "No matter your opinion of her, Sorcha would always put her patient's needs first. She would never put Angie at risk, so she clearly thought this was for the best. She is headstrong and willful but not reckless."

"She was this time! What if Miles finds out? He will kill me. Worse, he will complain to Raf, and we will be kicked out. Then where do we take the girls? We need the sanctuary here, at least until Tadhg finds out something, and we can go home."

"How will Miles know?" Cam pulled me down to sit beside him, our backs against the enormous pine. Homesickness gripped me.

"I don't know. I certainly didn't include it in her medical records for anyone to read. But what if he works it out? What if she regrets it in a few days and tells him what I did?"

Cam held onto my forearms as he observed my face. "Honey, how much of this is about what happened to you?"

"None. Of. It," I growled, not wanting him to see my distress. "This is about what your sister forced me to do to that poor woman."

"That poor woman has thirteen children after today. Do you not think she has the right to choose? Back home, she would have had the choice. So have we gone backward as a society, not allowing women choice?" His voice softened. "You know your nightmares are getting worse? It is every night, honey. You don't sleep. You can't keep this up."

I wanted to argue, fight him, but logic took the upper hand as my rage dissipated. "I know."

Cam watched expectantly.

"This *is* about me, isn't it?" I whispered as he pulled my head down onto his shoulder

"I think so, honey. You have always been a champion for other women. You would never have let Miles' wrath worry you before. So what has changed? You have. You had something done to you, against your will, and without your consent. Something awful, and even though it has been seven years, I know you aren't over it. It still haunts you. But this is different. Angie gave consent. Willingly. She wanted this fifteen years ago, only Sorcha left before she could assist. You gave her what she wanted—control of her own body. It was a gift. She is grateful, Frey. Isn't she?"

"She is," I acknowledged, opening my eyes and turning to him. "But I am scared of *him*. What he could do. Not to me personally, I don't give a shit about that. But to all of us, our children. He is controlling and manipulative, needing to be the center of attention. He is a narcissist, and that makes him dangerous."

"You don't know that." Cam gently held my face between his enormous garden roughened hands, studying me. But in that moment, I knew without a doubt that he would lay down his life for me.

"No, but Illy does. She pegged him the first time she met him. She says he sees those children as possessions. Narcissists are incapable of love. They further his self-interest as they contribute to the household. But he doesn't love them the way you love your children. Sorcha too. She says he is controlling and abusive."

"So, what do we do?" His thumb ran down the curve of my cheekbone.

"That is the problem. I don't know that there is anything we can do. We congratulate her on her child and say nothing. Though it goes against everything I want to do."

"What would you want to do?"

"I don't like keeping secrets."

"But sometimes, secrets are for the best."

As we sat in the forest, our backs against the large pine, I thought it through.

"It feels like a million years ago when we lived here, in the old world. There would have been choices, I guess, if she wanted to leave. Family. Friends. Shelters. Legal options. Medical options. But here? Where do we take her? We are stuck here ourselves. She has a shitload of kids, and she won't leave them. We can't take all of them. Besides, he is their father, and he isn't awful to them, as far as I am aware. Our options are exceedingly limited."

"They are. Do you think she wants to leave him? We could speak with Raf if that is the case."

I considered as I dropped my head into his chest. "I don't think so. She just wants no more children."

"And will she? Have more children?" he asked softly.

"No. Sorcha told me what to do, and I did it," I whispered.

"You gave her a gift, honey. She wanted this. You need to see that you gave her what she wanted."

"Maybe." I wasn't convinced. And it was so damned permanent.

"Have you thought any more about what you learned when we went to your house that day? I keep waiting for private time to chat, but we never seem to be alone. About your parents being related, that is."

I exhaled. "My parents, they were definitely second cousins."

"Cousins or second cousins?"

"From the family tree I found inside the old family Bible, it appears they were telling the truth, and they are second cousins."

"Is that even legal?" Cam was choosing his words carefully, fearful of offending me.

"In Australia, yes. Norway too, but it is frowned upon socially."

"What is the difference? It always confuses me with the once removed stuff."

"A second cousin is the grandchild of a great-uncle or aunt. So the way I read the family tree, Dad's grandfather and my mother's grandfather were brothers."

"What is the risk, genetically?" I knew what he was asking. Were our children really freaks?

"The risk is comparatively low, but it places any children at increased risk of autosomal recessive genetic disorders, and the risk is higher in populations that are already highly ethnically similar, such as Norwegians where there wasn't a lot of cultural diversity, at least not in their generation." I took a deep breath and exhaled before continuing. "But there is more. My great-grandparents were first cousins. So, I have a double whammy."

Cam exhaled through pursed lips. "Do you think this is why you have a modifiable genome?"

"I have given it a lot of thought, and I am almost certain. But likely in their assessment of me, the scientific teams never knew. They took my blood and a cell scraping for DNA purposes but never asked about my family history beyond a survey asking for risk factors. I didn't mention it. It just wasn't on my mind, and the great-grandparent part I had no clue about. As I have said, Jorgensen is a common name, and they would have needed to do a lot of digging into my family tree even to work it out. But I have been thinking, should I say something? Would it help future generations survive?"

"Whoa. That is huge, honey. You can't just drop that information and expect the scientific teams on Auckland and Clava not to act. You also can't change your mind and stuff it back into the box. Besides," his voice dropped, "there is what they did to your sister. To you."

"I know. But without my genome, these girls couldn't survive outside. Look at Ruby and Scarlett. Without them, we may still be stuck in the middle of the Indian Ocean."

"Agreed. But if your great-grandparents were related, and your parents were related, it would mean generations of crossbreeding to produce more children who have modifiable genomes like yours." He gulped. "Do you think our girls would be the same? Kat and Xanthe?"

"I don't know." I shrugged. "I'm not a geneticist, but I would assume so. They have my genes, although yours too. On that note, all the girls have my bloodline." So there is was. They were different, and it was all my fault.

"Do you know a geneticist we could ask?"

"I do," I growled. "Derek. And I wouldn't trust him farther than I could kick him. He was the one who gassed Illy and me."

Cam's mouth dropped. "I don't think you ever told me that. It was *him*?"

"It was."

"Well, that answers that question."

"It does," I responded firmly. "There is no way I will allow anyone to do that to our girls while I still have breath."

"So we keep it to ourselves. You can't even tell Illy, in case she tells Ashton."

"She would never betray my confidence. I trust her with my life."

"They are intimate, Frey. That bond overrides everything else. You might trust her with your life, but this is our girls we are talking about. I trust Illy. I do. But I don't trust him."

I didn't agree. There was no way Illy would ever do anything to jeopardize Seraphine's safety, but I changed the subject. "How long do you think it will take for Tadhg to learn something useful?"

"Well, he will need to set up all the equipment again and monitor transmissions. Not much is recorded, I don't think, but Ashton could assist there. He will know what recordings are kept, and how to access them. As much as I despise the man, he will have earned some brownie points if he can work out who is targeting you and the kids."

"You know, maybe it is the Miles situation, but I am feeling tense. I can feel my jaw set all the time. I keep waiting for the battle to show up on our doorstep."

Cam laughed and leaned back against the tree. The sun was dropping down the sky, the shadows were changing. "There is my warrior goddess speaking. What is Freyja the goddess of? In all these years, I never thought to ask."

I laughed heartily. "Love, sex, and war."

Cam stopped, his mouth dropping. "That is freaking hilarious. Do you think your parents knew?"

"Definitely. They both enjoyed mythology and read stories from the *Prose Edda* to us when we were young. They told me they wanted strong female names. I was also born on a Friday, and Friday is named for Freyja. Katrin is a Greek goddess of magic, although it is also a Norwegian variant of Catherine."

"I love that—love, sex, and war."

"Well then, you will love the part where the Goddess Freyja rides in a chariot pulled by two cats and chooses half of those slain in battle. You should have heard Kat tease me about that! She always said I was only studying to be a vet so that I could train those cats."

"I can see you doing that, driving a cat chariot. What would she think of you being a doctor?" Cam leaned back squinting as the setting sun broke through the branches before us.

"Proud," I admitted. "Kat was the artistic one. I think I told you once she wanted to be an architect."

"You did. So where does Freyja take her half of those who die in battle?"

"In Norse mythology, there are two places those who fall in battle can go. Half are chosen by Odin and are taken to Valhalla, an enormous hall in Asgard. The other half are taken to Sessrúmnir, Freyja's hall. Both are considered an afterlife paradise. Strangely, there are two. In most ancient myths, there is only one." I squirmed, trying to get comfortable. After standing for hours my lower back hurt, and the ground was hard.

"I've heard of Valhalla, but not Sessrúmnir. Does Freyja care for them?"

"Oh yes, they are treated very well as warriors. Only the brave are chosen. They feast and drink beer for all eternity."

"Priorities!"

"Well, what do you think our priorities should be?" I asked cheekily.

Instead of the flippant response I was expecting, Cam looked thoughtful. "Family and time."

I pulled my head away and stared at him as he leaned back into the tree, looking pensive. "Okay, not what I was expecting. Now you need to explain."

"Family is the reason for everything. Supporting them, loving them. I don't just mean blood relatives. Those we choose to be in our world, those we care for, and are part of the fabric of our life. And time, well, who wouldn't want more time to focus on the important things? To spend more time with someone we have lost, to spend more time doing something we love. I think the only people who truly value time are those who know that theirs is limited. People with terminal illnesses. They are the ones who take a holiday, buy a sports car, or get a tattoo and don't care what other people think. Because they know something we don't. Time is precious and something we have too little of."

"I didn't take the time to say goodbye to Ceridwen," I whispered. "Now I will never get the chance. I couldn't find her the day I left, but I thought I would see her at the birthday party in a few months. But now I will never see her again. My sister too. What I wouldn't give for more time with her."

Cam exhaled forcefully. "It is their birthday in ten days. Would you like to do something special? A memorial for Ceri, Soli, and Beth?"

"I would like that very much."

CHAPTER 24

"HOW IS ANGIE DOING?" Cam asked softly as he collected me from the clinic the following week. After Angie's impromptu cesarean, Sorcha had insisted that he drop me off and pick me up each day. Sorcha had manipulated the roster so that we were always there together but refused to let me walk to and from the clinic alone. "I just saw them leaving. She looked happy enough."

"I removed her stitches today. We couldn't talk as Miles was there. But when I asked him to hold the baby so I could lie her down, he turned away for a moment. She looked at me with such pleading. I gave her a nod. It was all I could do."

"How did she respond?"

"I don't think I have ever seen so much gratitude," I confessed. "Her face relaxed, and I felt the relief. She didn't need to use words. You were right. It was a gift."

"That is wonderful news on several fronts. Angie gets what she wants, and he never needs to know. But selfishly, our kids are safe. I just wish we knew who was behind it so we could take them home."

"Illy thinks Stefan may be responsible," I said and immediately regretted it. The last thing I wanted was to talk about my former boyfriend.

I could feel the tension ripple across his back as he walked beside me. The chasm opened up between us. When he responded, it was calmly, a fraction too chilled. "What do you think?"

"Honestly, I can't see it. He is a scientist. He pledged to save lives, not take them. What would he stand to achieve?"

"What does Illy think?"

"As for motives, who knows?" Cam's tenseness betrayed he was not happy with this response. I relented. "But she thinks he may have been the one who broke into our home so that I would rush into his arms."

"Would you?"

This was rapidly heading into dangerous territory.

"Not in ordinary circumstances," I admitted, trying to take the middle path. "I'm a fighter, not a runner."

"But had you come home that day and found the photos?" he pushed, ice rising in his voice.

"I would have gone to Illy," I said truthfully.

"And then?"

The pause was excruciating, and it was clear he would wait an eternity for my answer. I had never lied to him. "I don't know," I whispered, and felt my heart shatter into a million pieces as I watched his back disappear into the distance.

Sitting with my back against a tree, I wondered if it was worth it. The agony. Letting no one near meant not being hurt. Alone, but not lonely. Right now, I felt utterly alone, and yet I was married. Surrounded by family and friends. My children. But a void filled my chest. How did he have the power to rip my heart out and stomp on it again and again? Me. I had given him that power over me.

Fighting back the tears, I closed my eyes and tried to remember the last time we were truly happy. On Mousa? Maybe. But we were alone. No children, no work pressure. Before I was running across the world, fearful for my life, and that of my children. Hunted and persecuted. Had we just grown apart? We would never have been compatible in the old world. Different lives, different values. Can you move so far away from your roots? People make choices and can grow. Learn. But values systems are hard-wired, my mother used to say.

My thoughts ran rampant, threatening to drown me, pull me under. I needed to get out of here. This feeling of entrapment, that sense of foreboding loomed in my mind. *Should I go back to Melbourne and see how Tadhg is doing? I hate to leave Cait, but she is safe here.*

Standing to leave, I sensed I was being watched. Frantically scanning the forest, I saw Illy at the far side of the clearing, leaning against an ancient red gum, an empty basket swinging on her left arm. Seeing it was her made me relax slightly, still concerned it could be Miles hunting me down for what I had done to his wife.

She approached apprehensively, assessing. "You are running again." It was a statement, not a question.

Stiffening my spine, I answered. "No, I am going to check in on Tadhg. It is important we know what they have found and when we can leave. Just a quick trip. I'll be back tomorrow or the day after."

"You are running away from yourself. You can't escape your problems by running, Frey. You need to deal with challenges, not shut yourself off."

Just bloody watch me, I thought.

"We need to know what they have learned," I insisted as reasonably as I could. "I can act as a messenger. They don't know that we made it safely. They would want to know we are safe. All of us."

"They do. But Gerry could go. He doesn't have a child here."

"Gerry isn't Australian. I know my way around."

"True. Sorcha could go. Me even." I sighed. I did not want to get into a discussion over this. "Walk with me," she urged. "Tell me about this sudden desire to run back to Melbourne. You know I won't give up until you do."

I started speaking, slowly. Describing what I was feeling. That pervading sense of fearfulness, knowing we were vulnerable, terrified Raf could kick us out without notice. How I felt about being forced to operate on Angie and remembering waking from the surgeries I had endured. The nightmares. Fear of Miles learning what I had done. My fury at Sorcha. Before I could stop the torrent, it gushed out of me. All of it. My feelings. Cam railroading me into admitting that I would have gone to Stefan over him.

"I can't help but feel that I continually give him the power to wield over me. I wonder if I were fragile and vulnerable like *her*, then would he feel like I need him?"

Illy snorted. "Fragile and vulnerable are words that have never been used to describe you. Even with the trauma you carry, you are still a badass, and that is why I love you."

"But what if delicate is what he wants? Most men do, don't they? Luca did. They want to be the protector, and I don't need protecting. So when he realized I wouldn't run to him to protect me, well..."

"Luca knew full well that I could take care of myself. But yes, most men want to protect those they love. It is ingrained in them. Protector instinct. Particularly around their children."

"Will he always be looking for that in a woman?"

"Of course not. Cam loves that you are strong. You just told him that he is replaceable. That would have been hard to hear."

"I didn't say that at all."

"Look at it from his perspective. You did. You said if you were in danger, fearful for your life, you would run to someone else."

"*Fuuuccck*! Sometimes, I can't help but think that it is just all too hard, too exhausting. Is it even worth living if you are only half the person you once were?"

"That is a bit extreme."

Is it?

The first of the four enormous community greenhouses loomed before us, their tinted green rigid plastic panels glinting in the late afternoon sun. I turned to take the path away from the village, down to the lake. I wasn't ready to go home and see Cam or Sorcha.

"Hang on. I need some veggies for dinner," Illy noted, swinging the basket on her arm. "Come with me. I'm not finished with you. Frey, you have been together for the best part of twenty years. You have overcome far worse than this. Remember the mantra. This is a phase. This too will pass."

"Then why do I keep feeling like I just can't do this anymore?"

"You haven't told him yet, have you? About the PTSD."

"No," I whispered. "I can't. I don't want him to see me as weak."

Illy opened the door and held it open for me. "He has never, will never, see you that way. You aren't being fair to him or yourself. You aren't giving him the full picture."

"What do you need?" I sighed, still feeling the need to flee as far away as possible.

"Everything. We have over thirty mouths to feed, remember? Can you get twenty potatoes? I'll get the carrots and beans. Luca didn't need to protect me, and he knew it. But he could have if the situation arose. I guess that was why it worked. We loved each other, but we weren't needy."

"Was Lae needy? Is that what men want?"

Illy sighed as she shook the dirt from a freshly pulled carrot. "You are asking the wrong person, my friend. I never knew her. But from what I understand from Sorcha and Di, she wasn't as strong as you. Not needy exactly, but not the force of nature you are."

"Well, I don't feel like a force of nature. I feel like all I do is cause people pain, including myself. I can't help but think he would be better off without me."

"We both know that isn't true."

"I'm damaged, Illy. I don't think I can be repaired."

"No, you are traumatized. I hear you screaming, every night. It breaks my heart to know you are in so much pain. You need to tell him."

"I'm so sorry I woke you."

"That isn't the point, and you know it."

"I can't tell him. I don't want to be seen as pitiful. What else do you need?" I dropped the potatoes into the basket, watching Illy's arm sag with the additional weight.

She assessed the basket, nearly filled with vegetables. "I need some broccoli. Maybe spinach? You are so far from pitiful it isn't funny."

Ignoring the last comment, I scanned the planter boxes around the room. "I don't see any. But I think they grow brassicas away from tomatoes." I waved at the rows of tomato plants, carefully staked so that the weight of the ripening fruit didn't break the stem.

"Well, if Kendra is anything like Di, they will practice companion planting."

"Oh, aren't they so alike? I can barely tell them apart."

"Only in looks," Illy muttered as she rearranged her laden basket. "Come on. Let's check the next one. Di said she explicitly wanted broccoli."

"What do you mean, only in looks?" I asked as we moved toward the second greenhouse, catching the undertone. But she wasn't listening to me. Illy stood with her head cocked to the side, listening intently.

I did likewise and caught the voices. A man and a woman. She was speaking in a low, coquettish tone. Flirting. He was rumbling in a deeper voice, but I was unable to make out the words. Grasping from the tone that we were interrupting a private moment, we turned to leave. We would need to do without broccoli tonight.

Illy's eyes popped wide as she froze just outside the doorway. Furrowing my brow, I heard what she had. It was Cam's voice. Stepping as close as we dared to the opaque fabric, we listened intently.

"But you look so sad. I just wanted to see if I could help," the female voice purred.

"I'm fine." His tone was abrupt. My blood froze in my veins. *How fast can I get to Melbourne? Do I take*

Cait with me? She would be safe, even outside. I can leave now and be there in a few hours. I know my way in the dark. My parents' house. I will be safe there.

"You know," the sweet, lilting tone continued, "I noticed you when you arrived here. I hoped you would notice me. I would love it if you could stay. I really want to get to know you better."

"Umm, sorry?"

"You are here to stay now, aren't you? It must be awfully crowded in that old dormitory with so many people." I could feel the honey dripping from her words. "You could stay with me. I have my own place. It is only small but very cozy. I'm sure I could make you very happy. Your life is so fascinating. I'd love to hear all about your travels, about the world out there. You have been to so many wonderful places. I can't wait to hear your stories. Come, sit with me."

The tone was so full of infatuation; I felt the bile rising. The silence that followed was heartbreaking. I closed my eyes, seeing another woman in his arms, and turned to creep away. It was better this way. He could move on. Cam had better options.

I took two steps, but Illy placed a hand on my arm, shaking her head. *Wait.*

As my heart pounded out of my chest, I closed my eyes and counted to ten.

"Sophie," Cam's voice was low and choked. "Thank you for the offer, but you should go. I'm married."

My heart started to beat again, the first beat so fierce I thought it would pound out of my chest.

The silky voice tried again. "But you look so unhappy. She need never know. It can be our secret. The boys here are *so* boring. Kendra says you have been to so many wonderful places. Traveled the world. Your life must be so exciting."

"I've never kept a secret from Freyja," he choked.

"Secrets are so sexy. Let me show you," she hummed.

The pauses were killing me. What were they doing? My heart was pounding so loudly he must be able to hear it.

"Please ... don't."

"Don't you like what you see? You can touch me if you like. See how smooth my skin is? Feel it."

"Sophie, please. You need to leave. Someone will see you."

"I don't care." I could hear the haughtiness in her tone from where I stood. "I want you, and I know you want me. I can see it in your face. You can't lie to me."

I felt the vomit rise into my throat, choking it down.

I heard the voice, so low I had to strain to hear it. "I love my wife. We are bonded until the day we die. I promised her commitment until love lasts. The problem is it will always last. I have loved her since the day we met, and I will want her until I take my last breath. There will never be anyone else for me."

"That is beautiful," she simpered. "But she doesn't make you happy, does she? Sitting here all alone, you are miserable. We both know it. She need never know about us. I promise I won't tell. I know I can make you happy."

The sound of a metal zipper opening echoed through the greenhouse.

Illy nodded at me, and I opened the door as I heard Cam plead, "Sophie! Stop!"

She was kneeling before him naked, her dress on the ground. As the scene came into view, I realized her hands were unfastening his jeans.

"Get your hands off my husband," I growled.

Sophie's head snapped around, her dark hair flying, cheeks flushed. Cam's eyes widened in shock.

"Nothing happened!" he exclaimed, the words tumbling over each other in a rush to escape his mouth.

"That's not true." Sophie turned around, displaying her pert naked breasts and smooth expanse of creamy skin meeting womanly curves. She held her perfect inner arms out to me. "He loves everything I have to offer."

I looked away. Why wouldn't he? She was young and beautiful, her skin smooth and supple. My stomach was riddled with scars and stretch marks from forced surgeries, cesareans, and growing children. For the first time, I was ashamed of my arms, crisscrossed with old wounds. My face now had fine lines around my eyes, befitting my forty-two years.

"Which is nothing," Illy growled, stepping around the corner.

The movement caught my eye as Sophie draped an arm around Cam's broad shoulders, her ample breasts pushed flat into his sides. It was then I noticed how uncomfortable he was and not with me bearing witness. He was backing away from her. His eyes were cast down. The rage rose in me.

"You. Go, now!" I boomed, taking two menacing steps toward her. Sophie snatched at her dress on the ground, humphed at me, and stormed away, pulling it over her head.

Cam was still fidgeting, unsure where to look.

I heard Illy speak as she headed toward the door. "I'll deal with her."

After the footsteps had died away, I asked, "Did you want her?" in as calm a tone as I could manage.

"No," he whispered, unable to meet my eyes. "But I couldn't get her to leave."

"Why didn't you just push her away?"

"What did you want me to do? Drop her on her ass in the mud?"

Yes! My brain screamed. "I suppose not," I admitted, recognizing who she was. Raf's daughter. If Cam had rejected her, upset her, she would go running to her father and accuse him of assaulting her, and we would likely be kicked out. Then where do we go? Now I knew what Illy had meant by taking care of it. Ensuring she wouldn't blab.

"All I could think about was what you said about not getting kicked out of here. I knew I needed to let her down gently. But she wouldn't take no for an answer."

"How old is she?" I asked suspiciously.

"A child, not much older than Sam. Nineteen, I think."

"Fuck," I seethed as he got himself under control. Finally, I asked, "Did you mean what you told her about me?"

Cam looked at me then, full of surprise. "Of course. Have I not told you that a million times?"

"Not lately," I admitted.

"Did you need to hear it?"

"Maybe."

Cam grabbed my hand and led me to the back of the greenhouse, where there was a small room with potting benches, seeds and hand tools, trowels, and hand rakes. The walls were made of the same opaque green plastic. I could see the shadows of trees outside, darker, but not clear enough to make out the shapes. Purposefully, he locked and barricaded the small door behind him. Sweeping aside the envelopes of labeled seeds, he lifted me, sitting me on the potting bench. It was the perfect height. I wrapped my legs and locked my ankles behind his back as he gazed into my eyes.

"I'm sorry we fought. It hurt when you said you would run to someone else. After all we have been through, I wanted to be the only one you would turn to. The person you would trust."

"At that point in time, I was pissed at you," I admitted. "That doesn't mean I would ordinarily do that. I just feel you want more from me than I can give."

"What do you mean?"

Sighing, I tried to explain. "I feel like I am not who you need anymore."

"How can you say that?"

"It is just how I feel."

"Honey, what has happened to us?"

"I don't know," I said, although I did. I just couldn't say it. Not now. What if he ran off after Sophie, after learning she was the better choice?

"You are everything I want, could ever want. Why would you question that?"

"I saw her flaunt her arms. It was deliberate. I'm flawed, Cam."

"You will always be perfect to me."

I snorted, hiding my discomfort.

"I don't see your marks as I assume you don't see mine. They are souvenirs of a life lived, not damaged goods. Frey, I just see *you*."

"All I know is seeing you just now with that skank and you telling her no was the most romantic thing I have ever seen. I was so filled with love for you that I couldn't breathe."

Cam's mouth dropped. "Even after twenty years, I will never understand women! So all I had to do was be propositioned by someone else, drop her on her ass, and you would fall madly in love with me?"

"I'm already madly in love with you," I whispered in his ear. "You just reminded me why."

My head tilted back as Cam kissed my neck and throat. "Why?" he purred against the delicate skin of my neck.

My eyes closed as he held me against his solid chest. I could feel his heart beating faster. "Loyalty, honor, commitment."

"I have committed to you twice." His hands lifted the top over my head, pausing to search my soul. "Do you need to hear it again?"

"Yes," I whispered.

Cam pulled his t-shirt over his head and began reciting his marriage vows, slowly, enunciating every syllable, without breaking eye contact. For each line, he removed an item of clothing, alternating between his and mine. By the end, we were both naked and gasping.

"I can't promise to love you as long as love lasts," he breathed as his warm naked chest pressed me down onto the bench, and his husky voice caressed my skin.

A small gasp escaped as he pressed into me. "I will love you until my last breath," he moaned.

"And I you."

Unable to return to the dorm, we lingered in the greenhouse until it was dark, not wanting to be away from each other.

"We can't sleep here," he breathed as I lay across his lap in the corner.

"I am not ready to see anyone," I admitted.

"Get dressed. I'll deal with it."

As we approached the dorm, Cam scooped me up into his arms. "Pretend you are asleep," he whispered as he kissed my cheek. "I will tell them you are exhausted and take you straight to bed. Even if they know it is a lie, no one will challenge me."

"Mumma!" Cait cried as she saw Cam across the room.

"Shush, darling," he cooed. "Mumma is asleep. She is very tired, Caitlin. Can you open the door for me?"

Curled into his chest, I desperately wanted to see my daughter but could hear Sorcha talking in the kitchen. Conversations stopped as Cam walked through the living space and down the hallway. Cait stood in the doorway and watched as Cam laid me on the thin camp mattress.

"Come and kiss Mum goodnight," he whispered. "Then go and play with your sisters."

I felt the warm breath and child lips press on my cheek, but I didn't move. The door clicked closed, and I opened my eyes.

"Are you hungry?"

I nodded and heard the door click again as he slipped out of the room. I could hear the rumbling of voices in the main room but couldn't quite make out what was being said. Guilt wracked my body, making me tremble. I needed to tell him about Clava, the panic attacks, the nightmares. But not now.

Cam returned with a plate of bread, cheese, and fruit. Hardly a meal, but enough. I sat up against the pillow, and he lay beside me, watching me. Silently, we ate, not taking our eyes from each other, feeding each other pieces of cheese or grapes.

"I love you," I mouthed in the dark.

"We will get through this, I promise. We have been through so much together. No matter what happens, what challenges we might face, the one thing I know for certain is that we will always find our way back to each other. I can't imagine my life without you. I refuse to have a life without you in it."

"Thank you." It felt like a foolish thing to say, but they were the only words that popped into my mind.

"Frey, I have a million things to thank you for. A life filled with joy, five wonderful children. Every day I wake with you is a blessing. Now, get some sleep."

CHAPTER 25

EACH YEAR, ON THE 20th of March, we held a collective birthday for my girls and Katrin's. Kat's girls had birthdays in the latter part of the year, my girls' actual birthdays spanned eight weeks, but a common day of celebration had been chosen, the spring equinox. It felt fitting that Beltane, a fire festival celebrating fertility and new life, should be selected as their birthday. This year, we had three missing from our number, and the adults held a quiet memorial when the children were in bed. With the fall colors surrounding us, we remembered the lives we had lost. The girls didn't need reminding that they were targets.

Gerry was even more taciturn than usual, remembering his little Soli, who hadn't lived to experience the joy of turning seven. Recognizing that this day would be the most difficult for him, Cam had asked if he wanted to head back to Melbourne to see if Tadhg and Ashton had learned anything. He refused, wanting to stay with the Orkney girls on their special day.

"He is a good man," Cam noted as we found a few quiet minutes alone. "I'm not sure I could celebrate a day that should have been my daughter's birthday."

"I knew he was one of the good ones the first time I met him. When he offered to come with me to Mousa…" I trailed off, remembering that the first time I met Gerry was the same day Cam had lost Laetitia.

"Without you, he may never have married Saba."

While that was true, I wasn't sure what to say about the complex tapestry that life weaves. How one seemingly insignificant event impacts generations to come. When Luca and I went after Laetitia, Isla, and the others, we had stopped on Orkney. Gerry had accompanied us, and later married Saba, one of the rescued Orkney women. Without their gratitude to me, they would not have adopted Soli, but then, because of me, they had lost her. Every single thread of the rich tapestry forms a timeline that weaves in and out of others. How different would our lives be if I hadn't been on Lewis that day? Cam and I wouldn't have Katrin. Likely wouldn't be together now. Then none of our other children would exist. I could still be traveling with Angus, and he wouldn't have killed Luca, leaving Illy and her children bereft. He would never have used my sister to carry Ceridwen, but then I wouldn't have lost her.

"You need to stop blaming yourself," Cam said soothingly, pulling me out of the rabbit hole. "You can't predict what others will do, what impact one decision will have on the course of your life or the lives of others."

He was right, of course. The tiny pinprick of doubt needling me was that the common denominator was *me*.

Today we were determined to celebrate. These girls were away from their families, their homes, but we sought to make this a day to remember. They awoke to a delicious late breakfast, and when they had all gathered, they were each presented with their gift, sourced and carried from Edinburgh. The room was filled with the sounds of shredding paper, merry chatter, and peals of laughter.

"Di should have been a wedding planner," I noted, watching Di as she flitted around, making the final arrangements, crossing items off her list. For days I had watched her pleading, cajoling, and charming people to get everything she wanted: food, supplies, and assistance.

"She is a natural," Illy agreed.

Sorcha grinned. "She loves a party, does Di."

Di was now the unofficial event organizer of Lewis, arranging the annual Harvest Festival, meaning Cam and I no longer needed to endure the pain of planning a massive event. If you wanted something arranged, you asked Di. No one refused her anything, and she had a knack for making people want to donate or give anything she asked them for. She had spent the best part of a week inviting everyone to this event, sourcing food and decorations for the girl's birthday, and organizing the biggest party I suspected had ever been hosted on Kiewa.

"Do they know they are only getting one day off school?" I asked Di quietly as she passed with an arm full of colored paper streamers, assisted by Cait and Sera, who were yapping away madly behind her. I watched the two of them together. Sisters. Gestated by different surrogates, but full sisters. No wonder they were so similar. They had a love/hate relationship like any sibling. There was no middle ground—they were either inseparable best friends or screaming at each other, pulling hair, and trying to claw each other's eyes out. Caitlin was more dominant, but Sera had a sly streak. She had learned a lot from her older sisters, primarily how to lie and keep a straight face.

"No, and you aren't telling them either," she ordered, in her best Sorcha impersonation. "Let them enjoy their party. School can wait. Can you please go over to Tully's house and get the bread, please? She might need a hand. I asked her for quite a lot, and she wasn't done when I dropped by there an hour ago. Do you know which house it is?"

As I walked, sadness filled me as I grasped Cait was turning seven, and her siblings wouldn't be here to share her joy. Not all her siblings but her immediate family. Louis, Katrin, Xanthe, and Thorsten weren't here. Closing my eyes, I sent them a silent wish that they were okay, and everything had settled down. Cam had told Louis as much as he dared, knowing that he was likely to have filled in the blanks himself. In Sorcha's absence, I hoped Kat would still start her apprenticeship, perhaps with Hamish or Mel. Perhaps Stefan? With no suspicion pointing to him, there was no reason he would have been removed from the med team, especially now that they had lost Sorcha and me. He would have easy access to Katrin. My stomach cramped. If it was Stefan, then I had just left my daughter in easy reach of a murderer?

I conjured Stefan's slim, angular face and sandy hair. Freckles lightly spattered across his cheeks gave him a slightly bronzed look. I remembered how he looked at me when he had kissed me. *Was that the face of a murderer?* Kat was super sharp and could read people almost as well as Illy. The difference between them being that she had no filter. Armed with a cutting tongue, she could decimate people with a few sharp words. Sometimes I worried about her working with Sorcha, but now Sorcha was here, and Kat was not. For the millionth time, I prayed she was okay.

Tully was immensely grateful to see me and looked like she wanted to hug me when I offered to ferry goods for her while she cleaned up so she could attend the party. She was still dressed in a dough-spattered apron, and the kitchen looked like a flour bomb had hit it. I made several trips between her home and the long trestle tables in the village clearing, carrying biscuits, cakes, tarts, bread rolls, baguettes, and other pastries to the food tables, ensuring they were spread out between the plates of salad, fruit, and cheeses. The scent wafting from each tray I carried made my stomach rumble, and I wondered how long it would be before I could eat. They were only just setting up the biogas barbeque, so the main meal was some time away, planned for a late lunch and early dinner. *Could I sneak a cake or two in beforehand?*

Tully looked up from her kitchen cleaning as I collected the final three trays, and I thanked her profusely. She had done so much to make the girl's birthday special, and I genuinely appreciated it.

"My pleasure. We don't have parties often, so it is lovely to help. But I didn't make the birthday cakes, so please leave a space in the middle. We can arrange the other food around the outside."

"Well, it all looks delicious! I think we will be eating for days!"

"Have you met the men here? I'm scared it won't last the hour!"

As I carried the final trays, I watched the drinks station being set up, wondering how Di had convinced them to donate so much alcohol. While it was made here, it wasn't abundant. Unlike home, where we could raid the mainland occasionally, it was tightly controlled. As I watched, bottle after bottle of wine, cider, and beer was pulled out of a crate and laid out with glassware on a separate table. People were already milling around, waiting to source a glass. Raf's sangria-filled glass pitchers lay on another table, catching the sunlight and making the orange slices glow through the beautiful claret liquid.

Sensing movement behind me, I turned and watched Sophie approach with her long dark hair swaying sensuously down her back as she carried an enormous silver tray of vanilla cupcakes, each coated with thick white icing and a "7" decorated on top in pink. One for each girl. *Cait would love that,* I thought as she looked me up and down and smirked as if I were no competition. We rarely had time to ice cakes on Lewis. Usually baked goods were eaten hot straight from the oven. She had gone to a lot of trouble. Despite my feelings about her, I knew I should thank her. I cleared a space in the center of the table and turned to speak, but she pointedly ignored me, turning her head away. She spent a moment arranging the centerpiece. She wasn't even twenty, I realized, eyeing her covertly as she sauntered away. She was stunning. Every man here was watching her slim waist and curvy hips as she walked, swaying gently. She had a classic hourglass figure with rounded breasts, her cleavage on display in her floral v-necked dress. Her dark glossy hair was swishing down her back as she walked toward the houses, the sun catching the highlights. With large brown eyes with dark lashes and porcelain skin, she was aware of her attractiveness. She was one of those women who knew she was beautiful and thrived on the attention. She carried herself confidently and always got what she wanted.

Breaking my attention from the departing Sophie, I took in the grassy clearing surrounded by large eucalypts. Everything looked so beautifully festive in the afternoon light. Streamers hung between trees with paper lanterns hanging in all colors. The children had been busy. Seats were scattered around the clearing. Food was ready to be served. Closing my eyes and inhaling the scent of gum trees, I smelled home, making me feel almost nostalgic. Opening my eyes, I looked around for Cam and saw him speaking with Sorcha at the other side of the clearing. Sophie was nowhere near him. Good. She hadn't tried again after that day, and I was surprised at the relief I felt.

Everyone was here. The girls were running around happily, chasing each other, jumping to touch the streaming ribbons. I smiled as I saw Sera, Alasdair, and Rani run past, laughing, Rani's pink and white skirt billowing out around her. I couldn't see Cait in her navy polka dot skirt. She insisted on wearing her favorite top, a white tee with a blue butterfly. It was nearly too small, but she refused to give it up, even to Sera, who was slimmer in build. I scanned the crowd but knew she was safe with Di. Everyone was enjoying themselves. Music filled the air and merry chatter hung in a low thrum.

As I stood before the long trestle table laden with biscuits, cupcakes, and tiny jam tarts I had covertly eyed as I carried them from Tully's house, a muffled conversation reached my ears. Di's voice. I would have known it anywhere, even from behind the large tree some meters away. Putting two jam tarts onto my plate, I turned to look for where Cam had gone.

He was moving chairs under a tree, and I couldn't catch his eye.

"You have known I was with Sorcha for fifteen years. What's changed?"

Kendra's tone was arctic, making even me freeze where I stood. "There is knowing, and there is ramming it down my throat. It is unnatural. And to raise children like that? You should be ashamed. I'm so glad Nai Nai and your parents aren't here to see this. This would kill them."

"I didn't ram anything!" Di sounded perplexed. "How…"

"Getting around kissing and canoodling in public. In *my* house. People are talking, Diana. It is disgusting. I'm ashamed of you."

"Ashamed of me?" I could feel the hurt radiate from where I stood. "I've always supported you, no matter what."

"Then where have you been the last fifteen years? You could have stayed here with me."

"I followed my heart."

"Well, I followed mine."

"I was always there for you. Don't you remember?"

"All I remember is you abandoning me."

"Craig breaking up with you? Who went and got your stuff? Took you to the clinic for a termination when you learned you were pregnant? Sat beside you so no one knew which of us it was?"

"Don't you dare bring that up! If you tell Arjun…"

"I'm just saying I was there for you, Ken, in your darkest hour. It breaks my heart that you can't be here for me when I need you most. To protect my children."

"But they aren't your children, are they? Two women can't… ugh! I can't abide … this."

"I named my daughter after you." Di's words came out choked.

"I never asked you to," Kendra spat, the venom making my blood boil. "It is unnatural to raise a child without a mother and a father."

"Since when did you care? You were the one who rebelled as soon as you could. Drinking. Sex before marriage. Living together out of wedlock. Abortion. You never cared before. Why now?"

"It is unnatural," Kendra repeated stonily.

"Is that what you think of me?" I could hear the thickening of Di's voice and could visualize tears rolling down Di's sweet face. "Unnatural?"

Di was the sweetest, kindest person I had ever met. She was so wholesome, always had a kind word for others. It broke my heart to hear her tortured like this. Dropping my plate on the nearest table, I took four strides toward the tree. Stepping around the rough bark, I wrapped my arm around Di's shoulder and steered her away from her vicious cousin, glaring over my shoulder, daring her to say anything else.

Di's distress attracted Sorcha and Cam, who were seething when they heard my concise version of events.

"Fucking bitch. Unnatural, my ass. I saved her and her children when they were born. Did she tell you that part? I delivered them both, and they both would have died." Sorcha was bristling.

"I'm so sorry, Di," Cam soothed. "She is in the minority. Love is love. Not one person on Lewis has any issue with you and Sorcs, Bridget and Jorja, or any other same-sex couple there. I'm just so sorry that she can't see that."

"She is my family," Di wept.

"*Was* your family," Sorcha hissed.

"Frey!" The urgency in her voice jerked our attention from Di, making us turn and look at Illy as she came running up the path.

"Come!" was all she could say in her breathless state, and we followed, aware of the stares we were attracting. Di was still sobbing, her face red and blotched.

We hurried down the path away from the main village, passing people walking into town for the celebrations. Illy slowed and smiled as we passed, greeting everyone, telling them we were looking forward to catching up at the party. Just off to get a few last-minute things. It was a façade. She wasn't keen to let anyone know where we were going.

"What's up?" I hissed.

Illy kept the fake smile plastered on her face. "In a minute," she hissed as she smiled sweetly, slowing as we passed another small group of locals. Checking to ensure we weren't seen, she dashed off the path and into the shoulder height, glossy green reeds growing alongside the water's edge.

"Careful where you stand," Sorcha advised as we pushed through. "It was just over there that Tom was working when the snake bit him, and it is still warm enough for them to be active."

Di's hand shot out and gripped Sorcha's. She was deathly afraid of snakes.

We pushed through the reeds, trying not to trample a path that made it clear where we were going. Illy was setting a cracking pace, and we were all fighting to keep up.

"Where the fuck is she going?" Sorcha groaned. "We are missing the girls' party, not to mention leaving them unsupervised."

All became clear when we reached the water's edge. Gerry was sitting beside Cait, bedraggled and distraught, beside the picturesque blue lake that formed the town's primary water supply. Dropping to my knees, Cam shielding her on the other side, we hugged her as I quickly checked her over. She was filthy, coated in mud, and unable to form words.

"Is she okay?" Cam asked quietly, and I nodded.

I felt the fist fly past me and connect with the young man's nose. Blood spattered, some specks hitting me in the face. I hadn't even seen Sanjiv, Kendra's son, sitting quietly on the other side of Gerry. Gerry was gripping his arms behind his back.

"Wha…" I started as Gerry hauled the young man to his feet.

"I needed some time alone before I made an appearance at the party. I saw him from a distance," Gerry spoke with his characteristic softness. "He had tied her hands behind her back, gagged her, and was frog-marching her to the water's edge. She was fighting, and he punched and kicked her. Hard. In the stomach and back. I caught up with him as he…"

Another look at Cait's dripping hair and boot-printed white top, combined with the red patches rubbed raw around her wrists, indicated exactly what Sanjiv had intended to do.

"Why?" I boomed in his face, shocking him into speech.

"She is a freak," he spat back at me, the venom hitting me before the words registered. "One of *them. Witch!*"

"Them?" I growled, despite knowing precisely what he meant.

"Freak," he mumbled again before he clammed up and refused to speak.

Illy took a single determined look at Gerry, and they dragged Sanjiv off to the trees a hundred meters away. I lost sight of them as they pushed through the thick foliage.

"Find them all. Now!" I barked at Cam, who was still watching the trees sway back into place.

I carried Cait back to the cottage, tears streaming down her sweet face as she struggled to comprehend what had happened to her. Cam and Di headed back in the direction of the party, looking for the other children. I glanced across Cait's mud-matted hair at Sorcha and saw the grim determination in her eyes. I just wanted to hold Cait and never let her go. She was uncharacteristically silent, and I glanced at Sorcha, fearful for the long-term ramifications of this trauma.

We carefully removed her clothing, checking the bruising now forming across her face, where he had struck her multiple times, chatting away about the weather and what they were learning at school. Silently, I prayed she had no internal bleeding or injuries. As I removed her formerly white top, I steeled myself not to cry. The bruising on her poor, tiny body was horrific. Dark purple blotches already riddled her back and stomach, red rings still prominent around her wrists, skin rubbed off in places. I felt sick envisioning what my baby had endured at Sanjiv's hands.

While I assisted Cait to shower, Sorcha retrieved the smaller ultrasound machine from the clinic, and Cait giggled as the cold wand was moved across her bare stomach. Sorcha's shoulders relaxed, and I breathed more comfortably than I had since Illy had dragged us away from the party. Sorcha and I scrutinized the tiny monotone monitor. Internal bleeding, significant bruising, but no ruptures that we could see.

"Is she okay?" I mouthed over her head, and Sorcha nodded grimly. It wasn't like we could operate on her quickly.

I was just wrapping her up in a blanket and giving her a hot drink when Cam arrived with the rest of the children, all unharmed. I flashed him a look over the children's heads, and he grimaced. Neither of us had seen Illy or Gerry return. The conversation with Sanjiv was taking longer than expected.

Di and Sam ducked out and sourced food on several trips, advising us in a whisper that most people had not even noticed that the guests of honor weren't there. With Ruby, Scarlett, and Kendra's help, she served the younger children dinner, as stilted conversation took place between the adults at the far end of the room. We all knew what this meant. We weren't safe here. I noticed she had taken the platter of birthday cakes for the girls and smiled. Hopefully, no one had noticed.

She saw me watching and tried to smile, but it fell flat. "The alcohol was going down far too easily, and no one was paying any attention to what I was doing, so I took them. The girls shouldn't miss out, should they?"

"After dinner," Sorcha ordered, making Di wilt slightly.

"Oh, come on. It is their party, and they haven't had lunch. Surely just this once they can have cake first?"

"No!" Sorcha and I chimed in unison.

"I know when I am outnumbered," Di said haughtily, placing the platter on the bench as she supervised children eating hamburgers, salad, and bread.

The girls chattered away merrily, most not realizing that the party was going on outside. Sam had brought back some streamers and lanterns. Those who had finished eating were running around chasing streamers, wrapping each other up. Cait was subdued but warmed up as she ate in her pajamas, seated beside Alasdair and Taki. By the end of the meal, she was watching Sera and Fairlie chasing each other around the room, tucking streamers in the back of their skirts like tails.

Illy and Gerry returned, looking grim, just as the adults were preparing to eat. They sat silently with the rest of us, but I could see it was urgent. Di clapped her hands to get their attention, then shooed all the children into the bedroom. I could hear the squeals as they were changed into nightwear, running up and down the rooms. She called Sam, Kendra, Ruby, and Scarlett to assist and read books, knowing that we would need to talk. She would hear it all later from Sorcha, anyway.

"Take the cupcakes," I suggested. "But perhaps let them digest their dinner first. After all that running around, no one needs to clean up vomit tonight."

Several "eewws!" accompanied this, making Di smile.

CHAPTER 26

"THANK YOU!" I FLEW at Gerry as he entered, and he barely got his arms up in time to catch me. "You saved Caitlin's life."

Gerry flushed and stiffened. After a pause, he clasped me to his chest. We had always been friendly, but now I owed him. Caitlin was alive tonight solely because of Gerry, and I would never forget it.

"There was no way I would let any more be taken. And especially not today. I'm just glad I was there," he said in his quiet Welsh manner.

"Thank you. Truly." Cam stood back awkwardly, but I could tell he was fighting with emotion. Someone we knew had tried to murder our daughter and would have succeeded had it not been for Gerry.

"What the fuck happened?" Sorcha asked, deliberately keeping her voice low. We could hear Sam reading and the girls giggling and squealing, unable to settle.

Illy sighed. "He held out longer than I expected, but we have ways."

My eyebrows hit my hairline. I had seen Illy's interrogation tactics before. "He is only a boy," I whispered.

"He is nineteen, and he fully intended to kill your daughter," she said pointedly. "And mine. And all the others. He knew exactly what he was doing and came prepared, so let's get past the innocence of youth bullshit right now." She pulled the remnants of the cut rope from her pocket and dropped it on the table.

"Why?" Cam asked.

Gerry spoke. "He worked out pretty quickly that we were serious. He admitted his part, but I had seen enough that there was no point in lying about that. It was the rest of it, the *why*, that took some time. There is a radio study group, older teenagers. The Players they call themselves. The first-born children of each community. It is an elite group."

"Firstborns?" I asked.

Illy continued. "It was a group formed for study originally, but like many teenagers, they developed a God complex. They were the children of the original settlers and believed they were the chosen ones, the first to be born here. They said it was their right to inherit the earth, but they were kept in a cage. They bitched and moaned about the younger children in their communities, feeling superior. We were all in our twenties when we arrived, so they were the first children of the new world. There is quite a gap between the original settlers and the firstborns. Then they learned about the children of selected partnerships, and later, your children, the modified ones. They are desperate to see this world that they have seen pictures of, heard so much about, but will never see themselves. They feel trapped. So they started acting out."

Gerry spoke softly, "They found commonalities and played games."

"Games?" I asked. "I assume you don't mean chess?"

"Well, funnily enough, that was where it started. It is a straightforward game to play via radio, strategic. Queen to H5. Then they started giving coded messages to each other. Remember, most of these kids have never met, not in real life. The learning groups are age-based, so only a small number are from each community. The oldest ones. They were voices on the radio, egging each other on to do wilder things. It built up over time. Setting challenges, seeing who was game enough to do them. There were only a few common texts in each community. *Harry Potter, Alice in Wonderland...*"

"The Bible," Cam whispered, remembering what Illy had said.

"Exactly." Illy picked up the story. "So they started leaving each other missions in code. They used code-names in the game, so they don't know who is who. But as is the way with any gang, the stakes kept being raised. Soon enough, it was things that needed to be validated, significant enough that they would be reported by others in the community so it could be proven. Damaging property. Stealing things. Then a new player entered the game."

"Who?"

"D."

"D?" I knocked my drink over and jumped up to grab a cloth to clean it up. "Who is D?"

"Sanjiv insists he doesn't know."

"Does he know anything?"

"He started quietly, and they assumed he was a Firstborn, too. Then, slowly, he started challenging them to do more. Setting the stakes and recognizing within the group those who had achieved their goals. Remember the fire on the Shetlands? The massacre of livestock on Kerguelen? Children of the forced partnerships being injured? All missions. This D was behind them all. Sanjiv says he can't remember when D went from being one of the group to leading it, but over time, he did. They listened to him. Sought his approval."

"He manipulated them."

"Okay, so when did the stakes become human lives?" Sorcha snarled.

"It took a while. A year or more. After they all clamored for the recognition that the Players could give. First, it was about harming the children of selected pairings, those children resulting from the forced reproduction. Then it became about Freyja's children. It was the ultimate test to take out an immune one. Three of them have so far claimed the honors. Sanjiv thought he would never reach that status. After all, there were none here."

"Status?" I asked.

"Those that performed the mission were revered. Honored. Treated like Gods."

"Then we walked right in with all of them," Cam finished.

"We did. Sanjiv had the chance to take out several of them, and he intended to. He admitted that. Scarlett was his first target. He would have been the best of the best, with multiple targets acquired."

"Targets! They are children!" Bile rose into my mouth. Murdering children. For sport.

"How did Raf let this happen?" Sorcha asked. "I thought all comms went through him?"

"They do," Illy admitted. "But if he thought it was a study group and these kids are all aged eighteen and nineteen, likely he didn't stay to listen."

"Well, one thing is for sure. We can't stay here," Cam said, scanning the room and taking in the bombsite. The long dining table was still covered with dirty dishes and half-eaten meals. Sleeping bags and piles of clothing were scattered around, drying on various surfaces. Birthday gifts were still heaped on a nearby table. Caitlin's filthy clothes still rested in the bathroom sink, waiting to be cleaned.

"Bloody hell," Sorcha seethed. "Now where do we go? I'm assuming these murderous fucktards are in every community?"

"I'm not certain, but it sounds that way. Any that were part of the radio network, and I am fairly sure that was all of them," Illy finished.

"It was," Gerry confirmed, making me look around. I had forgotten he was here, sitting quietly behind me. "I helped set up the protocols. Timing and such. We have a schedule for each subject, each age group, and interest."

Fire rose in my belly. "Can't we just talk to the people here? Let's speak with Raf. He likes Sorcha and Illy. He won't want to lose his best surgeon."

"It is more complicated than that," Illy cautioned.

"Why? Is Sanjiv the only one?" I asked. "Maybe if it is just him, we can neutralize the threat. Even if Kendra isn't supportive, we can talk to the others here. They won't support children being murdered for sport."

"No, there is one more."

"Do you know who?"

Illy looked at Cam, then at me. "Sophie."

Cam gasped aloud, turning to look at me. Illy caught the glance.

"We need to go. Tonight." I stood and started clearing dishes. Sorcha joined me. As I turned to move the dirty plates from the table to the bench, I thought of the last time I had seen Sophie swaggering past me, all the men watching her. Mesmerized with her flawless skin... glossy hair... Shoving Sorcha out of the way, I sprinted to the bedroom.

"Hey!" Sorcha bellowed as she crashed heavily onto the bench. Di had the platter in her hand as I threw the door open.

"No!" My outstretched hand banged into the underside and knocked the platter from her hands. The cupcakes scattered all over the floor, twenty-four horrified girls staring at me and the smashed cakes. White and pink icing smeared across the floor, a single beam of evening light making the icing sparkle.

"What are you doing?" Sorcha roared at me, reaching the doorway.

"So...phie...baked the cakes," I forced the words out.

Several of the girls started to cry. Their much-wanted treat was now crumbs across the floor.

Illy entered with Cam. "Sophie?" she asked.

I tried to slow my breathing. "I saw her carrying them. She smirked at me. I swear. At the time, I thought it was just that she would try again. But now..."

"Cupcakes." Illy looked at me intently.

Di was trying to comfort the girls, who were all crying now, staring at the icing spattered in an arc around her. Cam was frozen, looking horrified.

"You need to start talking," Sorcha hissed in my ear as she helped me pick up the pieces of cake and clean the icing from the wooden floors. I nodded and blinked at her.

Once we had closed the door and left Di with the sobbing girls, I told Sorcha about the events of the last few days. Sorcha's mouth dropped when she heard of Sophie's naked proposition.

"She is a child! She was the first child born here. I delivered her!"

Illy interjected. "You know what this means? Frey, you are still a target. It is likely that she was using Cam to get him away from you."

"Why?"

"She is a nasty piece of work. I have only spoken to her three times, and each time I left with the feeling that she was manipulative and malicious. Now that we know she is a Player, likely her target was you, Freyja. Only, instead of just eliminating the target, she wanted to destroy you first. What better way to get you away from us than to seduce your husband, make you feel ashamed of your physical appearance? I saw her flash her arms at you. If you were isolated from Cam, and his attentions were elsewhere, then you were easier to pick off. When that didn't work, she targeted the girls. What she didn't count on was that we are a team. A family. Likely she has never experienced the type of bond that we all share. She views women as competition and men as sport. I doubt she has never known true loyalty and friendship."

"How did you know about the poison?" Sorcha asked me.

"Do you remember Summer being terribly sick about a week before we left?" Illy answered.

Sorcha's mouth quirked. "I do."

"She had eaten a poisoned cupcake left for Seraphine."

Sorcha was sharp. "Poison. A woman's choice of murder weapon."

"Exactly. We will never know for sure, but I think we can safely assume that Frey just saved all of their lives."

Sorcha watched me intently. "Thank you," she mouthed.

"You know what this means," Cam said, connecting the dots. "It was likely a woman who left the cake for Seraphine."

"Time for speculation later," Gerry interjected. "I promised to protect these girls. We can't do it here. Not if Sophie is Rafael's daughter. No one will believe us. We need to go. Now. It is good timing. Everyone will be at the party, drinking. We can walk to the dome before it gets dark. They won't even hear the cars with that racket going on."

"But where do we go?" Illy asked. "I can get into Army bases with barracks and dormitories, but how long will we last? This isn't a quick fix. This D is the ringleader, and he is still driving this. We pushed and pushed, but Sanjiv didn't know who or where he was. Or at least, refused to tell us. But I don't think he knows. Gerry and I pushed pretty hard. So wherever we go, we need to be prepared to set up for weeks, possibly months. We need to grow food and access fresh, uncontaminated water. There are other isolated communities in Australia, but from what we learned from Sanjiv, there is likely a player in every community. He knew a few from before, recognized some voices. But most used code names."

"What about a university?" I asked. "A hotel? Those monsters near Inverness survived on canned food and beer for years outside a dome."

"These are children. Much harder to keep safe. They need fresh food to remain healthy. They are still growing. We need a domed community to stay anywhere beyond a few days, even if the girls don't. There are twenty-seven children and six of us. That is a lot of mouths to feed."

"You know where we can go, don't you?" Cam looked over at Sorcha. "It would need some work, but it wasn't that badly damaged when we were last there. There is a house, albeit a tiny one. Greenhouses too. But it is safe. You and I are likely the only people alive that know where it is."

Sorcha exhaled sharply. "We didn't bury him."

Cam held his breath for a moment, remembering. "No. But what if Frey and I go now while we can still make it in daylight? Fix the shell, check it is all safe. Deal with ... anything that the girls shouldn't see. Would you be okay with it then?"

Sorcha's jaw clenched. "What I am not okay with is worrying 24/7 that my daughter is about to be murdered. So yes, I will be fine."

"Where are you thinking of taking them?" I asked.

"Do you remember how I told you that my parents owned a hundred acres of bushland near Mansfield? I told you they set it up with a makeshift dome, and Sorcha and I visited there when I found her on Kiewa?"

"Cam, that was fifteen years ago! Didn't you say that the integrity had been breached?"

"It had. But only in one spot. Gerry knows enough about the fabric to replace those sections. Remember when Orkney had that massive storm a few years ago? He was asked to help replace some panels."

Gerry nodded. "Aye, I did."

Illy piped up, "If you need replacement frames, I know where to source some. I was part of the settlement team, remember?"

"That would be great. It wasn't the largest space, but most of it was still alive. If we get back to the dock, I can take moss from the samples we took on Mousa to re-green the infected areas. Dad had boxes of seeds. Several greenhouses too. I saw them but didn't take anything."

"You kept the samples?" I asked. "I thought being dumped there was about us reconcile and make an international journey a lot more pleasant."

"I still kept the samples. I figured I had gone to all that trouble. Why destroy them?"

I wanted to smile, remembering that time, but the stress of the past hours was foremost in my mind. "Are you sure this place is safe for so many children? How far from here is it? You went there after you left here last time, didn't you? Could they locate us?"

"The girls are safe anywhere, although Alasdair, Kendra, and Sam are not. But in terms of physical safety, Sorcs and I are the only people in the world who know where that place is, could even find it. It is nowhere near the main road, and even before all of this, it wasn't easy to spot on a satellite being in a natural gully. It is about as safe as it gets."

"It is true," Sorcha admitted. "I doubt even Di could find it again, although she never left the car. And we certainly didn't tell anyone here about it."

"Fine. How long will it take you to mobilize the girls?" I asked. "We need to get away as quickly as possible."

"Well, if you and Cam head off now, we can start packing and mobilize the children."

"I'm not leaving Caitlin. I can't. She can come with us."

"Frey, I know this must be traumatic for you after what happened but treating her differently will only isolate her from the other girls. You know I would never let anything happen to her. None of us would."

"We can't," Cam whispered. "I need to bury my father first."

"Can you go, and I stay with her?" I pleaded.

It was Sorcha who answered. "I need you to do this, Frey. Please. Go with Cam and get things ready. She won't leave my sight, I swear to you. But Illy is right. The best thing you can do for her now is to treat her like one of the others."

Exhaling forcefully, I agreed, but wasn't happy about it. "What did you do with Sanjiv?" I asked. "Will he raise the alarm?"

"Left him tied to a tree pretty deep in the forest. Gagged, of course. With the party going on, hopefully no one will notice for a while. Most likely, he won't be found until morning. We have a few hours. But we need to move. Sophie might wonder where the girls have gone or go looking for Sanjiv if they planned the poisoning together."

"But what about somewhere to sleep?" Sorcha butted in. "The cottage was tiny. It won't sleep all of us."

"I can manage that," Illy piped up. "A trip to Puckapunyal army base should see us kitted out with tents, swags, sleeping bags, and anything else we need so we can leave a lot of this behind. I did some of my basic training there. I know where everything is and likely food stores too. It is only a few hours, round trip. We might take the kids and head there and spend the night. Load up in the morning and see you by mid-afternoon. That should give you enough time?"

Di had left the bedroom and was standing behind us, silent. I could still hear her daughter reading to the children in the adjoining room, Sam shushing them when they got too out of hand. A dark look clouded her face, very unlike Di. Sorcha looked at her enquiringly.

"Are you sure you want me to come?" she squeaked.

"Why wouldn't we?" Cam asked incredulously. "It wasn't you."

"No, but it was my family. Sanjiv came far too close to killing your child. I'm the one who trusted him with Caitlin. I should have looked after her, but I didn't. I wanted to speak with my cousin, and I trusted him when he offered to watch her. I trusted all of them."

"Di, it wasn't your fault," Cam replied. "We all thought we were safe."

"But you weren't, and it was my family who did this. Kendra and Sanjiv."

"I heard what she said to you, Di."

"She was so ... *evil*," Di whispered, her voice shaking.

"Was she always like that?" Illy asked gently, "Judgmental?"

"Not at all. She was the rebellious one, and we were as close as sisters. We shared everything. I thought she would always love me. Accept me."

"I think we can assume after today that we will get no support from her," Sorcha added.

"Can you forgive me?" Di whispered.

"There is nothing to forgive," I soothed. "Di, you didn't do this. I think we have all moved on from being punished for the sins of the fathers. What Sanjiv did, what Kendra said—those things are unforgivable. But it has nothing to do with you. I am so sorry you had to be on the receiving end of that. But she is still your family. Do you want to mend things before we go?"

"Not. Any. More," Di forced through closed lips. "Kendra has shown her true colors. Sorcha is my family. You are all my family. Family are the people who stick by you, no matter what."

"Did you tell her she was the spare?" Illy grinned, trying to lighten the mood.

Tears ran down Di's cheeks, and I stood up to embrace her. "This is not your fault. Can you help us pack up everything? We need to move."

As we raced around, packing up our clothes scattered around the main room and stuffing them in bags, Sorcha stopped suddenly, her arms laden with clothing.

"Cam, do you remember when Mum and Dad first bought the block? Before they built the cabin, I mean?"

"You mean when Dad bought that old blue school bus and dragged it in? Mum hated it and was so happy when he finally got rid of it. I loved that thing."

"Exactly. Surely we could find an old bus to accommodate the kids? We just need to find an old depot and could tow it into place."

"That could work if we remove the seats. I remember you and I being forced to work together to unbolt the seats from the floor. You hit me with a spanner because I wasn't working fast enough." Cam unconsciously rubbed his right temple.

Sorcha paused. "Well, you were pissing me off."

"I was given the disgusting job, by you if I recall correctly, of scraping the chewing gum off the bottoms of the seats."

"Eew!" I shuddered, listening and folding damp clothes. "Manky chewed gum under the seats of an old school bus."

"Did you not like chewing gum?" Cam asked, surprised.

"It was banned from my house. Mum detested it. Said it was cheap and made us look like cows chewing the cud. So, of course, Kat and I took every opportunity to buy it and chew it without her knowing. But I guess I grew out of it. Of all the things I have missed in the last twenty years, I can honestly say gum is not one of them."

"We were allowed it," Sorcha said with a twinkle in her eye as she stuffed jackets in a backpack. "Do you remember bubble gum?"

"I remember *you* getting it stuck in your hair," Cam shot back as he carried our bags from our room. "And Mum spending hours trying to get it out, threatening to cut it off if you ever got it in your hair ever again."

"I think that might have been the last time I chewed gum," said Sorcha thoughtfully.

"Did you always have long hair?" I asked curiously. Sorcha's long red plait had remained at waist length in all the years I had known her. But hairdressers weren't common, and we tended to cut our own, so simple styles were easiest.

"Not as long as now. But shoulder length. I've had so many hairstyles over the years. With a fringe, without. Layered. Now I am just lazy and keep it long so I can tie it back."

"So, when you got gum stuck in your hair, was that before or after cleaning the bus?" I asked, intrigued, zipping up the bag I had stuffed full of clothes.

"Before. Why do you think I made him do it?"

"As much as I am sure you two are enjoying this trip down memory lane," Gerry said softly, "perhaps we could return to the urgent matter at hand? I don't fancy being pursued with twenty-odd screaming children."

"Agreed," I said to Gerry, and picked up the over-stuffed backpack. "Your idea of a bus is a fabulous idea," I said to Sorcha, adjusting the pack and assessing how many bags I could carry the few kilometers to the cars. "They are enclosed, waterproof, and we can keep the kids together. One door in and out, so we can keep them safe, too."

"I can do one better than a commercial bus," Illy piped up from the kitchen as she loaded bags of fresh fruit and vegetables. "There are military buses. We used them to transport large groups of recruits. Large modern ones, well… twenty years ago they were modern and well maintained. Like touring buses, they had a toilet in them. It means we can keep them safe, even at night."

I knew the type she meant. My school had owned one. "Do you know where we can get one or two?"

"I do."

"Can you drive one?"

"No, but I would give it a red hot go. It isn't like there is any traffic anymore. How hard can it be?"

"I can drive a bus." Gerry's calm Welsh voice carried over the table, and we turned to look at him. "I was a drummer for the South Wales Police Marching Band. We had a bus to get to events."

"That would be very useful."

"Especially as Illy likely can't reach the pedals," Sorcha finished.

Laden like pack donkeys, Cam and I hastened along the main road between the two parts of the Kiewa settlement, sticking to the verge so we could duck into the foliage if anyone came past. Thank goodness the party was being held at the township farthest away from where we had left the vehicles. With any luck, they wouldn't hear us. We could hear the hum of chattering, laughter, and music filling the evening air as we moved along the road, the sun casting shadows along the route.

"Why do you think Sophie targeted me?" Cam's voice was barely audible over his footsteps plodding away in the dirt.

"Who knows what a spoiled, entitled brat thinks? Maybe she really wanted you."

"I would have thought you would understand the psychology of a spoiled teenage girl better than most." Despite the tenseness of our flight, I appreciated the attempt at humor.

"Spoiled, yes, but I was never homicidal."

"Oh, I don't know. You tried to drown me that first night."

I nudged him with my shoulder, unable to touch him with our arms filled with bags. That night, our first night together, was a lifetime ago, and yet somehow, just yesterday.

"Likely it was just a way to get close to the girls." I didn't actually believe it but tried to make light of the situation.

"Maybe." We both knew the truth. There wasn't a more satisfactory answer to this problem. Either Sophie wanted a much older married man for an illicit relationship, or she was trying to get close to him to murder his wife or child. Neither was a more attractive prospect.

"Goodness, I hope they can get those girls out quietly," I said, my mind still on Caitlin and her injuries as we headed toward the dome opening. Both the physical and emotional ones. We had left Sorcha, Illy, Gerry, and Di to round up the children, packing anything urgent and making a detour via Puckapunyal army base where they would spend the night, and the best part of the next day, sourcing more supplies, suitable for bedding and feeding us all for the medium term. Everything replaceable we would leave behind, partly as we could source more, but mainly as the residents may not immediately realize we had left if we left bedding scattered around.

We had taken the keys to my father's vehicles but agreed that we would take the original one with the new battery Tadhg had rigged in Melbourne as that one needed to be hot-wired. Cam knew how, but we also had the most time. The last thing we wanted was for someone to pursue the others and get caught trying to start a car. There were four vehicles parked outside, Sorcha and Di in one, Illy driving the Unimog, and Gerry driving the others, splitting the children between them. It wasn't like we were going to be arrested for overloading a vehicle.

"How will we get the buses in place?" I asked as Cam slid back the access panel, and I stepped through the opening. "Leave it open. It will be easier for them with the kids. It isn't going to rain."

"Illy says the Mog can tow them. We don't even need to start them."

"I meant, actually through the dome itself. The openings here aren't large enough."

"Dad's dome wasn't quite as high-tech as the ones here." Cam grinned as he dropped his bags on the far side and fossicked around in his pockets for the keys. "Dad used industrial strength tarpaulins over a thin metal frame. They will have lasted in most places. It was a clear domestic one that had split. He must have run out of stronger ones. It is a very protected piece of land in a gully."

Cam pushed his way through the dead forest to the hidden vehicles and started Dad's Cayenne, shining the headlights on low toward the other cars, illuminating the scene. As I loaded the bags, I heard him hot-wiring ours, letting it idle as he started the second, then the remaining two, moving them into the clearing, checking the fuel level, and leaving them running. The Unimog worried me, the loud rumbling noise of the engine piercing the still air.

"How on earth do you know how to hot-wire a car?" I asked, amazed. "Misspent criminal youth that you neglected to mention?"

"Not exactly. Dad taught me when we used to go camping, just in case we ever lost the keys or if we were ever in an accident in a remote area. With no phone service, we may need to start any car, so it was a useful skill."

Cam reversed the last car into the dusty space outside the dome, slowly pulled it down the road, and parked it in front of the others.

"What other useful skills did he teach you?" I asked as he got out and started loading bags.

"How to break into a house. You have no idea how many times paramedics or water fairies need to do that. Nanna fallen and broken her hip. Could reach a phone or medic-alert button but doors locked. They had ways of getting in."

"Water fairies?"

Cam snorted. "What ambos called firefighters. They were often based in the same building or went to jobs together, and there was a great camaraderie between the services. Dad was friends with many of them. Always loved it when they were called to jobs as they turned up in big trucks and en masse. Do you want to drive? Your hand is better."

"No, you can," I responded, thinking back to what he and Sorcha had said.

"If it was only a small section of their dome that was damaged, why..." I couldn't think of the words to ask why his parents hadn't survived. Why he suddenly thought it was safe for all of us. Fortunately, he knew what I was asking.

"Mum passed first. I think, or rather, I am fairly sure, she ate something that was contaminated without knowing it. Dad took his own life, not wanting to be without her. He still had the tablets beside him. But when I left, there was only one damaged tarp, and it was a small patch of dead vegetation compared to the entire block, much of which was planted out. I am hoping it was just bad luck that Mum ate something from the infected part."

I clicked my seat belt as we moved down the road, the car bouncing roughshod over ruts and potholes. "Wow. You never told me about your father. I always assumed that you found them both dead. Well, you did," I corrected myself. "But I assumed the protozoa had taken them both. He must have loved her."

"He did. He also would have been all alone. It wasn't an option, I guess."

I paused, wondering what I would do in that situation. Alone in the world, grieving. Knowing my children were out there, but no idea where and how to get to them. Would I do the same?

CHAPTER 27

"**YOUR PARENTS BROUGHT CASSETTES** out here?" I lifted the dusty tapes from one side of the book-case. Turning them over, I could just make out the handwritten scrawl in smudged blue pen, the writer struggling to keep on the lines beneath the brittle and yellowing plastic case. The sun was setting, and we had rushed to get the cabin set up before we couldn't see at all.

Cam peered over my shoulder. "Bloody Mum. Those are my mixed tapes."

"Mixed tapes?" I smirked, trying not to sound mocking.

His arms came around me as he whispered, "I would have made you one."

"You dork. You made mixed tapes?"

"Of course. Every Saturday night, I would listen to Take 40 Australia and record the songs I loved. I used to run to the loo or to get a drink when a crappy song came on and cursed Mum if she called me to put laundry away or something that took me away from the radio. Sorcha did too and all the kids at school. We used to talk about it on Monday. Didn't you?"

"Not really. I mean, we talked about popular music, what was on the charts. But we just bought the songs we liked. Besides, we went out most Saturday nights. If we were at a private party, sometimes it was on the radio, though."

"Rich bitch."

"Dorkus," I shot back with a kiss and reached for the old cassette player stashed on top of the bookcase, plugging it in. "The 90s called and want their music back. We'll need to get the generator running if you are going to serenade me with songs from your awkward teen phase."

"You'd love it."

"Guns and Roses?" I read from the cassette in my hand, my eyebrows hitting my hairline.

"Sorcha said she would liberate some algae from Kiewa to kick start us when she comes," Cam spoke, ignoring my taunts as he moved our bags out of the way and shook the dust off the quilt cover. "The photobioreactors worked better on Kiewa, although they had biogas too. More daylight, I guess. Mum and Dad just ran a diesel generator and solar panels, so that will need to do until they get set up."

"Wham? Duran Duran? *Cyndi Lauper*!" I squealed.

"Okay, those are Sorcha's."

I scrutinized the handwriting. The neat, tight cursive script. It was undoubtedly a teenage girl's handwriting. "I can't tell you how much fun I am going to have with this!"

"Careful—she doesn't cope well with being teased."

"I know, but this is far too good an opportunity to pass up... *Richard Marx*!"

Cam disappeared to start the generator as I poked around the room, banging dust off the pillows and using a cloth to wipe over the tables and benches. As I worked, I carried the many photos scattered around the room to the window and looked closely. Every one was a photo of them as a family, a much younger Sorcha and Cam fake smiling for the photographer. Sorcha was unmistakable, her copper-red hair falling to her shoulders, wispy fringe framing her glaring green eyes. Cam was softer looking, more babyish in the face. The same dark hair and blue eyes, but gentler looking. The years and outdoor labor had chiseled his features, made him more handsome.

I jumped, dropping the photo I was holding as the gravelly tones of Tom Cochrane filled the room, with the opening bars of "Life is a Highway." A single lamp flicked on, casting a warm glow around the room.

Cam stood at the open door, watching me as I picked up the photo and replaced it on the bookcase. He held out his hand to me.

"Seriously?"

"Come on. No one can see us."

Reliving our teen years, we danced wildly to Cam's rock classics and some of Sorcha's in the dimly lit room. Van Halen, Hunters and Collectors, INXS, Cam spinning me until my hair flew, laughing hysterically until we flopped on the bed, exhausted.

"They would be so happy to know we were here," he spoke in my ear. "It is the closest my parents came to meeting you. I don't have many regrets, but I do regret that they never met you or the kids."

"I need to tell you something."

"You can tell me anything. You know that."

I sighed. "I should have told you weeks ago." Cam looked at me, listening. I curled away from him, facing the darkness outside the window. "Illy says I have post-traumatic stress disorder."

Cam paused for a moment before responding. "Is that why you cry out in your sleep?" he asked gently, stroking my hair away from my temple. "Memories? Nightmares?"

"It is more than that. Since I returned to Clava and needed to work in the operating theater where they performed my surgeries, I have panic attacks. I hear a door slam off in the distance and feel trapped. Once, the scent of the anesthesia when I worked on a patient gave me flashbacks of losing consciousness. The clang of metal reminds me of the feeling of restraints against the bed rails. I fall into a dark hole, my heart races, my chest tightens, and I lose control. I feel detached from people and places. Sometimes I need to run, to get away and stay safe. Others, I just want to hide in a corner and hope no one notices me."

"Oh, honey. I wish you had told me. Lots of emergency services workers had PTSD after the things they had seen, including my father. Often it wasn't one job but the culmination of many cases they had seen over the years. This is nothing to be ashamed of."

"I couldn't admit it to myself. I want it to go away, but the attacks are becoming more unpredictable."

"How long does it take for you to recover?"

"Sometimes it doesn't take long, and I can force myself to focus and get through. Other times it completely consumes me, and I lose hours. Illy says I am feeling devoid of emotion, and this is why I push you away."

"Is it?"

"Probably. When I came home, I was so angry. With you, with everyone. But I didn't know why. I would have sworn it was your accusations or the photos, and I admit, they still haunt me. But Illy is right. When I returned, I couldn't feel anything for you or the kids, and the anger was partly frustration at being numb. It was like a brick wall had been built around me, insulating me. To let you in meant breaking down the wall that kept me safe. Being angry at you and keeping you at arm's length was easier than admitting I felt cold."

His arms tightened around me. "I felt like that, after Inverness. But you were there, and we moved on together. I am so sorry I wasn't there for you."

"It wasn't your fault. I blocked you out. You didn't know."

"I should have seen it. You were cold, even to the kids. You were just going through the motions. It was like you went to Clava, but someone else came home inhabiting your body. It looked and sounded like you, but it wasn't the woman I loved."

"I'm so sorry."

"Don't apologize. After everything you have been through, it was expected that the trauma would impact you at some point. I kept waiting for you to drop your bundle, but you didn't."

"I came close so many times. I tried so hard to hold it together. Illy was pregnant, grieving for Luca. She needed me. Then we had Caitlin. I put one foot in front of the other and focused on the next step. It wasn't until I started my training that I couldn't hold it together anymore. I thought it was the stress, the pressure they put on me."

"That probably didn't help."

"It was extreme, and I was exhausted on a level I can't even describe. Fatigued beyond physical tiredness. But it was more than that. I felt so helpless, out of control. I needed to be successful in my placement. People were counting on me. So I blocked out everything and just focused on the learning. Finish that, and I could go home."

"At the detriment of your wellbeing? Everyone would understand placing your mental health first."

"I never wanted you to see me as weak."

"I could never see you that way. No one who has ever met you sees you that way. Even after everything that you went through, you are still the strongest person I know. This isn't you. It isn't who you are. This is a natural response to something that happened to you. I have struggled with anxiety my entire life. It doesn't define me. You know we will work through this, together. I will always be here, no matter how awful you are to me."

I squirmed uncomfortably, and he gripped me tighter. "I will never leave you. Know that. You are mine, and I am yours. No matter what happens, I will always be here. Do you remember when you described us as two halves of the same whole? We are a team, Frey. I love you more than I can put into words. You let me know what you need, and I will give you that. Space. Time. Love. Just listening. Anything you need. Tell me what you want. It is yours."

"Can I have all of it?" I whispered.

As the dawn light pierced the cabin, we knew what we needed to do. Following Cam out the front, he handed me a shovel, and solemnly we dug in the rich red earth. After burying Cam's father alongside his mother, we set about cleaning out the dead plants, clearly demarcating the lines and allowing several meters of clearance. Cam was right. There were only two tears in the makeshift dome fabric, and both could be easily replaced. There was one other torn section, but it was at the far edge, close to the ground, and the dead earth surrounding it wasn't an area they had used to grow crops. In the meantime, when we could recover them, we would use the moss samples to rehabilitate the infected earth.

We worked in silence, both of us replaying memories of our parents. I found a notepad and pencil, shook off the dust, and started to take stock of what food we had while Cam went to investigate the outer buildings, sheds, and greenhouses. There were cases of canned foods stacked neatly under the veranda and many more in the various sheds and outbuildings. Counting carefully, I noted the quantities of baked beans, canned lentils, chickpeas, and the enormous variety of canned and jar foods, checking them carefully for spoilage. Yelling broke through my concentration, making my heart lurch, and I dropped the notepad and bolted, wondering what I would find this time. After Caitlin's attempted drowning only yesterday, then leaving her with Sorcha, I was still a little jumpy.

"Where are you?" I called frantically.

"In here." Cam's head popped out of a largish greenhouse toward the end of the row of outbuildings and disappeared.

What now? I ran, panicked, recalling the last time I had seen Cam in a greenhouse.

As soon as I entered, I realized that this was like no greenhouse I had ever seen. Despite the transparent plastic walls and ceiling, rectangular tanks ran the length of the building in four distinct rows. Although the tanks sat on the floor, the vegetation growing on top of the tanks at chest height was crammed in, plants bursting from every available centimeter of dirt.

"Aquaponics!" Cam breathed from where he stood beside the nearest tank. "Can you believe it! The fish are alive. The plants are alive! After all these years."

"You mean like what Kai raised on August?" We didn't have aquaponics on Lewis. Partly as we had vast lochs and streams with fresh fish, mainly as it was considered too cold, but I remembered the set-up clearly enough.

Cam slid one tray aside, and from the murky green water, lifted an enormous trout to show me. I stepped closer to look. He was healthy, of a good size, with crystal clear eyes and no visible diseases. Cam let the wriggling fish slip back into the water. Standing beside him, we could see the fish were packed in hard with barely enough room to move.

"We might have fish for dinner," I said, amazed, watching them wriggle past each other.

"They have been breeding in here all these years. I didn't even know my father knew anything about aquaponics. I had a uni textbook I was always bugging him to read..."

"Well, he must have made the time." I slipped an arm around his waist. "This is wonderful. I was wondering how we were going to ensure the children got enough protein to keep them well. A vegetarian diet is fine when food is plentiful. But for growing children who need protein to build muscle, I was worried. But now … this is wonderful."

"My father's fish," Cam breathed. "Or perhaps, ancestors of his original fish. I'm not sure how long they live. Do you know?"

"Around five years, I think. Did you not come here last time?"

"No. Sorcha and I walked up the driveway. We could see all the living trees and that one dead patch, so we called them, thinking they were alive. I went into the cottage, which, as you saw, was empty. It was dusty even then, so we knew something was wrong. Sorcha followed me in. When we realized they weren't there, I headed around the back when I heard her screaming. Once we saw my father, and Mum's grave, we left. We didn't look any further."

I nodded. They were only looking to see what had happened to their parents. Like me, only my visit was many years later. But we both had closure.

"I'm going to need to thin the crops. But this is a wonderful head start. So much salad and a wonderful array of vegetables." Tomatoes were growing everywhere, even in the dirt floor where overripe tomatoes had fallen and sprouted.

"We are going to be okay." He turned to look at me, relief softening his features.

"You didn't believe it? It was your suggestion."

"I admit, I was concerned. It has been fifteen years. What if the dome was gone and everything dead? But now, even if the trees were dead, we have enough food to feed us for weeks supplemented with all the canned food they have. Plus, what Illy will bring back. We really will be okay."

Cam lifted me and swung me around with some difficulty given the tanks and limited space between them.

"Rather than thinning them, should you just build more tanks and relocate some of the fish?" I asked. "You can propagate seedlings from here and replant them so..."

"Listen to you, Miss Agriculture! I always thought you were ignoring me when I talked about projects."

"Sometimes," I admitted. "Not always. But there are far more of us, so we need to plan. How will we ensure that the contaminated area doesn't spread?"

"The protozoa are possibly dead now with no water to spread it. I just don't know how to test for it."

"Shame Ashton isn't here. I am fairly sure they have a simple test kit for their re-greening areas. He told me they can test that the protozoa are no longer active and how much moss it takes to reverse the process."

"You want him here?" Cam's eyes widened.

"Not on your life." Illy and I hadn't discussed her relationship any more than that one day. I loved her, wanted her to be happy. But I couldn't see him with her. "We see him every year at their birthdays, and without his help, we would likely have starved to death in the middle of the ocean, but is it wrong to admit that I still don't trust him?"

"I would worry if you did. I can't fathom how Illy does."

"Emotion clouding her judgment? She is also terribly lonely. Luca has been gone for seven years. That is a very long time to be alone."

"But why him?"

"Who else is there? There are very few single men on Lewis. I tried to set her up with Aidan, but she told me she would likely kill him within a month."

"Would she ever! She would eat him alive. Besides, Aidan is a lifelong bachelor." The dark look on Cam's face proved his mind had gone to the same place as mine. "Well, we can rule out Stefan, can't we? Older teens, the Firstborns. Not to mention poison. Clearly a woman's choice of murder weapon."

"It is looking likely," I admitted, somewhat relieved. "I have been worrying about Kat being in such proximity to him at work. At least if we know it is a younger person, and likely a girl, that narrows the field a bit."

"Of all our children, she is the one I worry about the least. From the day she was born, our Miss Kat was no victim."

"Do you need to finish up here?"

"No, I was just poking around to see what tools Dad had left. But when I saw this, I needed to show you. Di will be thrilled. What were you up to?"

"I've nearly finished taking stock of long-life food on the verandah. I was just heading to the sheds, but I could use a hand. I need to move the stacks to see what is there and get all this done before they arrive with the kids. We will be too busy setting up sleeping areas, orienting children, and working out how on earth we are going to feed them all."

"Give me five, and I will meet you there."

"I wish I had met them," I said, making Cam look up at me as he stacked crates of canned food. "But being here, being close to all their things, makes me feel a little closer. Is that silly?"

"Not at all. I got a better feeling for you when we visited your family home. Mansion, I should say. No normal family lived in a house like that."

I wanted to argue, but it was true. I had been fortunate. But in the end, it hadn't saved them. "What did you do with the albums?" I asked.

"I slipped them under the bed. Isn't that where memories belong? Close to us when we dream?"

I smiled, then frowned as a memory struck. "Who do you think it was? On Lewis. Who damaged my photos?"

"Oh honey, you know I am not great at reading people. Truthfully, I have no idea." I nodded, unsure if that was a good thing or not.

The sound of a vehicle in the distance made us both sit up, alert. They were here.

The fortnight that followed was manic, setting up a permanent camp for so many people in a comparatively compact space where growing food was of paramount importance. Illy and Gerry were sent to source as much as possible, initially towing back three buses to use as bedrooms. Sam, Kendra, Ruby, and Scarlett set to work removing the seats, lining them with foil insulation and timber panels sourced from a hard-ware store. Illy and Gerry made daily trips to and from warehouses, sourcing dome panels to replace the few damaged ones, which Gerry had begun to install. Over time, we planned to replace all of them and ensure that this place was as safe as Kiewa or any other domed community, but right now, he was needed to help build new tanks, new garden beds and help establish more food crops. Cam's parents had set this place up for two, not thirty people. While Cam and I were sourcing bottled water to empty and fill the tanks, Illy made a trip back to the *Damara* to collect the moss samples, and Cam and Di set about using them, rehabilitating the area that had been infected.

As our community took shape, our minds turned to our security once more.

"We need to get back to Melbourne to check in on Tadhg. Find out what he has learned. But there is a chance it will involve investigating what he has learned. I can't see Tadhg saying, 'So, I found out nothing.'"

I glanced at Illy. "You were there only a week or so ago. Why didn't you stop in then?"

"Mainly as I was in a rush to get back. But also because I knew it wouldn't be a quick trip, and if I learned anything, it would derail the establishment of our little settlement here. Keeping the girls safe was more important at that point than finding out who is behind it."

"It is time," I said firmly. "I'm not adding any value, and I can't sleep easy knowing that someone is out there gunning for us. The players will all know that we are in Australia now. They must be looking for us."

"I'll come with you, Frey," Illy said firmly. "We need to leave the others here. Sorcha for her medical skill. Di and Cam to continue planting. Gerry to protect the children. Goodness knows how long we will need to live here. You and I can do this."

Cam slammed his hand on the table. "No. Remember what happened the last time you two had a girls-only adventure? You barely escaped. I can't go through that again. You were gone for months. I can't."

"You need to, Campbell," Sorcha reassured him in a gentle tone, unlike her. "Illy is right. If Tadhg has found out something, they need to investigate. They are highly capable women, both of them. What happened last time was a freak event. There is next to no chance anything like that will happen again. We need you here, and we are heading into fall. We have thirty people to feed and a mostly vegetarian diet aside from those fish. You need to get a move on and need Diana's help to grow at maximum efficiency. Now that Illy has found the warehouse, we need Gerry to replace all the panels to ensure the dome's integrity for the long term. These tarps are twenty years old. It is the only way."

Cam clamped his mouth closed. He wasn't happy. My revelation about my mental health was foremost in his mind, but he realized this might be the only option with the resources we had.

"Tomorrow?" Illy looked at me, her blue eyes guarded.

I nodded. "In the morning. We can take one of the cars. But I feel bad about taking one. They would struggle to move all the girls quickly in a pinch. Maybe you should teach Gerry to drive the Unimog?"

"It is too big and uses too much fuel. What we need is a people mover. A four-wheel-drive one. A Landcruiser troop carrier, or something similar," Sorcha surmised. "Capable of driving off-road, any of us can drive it, and we can fit all the children in together in a pinch. The buses are here now and not exactly versatile if we needed to escape."

"Well, we can't exactly just log onto car sales and buy one. Don't forget we are in the middle of nowhere," Cam added. "Did the army base have anything smaller but large enough to carry all the kids?"

"Not that I saw," Illy thought aloud. "I can go back and check..."

"Hey, didn't your girlfriend Natalie's parents have one? They lived in Mansfield, didn't they? That isn't far. Hour round trip, tops." Sorcha's eyes twinkled with mischief.

"They lived just outside of Mansfield, and yes, they had one. But that was twenty years ago, Sorcs. While that thing was bulletproof and easy to work on mechanically, there is absolutely no guarantee it is still there and that we could even start it."

"Girlfriend?" My eyebrows raised.

"Oh yes," Sorcha taunted, enjoying making Cam squirm, and I suspected me too, in retribution for teasing her over her teenage music choices. "Cam's long-term girlfriend before he left Australia. They used to go away for dirty weekends in her parents' troopie."

"Camping," he spat.

"Same, same." Sorcha smiled sweetly. "I think you should go and look. Take someone with you. It would make it easier to have one solid four-wheel-drive capable of transporting most of the kids."

"Fine. Who's coming with me?"

"I'll come," I growled. "You can tell me about this girlfriend I have never heard mentioned before."

"We broke up!" he protested. "Months before I came to August. There was nothing to tell."

"Then why haven't you mentioned her before?"

"Because she was a psycho!" Sorcha sang over my shoulder, making me look back.

I turned back to Cam, my mouth open, awaiting a response.

"She wasn't psycho," he muttered. "Maybe just a little clingy."

"Oh, come on. She was more clingy than super glue stuck to velcro." Sorcha turned to me, gloating. "Cam broke it off because she desperately wanted him to propose. Thank goodness he came to his senses. Took him long enough, like several years too long. Mum was dreading them having kids and passing on her nuttiness gene. Nutty Natalie, she used to call her."

My eyebrows raised even higher.

"There was nothing to tell. I was single when I left Melbourne."

My silence indicated that I was not satisfied with that as a response.

Cam's face reddened, aware that we had an audience. "We were together for a few years. I wasn't ready. She pushed. I said no. We were still at uni. I was living at home, she was in a share house, and I was in no way ready to be married. So we broke up."

"When was this?"

"Three months before he left for August," Sorcha piped up. "The psycho called quite a few times after you had left, looking for you. Wanting to catch up. Rec-con-cile," she purred.

Cam glared at her. "Bloody hell, some days I regret coming and getting you from Kiewa."

"When she called for the third time, I can't tell you how much I enjoyed telling her you had moved on. I may have implied that you found the right woman and were blissfully happy. You should have heard her lose her shit before she slammed the phone down on me!" Sorcha cackled, then added a touch more softly. "What I didn't know at the time was that I was telling the truth."

"You are such a bitch."

"And you love me. Now, as much as chatting about Nutty Natalie reminds me of how super pleased I am that Freyja is normal, can we get back to the problem at hand? If Freyja and Illyria are heading off to goodness knows where, then we need a more capable vehicle in case we need to mobilize quickly."

Cam returned his attention to me. "Are you sure you don't want me to come?"

"I am not ready to be separated again, potentially for months. But Sorcha is right. They need your expertise with the crops and aquaculture if we are to survive here for any length of time. The girls need as much protection as possible, especially now that we know there are people in all communities who consider them a trophy, and Sophie and Sanjiv will let them know we are in Australia. There is also the medical risk to you we need to consider."

"Medical risk?"

"You have no spleen, remember? We knew Kiewa was likely safe. Di knew that no one there had been outside for nearly twenty years, and Sorcha says they were all healthy to begin with, so the chances of you being infected with a virus or bacteria was minimal.

But we don't know what we could be exposed to elsewhere. When I was on Clava, I learned that other countries were not quite so vigilant with their medical screening. In some places, it was socio-economic status, social standing, position, or even appearance that saw candidates chosen. So we can't take the risk that you will get a bacterial infection, and we can't treat you."

"I'll be fine. I've not been sick in seven years."

"And likely you will continue to be fine. But will I run that risk? No. I won't take any risks with my family."

"But you are quite happy to place yourself in harm's way?"

"Do I have a choice? These are my daughters they are targeting. Me."

"Caitlin is my daughter. You could let Gerry and Illy go. They are better equipped."

"I'll go," Gerry spoke in his low Welsh cadence behind me. "I'll see them safe, Campbell, though your lovely wife here can teach me a thing or two. She is a highly competent woman, and I have seen her in action. I'll teach Sam how to replace the panels before I go. He is quite good with tools."

Cam didn't relax hearing this but sighed, acknowledging he had been defeated.

"Come on," Sorcha announced, a fraction louder than required. "Let's give them some privacy if they are about to be separated. But you need to get going if you are going to find that vehicle and return before dark."

CHAPTER 28

WE DROVE THROUGH COUNTRY lanes, frequently stopping to move fallen trees, fences, or other obstacles. Slowing, Cam pulled the Cayenne into a driveway still marked with an old milk churn mailbox but braked unexpectedly.

"What?" I asked, peering out the windscreens. There were no obstructions.

He turned to face me. "Before I left Lewis, I ran into Toby."

I crinkled my nose. "Which one?"

"The jeweler. Well, the plumber, but you know he makes jewelry in his spare time."

"I did, not that I have seen much of it. It isn't like there is a great need for jewelry here. I was never really a bling kind of girl, even before I left home."

I held my breath as Cam unfurled his fingers, revealing a blue gemstone set in a simple silver pendant. "Is that?"

"It is. Would you like it?"

Cam had told me the story of Lae and the necklace. Her mother's and this one. I hadn't thought of that in years. "How did Toby come to have it?" I asked as it glowed in the afternoon light streaming through the windscreen.

"After Lae was taken, I couldn't look at it. So I gave it to Fraser. Fraser gave it to Toby and told him the story. He held onto it. Just in case."

"I'm not sure it is appropriate to give it to me. I mean, didn't you say this was what you fought over that day?"

"It is. But we would have argued, regardless. You had returned, and Di was here. She was jealous of you both, catching up and spending time together. She felt left out. I know that now. It wasn't about an inanimate object, no matter that it brought up terrible memories for her. Ultimately, she was fearful that I would leave her for you."

"But you ended up with me."

"I didn't *leave* her for you. She was already gone."

"I know that, but… Cam, I can't. It was never mine. It was hers. I realize it is a little odd, but why don't you give it to Louis? Perhaps without the end part of the story, but that it was a gift for his mother?"

"Are you sure?"

"I am. One day soon, he will meet someone special, and it can be for her. Our daughter-in-law."

"Don't! We have a seven-year-old! I am not ready to be a grandparent!" He paused. "What about you, then? I never gave you a wedding ring."

"Most people don't have them. We have been together for the best part of twenty years. It has never been important before. Why now?"

"I brought it with me as I wanted you to have something. Something you wear, to remember me when we are apart. It feels even more important now after what you told me. I want you always to know how much I love you. Remember what Luca said about his Mum giving him the watch?"

I smiled, recalling the story. "I do." A thought occurred to me. "We weren't together when we left for this trip. Why did you bring the gemstone?"

Cam smirked. "You don't think I would travel all the way to Australia, by sea, and not break down your defenses?"

"Cocky little bastard, aren't you!"

"Maybe. Once I knew we were leaving Lewis, again, I figured I had the time to give it one more shot. After all, you did it once. In Edinburgh. What I didn't count on was that my pain in the ass sister would bring that reconciliation to a head quite a bit faster than I expected."

"I am thankful to her for that," I admitted. "I wasn't at the time, but I suspect she knew better than I did."

"The way she tells it, Illy played a key role."

"Oh, the whole manipulative scenario reeks of Illy, too. Both of them. Goodness, can you imagine those two in leadership roles together? They would beat everyone else into submission within a week."

"A week? I think you underestimate my sister! Anyway, that wasn't the point. I just... well..."

His face flushed. I sucked my breath in as he fished the small dark blue box from his pocket and snapped it open, displaying the contents.

I gasped at the glistening brown jewel encased in a rose gold band nestled into the white velvet. "What is it?"

Cam pulled it out of its white pillow and took my hand. "It is an argyle diamond. A champagne diamond, it is called. They were mined in Western Australia, which is where I picked it up, incidentally. I want you to have something, from me. Something Australian. A symbol, I guess." Cam started to stammer.

"It is beautiful," I breathed, genuinely awed by the sparking ring now adorning my left hand. "I love it. Truly."

Holding my ring up to the window, I was mesmerized by how it sparkled in the light. "Why now?" I turned back to him.

"We will have been together twenty years soon. I was holding onto it for our anniversary, but now that you are leaving me... I thought... Well, I want to give it to you now. Especially after what you told me. I want you always to see how much I love you."

"Our anniversary?"

"You don't think that is worthy of remembering?"

"Yes, but we weren't together all of those years."

"But we should have been, and I intend to make all those missing years up to you. If I had kissed you once a day, and we missed four years, how many kisses do I owe you?"

"Well, we missed closer to five," I hummed in his ear, suddenly overcome with emotion. "I didn't know you for the first year we were on August."

"Hmm, somewhere in the vicinity of two thousand missed opportunities?"

"Better get started then."

CHAPTER 29

ILLY SOUNDED THE HORN as we pulled into the government facility in Melbourne. After I was processed here, I had returned once with Angus and Luca, when we found the list that had seen Cam reunite with his sister. Unfortunately, these buildings had fared no better than the homes near my parent's house. Filthy windows, gutters falling, and roofs sagging. Tadhg and Ashton came rushing out of a building ahead of us, looking crumpled and apprehensive. As we exited the car, Tadhg's shoulders slumped, and he returned the gun to the back of his jeans.

"You always loved to make a grand entrance." Ashton leaned into Illy for a kiss, barely recognizable with uncharacteristically scruffy hair and an unkempt beard. Unable to watch, I turned to ask Tadhg, "How did you go?"

"You have amazing timing. It took us forever to get the generator started, and then we spent weeks listening to radio transmissions. But we found what we were looking for. We were just downloading data and were planning to head off to find you in the next day or two. Can you come inside for a bit while we finish up? We only have a few more hours of work, assuming the power remains stable. It can be a bit sporadic on generator power, but I rigged some solar panels to boost it."

Carl offered to make us tea while Tadhg buzzed around attaching and detaching portable hard drives to servers. Gerry and I followed Tadhg, not wanting to bear witness to Illy and Carl's reunion. The roar of the generator was deafening, making conversation impossible, and I was pleased to return to the staff room that they had set up as a living space. Making some noise as we advanced down the corridor, I was relieved to see them sitting on the couch, drinking tea, although Illy was slightly flushed.

Gerry, Tadhg, and I settled in on the opposite couch, and as Carl poured us tea, Illy gave a quick summary of what had happened on Kiewa. I saw Tadhg's face blanch.

"It is fine," I said, placing a hand on his arm as he bristled. "Fairlie is fine and all the others. It was only Cait that the boy attacked. We left within hours; they are all safe. Though, the second Player tried the same night."

"Thank goodness Freyja stopped that," Illy said, explaining about the cupcakes.

"Jesus, Mary, and Joseph," Tadhg muttered. "I thought they would be safe here."

"So did we. Did you learn anything?" Illy asked. "We learned from Sanjiv that it was someone named D behind it all. But he refused to tell us much more. I'm not sure he knew anything else."

"And you know him," Carl said bluntly. "Dale. After he assaulted you, we expelled him from Clava. We watched him for a while but then lost track of him. After all, it has been years. Goodness knows how or why, but he turned up in one of the isolated communities in India. There was a split in the community there, and he joined the more conservative religious faction. It appears he told them about you, your sister, and the plans to recolonize the world with genetically modified children. Superior children. Of course, they were outraged that their children were not selected, and he fueled it."

"Is this religion versus science?" I asked. "The Biblical references, I mean."

It was Tadhg who answered. "This is not about religion at all. Where there are groups of people, unhappy people, there will always be elitism. People who want more or who are envious of those who do. People will always cling to an ideal."

"Killing children? How could anyone who believed in any God condone that?" Gerry asked.

"I'm not justifying it in any way. But if you were a believer in true equality, then you would consider these children as abominations. They were selected eggs, genetically modified, and grown in surrogates. Nothing about their conception or gestation was natural. We see them for the children they are, but they are unique. They are special. But it was a manufactured kind of special. Does that make them evil? Of course not. But they are different, and that makes them a target." We all stared at Ashton and his cold, scientific analysis.

"They are just little girls." Tadhg was more emotional than I had ever seen him. I placed an arm around his shoulder. He was tense.

"It would be easy to think that, but it isn't quite that straightforward," Ashton said, looking directly at me. "Dale has convinced them that your children, and Katrin's, are an abomination. A scientific creation. Freak is the word they used. When he took over the radio transmissions from India, he encouraged the eldest in each community to believe that only the strongest were chosen, and only the elite will survive under the geodesic domes. These children threaten their role."

"My children are not freaks," I growled. "They aren't here to threaten anyone."

"This is revenge," Illy interjected. "Classic revenge."

"But these are children he is killing!" I protested.

"I don't think it has anything to do with the children. It has everything to do with getting back at you and me. He was expelled and estranged and has wandered looking for a new place to settle. You were the one who screamed, drew attention. He likely bears a grudge. What better way to get back at you than to pick off your children, one at a time?"

Illy was right. This was about her, and me. "What do we do?"

"I've always wanted to visit India."

CHAPTER 30

AS WE NEARED THE dock at Port Melbourne, a familiar vessel was mooring. My mouth dropped. "Is that..."

"It is."

From the sparkling white deck of the *Eurydice*, Isla waved madly, sunlight catching the auburn highlights in her long black hair. A stocky man stood behind her.

"Who is that?" Illy asked and then gasped as he drifted into view. "It's Jake!"

Isla squealed as she staggered along the pier, struggling to get her land legs after so long at sea. Isla knocked me flying, and we both landed on the deck with a thud.

"Oomph!" I exclaimed as the wind was knocked out of me.

"Who is with you?" Tadhg asked as he gave us both a hand up.

"Just us," Isla twinkled. "Though if I had known how well I would sleep in a bed, alone, with just the gentle rocking of the waves, I would have run away years ago!"

"Fraser let you come alone?" I asked incredulously. Fraser was a darling, but so besotted with Isla that he didn't even like another man speaking to her, let alone let her travel across the world with one other man.

"I didn't give him a choice," she twinkled, knowing my question. "Besides, it is Jake. He rescued me from Mousa, and we see him annually at the kid's party, so he has some deposits in the emotional bank account. Besides, with all of you gone, people left to look after the children were in short supply."

"Wow. And you are okay traveling by boat?"

Isla growled, deep and low in the back of her throat. "I can't swim, Freyja, but I'm not about to lose my mind over it. Besides, this was for all of us, not just me."

"How are they all, the kids?"

"I wondered how long it would take you to ask," Isla smirked. "For someone who insists they aren't a natural mother, it took you all of thirty seconds to check. I have some things to tell you, but best in one sitting. Where are you off to?"

"We came to check supplies and restock the vessel. We have a trip to make. We have news for you too."

"But," Illy looked at me. "I think we would all prefer to take the *Eurydice*? Especially after what happened on the way over?"

We spent the next few hours loading the *Eurydice* with supplies capable of seeing us through another long voyage. Cracking a fine bottle of pinot noir, we sat on the deck and enjoyed the sunset, watching the reds, oranges, and purples of the sky as it sank into the bay.

"Can I tell you: I don't think I have ever been so relaxed?" Isla said suddenly. "No livestock needing me in the middle of the night, kids moaning about something, meals to make, and cleaning up after other people. I think I've worked out why you two keep disappearing on missions."

"What is it you needed to come all this way tell us? But the kids first, please," I asked.

"Well, it is all intertwined. First, your kids are all fine. Louis is a champion and has stepped up like you wouldn't believe. He ensures Katrin and Xanthe are up, dressed, breakfasted, and off to work. Kat is hanging for Sorcha to return, to start her apprenticeship properly, but Morwenna has taken her on temporarily. The problem is, Kat is so damned sharp that she is learning faster than Morwenna can teach. It is frustrating both of them, and there have been tantrums on both sides."

I grinned at Illy. I could see Katrin and Morwenna butting heads.

"Xanthe is fine but not coping with you being away. But she helps me on my rounds most days, not wanting to be away from me. She says she wants to be a vet, but I keep finding her cuddling the livestock so I wouldn't bother thinking about apprenticing her."

I smiled. Xanthe had always had a soft spot for animals, but I couldn't see her performing the less desirable parts of veterinary work.

"Thorsten has adapted. He happily lets Louis walk him to school at Bridget's. She is running it from home now, partly as there are fewer children, but mostly to keep them safe. She doesn't let them out of her sight."

"Good," I murmured, not wanting to interrupt the story.

"Summer and Ally are having the time of their lives. They wanted to stay at your place, Illy, alone, and I refused. I had visions of boys staying over every night and coming home to two knocked-up teens, and I will not be responsible for that."

Illy groaned, her head dropping into her hands. "Are they even going to school?"

"Yes, but begrudgingly. It is Jorja who has the best relationship with them and has taken them in. She understands them and is keeping them on the straight and narrow. Well, at least until you get home. But Ally is eyeing off one of Mike's boys, so you need to have 'the talk.' And soon."

"Bloody hell," Illy groaned. "How am I supposed to deal with two hormonal teen girls?"

I laughed. "Did I ever tell you that when I went on international trips with my school, it was expected that all the girls took the pill? We used to have to line up every morning, and the teachers watched us take it. There was no way the school was going to be responsible for an unplanned pregnancy and ruin the school's reputation."

"You can't be serious?"

"Deadly. I suspect all the parents knew that a bunch of rich teenage girls, overseas, and unsupervised at times, were a disaster waiting to happen, so no one complained."

"Maybe I need to do that with mine!" Illy grimaced, and I noticed Carl watching her intently.

"They will be fine," I assured her. "But Sorcha has an interest in women's health. Have a chat when we get back. And yours?" I asked Isla.

"Mine are fine. Fraser is there. Louis still works for him. They are well supervised and have no time to get into trouble."

"Not that we aren't thrilled to get a report on the kids, but why are you here?"

"After you left, there was a lot of talk. Scuttlebutt. The usual stuff. Why had you all left in the middle of the night? Had someone died? So that went on for a few weeks. It got to the point where I actively avoided people as I knew they would ask me questions I wasn't prepared to answer. It was Xanthe who worked it out. I had asked her to collect some wormwood from Jacinda so I could worm the cats. Aroha was in the surgery, preparing herbs. Xanthe talked to her while she waited but couldn't shake the feeling that Aroha was grilling her for information on where you had all gone. After all, you had taken Arataki. Xanthe kept insisting that she didn't know. No one had told her. But she felt uncomfortable. She told Aroha that she would come back for the wormwood, and Aroha dismissed it, telling her it wouldn't take long to prepare. Then Aroha offered her a cupcake."

My heart stopped.

"Xanthe politely refused and made her excuses to leave. Aroha tried to stop her, forcibly. Fortunately, Summer and Ally were walking Thorsten home from school and saw Aroha backing Xanthe up against the wall through the window. They crept in the side door, pounced on Aroha, and ahem ... interrogated her."

"Interrogated?" Illy asked, barely able to look up from her face in her hands.

"They tied her to a chair and threatened her with a knife."

"Oh, fuck."

"But it worked. Aroha confessed to it all. She wasn't originally part of the group, the radio group, but had been asked to share some of her knowledge about herbs, mainly for acne and contraception. But she felt valued. The others sought her advice and listened to her. She became a regular part of the radio learning network and was a Player. She denies breaking into your home, but she admits to poisoning Seraphine and trying to harm Mei as well. She had access to all the children as she picked up Arataki from school every afternoon. She has extensive knowledge of herbs and knew how much would kill Seraphine. It was a toadstool she used in the end as she knew it would look like she had eaten it accidentally."

"But she knew it was deadly?"

"She did. She had been testing it on small animals but just wasn't sure how much was a deadly dose on a child. Ironically, Cam was the one who taught her about edible and non-edible fungi. She tried to blame him at one point."

"Aroha? But Taki is her sister!" I still couldn't process this news.

"And you don't think she could be jealous? Her family expanded by one more, a special child, doted on, but one that isn't a blood relative? She couldn't target her own sister without arousing suspicion. It makes sense to start with another, one she wasn't close to. And she doesn't know Seraphine well. But more than that, these children were the firstborn children under the domes. We told them they were special. Millions had died, but they survived. They were the future of the human race. After all we had lost, we doted on them. Then these special little girls came along. The true inheritors of the earth. They can go outside with no consequences. It was part jealousy, part God syndrome."

"Most teenagers are arrogant. It comes with the territory," Illy added.

"She tried to murder a six-year-old?" I seethed. I knew Aroha well. Until I had traveled to Clava for my training, we had shared dinner every Friday night for years. Many nights she and I had discussed naturopathic and traditional medicines for both people and animals.

"What did Jacinda and Jamie do?" Illy asked.

"They were mortified. Angry at first with Summer and Ally but soon realized it was the truth. Jacinda was hysterical and wouldn't stop apologizing. You had taken Arataki to protect her, and yet her daughter had tried to kill Illy's. Jamie was morose. Speechless. I don't think I heard him speak. They barricaded themselves within their home, wouldn't speak to anyone. Then they waited until the equinox and left."

"Left?"

"They packed up and went back to August Island."

"But what about Taki?"

"They left you a note." Isla fossicked around in her pocket and pulled out the crumpled envelope, still sealed.

I read aloud.

Dearest Freyja, Campbell, and Illyria,

We have been friends for a very long time, and it breaks my heart to do this. But you will soon learn what Aroha has done, and we have no words to express our sorrow at the pain she has caused. But she is our daughter, and above all else, we need to support her. We can't stay here. People will know, and she will never be able to look people in the eye again. It will be a death sentence. For all of us.

We will return to August at the next opportunity. Please take care of our little Taki as we know you will. We have no idea how long it might take for us to see her again, and that breaks our hearts. She is part of our family and always will be. But we need to deal with the problem before us, and that is Aroha.

As for you, your friendship means the world to us, and that will never change.

Cam, since we met on August so many years ago, you have been a kind and loyal friend. You took us into your home and your heart, and we will be eternally grateful for your friendship.

Frey, you are the strongest, most loyal woman I know. I keep asking myself, how would Freyja deal with this? But then the tears start, and I know I will never be half the woman you are.

Illy, life dealt you the worst hand, and I cannot express my despair that it was my daughter who sought to take even more from you. I hope one day you can forgive me, and her.

Please tell Taki how much we love her. She will always be in our hearts.

Kia Ora,

Jacinda

Holy shitballs.

Illy's face was blank, drawn, and white. I couldn't read her but knew not to ask. Now was not the time. Jake poured another glass of wine each, and we sat sipping, staring out at the darkening sky.

"Why did you come?" I asked when I finally managed to organize my thoughts to enable speech.

"Jacinda found Summer and Ally torturing Aroha with a knife and went ballistic. Thorsten ran to get Bridget. Jorja heard the yelling and came running, which also attracted Fraser. With three screaming girls, Jacinda's fury, and Xanthe's crying, it took some time to get to the bottom of what had happened. Jorja was amazing at getting them all under control, Fraser told me. But it was your daughters who got the most out of her. Aroha clammed up by the time the adults arrived and would only admit to what Summer and Ally had already managed to get her to confess."

Illy groaned. "Those girls could get her to confess to being the Archangel Gabriel with enough time and motivation."

"What the twins learned from Aroha was that the main instigator of the Players is in India. She wouldn't tell them anything about the other players, refused to give names, and didn't know which community in India they are in. Apparently, there are several, one connected via the Nexus and several others. But all have radio transmissions. So, knowing that Bethany was murdered on Newgrange, I called Jake and asked him who the eldest children were there. It didn't take him long to work out who it was. I made the same call to Clava and Orkney, but they hadn't responded by the time Jake arrived at Lewis, and we left."

I looked at Jake, my eyebrows raised.

"I got onto it straight away and worked it out fairly quickly. There were only three children born on Newgrange within the first eighteen months, so there was a limited pool of candidates."

"Who...?"

"No one you know," he said firmly. "But they will be dealt with for Bethany's murder. As part of the interrogations, one of them confirmed that someone called D was the leader of the group, and he was in India, but again, the specifics are vague. So, Eoghan took me to Lewis, Isla met me at the dock, and we came straight here. Now, why are you here?"

I told them briefly what had happened in Kiewa.

"Oh my God, I am so sorry!" Isla's words flowed in a torrent. "You brought them here to keep them safe, and they attacked Caitlin? Then they tried to poison them? Where are they now?"

"Safe. But not in Kiewa. But that is why we were here. To find who is behind this and put a stop to it. If we can find the ringleader, then..."

Jake interrupted, "Did you know Isla speaks fluent Hindi and Gujarati?"

I didn't and turned to look at Isla, who blushed under her tanned skin.

"Well, I am not exactly fluent after many years of limited use, but I am fairly certain I can be understood. We used to go back to India every summer and visit Mum's family. Some spoke English, but most didn't."

"Knowing you, Isla, you will be understood no matter what language you speak!"

Isla grinned.

"So are they Hindu or Muslim in this community?" Jake asked.

"Neither," Tadhg replied. "Christian."

"It would be possibly easier if they were Hindu," Isla noted. "Most Hindus believe in the principles of ahimsa, or non-violence, and I think we could argue that principle in this case. Many believe in the death penalty for violent crimes as it protects the innocent, but that isn't what has happened here. These girls are innocent, so I doubt many Hindus would support killing them."

"I think the Biblical references found at the murder scenes tell us quite clearly this is a Christian community we are looking for," Illy noted.

"Agreed. This community is Christian," Tadhg advised. "It took us some time, but finally we heard the Players in their weekly group. There are more than we realized. But it wasn't a Bible group—as in the point of the meeting wasn't about religion. It was just standard teen stuff, a whole heap of nothing, to be perfectly honest, so it took us some time to work out that we were indeed listening to the correct group. Then a girl asked if anyone had seen the freaks since they had run away like scared mice."

Illy's hand reached over and placed pressure on my arm.

"And?" she asked.

"This was maybe four weeks ago, and the answer was yes. Another girl, arrogant and fancied herself as something special, advised they had all of them and would handle it. She had a soft Australian accent, I was fairly sure, but it was faint, and it was hard to detect over the satellite radio. So, of course, that started a mad flurry of chatter about helping and where was she located. But she refused to tell, saying it was her mission and she could handle it."

"Sophie," I muttered, looking at Illy.

"She certainly fits the description," Illy agreed.

"And after that?"

"She dropped off the transmission or at least stopped answering questions. The others tried to work out who she was for a while but got nowhere as they kept disagreeing and talking over each other, and soon that conversation ended. They thought she was just bullshitting them, and they started talking about sex positions. That was hard to hear as a parent of teenage girls, let me just say."

"And the following week?"

"The same group met, but the girl didn't connect. So after asking if anyone knew where they were, it wasn't spoken about. Two weeks later, we heard Dale speak, and your friend here confirmed his voice," Tadhg finished.

Ashton is not my friend, I seethed, but kept my face pleasantly neutral, ensuring I didn't look at Illy.

"Well, it is good you could confirm that it is him. How did you verify he was in India? Did he say something?" Illy asked.

"Not exactly. He was talking, so his microphone was on, and we heard chatter in the background. We were recording, of course, so we caught some of the words. It took us days to work them out phonetically, and even more to work out what they meant. But finally, we worked out that the words were Urdu. Can I tell you how hard that type of research is now without Google?"

I grinned. "I can imagine."

"What were the words?" Isla asked.

Tadhg rummaged around in his bag and pulled out a notepad, flicked through a few pages, and read: "*Aap iss naasut pe ek aamaas hain.*"

"What does it mean?" Illy asked.

Isla grinned, her brilliant white teeth gleaming. "I speak very little Urdu, but I know that. It is a classic insult. 'You are a tumor on the world.'"

"Can't say I disagree."

CHAPTER 31

THE EURYDICE BEING SMALLER and slower, and with fewer places we knew where we could refuel, we spent several weeks traveling, and each day my heart broke a little more for Cam, leaving him alone and with so many children. We had sent Gerry back to Cam and Sorcha to pass on the message that we were headed to India when we realized Jake would accompany us. Gerry was given the full briefing from Tadhg and Jake and asked to return with a vehicle we could use when we arrived back in Melbourne. I rested a little easier knowing Gerry was there to protect the girls, and Sorcha, Di, and Cam at least knew where we were going and why we might be gone for months. Every time I felt or saw the ring on my finger, I thought of him and sent a silent wish that he was okay.

Caitlin's trauma plagued my nights, and many times I woke in a cold sweat, feeling each punch and kick of the beating she had endured. I had treated her wounds daily, applied arnica, and I knew the patterns well enough to know exactly how many blows he had landed on her tiny body. "I will find out who is behind this, baby girl," I promised her every night.

"And I will put an end to it. We will go home. Soon."

Reunited after weeks apart, Illy and Ashton spent much of their time together, leaving Isla and me with Jake and Tadhg. We shared cooking, piloting, and general tasks, but much of the day we lazed around, looking for something to do. I often strolled the upper decks, using exercise to keep my anxiety in check. Finally, I understood why Cam would walk in the mountains on his days off. Fresh air and exercise did help, partly as I had something to focus on that wasn't the whirring of my brain, thoughts threatening to drown me with the rapid-fire changing of topics. I could barely grasp one concept before the next jumped in on top.

"Come on," Jake pushed me one evening after dinner. It had been raining all day, and I was pacing like a caged tiger. "I'm setting up the machine. You used to love karaoke."

Isla's eyebrows raised, and I rolled my eyes. "Luca loved to sing," I protested. "I think you have that wrong. I used to love laughing *at* him."

"I remember you singing 'Jolene' on more than one occasion."

Isla's eyes sparkled with mischief. "Oh, go on, do. I love that song."

"Fine," I growled, realizing I wouldn't get out of this.

Jake finished setting up the DVD and handed me the microphone. Tentatively, I started the opening lines. As I sang, I relaxed, letting go of the tenseness that had built up in me since we had left Australia. After applauding madly, Isla came up and joined me for a few duets, and after half an hour of hilarity, Illy appeared, her hair looking suspiciously neat.

"I have never heard you sing!" she exclaimed. "Luca always said you could but listening to you belting out 'Holding out for a Hero.' Wow! I thought it was a recording at first."

"Your turn," I said cheekily, handing her the mic as an early Madonna number came on.

Several bottles of wine later, and everyone had humiliated themselves singing cheesy numbers amid hysterical laughter, especially as Jake tried to sing women's ballads mimicking various singers. Badly. Carl had surprised me with a solid tenor and excellent range, not exactly suited to most of the popular music we had here, but he could hold a tune and wasn't unpleasant to listen to.

"I needed this. Thank you," I said to Jake as he crashed beside me on the sofa, and Illy and Isla negotiated a song to sing together.

"I've known you for a lot of years, my friend," he said, beneath the giggling. "I know you better than you know yourself sometimes. Do you still miss him?"

"I will until my last breath," I admitted. "I didn't realize what a big part he played in my life until he wasn't in it. It feels like every inhalation is a half one because I am missing some critical element."

"He adored you, too. It would kill him to see you like this."

"Like what?"

"Hunted and afraid."

I dropped my head onto his shoulder. "I'm so glad you are here."

CHAPTER 32

"FREAKING HELL, I HAD forgotten how much I detest humidity," I seethed as I looked at my hair frizzed out like a cheap party wig, three times its normal volume. Isla, brushing her lustrous black locks in the mirror beside me, stopped and grinned.

"At last! How many years have we been friends? Finally, I find something where I feel superior!"

"I'm jealous," I admitted. "Look at my hair! Cam would laugh if he saw me now, fluffed up like a poodle. I hate crossing the equator. I miss smoothing serums."

"Cam would love you even if you were bald."

"Humph," I grunted, watching her resume brushing. Isla's hair was thick and smooth. Not fine and fluffy like mine. "What I wouldn't give for your hair."

"Can I tell you how many times my girls have grizzled for blonde hair like you and your girls? They think you look like angels. Iona keeps telling me she wants to bleach it to look like Xanthe."

"Iona has beautiful hair. We are never happy with what we have, are we?"

"I don't know. I think we both have it pretty good," Isla said, surprising me. "I know you have had a rough time, Frey. But I can't tell you how much I am enjoying being here with you. Knowing that in some small way I might be able to repay you for all the wonderful gifts you have given me over the years."

"Oh, don't start that again."

"Don't brush me off. You saved my life. Then you gave me Rani. I want to help."

"Well, can you start by giving me ideas on how to not look like a Labradoodle?"

Moving behind me, and with three deft strokes, Isla brushed my fluffy hair and was braiding it down my back.

"It is so fine!" she said, the amazement evident.

"What I wouldn't give for thick hair like you and your girls," I replied wistfully.

"Rani's hair is fine, like yours," she said conversationally. "Poor kid, she desperately wants hair like Niamh and Iona, and without going into genetics, I can't explain why her hair isn't the same and never will be."

"I'm not sure if I told you, but on the journey over, we needed to tell them about their parentage. The girls were terrified and didn't know why they had been ripped away from their families and sent on this terrifying journey across the world."

"How did that go down?" Isla asked, tying the elastic hair tie around the end of my now neat braid.

"Better than we expected. The girls on Lewis all knew, of course, and some others did as well. There were a few tears, but they were old enough for it to make sense—why they look alike. Why we meet up every year for a common party. But quite a few didn't know that they were special and able to be exposed to the protozoa. That came as a shock, especially when we needed to send Ruby and Scarlett out to source parts for the yacht. Those girls stepped up. They have matured more than I would have thought possible in such a comparatively short time frame, some of it not ideal."

"How did Rani take it?"

"Like everything else, she took it all in her stride. She cried the first few nights, being away from you. But she is close with Arataki and Orla's daughter, Mica. She desperately wants to be friends with Sera and Cait, but they are such hard work. It took us about a week to sort out sleeping arrangements, making sure they were with someone they trusted. That made an enormous difference. Then, when Kendra, Ruby, and Scarlett agreed to sleep in a room, supervising the girls, that made an even bigger difference. They trust them and look up to them. It was Cait's reaction that perplexed us."

Isla laughed when she heard of Cait's tears about not being unique enough.

"Did I tell you that Luca was her biological father?" I said, unsure of how she would react.

"Really? That is wonderful. How amazing to have a child with your best friend and full sisters with your other bestie's child. How does Cam feel about that?"

"He took it surprisingly well," I admitted. "He always knew Cait wasn't his. I think Luca was the best outcome after her being biologically his. We both loved Luca, and he is gone, so there is no threat of him wanting to be her father or taking her away."

"Do you know who Rani's father is?" she asked gently.

"No. But Carl does. Do you want to know?"

Isla tilted her head, her long hair flowing past her hips. "I don't think so. It is enough that she is yours. I see her as ours, and I don't think I want to change that vision."

"She is, you know."

"What?"

"Yours."

CHAPTER 33

"FREY, YOU AWAKE?"

Opening my eyes, I smiled in answer.

"Can we talk?"

"Always." I sat up in bed, and she closed the door, slipping into the bed beside me, snuggling close to my warmth. We gazed out the window. The one I had spent so many days staring out of when we had traveled to Auckland to find Katrin.

"How would you feel if Carl returned to Lewis with me?" Illy asked finally.

"Are you sure?"

"Honestly, no. But I am not getting any younger, and we care for each other. I don't want to live in Clava or Auckland, but I needed to ask you before discussing the next steps. Would this traumatize you too much? It is okay to say what you truly feel. I won't be offended."

What a question. I want her to be happy. But with him? And living in a house that connects to my own?

"I don't know," I confessed. "The more I am around him, the more I realize he isn't the monster I feared him to be. But unlike you, I didn't know him before. He knew what they did to me, and he did nothing. I can't forgive that, now, or likely ever. But I want you to have someone in your life. A partner. Someone to help with the kids. On that note, how do you think they will take to him?"

"Summer and Ally will eat him alive." She giggled. "I have warned him they are hard work."

"What did he say to that?"

"That he would do anything to be with me. If that means being tied up, tortured, and interrogated at knifepoint as they did to Aroha, then that is fine."

"That is beautiful," I admitted. "Few men would take on another man's children. Especially your four!"

"I know," she groaned. "He has met Sera and Alasdair, of course. But they are easy in some ways. They never knew their father, so they won't assess him against Luca. But Summer and Al will put him through his paces. Test him. Likely terrify and traumatize him and make him run for the nearest vessel, screaming. Look, there is no rush. We are a long way from going home. I just thought I would ask. Give you some time to think about it."

"Thank you for considering me. But I have Cam and my family. I want you to have that sense of family, too." I paused before pressing on. "Can I ask something?"

"Of course."

"What is it like to be with someone new?"

"Are you thinking of Stefan?"

"I guess. Not regretfully," I hastened to add. "I have only been with Cam, on and off, for twenty years. Every time things were about to get intimate with Stefan, I felt awkward."

"I knew Carl before, of course. We had kissed, but nothing more, before I pulled away."

"Do you compare him to Luca?"

"How can I not?" she whispered, even though there was no chance of being overheard. "Luca was an enormous part of my life. He was generous, playful, and..." she giggled, "*really* good with his hands."

I snorted without meaning to. "And Carl?"

Illy sighed. "He is so vanilla."

"Vanilla?"

"He is so respectful that he keeps asking me how I am feeling and if I am okay. Do I like it? He never wants to experiment. Bloody hell, it is driving me mad!"

"Missionary not doing it for you?"

"I can't believe I am telling you this, but I don't think the man knows any other way! You should have seen his face when I suggested we use toys. He turned purple and was unable to form words. I thought he would blow a gasket!"

I collapsed into her, trying to repel the image of staid Ashton using sex toys, and the bed shook as she dissolved into giggles beside me.

"But," she said, when she had regained control, "it isn't fair to compare him to Luca. They are different people."

"They are. I guess that is what I thought about Stefan. I wasn't physically attracted to him but knew he was a good man."

"Do you still feel that way?"

"I do. And after what we have learned, he is likely innocent, so I feel guilty for suspecting him and running away with no warning."

"Have you told Cam?"

"Which part?"

"About you."

"The PTSD? I have."

"And did he run?"

"No," I admitted. "He told me he would give me anything I needed."

"And that doesn't tell you everything you need to know? He knows you are suffering, yet he trusts you enough to come on this mission."

"He does," I admitted. "He has always trusted me. Sometimes I can't work out why."

Illy rolled over to look at me. "I have been thinking a lot about that conversation we had on the way to Australia. The one about soul mates."

"When you called me an idiot?"

"That one. I am starting to think maybe you are right. Maybe we do find that person who completes us, makes us whole. Luca wasn't my first partner, not by a long shot, but he was the first one I could relax with. Let my guard down and trust him implicitly. Even after years together, he could take my breath away, just with a look. Maybe it is chemical, but I think maybe you were right. Maybe some people complete us. I heard what Sorcha said that day, and that was what got me thinking. Watching her with Di, and you with Cam. Really watching. You complete each other."

"Cam used to describe us as two halves of the same whole. I used to think that of you and Luca."

"So did I."

"And you don't feel that way about Carl?"

"It isn't the same. Logically I know it never can be. He isn't Luca. It isn't fair to compare them."

"But..."

"Is seventy percent enough?" she whispered.

"I don't know," I confessed. "I was about to throw away my marriage for less than that."

"You know, that is the first time I think I have heard you admit that you were jeopardizing your marriage. You blamed him for what happened."

"It wasn't him. Never was. It was all me."

"How are the panic attacks?"

"Lessening," I admitted. "Exercise helps, staying busy. But sometimes they just hit me out of the blue, for no reason at all."

"It is good that they are improving. I was wondering how you would go being away from Cam and the kids."

I sighed. "I am bored stupid and desperately want something to do."

"You could help me make a sex swing. I know how."

"Eww! I do not need that visual!"

Illy cackled madly. "It's okay. He would dive overboard with panic, I think." Finally, she calmed and looked at me. "I know I haven't been around much, but I will always be here for you. I love you. You know that, right?"

"And I, you."

CHAPTER 34

IN MELBOURNE, TADHG AND Ashton had triangulated the radio signal, pinpointing which community they suspected Dale was in. There were several in India, one connected via an antipode in northern Jaisalmer. There were also three others, isolated communities, settled later, and a fourth in Sri Lanka. They strongly suspected Dale had joined the coastal community on the now dammed Krishna River on the east coast, incorporating the former Krishna Wildlife Park. Tadhg knew from listening to transmissions that the community had split fairly early along religious lines. Two townships under the same dome. Not acrimonious but not exactly collaborative either. We knew Dale had aligned himself with the religious right. What we didn't know was where within the domed community he was located.

"Does that mean he traveled by sea to Krishna?" Illy asked. "I would have thought he would have used the Nexus?"

"We don't know," Ashton admitted. "He left Clava by bike, and we saw him arrive in Inverness.

We watched for a bit, but then he disappeared. We suspected he made his move at night, so we never knew if he had traveled overland to another mainland community or by sea. We didn't want to alert other communities to his wanderings as they might confront him, so we just let him go. That was the last we saw of him."

I raised my eyebrows at this. "You let an attempted rapist wander around unsupervised?"

Ashton looked abashed. "We were more concerned about you, Illyria, and ensuring the embryos were successful at the time."

"You let him go before you released us?" I jumped out of my seat. "What if he had followed us and tried again?"

Ashton held a hand up to me. "After. He was held, secured, for a few days. A trial of sorts was conducted, and it was agreed that he couldn't stay. You had already destroyed the harbor, so we knew he couldn't pursue you, although a few vessels were still usable."

My shoulders dropped at that. Only we had traveled to Edinburgh. He could easily have followed us, tried again.

Ashton read the displeasure on my face. "What would you have preferred we do? We had no capacity to keep him incarcerated. No one wanted to escort him anywhere. So we thought that banishing him and making him find his own way was best. Perhaps another community would take him in, after he had time to assess his actions and make better choices."

"Instead, he orchestrated the murder of three innocent children, and with time, would have killed them all, and my friend too," Isla said sweetly, making me flash her a look of gratitude.

After a period of uncomfortable silence, Ashton stood and left the room. Isla stood purposefully and sat next to me on the navy sofa. I smiled at her as she reached for my hand and asked me what I wanted for dinner. Illy slipped out of the room, unnoticed. The door thudding closed made me jump.

Maybe I don't want him in my home. What if I hear him, with her? My brain whirred, and I felt the familiar sense of my throat closing and chest tightening. I tried to focus on my breath, like Illy had taught me, but couldn't stop the feeling of losing control. I needed to get out of here, now. Not wanting to draw attention to myself, I bolted.

As I sat on the cool bathroom floor, knees drawn up and head dropped, I could hear the voices. Distant. A sweet, lilting voice. Isla.

"Is she alright?" Illy was asking.

"I don't know. After you left to go after your boy-friend, all the color drained from her face, and it was like she couldn't breathe. She ran, and I have been looking for her since. I keep knocking on her door, but it is locked, and she doesn't answer. I'm really worried. I've never seen her like this."

"Fuck," Illy muttered and pounded on the door. The banging made me crawl deeper inside myself, hiding.

Abstractedly, I heard the click of the lock being unlatched and the door opening.

"Get out, all of you," Illy barked, and I heard the door close again but couldn't pull myself out of the pit to look up at her.

I felt the small cool hands hold mine, but I was numb, like I had taken painkillers. I could feel the sensation, but it was muffled.

"Focus, Freyja, listen to me. Breathe. Slow your breathing. Squeeze my hand."

I could hear the words but couldn't get my hands to comply.

"Go away," I wanted to say but couldn't. My body was no longer under my control. I was here but detached. My throat had closed over, and my mouth was so dry I thought it would crack.

"Squeeze my hands," she ordered, and I focused as hard as I could to squeeze.

"Good. Again."

I couldn't. I didn't have the energy. I felt faint, so weak I thought I didn't have the strength to breathe anymore.

"I am not leaving you. I'm here, Frey. We do this together."

I could hear her speaking, but the noise was like someone was talking to me underwater. Muffled and indistinct. But the solid presence of her hands grasping mine pulled me back.

Slowly, I lifted my head and cracked open an eye.

"There you are." She handed me a glass of water, and I gulped thirstily. She nattered away as I tried to summon the strength to speak.

"I'm sorry," I finally murmured.

"I am going to slap you if you apologize again. Okay?"

"Okay."

Sipping the water and listening to Illy chatter away about romance novels, I finally managed to say, "Still not my thing."

She grinned cheekily. "Yes, but I have been talking about them for nearly twenty minutes now. How much did you take in?"

"Not much," I admitted.

"As I thought. You are dissociative. So what we need are some tools to help you when you can feel this coming on."

"Tools?"

"I suggested a journal before, but sometimes something as simple as a mantra can help. Something simple like, 'this will pass.' Repeat it over and over and truly believe it. You keep saying it until you feel it. Can you try that?"

I nodded gingerly. I had a cracking headache forming. Illy saw me wince.

"I'm going to get you something hot to drink and some pain relief. But first, let's get you to bed. And before you say anything, I am staying with you tonight."

"Captain Vanilla won't object?" I whispered.

The bubble of laughter broke from her chest as she wiped tears from her eyes. "God, I love you. It will do him good."

CHAPTER 35

WE MOORED ON THE far side of the dome and agreed that Tadhg should remain with the vessel, heavily armed, although there were other vessels moored here. There was no way we could let the *Eurydice* be stolen or sabotaged. Ashton insisted on coming with us but refused to carry a weapon. While having no experience with firearms, Isla would do anything to protect her children and agreed to carry one. She looked rather fierce brandishing it. Jake had spent days aboard the *Eurydice* setting up targets on the deck, teaching her to load, aim and fire it, and she was quite an excellent shot. Not as good as Illy or me, but she could hit a moving target at a decent range.

"He is a liability," I breathed in Jake's ear as we kitted ourselves. Jake inhaled and nodded.

With Ashton and Isla between us, Jake led the way, leaving Illy and me to bring up the rear. We located an access panel and let ourselves in, wading through the mangroves toward the center of the dome. Fields of green stretched before us. Trying to avoid damaging the crops of rice and sugarcane, providing evidence of our presence, we soon found a dirt road and began walking inland, wondering how on earth we were to work out which of the communities Dale was in. There were several here; we knew from the satellite footage. We just didn't know which was which.

We had discussed what we would do if we found him. Take him with us was the consensus, although I knew Illy was concerned about me if that occurred. As much as I never wanted to be in a room with him again, if he was removed from the team that supported him, and no longer controlled the Players, perhaps the game would stop, and the girls would be safe? We didn't have the stomach to harm innocent people. But we had all agreed that the safety of our children was paramount. Ensuring they could go home and live without fear was our endgame, and if taking Dale from this place meant we could achieve that, I was all for it.

Watching Ashton trying to be stealthy in front of me, I grimaced. For the hundredth time, I wished he had stayed with Tadhg. This would be so much easier if it were just the four of us and only Isla to protect. Illy, Jake, and I could take care of ourselves, and we needed her linguistic skill. She also wasn't afraid to use a gun, knowing the stakes.

The sound of a group singing reached us, and we stopped in the road. Isla listened intently and smiled. "That is a Christian hymn," she whispered. As we listened, I recognized the cadence but couldn't recall the name of the hymn in English.

We reached a crossroads, and it was evident by the well-worn grooves and footprints that this was a well-worn road between communities. Pausing momentarily, we turned toward the pleasant sound.

It was a choir of sorts, and despite not knowing the words, they were quite good. Reaching the outskirts of a sizeable township, we ducked into a cluster of trees to confer.

The audible click of a gun being primed made us freeze. Armed with small automatic weapons, three men stepped out of the bushes; the guns aimed squarely at us.

"Well, that was a monumental fuckup," I muttered, conjuring an image of Luca facepalming at our being caught so quickly.

They fired sentences at us in a language I didn't understand, and Isla struggled to interpret. It was swelteringly hot. Rivers of sweat were running down my back. The leader prodded Jake in the chest with his weapon and shouted in his face. Isla waited for a pause in the shouting and asked something haltingly. The leader slowed down his speech and fired something at her. She replied, gesticulating earnestly.

The back and forth went on for some time. I was fighting not to pass out from the heat, the weight of the strange words settling over me like a heavy cloud. Finally, Isla turned to us. "He was speaking Urdu, and I only speak Gujarati and Hindi. Fortunately, he also speaks Hindi. He knows who we are. They received a radio message from Kiewa that we knew about Dale and were likely on our way. They have been waiting for us."

"Fabulous," I mumbled. "What now?"

"They insist we accompany them into town. I don't see we have a choice?"

Confiscating the weapons we held and with the muzzle of guns poking in our backs, we began the short walk into town, dust kicked up from the road, making us cough. On the outskirts of the village, houses lined the street, smaller streets branching off to either side. The houses here looked older, more dilapidated than those I was used to seeing in planned communities. A shout halted us, and we were shoved into a shed laden with boxes, crates, and hay bales, barely large enough for the five of us and the contents. The temperature in the tin shed was significantly hotter than outside, and the wave of stale, suffocating heat hitting my face was like walking into a sauna. The confinement, stench, and dusty floors conjured images of being held captive in Inverness, and I closed my eyes, swaying in the heat, willing my brain to focus. *Not now*, I repeated to myself, feeling Joey's tongue on my face. *Not now.*

Illy gripped my hands as I perched on an old wooden crate. "Look at me, Frey. Focus on my eyes. Stay with me."

Blurred as my vision was, I looked into her blue eyes, grounded myself, and nodded. I could not lose it now.

"Breathe. In. Out. This will pass. Repeat. This will pass."

"I need to get out of here," I croaked through my constricted chest.

Staring deep into my eyes, Illy said, "There is no point in escape, Frey. We are here to talk, to negotiate. If we escape, then the trip here was pointless. We need to see Dale, convince them to stop targeting you and the girls. They will come. We just have to wait."

A tiny prick of logic in my brain recognized this as a good idea, but the panic of being trapped set in, making the brick wall rise, and I shrank inside to stay safe. I closed my eyes again and tried to focus on my breathing, repeating the mantra. In. Out.

I could hear Illy talking to me through the solid wall that surrounded me. A calm, lilting voice, but I couldn't distinguish the words, just saw the pleasant buzz floating around my head, thick and cloudy. But she was there. I wasn't alone as the chasm threatened to suck me down. The darkness swirled before me, and I felt myself weightless, falling. As I fought to pull myself out of the fog, I felt her arm bearing weight on my shoulder. It was grounding. Pleasant. An anchor I could attach myself to and pull myself out.

"I'm okay," I croaked, my voice hoarse from the dust.

She held me then, sat beside me, and cradled me like a child. *It is comforting*, I thought, *reassuring*.

"Frey," she murmured in my ear, not wanting to be overheard. "Did you speak to someone when your sister overdosed?"

I had to cast my mind back, fighting the swaying sensation in the oppressive heat. "I did. One of Mum's colleagues. But it wasn't private, so Mum found someone else. Someone who didn't know my family. But I didn't go for long."

"Did they diagnose anything?"

"I can't remember. That entire time was a blur. I had flashbacks of finding her lying there for years. Nightmares. I was angry at them, so much so that I moved out."

"When did you isolate yourself from people? Emotionally."

"After that, I guess. I mean, I was never the life of the party. But that was when I pulled away. Stopped letting people hurt me."

"And your therapist said nothing?"

"I think I just stopped going. I returned to uni and just avoided places and people that reminded me of her."

"I remember how you reacted when we visited Auckland. I wondered at the time if you had worked through your trauma from earlier. I think it has stayed with you, compounded by each additional challenging situation you have been placed in. I used to describe it to my patients as a clear bucket of water. The bucket is full, but people can't see that it is full. To the outsider, it appears calm and still. One additional drop and the torrent starts as the bucket overflows. People think, 'Why would that one little thing set her off?' But the bucket was already at capacity, and that tiny little thing was the tipping point. Does that make sense?"

"It does."

"I am wondering if you already had PTSD. First, finding your sister in Melbourne, then what happened to you on August, being sucked away unexpectedly. Being held captive in Inverness, finding your sister again and what you needed to do, then our situation on Clava. Now your girls. You have dealt with more trauma in twenty years than most people do in a lifetime."

"I'm fine," I whispered in her ear, aware Isla was watching me, concern engraved into her delicate features.

"No, you aren't. But I can't do much to help you right now. But I will, Frey. I promise. We will get out of here. You will see your children again."

"I just want to go home," I spoke more loudly, making them all look at me from where they sat on random items scattered around the small space. "I'm sick of running, of feeling stalked. Being dragged away from people I love. I just want to take my family and my friends and go home. Be safe. Live a normal life. Is that too much to ask?"

"We all want that, Frey. Truly." Jake looked at me across the room. "I'm sorry about this. I keep thinking if Luca..."

"Nothing would have changed if Luca were here," Illy interjected. "They were waiting for us. We would still be in this situation."

The door flew open, kicking a cloud of dust into my face and making me cough. Two men stood in the doorway, blocking the daylight, but didn't enter.

"Couldn't stay away, could you?" the familiar greasy voice jeered at me as I blinked in the onslaught of brightness. "Want me that bad, do you?"

I could sense Jake wanting to pounce, but I spoke calmly enough as the cooler air rushed into the shed, reviving me slightly.

"Good to see you haven't changed. So, you still need to take women prisoner for them to be in the same room as you?"

Taking two steps across the room, he bent down to slap me across the face.

I grinned up at him, refusing to react. "Ah, still need to beat them too, I see. Such a class act. Your mother must be so proud of the *man* she has raised."

His fist clenched to match his jaw. As the hand swung back, ready to strike, I swiftly pulled the tiny knife Luca had given me years ago from the center of my bra and embedded it into his chest. Angled directly upward and under the ribs as Luca had taught me. I had carried it for years, never needing to use it. Instinct had told me to bring it this time. I was a surgeon; I knew where the heart was. One quick thrust with as much force as I could manage was all it took. Dale dropped onto the filthy floor, his mouth opening and closing.

"Never telegraph your punches," I could hear Luca say in my ear as I watched him gurgle.

Jake moved quickly and overpowered the other man, who was still gawking at Dale, gasping on the floor. A single blow and he was out cold. Jake dragged him to lie beside Dale before returning to the door.

He brought a single finger over his lips as a couple passed.

"What now?" Jake asked Illy.

"I think we try to find someone in charge and talk," Illy suggested.

Isla was still standing in the shed, gaping down at Dale, bleeding out on the floor.

I heard Illy speak in her ear. "That is Dale. The man who orchestrated the murder of our children and tried to rape Freyja on Clava." I watched Isla's face as it went through a bewildering series of expressions before she booted him solidly in the stomach and moved to the doorway without looking back. She slipped her hand into mine and looked up into my face.

"What do you want me to do?"

"Ask for the most senior person here, I guess."

To my utter astonishment, Isla stepped out into the street, put two fingers into her mouth, and whistled. An ear-piercing, glass-shattering whistle. Everyone stopped and stared.

"How did I not know you could do that?"

"My parents taught me how to catch a taxi." She grinned. "It has come in useful a number of times."

Isla strode boldly up to the nearest person, an older woman carrying a basket of leafy green vegetation I didn't recognize and fired off a question.

The woman jerked at Isla's brusque tone and words but responded cautiously with a gesture toward a large building in the distance. The only two-story building here, it loomed over the others, its whitewashed bricks glowing orange in the late afternoon sun.

Isla turned to us. "Come on. We can find the village elders there. It is a meeting place of sorts. Kind of like a hall but also a court. If people have problems, they take them to the village elders to mediate three afternoons per week. She said they should be there now."

"Sounds good to me," Illy stated. Jake shrugged as we followed Isla toward the building, Ashton silently bringing up the rear.

Halfway to our destination, a group of men surrounded us, shoving us roughly. Isla fired off something in Hindi, and they replied just as rapidly.

"They are here to take us to the court. I tried to explain that we were taking ourselves there, but they insist that we are escorted."

"Overkill," Jake muttered, but I sensed him tense, keeping a wary eye on each of the guards and where they were. Ashton looked fearful. I doubted he had ever been in a hostile situation.

The guards pushed us sharply in the back with their guns every few steps.

"It would be so much easier if they just let us walk," I grumbled as I helped Jake up after he had been pushed onto the dirt road for the fourth time. His face was as black as thunder, and I wondered how many more assaults he would bear. Jake was smaller than Luca, but he was strong and had been his equal in hand-to-hand combat. Many nights, moored on an abandoned beach, Angus and I had watched them practice their sparring skills. Regularly I teased them about it being a display of testosterone-fueled chest-beating, but I never admitted to them that it was impressive to watch.

Upon arrival, we were forced to sit in the large, swelteringly hot hall, the humidity so thick it felt like we were swimming through it. Three men, elders, dressed in long white robes, sat at the far end behind the single long table, with a fan behind them blowing their hair. People sat in the four rows of elevated stadium seating that ran along both long walls. We were forced to the floor at the opposite end of the room from the elders but with a direct view. The floor was filthy. Dusty footprints of all shapes littered the open space before us. I felt myself wilting from the temperature, and Illy nudged me in the ribs. Be alert.

Isla did her best to translate as each case was called. Mostly neighborhood disputes. A cow grazing in a neighbor's crop paddock and the farmer seeking compensation for lost crops. A borrowed tool never returned. A disagreement over the price of rice.

"Bloody hell, they couldn't prioritize?" Jake grunted and received a sharp jab in the back with the butt of a gun for his trouble.

Bored stupid, and mostly unable to follow, I watched the sun as it dropped in the sky. Stifling a yawn, I desperately wanted to lie down and sleep, the oppressive heat sapping the life from me. Slumping, I felt Jake's arms adjust me to rest against his reassuringly solid and comfortable chest.

After an eternity in that scorching, stifling hell, it was our turn. We were dragged from our place on the floor and thrown in front of the long table. All three of the seated men glared at us, and one of our captors started to speak. Others joined in, with the judges intermittently asking questions. There appeared to be no structure to the proceedings. Isla did her best to translate, but with so many people talking, it was difficult to follow who to listen to, and she could only translate parts of disjointed sentences. I could sense her frustration as they kept speaking over each other, pointing at each of us in turn, arguing.

"We are being accused of murder," she finally said.

"I gathered that. What is the sentence?"

"First, they want to know which of us killed Dale."

I raised my hand. The man behind me grabbed me by the hair, half lifting me from my seated position on the floor and jerking my head back.

"You took one of ours. Now we must take one of yours," Isla translated haltingly.

"You have already taken three of mine!" I couldn't contain my frustration. One elder frowned at my outburst.

"You speak English," Illy accused him.

"Some," he admitted. "I was a university lecturer a long time ago. What do you mean we took three of yours?"

Illy filled the council in as best as she could. My children. Dale. The Players here and in other communities. The murders. The judge interpreted for his peers, and they spoke for a long time. My neck was hurting from the position my head was being held in.

"Be this what it may, we did not kill your children," the middle judge announced after a long consideration.

"But you allowed it," Illy spoke calmly. "Had you not sheltered this man, three innocent children would still be alive. Does that not make you an accessory to murder?"

"Fuck, this will never be over," I muttered as the hands tightened on my hair, pulling my head all the way back and exposing my neck. I could see Jake like a tiger, ready to pounce. His eyes not leaving me. He wouldn't let them hurt me, I knew. Neither would Illy. But with one quick swipe of the blade my captor held...

"We were not aware of his past. When he came to us, we felt it was our duty to accept him. We also did not know about your children or what he did before. He told us he was a teacher. We allowed him to teach our children English so they could communicate with others in the world."

"But what they communicated was how to kill my friend and her children."

"Of this, we were not aware. Had we known, we would not have permitted this."

Another of the judges asked something in Hindi, and Isla translated. "He wants to know why your children were targeted."

"Isla, explain, please," Illy spoke aloud, murmuring under her breath. "I trust your translation."

Isla spoke for what seemed to be a long time, earnestly and with passion. She touched my shoulder at various points, and I tried my hardest to look like a persecuted mother, which was rather difficult with my hair being pulled tightly and only able to stare at the ceiling.

More conversation took place behind the bench.

"What are they saying?" Illy whispered.

"I don't know. They are speaking Urdu, and I only know a few words. I can't follow, and they know it."

A heated discussion was taking place, voices getting louder and more aggressive.

"This isn't good," Illy muttered, her eyes not leaving the three men.

"You are the mother that created these children?" The middle judge looked directly at me.

"I am."

"What threat do these children pose to us? I cannot imagine our friend would have considered them a threat for no reason."

This was a challenging question. I looked at Illy for guidance.

"Tell the truth," she said, loud enough for the judge to hear.

As succinctly as I could, I explained why these girls were different. They were immune to the protozoa that still decimated the planet. One day, they could live outside.

The collective intake of breath from the crowd made the judges look, and I knew this couldn't end well. Freaks. People would always consider them monsters.

"So they *are* unnatural," he spoke aloud, to murmurs of agreement from his peers.

Rage rose in me, but before I could answer, Ashton spoke. "No," Ashton spoke from behind me, raising his hands to show he wasn't being threatening. "Isla, if you would. As accurately as you can, please."

Isla nodded consent.

"Ms. Jorgensen was an unwilling victim in all of this. I was in charge of the scientific communities on

Clava and Auckland Island. I led the teams there, those that chose all of our surviving people. We kidnapped her, kept her captive, and stole her reproductive material without her consent to create these children. Dale, your colleague, was once part of my team. Unbeknownst to us, he attacked her. We expelled him, and as retribution, he sent assassins after her children. She is innocent. She played no part in this."

There was a collective gasp among the audience and low chatter. Ashton waited until the judge raised a hand to quiet them. "Don't blame the victim. If you need to blame anyone, it is me." Ashton paused, waiting for Isla to catch up. We saw the look of shock on their faces. The audience had quieted too, stunned into silence.

"I am the orchestrator of all of this. It was my grand plan. I am responsible."

The center judge, the one who spoke English, silenced the crowd before speaking. "Regardless, she is responsible for these children. How do we know we aren't at risk of all the people she can bring into the world? If her offspring can live outside the domes, then aren't we trapped? They will target us. Keep us caged, like animals."

"No, we need everyone to survive. These children are only little girls, and there are very few of them. They will need to choose partners from within the protected communities to have children of their own. Over several generations, we want *all people* to be able to live outside, be immune. Your future generations too. This was for the benefit of everyone. The world will not be overrun. Ms. Jorgensen cannot bear more children. During the first surgery, the medical team accidentally scratched one of her fallopian tubes, causing an infection and rendering that ovary use-less. In the second surgery, they took as many eggs as they could make her produce. She is infertile. There will be no more. It took us over a decade to produce this small number of children. We have never been able to produce any more, before or after."

Shellshocked from what I heard, I pulled my head down slightly to try to see the judge's face. My captor was also entranced by Ashton's words and allowed my head to lower, without releasing his grasp on my plait.

"I'm the one responsible for it all. If you need to take a life, take me. Please. Let her go and be with her children. They are only children. No different from your own. They pose no threat to anyone. Quite the opposite. One day, their future generations will help *your* descendants survive once more. Isn't that what we all want? To leave the best legacy we can to our own children and grandchildren?"

Everyone stopped and stared as the gasp I had desperately been holding in broke free from my chest.

"Is that why?" I whispered, tears filling my eyes.

"Why we let you go? Why you had no more chil-dren? It is."

"You did this to me?" I blurted, tears blinding me. "You ... did ... this. You have known all this time, and you never told me?"

My captor let go of my hair unexpectedly, and Illy caught me as I sprawled forward across the dusty floor. After she assisted me to stand, I could see the pain etched into her fine, bird-like features. She clutched his arm and stared up into his face.

"Truly, Carl? You did that to her?"

Ashton shuffled uncomfortably as he gazed down at his feet. The man who had held me lurked nearby, unsure what to do as the crowd started chattering and escalated into a roar.

"This is acceptable," the English-speaking judge announced. The noise was deafening, everyone speaking at once. Once more, he raised his hand and waited for the crowd to settle.

"Promise me our children will be safe," I demanded.

The judge nodded. "I will make an order that these children are to be protected. You have my word."

"There is one more thing I need to tell you," Carl mumbled, looking down at his dust-covered feet.

"What?" Illy snarled.

"Arataki and Solstice are my daughters."

"Is that why you came to our aid? Because you knew Taki was with us?"

"Partly," he admitted, pleading for understanding in his eyes. "They are my daughters, but they will never be my children. Every year I watched them and felt a sense of pride, knowing that they were mine. Intelligent, beautiful young women. It broke my heart to hear what happened to Solstice, and I swore I would do anything I could to stop that from happening to Arataki. So I watched to see if I could work out who was behind it. I saw you leave and watched to see where you were going, hoping you were coming to us on Auckland Island. When I saw you stop, I knew something was wrong."

One of the judges issued a short sharp directive.

"Can I ask one thing?" I asked as Ashton was grabbed, his arms thrust behind his back.

"Anything."

"Did Dale father any of these girls?"

"No. He and I were the last two candidates with no children of our own. Arataki and Solstice were conceived in the first round. He was scheduled to father two in the second. But then... well, we chose Mr. Cadman for both embryos instead. He is the only male genome from our team not to be replicated."

Two of the men standing behind us hauled Ashton to his feet and started pushing him toward the open doorway.

"I am so sorry, both of you," he called back as he was taken away. "For everything. Illyria, you know what you need to do."

"Let's go," Illy said stiffly, clutching my upper arm and grabbing at Isla, Jake hot on our heels. No one stopped us.

Three steps out of the village, I stopped and turned to Illy. "But it isn't over, is it? It will never be over. The girls will never be safe. Someone will always be after them. If not these people, then someone else."

"It's okay," she soothed, pulling me along.

"But it isn't," I protested, digging my feet in. "Where can they be safe?"

Illy's face was tormented. There was something she wanted to say. But not now. Picking up the pace, we veritably ran back to the harbor, not speaking until we were well clear of Krishna.

As we approached the mangroves near the beach, Jake rushed ahead and called to Tadhg. He returned with a gun, rounding Illy, Isla, and me up like a cattle dog on high alert. But no one followed as we closed the access hatch behind us. Tadhg had the vessel started, and we were pulling out of the harbor within seconds of stepping foot on deck.

Illy's face was unreadable, dark, and broody.

"What is it?"

"Carl told me a place we can go to deactivate all the portals, knock the entire Nexus offline. He also suggested we block the radio signals. He always worried it would come to this. Science versus religion."

"But it wasn't religion at all. Just some asshole seeking revenge. And we can't escape that. Ever."

"True. But we can insulate ourselves. Each community focused on its own needs."

"Can we? People have been traveling through the Nexus for years. Even on Lewis, we have been using it quarterly for over six years. People visit family and friends. Isn't this kind of like the Berlin Wall? People will be off visiting and get caught out?"

"I don't see another way of doing it. If we warn people, someone will try to stop us. It is best if they believe it is an accident. If no one knows for sure, then there will be no retribution. People desperate to get home will travel overland or by sea. It isn't insurmountable. But we need to protect our children, Frey. If they can't travel easily, if we remove cross-community communication, they are safer. We will learn who the players were on Lewis and eliminate that threat. It is the only way."

"I see that. I just feel like it isn't my place to make this decision."

"After what you just learned, you don't think you have earned that right?"

I considered that. "No, I really don't. I admit I have probably suffered more than most. But that doesn't make me special. We are talking about tens of thousands of people, and I am stopping them from traveling through the Nexus to their own families."

"Correct. Traveling through the Nexus. You aren't killing anyone or stopping movement. We are just preventing an uprising that could harm these children. I believe that there is no further risk from here. They believe in a life for a life. They have that. With Dale gone, and their ruling, I genuinely believe the girls, and you, are safe—from them. But in case what they said in Krishna wasn't true, or the other Players continue, we need to take steps to isolate them. They were given to us to protect. We need to take every step possible to do that, don't we?"

"I guess..."

"What would you do to protect Cait?"

"Anything necessary," I answered in the same heartbeat.

"Can you not see that this is necessary?"

I could. I just didn't see that it was my place to make decisions to affect the planet.

"Frey, you affected the future when you had those children. I know you didn't choose that, but that path found you. Like it or not, you are the mother of the future human race. You have kind of earned this. But I won't put that pressure on you. I have made this decision. I'm going to do this. For my daughter, yours, and all the others. Maybe this will be my legacy."

"Oh, Ils." I held her close. "Thank you."

"And if she doesn't, I'll do it." Isla's voice sounded in my ear as her arms embraced us both. "I owe you this, Freyja. A life of peace. You gave me my life, my family, and the gift of Rani. Every day I am alive is because of you. I would do this for you a hundred times over."

"What about the Players in each community? How will we know who they are? Get them to stop?"

"Leave that with me. It won't be hard to work out the oldest children born there. They will rat on each other with enough pressure applied. But, I promise you. They will all be identified."

"Am I setting a course for Melbourne?" Tadhg's voice rose from the bridge as Jake returned to us after ensuring we weren't followed.

"Just head south," Illy called.

"Where is this place?" I asked.

"Borneo. Inland, of course. The tricky part is that it is bloody hard to get to. Even before the pandemic, the journey was a helicopter or long-boat in, through the thick jungle. There is an enormous cave system that straddles the equator, extends for hundreds of kilometers. If we set the charge, it will decommission the Nexus. All antipodal travel goes through the equator. If we destabilize the central point, none of it will work. It knocks them all offline."

"How do we get in? Borneo was fairly isolated, even before."

"I'll get you in," Jake announced.

"What do you need to deactivate the Nexus?" Isla asked quietly.

Illy was gazing out to sea. She was still dealing with the emotional trauma of leaving Ashton behind. I was conflicted, equally pleased to never see him again, furious to learn what he had known for the past seven years and had never told me, and distressed for my friend losing her partner.

"Explosives," Illy admitted. "And a lot. It is a bit of a detour, but we can travel via Butterworth in Malaysia."

"There is an air force base there, isn't there?" I asked. "I remember Luca mentioning it once. We were in the area, and he was trying to convince Angus to stop and collect weapons. We didn't for some reason that I can't recall, but I remember the conversation."

"There is." Illy smiled wanly at the mention of Luca, so close to the loss of Ashton. "I have been there. I went to a conference there early in my career. Unless they have cleared the place out, I think I can find weapons and explosives."

"That would be great," Jake said. "I'll tell Tadhg to set a course to Malaysia."

CHAPTER 36

"**WHERE EXACTLY ARE WE** headed?" Isla asked as we leaned over the railing, the jungle looming before us. Where once the landscape had been lush tropical rainforest, pristine sand meeting the turquoise ocean, now brown piles of rotting leaves and trees lay decaying against the water's edge. It was a mess. A pile of slush. The pungent odor of rot wafting over the ocean towards us was bracing.

"Gunung Mulu National Park. It is quite a way in, and the rivers are likely blocked if that mess is anything to go by. Goodness knows how long it will take us. But I don't see we have any choices other than by boat, slowly, and moving obstacles as we go."

"What precisely are we looking for?" I asked.

"*Gua Air Jernih*, Clearwater Caves in English."

"Assuming any signage is still standing."

"Agreed, but we might be able to find a map."

"Where are you taking us? That looks shallow, and we can't swim."

"The nearest port, according to our GPS, is Brunei."

"That works," Jake piped up. "There will be aircraft there."

"Aren't you forgetting something?" Illy's light voice cut through my daydream as I gazed over the tropical beach. "None of us can fly."

"Well, I can. Badly."

I spun around from the railing and stared at Jake incredulously. "We have known each other for how many years, and you never told me that?"

"Because I was trying to impress you. If you must know, I failed my flight training. But instead of kicking me out, the military offered to retrain me as an engineer."

"Flight training?" I couldn't quite believe my ears.

"Helicopter training specifically. I enlisted to become a rescue pilot. I can fly fine; only I kept failing the simulation test. It turns out I have no concept of spatial depth. I kept landing the chopper on top of the other craft. In the simulator, of course. You'd think they would have assessed that before I enlisted and underwent basic training, but no. Anyway, so I failed."

"And you don't think not being able to land might be a minor issue?"

"Well, there aren't likely to be other craft there, so as long as we pick a large area, it should be fine."

"So you can fly okay; it is just the landing?" Illy questioned, her face serious.

"Well, it has been more than twenty-five years," Jake said, his eyes twinkling. "But sure. The basics won't have changed. The bigger issues are going to be finding one, getting it started, and ensuring we have enough fuel for a return trip."

"Leave that to me," Tadhg said. "I love a challenge."

"Well, you married Callie," I teased.

"Still a work in progress," he fired back.

"It is nearly monsoon season." Isla looked at me. "Rain daily. You can set your watch by it, well, assuming we still had watches. Every afternoon, the sky opens up, and it pours, usually for less than an hour. Then the sun comes out, and it is fine until the following day."

"When is the safest time to move?"

"Dawn."

"Then we wait."

CHAPTER 37

After the afternoon showers ceased, we headed to the airport, which fortunately was only a short walk from the pier in the steamy, unpleasant heat. Hours of swearing, yelling, and throwing tools ensued as Tadhg and Jake worked on one craft after another. Scanning the airfield, it looked like every chopper here had a hatch open and parts strewn across the tarmac. The girls and I kept a close eye on proceedings, mainly as we were fearful that we might be making this trip by longboat and dealing with the hazards found along a river unused for twenty years and likely blocked by fallen trees. We all breathed a sigh as Tadhg and Jake finally managed to get one started. Jake tested it by hovering over the ground and flying short distances, declaring it safe. As Tadhg sought avgas, Illy, Isla, and I, knowing little about machinery, and nothing at all about helicopters, loaded it with fresh water, food, a medical kit, and the fully enclosed protective suits with fitted rubber boots we had found at Butterworth to keep us dry. We had taken a suit each in case we needed to wade some distance between where we landed the craft and the cave entrance. We left Jake to load the explosives, the only one among us comfortable in handling it. Isla kept her distance, I noted. I wasn't scared but had no experience either, aside from watching Luca detonate the facility in which they had kept my sister.

As the sun returned and the intense heat evaporated the surrounding puddles, I remembered what Cam had said about the thinness of the air becoming an issue for the earth. With no plants to create oxygen, we were rapidly using up what little we had. Within a few years, we wouldn't be able to go outside at all. Guilt at this thought pricked at me, realizing that people really wouldn't have an alternative after we deactivated the Nexus. We would be stuck.

Safe, a tiny voice reminded me, and I pushed it down.

Returning to the *Eurydice* for dinner, we paused to watch the spectacular tropical oranges and reds of the sun setting across the turquoise horizon. As night fell, we reviewed the maps, plans, and layout of the cave system. Jake and Tadhg plotted how to get the most effective shock to jolt the Nexus out of alignment.

"Do you think we can carry all of it?" Isla asked Jake.

"We need to try. We only get one shot at this."

Dawn broke as spectacular as the sunset the previous evening. Pink-gold tinted the horizon, and I twisted the ring on my finger as the light rose and illuminated the white paint of the *Eurydice*. Closing my eyes, I pictured my family. *Soon, my love. I will be home soon. Look after my baby for me.*

Jake managed to start the helicopter and, after a shaky start, was soon doing steady circles as we shaded our eyes from the brilliant sunshine. The sun's rays were burning my skin after so many years of living under a protected layer of fabric, better than any sunscreen. Illy waved, and Jake came in to land, bumpily, but securely enough. Climbing aboard, we followed the map she had sourced and were soon rewarded with enormous rocky outcrops looming from the formerly tropical landscape.

"It must have been spectacular," Isla murmured beside me. "Look how dense the forest is, the river meandering through." The river was a deep green, flowing slowly past fallen trees and foliage, now brown and dead, rotting away into nothingness.

"What am I looking for?" Jake called back.

"That." Tadhg, seated up front with Jake and armed with the map, pointed out a flattened patch of brown earth, and Jake shakily lowered the craft. I closed my eyes, silently hoping this wouldn't be the last time I would see my family. He wasn't instilling me with confidence, swearing and muttering under his breath. The girls and I, seated in the back, gripped the armrests tightly. But aside from a whiplash-inducing jolt as we hit the ground, we were down. Casting my eyes over at the others, they were as relieved as I was. We waited for the rotors to stop spinning and tumbled out.

"Sorry," Jake mouthed over the noise. "It has been a few years."

I lay my hand on his shoulder. It was reassuring to have him along.

The signage, broken and dilapidated as it was, was still legible, and it wasn't hard to find the main path. Stepping carefully to avoid falling down concealed holes, we made our way to the cave entrance, moving fallen branches and trees rather than stepping on them, unsure what could lurk underneath. No one had time for a broken leg today. The suits were large and cumbersome, and the inbuilt rubber boots were several sizes too big. The result being that we were clumsy and ungainly, especially Illy. Her suit swam on her, making her look like a child in a clown costume.

Tadhg and Jake had spent much of the night discussing the best way to jolt the Nexus out of alignment. The fundamentals they had agreed upon. Setting the charges as close to the Equator as they could get and with as large a blast as they could manage with the explosives they had.

"But is it enough?" Tadhg kept asked Jake, knowing he had significantly more experience with explosives. Tadhg, we learned, knew about the impacts, how to set them and detonate, but had never done it in the field. Several times, Jake had done the physical work but hadn't been the person to calculate the quantity required.

"Should be, but this is so different from any of my other jobs. Those were all buildings, not caves. And nothing of this magnitude. We will need to generate the biggest focused jolt we can, as deep and as close to the equator as we can. The materials are old, but PETN is one of the most powerful explosive chemicals available. Was available, I guess I should say. Not like anyone manufactures it now. But it was stored well enough, so it should work."

"More powerful than TNT?" Isla asked innocently.

"Similar, but this explodes with more power. Regardless, we have some RDX and C4, so we will just set it all and hope for the best."

Isla nodded. I knew she was as clueless as I was when it came to the benefits of one chemical explosive over another.

"We need to get as far in as we can. Deep, I mean. It could be a long way, and the oxygen will be thin in places. Are you prepared?"

As much as I didn't want to go underground, we were all required to carry the large quantity of explosives we had taken. We would need to move slowly and gingerly, careful not to bang it against the wall, exploding ourselves in the process.

Arriving at the cave entrance, we stripped off our waterproof suits, and I breathed a sigh of relief as I hung the sweaty plastic suit on a rock inside the cave's entrance to air. Removing my hiking boots from around my neck and untying the laces so I could wear them, we reloaded ourselves with the heavy backpacks containing the explosives and detonation equipment. It was hot and steamy in the caves, and the deeper we traveled, the more oppressive the air became. Stripping off as much clothing as I could, I was soaked. Rivulets of sweat ran down my torso and uncomfortably down my back beneath the backpack, making me squirm.

We only had two solar-charged lanterns, so we stuck close together. In places, there were cracks in the rock, and tiny streams of daylight filtered through. But mostly, it was pitch black and slow going, resulting in us tripping over boulders and banging our elbows and heads on rocky outcrops. We tried to keep up a steady stream of chatter, mostly warning each other of hazards. Illy was quiet, thinking of Ashton, I guessed. It was his knowledge that had led us here. He had sacrificed himself to save me, but I was still seething with the news of what he had sanctioned. Not done himself, and I had no doubt it was an accident, rendering me infertile, but he had known. I had seen him annually for the past six years, not to mention the time spent on the *Damara*, and never once had he said anything. But then again, how could he?

"Hi Frey, fancy a drink? By the way, when we kidnapped you and raided you, we accidentally nicked you. Sorry about that! No hard feelings?"

Just as I was about to call time out, the air thinning beyond comfort, Tadhg, who was leading the way, stopped in an open area wide enough to park a compact car.

"Can we rest?" I gasped, my lungs struggling for breath.

Jake nodded. "It is getting bad down here," he wheezed. "We can't go any farther."

Jake and Tadhg gave instructions on where to lay the explosives, and we all helped to run the wires and charges, Jake checking the installation over and over. We all knew we had one shot at this. No one could face coming back down if it didn't detonate. The lack of oxygen was making me tired, and black spots were dancing before my eyes, making me fear I would lose consciousness.

"Come on. Let's start heading up," Illy suggested as Jake checked the layout and connections for the fifth time. "We know the pathway is clear. The guys will be right behind us."

Dragging my weary body along, I helped Isla, who was struggling as much as I was. Illy was flushed, her hair plastered to her face and gasping for air. The tunnel was wide enough in places that we could walk three abreast, in others, single file. The stone walls impinged uncomfortably around us, scraping my head and making me feel like I was trapped in an airless coffin. Despite no longer carrying the heavy contents of my pack, the return was uphill, and each breath was a struggle as we needed to stop every few hundred meters to catch our breath. As we walked, a strange sensation pricked down my back, and I stopped, turning.

"What?" Illy asked. "They are right behind us. I can hear them."

Listening, I nodded. I could hear the footsteps echoing up the tunnel. "Not that. Jake and Tadhg, I mean. It is … something else."

"Something else?" Isla's eyes popped wide, and I placed a finger over my lips. She quieted immediately, but terror replaced the look of shock.

"It's nothing," Illy grumbled. "Come on. They are right behind us. It is hot, and I am exhausted. Let's go."

Isla stood ready to go, but I stayed still.

"You go."

"For fuck's sake, Freyja, can we just go? There is nothing here."

Closing my eyes, I swayed, wondering if I was hallucinating from the heat and lack of oxygen. I tried to pinpoint the source of the feeling, slowing my breathing. *Focus,* I ordered myself as I removed sight and focused only on sound and sensation. *What is it?* It was a feeling, a sense. Something I couldn't quite put my finger on.

Opening my eyes, I took three purposeful strides to a large rock and reached behind.

A high-pitched scream filled the cave, and all hell broke loose.

Within seconds, we were being attacked. The lantern Isla had been holding smashed on the rocky floor as she was tackled to the ground, pitching the cave into total darkness. Tadhg and Jake came roaring into the clearing with the remaining lantern illuminating Isla, Illy, and me fighting off unknown assailants.

Jake put his fingers in his mouth and whistled, the deafening sound reverberating around the cavern. Everyone froze and looked at him. Pushing the hot, sticky body off me, I realized it was a young boy, a teenager perhaps, but so small and painfully thin I could count every one of his ribs. His hip bones protruded at strange angles, and his face was sunken painfully. He pulled back, but the oversized eyes looked terrified rather than aggressive.

Illy recovered her composure first.

"Berbahasa Melayu?" she asked haltingly. *"Awak cakap Melayu?"*

The boy fired off something unintelligible, but a thin, reedy voice sounded behind him.

"Saya berbahasa Melayu. Siapa Awak?"

Illy fired off some questions and was answered in return. A terse conversation followed, sweat dripping from me, making me squirm and needing to wipe my face constantly. Illy's posture was relaxing in the dim light. Finally, she turned to us and translated from her rusty Malaysian.

"When the jungle started dying, a group of local tribesmen, Dayaks, Punan specifically, came underground, hoping to escape the protozoa. Initially, there were a hundred of them. Now there are..." she stopped to check, "there are only twenty-two left, mostly children who have never lived outside, plus two elders. They moved their entire village here. They started with animals, goats, and chickens. But they all died. They brought crops to grow in wooden boxes and did their best to expose them to some sunlight and keep them out of the rain, but they provide little food for them. They are starving and only eat when they must."

"Have they truly lived underground for twenty years?" Isla asked, shocked.

"They have," Illy confirmed. "They try to get a little sunlight first thing in the morning but avoid the rain. They have a cavern filled with clean water, but it is the only safe water left. It is drying up. They had fish in there initially, but now, they have all died too."

"They likely have terrible medical conditions," I murmured to Illy. "Malnutrition, rickets, lack of vitamin D from living under here. No protein. Look at that boy. I can see that he has soft bones and fractures that haven't healed well." The boy I had been grappling with had a nasty break in one forearm that had healed at an odd angle. He was holding it gingerly. I hoped I hadn't inflicted any further injuries on him in our scuffle.

"What do we do with them?" Isla asked. "We can't leave them here."

"Not when I set off the explosives," Jake confirmed. "The roof will cave in."

"You saved them, Freyja." Isla looked at me suddenly. "It was you. You sensed them. We would have walked right past and blown this place up, killing them all."

I shrugged, unsure of what to say.

"But where do we take them?" Isla pressed. "There is nowhere to go. Is there another way? Can we set the explosives somewhere else?"

"We can't leave them here." Illy was firm. "They will die. If not from the explosion, but they are running out of food and fresh water. Medical conditions. Slow death or a fast one. But leaving them is a guaranteed death sentence."

"You know who can help them?" I thought aloud. "Sorcha. She spent many of her summer holidays helping in developing countries. She was training to be a doctor in communities like the Dayaks. She spent time in Timor, Papua New Guinea, and I think even Kalimantan. She will know how to treat them."

"So we take them with us," Illy decided. "We will need a few helicopter trips, but we can accommodate them all on the *Eurydice*."

It was a slow process: Illy communicated to the single elder who spoke Malay, he interpreted to the rest of his people, and Illy to us. Illy carefully explained who we were and what was about to happen. Although I didn't understand the words, she spoke kindly and warmly, initially to protests. They would be fine, but could we leave them some food and fresh water? Illy persisted. How could they continue to live here once that food ran out? Their children wouldn't survive long. We could relocate them. Help them survive into the next generation. Soon they were listening. I could see the nodding among the younger people. They knew they were dying but were reluctant to accept help from strangers.

"Frey," Illy said softly, "Speak to them."

"I don't speak Malay," I protested.

"It doesn't matter. Just talk, slowly and calmly. They don't understand your words, but they want to hear it from you. You sensed them. They think you are special. Just speak, convince them that coming with us is the best thing to do."

I spoke as engagingly as I could, using my hands to convey our willingness to help. They were terrified, but bizarrely, watched intently and listened to me. They didn't understand me, that was plain, but they were fascinated by me.

"Your hair," Illy explained. "Other than the older man, who once lived in Jakarta, the children have never seen light-skinned people, but they are fascinated with your golden hair. Jake, can you bring the lantern closer to Freyja?"

He did, and I caught the gasps of amazement.

"Take your hair out," she encouraged. I did, pulling the tie from my ponytail and trying to fluff my sticky hair around my face. The gasps made me smile, and I gently encouraged them to collect all of their belongings, gesturing that we needed to go.

Murmurs of assent filled the cavern, and I wiped the sweat from my brow.

Illy explained about the helicopter and the yacht, and the journey we would need to undertake to reach safety. I smiled as she placed her hands over her ears and scrunched her eyes closed, making them laugh. Despite never having been on a helicopter, the older man had at least seen them and explained to the others that they were noisy but safe. He offered to go first and suggested that I accompany him.

"They think you are a goddess," Illy explained, making me blush.

"She is," Isla whispered.

Several hours later, as Illy, Isla, and I stood on the deck of the *Eurydice,* we felt the tremor as Jake detonated the explosives deep in the earth. He and Tadhg had remained behind and set it from the helicopter. Our new friends were huddled in a cabin. Safe but terrified. Unable to stand the direct sunlight on their skin and in their eyes, we had hastened them into several rooms and drawn the curtains. When I had checked on them, they were all huddled together in one. Several smiled at me through their fear, and I tried to be reassuring as I gave them dry crackers to eat and bottles of fresh water, hoping to settle their stomachs before embarking on our journey back to Australia. The look of glee on their faces as they bit into the crisp cracker and it made a crackling sound was a delight, and they giggled softly.

"They are going to experience so many firsts," I said quietly to Illy as she stood beside me.

"I can't even imagine the mind fuck this will be. Twenty years underground, nearly all of them were born there. No experience of the ocean, wind, proper food. Thinking they are the only people left alive, only to learn they are not alone."

"You should have seen it!" Jake buzzed when he and Tadhg returned. "The rocks fell, and it was like a cavern opened up, and the earth tipped in. I thought it would suck us in, and I had to fly higher to be safe!"

"It was pretty impressive," Tadhg admitted, not with quite the same enthusiasm.

"Luca would have loved it," Jake said to Illy, grinning.

"I know. He would have hated to miss this adventure."

CHAPTER 38

SORCHA WAS IN HER element. Even after several weeks at sea, feeding them small quantities, and slowly increasing the quantity and variety of foods, they still struggled with digestion and were regularly sick. I had limited experience with malnutrition but knew to take it slowly. The children, who had rarely been exposed to the sun, had poor eyesight, and their skin had various fungal infections. All the children were aged ten to eighteen, we ascertained. Sorcha and I assessed them all, one by one, taking copious notes as the baseline. Hypocalcemia, hypophosphatemia, vitamin D deficiency, generalized osteopenia, multiple vertebral and costal fractures, and osteomalacia secondary to vitamin D deficiency from lack of exposure to sunlight and the inadequacy of their diet were diagnosed.

Much to my surprise, Sorcha also spoke basic Malay. Indonesian technically, she told me, from her time on Kalimantan. But the languages are similar, and many of the root words are the same. So with Illy and the Punan elder Rudi's help, she made herself understood quickly.

Like me, the children were fascinated with Sorcha and her long, red hair, touching it constantly. To my immense surprise, Sorcha found it amusing and didn't react when they crept up behind her as she worked, tugging gently on her long plait. Di, they were more relaxed around. I couldn't work out if it was her Asian appearance or her gentle manner, but the children followed her around like the Pied Piper.

"Tell me about the living conditions," Sorcha asked me between assessments. She and I took extensive notes on each of the immigrants, discussing areas of concern and possible treatments. Sorcha was the perfect mix of kind but firm. They recognized her authority immediately, but the respect she showed each of them was returned.

"She was phenomenal," I told Cam later that night when we finally managed to get five minutes alone. "You should have seen her. She was calm and patient and checked every one of them thoroughly. She took the time to ask each of them questions. After the fifth child, it was plain that they were all suffering from the same ailments. But she treated them all as individuals. Made them all feel special and cared for. I have never seen her like that. It was a gift."

"Sorcha always knew she wanted to be a doctor." Cam snuggled into me and whispered into my ear, careful not to be overheard. "From the time we were children, and she was given a toy stethoscope, she knew it was her calling."

Cam and I had chosen to sleep in the troop carrier we had taken from his former girlfriend's house. Parked alongside a bus, we could still hear voices outside. The original bus was filled with our children and Gerry. Di and Sorcha and their children occupied the cabin. The two other buses Illy and Gerry had brought were still sitting just outside the dome, and while they had been stripped of seats, they hadn't been finished with insulation and lining boards. Gerry had prioritized repairing the dome and building additional tanks for Cam in our absence. But for now, Isla and Illy slept in one, and Tadhg and Jake in the other. For the first few nights, the new arrivals would sleep in large ex-military cooking tents, all piled on top of each other, until we could finish the buses for them. They had slept in proximity for years and couldn't bear to be apart. The new children were exhilarated with the cool, fresh air and, after a lifetime of living in the dark, loved seeing the stars through the transparent sections of the dome. We had sourced clothing for each of them in Melbourne and warm jackets. Even though I was comfortable in a t-shirt, they were freezing, especially at night, never having experienced temperate climates.

"What did they eat?" Cam asked, snuggling down on his pillow.

"Their animals all perished in the first few years, so after that, they survived on a purely vegetarian diet."

"Did the plants grow without sunlight?"

"Not well. They are starving, as you can see. But yes, the plants adapted. I wasn't paying much attention, but they were stunted and oriented toward what little direct light there was."

"Will they ever really recover?"

"I don't know," I admitted. "There have been no children born for nearly ten years. Mainly due to all the nutritional deficiencies, the women couldn't carry them to term. Plus, like all parents, what little food they had was given to the children first, the elders, second. Most of the adults of reproductive age passed in the last few years as things got really dire."

"Tell me again how you found them?"

"It was dark, and the air was thin. I was struggling to breathe. You know that sensation when you have a fever, and everything feels surreal? It was like that. I just *sensed* them there. They alert us. We didn't see or hear anything. I just had that unshakeable sense that someone was watching me. I checked behind an enormous boulder and found a child. Then they all came out."

"You saved them all, Illy says. Jake would have blown the cave apart—with them in it."

I shrugged, unsure of what to say.

"What did you say Freyja's version of Valhalla was called again?"

"Sessrúmnir."

"I think we have just found the name for our new community. Freyja's chosen ones."

"I don't think..." I protested, but he cut me off with a kiss.

"It is decided. Those girls are special, your chosen ones. You saved those people. All of them. I say it is a fitting choice of name, and I can't imagine anyone would argue with me."

Scowling, I didn't persist, knowing that he was right. I just felt that it was a bit over the top.

I kissed his neck. "Tell me more about this girl-friend of yours that you took away for dirty weekends in this very vehicle?"

"She wasn't a patch on you, my goddess."

"Why didn't you mention her before?"

Cam paused, considering. "Because I haven't thought of her in twenty years," he finally admitted. "She wasn't my first girlfriend, but she was the one I was with the longest, before you. But even then, I guess I knew. It was easy, comfortable. She called the shots, and I was okay with that. But I think deep down, I always knew she wasn't the woman I would marry and have children with."

"Why stay with her?"

"Because I hated conflict, and we got along. We enjoyed spending time together, bushwalking, camping. It was just the long-term part I had an issue with."

"You don't think that was a little unfair to her? Wasting her time if you never intended to stay with her?"

Cam pulled back slightly. "Do you know, I never really thought about it like that. We spent most weekends together, some weeknights too. It was never an issue until she made it one."

"Did she actually want you to propose?"

"Oh, most certainly. She told me to put a ring on it. I was twenty-two, not ready for a lifetime of commitment. Then Sam, Sorcha's fiancé, passed, and I realized, watching Sorcs fall into that pit, that I didn't feel the same way for Natalie. That depth of emotion. So I broke it off. I was single for several months before I attended the selection and left for August."

"Do you think you would have ended up with her?" I knew I was pushing the boundaries, but I needed to know, after all that had happened.

"Probably," he admitted. "Had Sam not died, and she hadn't pushed, I suspect at some point, it would have just happened. All of my friends were in and out of relationships. Some were getting married or moving in together, so it just felt like what you did. Found someone you were mostly happy with and paired up. But when I met you, it was like a thunderbolt that knocked me for six. I knew. That first night. I knew."

"The first night?"

"Not the night we met in the dorm, but the night in the hot springs. That night, I remember it clearly. Lying on the rocky outcrop on the far side of the cave, a jagged piece of stone stabbing me in the back. You were lying in my arms, and it was like my heart changed rhythm and never reverted to its old pattern. In that moment, I knew with absolutely crystal clarity. *You* were the one I was meant to spend my life with. I just didn't want to freak you out, along with me."

"I felt the same," I admitted. "My relationships were all short term before you, but something in me just knew it was you. Illy described it to me once as finding your best friend, the piece that had been missing from your life. Only you didn't know until that moment that it was missing."

"I think that sums it up perfectly. You were always mine."

"Well, perhaps we need to make this place ours," I whispered.

CHAPTER 39

"WHY DIDN'T YOU TAKE them to Auckland Island?" Sorcha asked Illy as we gathered for drinks in the cottage the following evening after our return from Borneo. "Surely they could be better cared for there. They have specialists and diagnostic equipment. I don't have much more than a first aid kit."

"Perhaps, but they want to be independent. They are sick, yes, but not pathetic. On Auckland, they wouldn't find meaningful work and would always be treated as a curiosity. Here, they can farm, raise their children, and live the way they wanted. Safe, but in peace."

"Are you sure they will be okay here? I mean, everything is so new. The trees, the crops. They don't know what half of the vegetables are," Cam asked.

"They will be fine," Sorcha interjected. "We have a protein source with the fish, and we are lucky that Dad stocked the ponds with trout and salmon. Those varieties are high in protein but provide healthy fats that they lack too."

"Well, you and Di had better get growing if we now have nearly sixty mouths to feed," I said. "Not that they eat much now, but they will."

"I have decided on a name for The Block," Cam announced, making Sorcha scowl.

"What? You single-handedly think it is your place..."

Cam held a hand up to her. "Let me finish." He picked up a large, hardbound book from the table. *World Mythology*, I noticed as he flipped through pages, opening it on a double page, with colored illustrations of the goddess, Freyja, her golden hair and cloak billowing behind her as she rode in her chariot pulled by cats.

"Mum and Dad chose this place to be their escape, their piece of paradise. Both of them lived a life where they helped others. It was what they believed in. Finally, we can put this place to its true purpose and fulfill their vision."

Sorcha's scowl lessened, but she still wasn't happy.

Cam pointed to the enormous, decadent building rising from the grassy field in the book. "In Norse mythology, Sessrúmnir is the hall where Freyja's chosen ones live. They are treated well and live a wonderful life. Without our Freyja, these girls would not exist. These people would not have survived. Sorcs, without Freyja, I would never have found you again. Without her, you would never have met Di. So I think it is fitting that we name this place after her."

Cam handed the book to Sorcha, who scanned the content. There was a moment of silence before Di clapped her hands.

"I think that is wonderful!" she gushed. "Freyja's chosen ones. Sessrúmnir. I love it!"

Illy smiled but said nothing, recognizing that this decision was Cam and Sorcha's.

Sorcha nodded begrudgingly. "I like it. And yes, Mum would be beyond thrilled knowing that their little block had become a home for people in need."

"I propose a toast," Gerry spoke softly. "To Sessrúmnir."

"To Sessrúmnir," we echoed.

***

"What happened to Ashton?" Sorcha asked me the following afternoon as we cleaned up after our daily check-ups. She was having some success treating the fungal infections with the natural therapies Jacinda had taught me over the years, but many were still struggling with the change in diet.

"Wow," she said when I told her. "And how do you feel about that?"

"I'm not sure," I responded. "I am furious at what he did, what he knew. But I didn't want him to die, and now poor Illy is alone again."

"You are a better person than I am," she announced as she snapped her kit closed. "I would have pushed him overboard."

"I just wish he had told me. It feels like as soon as I deal with something, another knife comes and plunges into my heart. It is stupid, I know. I don't want more children. But to know that they damaged me? I always thought it was because he felt guilty that he let me go. Now I know I was useless to them."

"You aren't useless to me."

"You don't need me. You have this under control. I've always known you were an exceptional physician, but I have never seen you more in your element than you are here. This is your calling, Sorcha. Helping people like this."

"Perhaps. But I love having someone to talk to and bounce ideas off. We can talk about treatment options, what might work. I have always loved the collegiate part of medicine."

"That was something that took me by surprise with medicine. Not that Isla and I didn't talk about veterinary treatment. Of course, we did, but it isn't the same. With people, there are so many variables to consider."

"Despite what it cost you, I am pleased you did the ortho training."

"What do you mean, what it cost me?" I asked cynically, wondering who had betrayed my confidence.

"Despite what you think of me, I'm not an idiot, Freyja. Di and I both noticed that you came home a different woman. What did they do to you?"

"Nothing, other than work me into the ground. That wasn't it."

"PTSD?" she asked softly and watched as I sank into a chair.

"How did you know?"

"I suffered myself after finding Sam's body," she admitted. "Cam never knew. It was Dad who spotted it. After years as a paramedic, he had suffered himself at various points. Sometimes he lapsed into depression after attending one really awful job like a child murder. Other times, a culmination of shitty jobs left him feeling numb. But he saw it in me and got me help."

"Illy worked it out when we were on the *Damara*," I confessed. "After I broke my hand. I just thought I was empty."

"I'm so sorry. I should have seen it. I just thought you were being a bitch. I started wondering when you told me about the photos, the day we arrived in Kiewa. But it never seemed the right time to ask."

"Because I was being a bitch. Allegedly."

"Oh, not allegedly, you were. You lashed out at everyone. But it is me who needs to apologize, Freyja. For not offering support. You are the best thing to ever happen to my brother. Without you, he wouldn't be the man he is. And he was right about what he said yesterday. Without you, Di and I wouldn't be together, and we wouldn't have three amazing children. I have never said it aloud, but I truly mean it. I love you like a sister, and a best friend. But more than that, I respect you as a professional. My parents would have loved you. They would have welcomed you with open arms and had your back. You are the missing piece to Cam's life, and they would have recognized it, too."

"Really?" I fought to keep my game face, not wanting to show how much this meant to me.

"Bloody hell, I can't imagine my poor dad with you, me, and Mum in a room! Add Katrin and Caitlin to the mix, and I think Dad would have run away to the block to live years ago."

"What was he like? Cam talks about your Mum, but less about your dad."

"Dad was just like Campbell. In looks and personality. Dad believed he was undiagnosed neurodiverse, like Cam. He told me when I was seeing the therapist for my PTSD. He drove me to my appointments, and we would go out for a drink and talk afterward. But when he was at school, he was just the quirky kid who was quiet and couldn't make friends. But he plugged away, went to university, traveled, and met Mum. Mum was super organized and logical, so she took over the organizational stuff, which freed him from stress. You do that for Cam, I notice. One of Cam's psychologists, many years ago, said that super organized women tend to pair up with neurodiverse men. The caring types, nurses, teachers, doctors. They are the ones who can see past the quirks and understand the person underneath. I thought that when I first met you. You and Cam are so much like my parents."

"But it worked? They were happy?"

"They had their disagreements like anyone else, but yes. They were a team. I think that is why I was so pissed at you when you came home from Clava. You broke up the partnership. It was like watching my parents separate. Watching the train wreck as an onlooker and wanting to stop it, bang your heads together and give you a jolly good shake, but knowing I was powerless."

"I am sorry about that."

"Good. Don't do it again."

"Any hot tips on dealing with PTSD?"

"One. Healing isn't linear."

I crinkled my brow, pondering that. I was just about to ask what she meant when she said, "By the way, it is your turn to wash the bedding and soiled dressings from the clinic."

CHAPTER 40

"HONEY, HOW DO YOU feel about heading home? We have no reason to think we aren't safe. The Nexus is out of action. Tadhg is champing at the bit to head home to interrupt the radio signals. Dale is gone, and you said that the elders in India wouldn't allow any more attacks on the girls. Nothing is stopping us."

"Really?" I stopped pegging the washing I was hanging and turned to him. "Do you mean it?"

"I do."

Dropping the freshly washed clinic bedsheet in the dirt, I threw my arms around his neck.

"Hang on. The judges only said they would issue a directive. That might stop attacks by their children. They have no control over any other community. Why would someone like Sophie listen to what some old men in India say? We know about Aroha and a few others, but we don't know who killed Ceridwen or Solstice."

"I promised you I would work it out, didn't I?" Illy's voice reached me before I saw her come into view. She stooped to pick up the now filthy sheet. "I think a detour via August Island might be prudent. We can return Arataki to her parents and have a chat with Miss Aroha while we are there. Enough pressure and she will cave."

"If it is *you* applying the pressure, I don't doubt it." I grinned. "But what makes you think Jamie and Jacinda will allow it?"

"Of course they will. We will show that there are no hard feelings about the attacks on Seraphine and Mei, and we return Arataki to her family. If someone proved they trusted me enough to give me back my daughter, I would certainly encourage a child who had done the wrong thing to spill."

"True. When can we go?"

"A week?" Cam said thoughtfully. "I need to finish teaching the Punan how to propagate seedlings and care for the fish. It is slow going, and I need you to interpret, Illy. But it isn't that hard. They are taking to this life like they were born here."

It had surprised me how well the younger children from Borneo had taken to engaging with our girls. They learned together, although Di was still trying to teach the newcomers basic English.

"I'm learning more Punan than they are learning English," she told me one day. "But they are wonderful students, even if they have never had any form of formal learning."

"I'm so worried about those children," I admitted when we met for drinks in the cabin that evening. "Rickets takes such a long time to overcome, and so many of them have badly healed breaks. Do you think this generation will ever develop normally? Are we not better to take them back to Lewis with us? We have several vessels. They can come. I am sure they will be accepted."

"They are better off here," Illy said. "They have adapted well, and I don't think taking them somewhere new, and a freezing climate is in their best interest. It is warm here in summer, and at least the winters are milder here than Scotland."

"Ireland, too." Tadhg grinned.

"Hey, try Orkney!" Gerry interjected. "In winter, we get less than six hours of daylight! They'll think they are back in those caves."

"I just don't feel like we can't leave them," I said. "I know we said we would leave next week. I am so desperate to get home. But I feel terrible abandoning them."

"We won't be." Sorcha's voice was low but firm.

"What?" Cam snapped out of his daydream. "No. You can't. I didn't come all this way all those years ago to lose you. We are leaving in a week, Sorcs. We agreed."

"*You* are leaving next week," she corrected. "*I* am staying here. The Punan need me. If they are to survive here, at Sessrúmnir, then I need to help them."

"Wha...!"

"Stop being melodramatic, Campbell. It isn't forever. But I miss this. Helping people."

"You help people on Lewis," I pointed out feebly.

"Not the same. This was what I trained to do. I always planned to join *Medicin sans Frontieres* when I graduated, only that never happened. This is my dream, helping people who need me. I admit, at the time, I thought it would be short-term deployments after natural disasters or in warzones and refugee camps. But this is close enough. After twenty years underground, they are suffering from an enormous range of ailments. I can help, so I will."

"Are you sure you don't want them to come back with us?"

"No. They like it here. They hated the short time to travel from Borneo to here. Imagine a trip to Scotland. Besides, the winters will kill them."

"Do you want us to stay?" Cam asked, flashing a cautious look at me.

"No. This could take a few years. You have children on Lewis. They need you."

"Years!"

"This isn't a quick fix, Campbell," she rebuked him. "You have already confirmed that there is adequate space here for us to feed everyone?"

"There is, if you are careful. Save seeds and waste nothing."

"Then we stay." Sorcha was resolute. Even I knew that tone. Only a complete idiot would take her on when she spoke like that.

"Di? You are okay with this?" Cam asked anxiously.

Di flashed her charming smile. "We talk, you know! I am happy to be anywhere my family is. But yes. I got into agriculture to grow things. So now I get to mentor these people. Teach them what I know and everything I have learned from you over the years. Help them be self-sufficient in an environment I know but is foreign to them. Sam, Kendra, Mei, they are all here. My gorgeous wife. There is nowhere else I would rather be. Sam is eighteen. He can teach the children, and Gerry has already taught him a great deal about maintenance and repair. Kendra can help teach the children and assist us. This is what we always wanted for our children—for them to live a life helping others. What better way to teach them about their place in the world than for them to help people who need it?"

"Mum would love this, you know," Cam said quietly. "She would be so proud of you."

"And you," she said pointedly. "Look at everything you have achieved. All of you. Without you, I would still live alone on Kiewa. Look at all the living I have done because of you. The two children I never expected to have. Now it is my turn to give something back. But now you can leave and not feel guilty. Tomorrow if you like."

"Tomorrow then?" Cam asked, turning to Illy, Isla, Gerry, Tadhg, and me.

"Tomorrow," I confirmed.

CHAPTER 41

CAM AND I WERE silent for most of the bumpy drive back to Melbourne. Illy was in front of us, driving the Unimog with Gerry and the girls, Alasdair, Ruby, and Scarlett. Tadhg and Jake were in the back with the kids, taking turns to jump out and move obstructions from the road.

"She will be fine," I said finally, placing a hand on his knee.

"It isn't her I am worried about. Sorcha is a survivor. She will thrive. I'm pleased we can leave her Ashton's vessel. At least we know she can get home when the time is right."

"Then what is it?"

"I worry about you, funnily enough. Our girls, taking them to August."

"You know we need to take Taki back to her parents. You know how I feel about going back to August. But we need to. We can't keep her."

"Agreed."

"Do we tell them who her father is?"

Cam exhaled forcefully. "I think so. If Jamie is anything like me, it will change nothing. But there is a tiny sense of peace that comes with knowing that no one will ever come looking for her, seeking to play a role in her life. Does that make sense?"

"Of course it does. That is how I feel about Louis. It was easier for me to accept him, knowing that he will always be mine. What exactly are you worried about?"

"It was Aroha who tried to murder Seraphine, and Illy knows it. There were likely Players on August, and we don't know who. Are we just walking into another Kiewa?"

"Not exactly. We know there is a risk, and we take steps to mitigate the risk. But we can't just hide on Lewis. There are others there, too. Plus, Taki is so desperately sad. How do we take her back to Lewis, and her family is no longer there?"

"I know. It is the right thing to do."

"Bloody hell, I hate this enormous beast," I seethed as I performed pre-departure maintenance on the *Damara*.

"It's fine, Frey," Jake's voice cut over the engine noise. "We have talked, and Tadhg, Gerry, and I will take her home. We will take the Orkney and Newgrange girls on the *Damara*. You can take yours on the *Eurydice*."

"Splitting up? Why?"

"How about we take both to August?" Illy suggested.

"Because I want to get home," Tadhg cut in. "Not just to my family, but I need the equipment I have at home to block the radio transmissions. The sooner I get there, the better. We can manage. It will only be thirteen of them. But they won't do any learning. I can just about guarantee it."

"Is it even possible?" I asked, still fearful that there were Players out there seeking my head for a trophy. "Blocking radio signals, I mean."

Tadhg grinned broadly. "Of course! Radio jamming has been performed for decades. China, Russia, Cuba—they all blocked radio signals. During World War II, radio transmissions were jammed. The UN even passed a resolution on it in 1950, although I can't imagine anyone will care now. The issue I have was amplifying it. But with Jake's help, we have an idea."

"If you are sure, let me help you source as many spares and tools as we can. I don't want to find you adrift on our way home."

I sighed with relief as I stepped foot aboard the *Eurydice*. We had agreed to leave Ashton's smaller *Belisama* for Sorcha if she needed to move, mainly as it was solar powered with batteries, and she had some experience with it.

"She will come home, you know." Illy smiled into Cam's downcast face. "You are her family, too."

Cam's sapphire blue eyes turned on Illy mournfully. "I feel like I have abandoned her. And Di."

"She chose," Isla assured him. "She was glowing. Could you not see how complete she feels? Those people need her, really need her in a way that no one on Lewis ever has. We have other doctors. We will be fine. But she will help those people thrive. With her help, they will have children and ensure their culture survives. I can't imagine a better legacy."

"What do you think they will have done with Ashton?" I asked Illy as we curled up on the couch together a few nights later. Cam was piloting the vessel. Isla was sitting opposite us.

"Sacrifice. Their laws were very much an eye for an eye."

"Well, I am glad I ended Dale. I sleep better at night knowing he will never come after me again. I just wish I had prolonged it a bit."

"You didn't need to," Isla chirped. "Did you not notice he was suffering?"

"At the time he was slapping me around, I didn't. He looked thinner and sweaty. Why?"

"He was ill. Really ill. If I had to guess, I would say he had a parasite. I studied parasitic infections in animals back at university. Then one of the infectious diseases specialists from Auckland and I spent some time discussing the similarities between animals and humans at one of the girl's parties a few years back. Had a wonderful natter we did."

"A parasite infecting the parasite?" Illy quipped.

Isla laughed. "Well, my guess is that didn't have longer than a few months to live. And it would be painful if that makes you feel any better."

"Couldn't happen to a nicer person." Illy grinned.

CHAPTER 42

"**STOP PACING, WILL YOU!**" Isla snapped at me, making the girls gape in shock. "Illyria. Take her for a walk. A drink. Something! I can't teach when she is lurking like this."

Illy grinned and dragged me off the *Eurydice*, out into the blinding sunshine. Even though we knew Aroha posed no threat, and the only other Player here, a daughter of Jenny's, had also been identified, I was still reticent to leave them. But Ruby and Scarlett were here, so the younger nine were safe enough.

Illy slid back the access panel, and we stepped into the cool greenness of August. Strange how I had once considered this place home. Despite it being familiar, I felt oddly detached. Like a place I had visited many times on holidays, it was temporary. But as the pure air filled my lungs, I relaxed. Being inside made it easier to breathe. As we walked between the old dorms where we had been housed in those early months, a familiar, shadowy figure slipped into our path.

"Illyria. I would like to speak with you."

Illy drew back and looked at Derek, suspicious. "What?"

"In private, please." His tone was low, but not threatening.

"Do you want me to come?" I asked Illy, ignoring Derek.

"She is not in any danger, I assure you."

"Forgive me if I don't believe you. The last time we met with you, we were chained to beds for months. Then I was violated, assaulted, and nearly raped."

"I just want to talk. I promise. She won't come to any harm."

"No, but *you* might if I hear something has happened against her will," I growled.

"It's fine, Frey. I will see you in an hour. Meet me down at the river? You can show me this special place of yours."

I grimaced, assessing Derek's motives as she handed me the backpack. "It's a date," I promised.

I went to find Cam but found him deep in conversation with the agricultural teams about seed banks, so I slipped away before they could draw me into the conversation. Planting stuff was not my thing at all. Kelly and the team had struggled since Cam, Di, and Jamie had all left, although Jamie's red hair was visible as he worked the orchards in the distance.

I wished I had a book. I contemplated going to the library but remembered that Lena, the psychotic bitch who had left me with a decent scar along my arm worked there, so I gave up on that idea. While many years had passed, I had never forgiven her for the years of pain she caused me. Fuck. We had returned Taki to her parents. One look at their faces confirmed we had done the right thing, as awkward as it was for them and us.

I wandered aimlessly, passing people who smiled and said hello but didn't stop to chat. We had been gone too long now. We were strangers, and I was a person to be gossiped about. The mother of *those* children. Not that I had so many friends when I was here. Cam, Di, Jamie, and Jacinda. I pondered visiting Jacinda but dismissed the thought. We had parted on good terms. Aroha had apologized, but I still didn't trust her. She had tried several times to harm my children, she confessed. I was pleased she was here and not on Lewis. With little prompting, she told us about the other two Players on Lewis, Mike's twin sons. The Firstborn of Lewis. Knowing that I would check in on their father after his surgery, but not knowing that Cam and I had separated, it was they who had raided our home, vandalizing my photos, and left the knife in the door as a warning.

Jake, Tadhg, Gerry, and the girls from Orkney and Newgrange must be halfway home by now, I thought longingly as I wandered along the riverbank. This river hadn't been here when Cam and I lived here. The engineering team had constructed it to accommodate additional water flow from the water storage lake to the settlement, which had almost tripled in size. I desperately wanted to go home when we had departed from Melbourne but acknowledged that we needed to return Arataki to her parents. Seeing them reunite, I knew we had made the right choice, but it was still tense between us. They had made no request to return to Lewis, and we hadn't offered. Some time would need to pass before that relationship could be mended. Hearing footsteps, I glanced up and saw Illy walking toward me, a thundercloud over her head.

"What?" I asked before she could speak.

"Not now. Take me to the hot springs?"

I scooped up the backpack containing two towels and set a cracking pace up the hillside, one I knew well. But now, the foliage was dense, crossing the path entirely in places. Perhaps it wasn't as well-traveled as I had feared? I had conjured images of a well-worn highway to our special place, but it didn't look like anyone had been here in a while.

Illy kept pace, and we made it to the clearing. I paused, remembering the last time I was here.

"You okay?"

"I am. The last time I came here, I was sucked away."

"You didn't visit again when you returned?"

"No. Partly bad memories of what happened, and partly as I was alone. I had Luca, of course, but this was where Cam and I..." I trailed off, thinking of all the things we had done here. Made love, become a couple, pledged our lives to each other.

"Come on." The inaka bush had been hacked down, although recent growth was sprouting from the sawn-down trunk. But it no longer blocked the cave entrance. I stepped through the opening and crouched as I made my way into the outer cave. Crates were stacked along each wall, making me grimace. So they were using it. *Of course they are, you fool!* I berated myself. *The portal is here to the Nexus.* The now deactivated Nexus. Only they didn't know that. Likely wouldn't until the next solstice.

Using my hands, I felt my way to the back of the cave where the tunnel entrance began and warned

Illy. "It is quite confined. You will need to stoop, but the tunnel itself is only short."

Illy laughed, and it echoed pleasantly around the chamber. "So I can walk it with no problem then?"

I led the way and gasped again as I entered the beautiful cave. My grotto. The turquoise blue glowed eerily in the muted light, illuminating the walls and curved ceiling. Our sacred space. But ours no more. There was equipment everywhere, lifts and trolleys to aid the transportation. But no one here. *Just as well,* I mused. *We don't have swimsuits, and I don't feel like having an audience.*

"The stones we found are over there." I gestured to the sides where Cam had found the carved menhirs so many years ago. Illy traced the carving with her fingers. I dropped the bag and stripped off. Illy looked at me for a moment before following suit. She dipped her toe in the water beside me, and her mouth dropped.

"It is hot!" she gasped.

"Well, we didn't call it the lukewarm springs!" I laughed as I plunged in and instantly felt my muscles relax. "Oh god, how I have missed this!"

Illy entered more tentatively, but the look of delight on her face made me smile.

"Oh, my goodness! I can see why you would never want to leave!" She took the few strokes to the center of the pool and floated beside me, sighing. "I can't tell you the last time I had a bath. Or was submerged in hot water of any kind."

"Best part of twenty years?" I sighed beside her.

"Uh-huh."

We floated with our eyes closed for an eternity, yet no time at all. Feeling my muscles soften, I let go. My mind went blank, and I forgot everything. As the heat overwhelmed me, I swam the few strokes to the ledge and pulled myself up, gazing back over the pool. Illy sensed the movement and followed.

"The ledge?" she asked cheekily.

"The very one."

Illy sat beside me, gazing out over the cave. "It is magnificent."

"It is. Serene. Unique. And special, to both Cam and me. We pledged our lives to each other here, the first time. Once I would have said otherwise, but now, it isn't home. I would sacrifice any number of hot baths to get home. So tell me, what did fuck-knuckle want?"

Illy sighed. "They have made me a very interesting offer."

"Offer?"

"They want me to replace Carl as head of the project."

"What?" I just about fell off the ledge in shock.

"Tell me you told Derek to go screw himself with a jackhammer?"

"Not exactly."

I gripped her arm in fear. "You didn't accept?"

"No. I didn't do anything. I told him I needed to think about it."

"You can't. After everything they did?"

"What better way to ensure it never happens again?"

"Not that I don't think you would be awesome at it, but why you? You left them years ago."

"Apparently, they had a meeting after they heard Carl had … died."

What I desperately wanted to ask was, "Are you sure he is dead?" but that felt callous. Instead, I asked, "How did they know?"

"There was a transmission from India to the other communities after we left. Before we reached Malaysia."

"A transmission?"

"Ordering all the Players to stand down. That Dale had died, reparation had been made, and that the game was no longer sanctioned. There would be consequences to any Player who harmed a child."

"Did they? Stand down?"

"Nobody knows for certain, but it looks that way. There was a flurry of communications between the Players, asking if it was for real. It reached a crescendo as we were heading to Malaysia and then Borneo but tapered off around the time we headed back to Australia. It seems they all moved on. But there weren't any more transmissions about it before the Nexus was knocked out of alignment. So as soon as Tadhg can get home and block the radio signals, we are even safer."

"Why you?"

"You don't think I asked that? They said they wanted someone balanced and reasonable. They wanted someone with a unique leadership style to take the Collective forward. They recognized decisions had been made that were ... less than ideal ... were the words I think he used."

"Less than ideal!" I was just about levitating off the ledge. "Are you fucking kidding me?"

"They had a meeting, my name was suggested, and it was almost unanimous."

"Wow." I was speechless for once in my life.

"Your thoughts?" she asked after a few minutes.

I didn't know what to say and wasn't sure what role to play. Did she want me to play the supportive friend, encouraging her? Or devil's advocate? She was giving me no clues on her perspective, which made tailoring my answer difficult. I aimed for supportive but honest.

"It is a wonderful opportunity and one I can see you would be amazing at. We could all live in peace knowing that you would be the one to make any decisions, and they would be made in the best interest of everyone. The girls and I would be safe, and that means the world to me. It is what you were born for."

"But...?"

"But ... I don't want to lose my friend."

"You will never lose me."

My stomach clenched, knowing this wasn't the case. If Illy took over running the Collective, she would move to Clava or Auckland. Take her family. Seraphine. Those I loved as an extension of my own. The wave of anxiety rushed up my gullet, and I tried to muffle it.

"Come on. We need to get back."

Illy paused for a moment, sensing my distress, but followed me back across the pool. We dried and dressed in silence and began heading back down the hill into town.

Unable to sleep, I tossed and turned and finally padded out to the kitchen. Quietly, I checked on the children in their rooms, but they were still asleep, so I returned to bed and curled into Cam.

"What happened between you two yesterday?" he whispered into my ear. "I've never seen you two go so long without speaking, except for those three days at sea when you broke your hand. Has she met someone? Did you argue?"

"No. Nothing like that."

"Okay, but last night was like an iceberg between you. Then you went to bed early, which I have never known you to do. What happened?"

"Come with me? To the springs? We will never get to visit again, and it means a lot to me that the last time I am there, it is with you. The way it should have been. It is hours until dawn, and we can be back when the kids wake."

It was slow going in the dark, with only the stars twinkling through the dome. I pointed out the constellations I had seen at the Clava Cairns to break the silence, and Cam snuggled closer, remembering our time there. As we entered the inner cave, his arms came around me, and his larger frame engulfed me as his lips sought mine. The warmth of his skin against mine matched the humid air, and I melted into him. He scooped me up and held me against him as we entered the water. Together. Safe.

Reaching my face up to be kissed, he adjusted my position to face him, my legs wrapped around his waist.

"I remember the very first time you did that. I thought my heart would pound right out of my chest."

We soaked in the healing waters for the longest time, and for the first time in months, I switched off my brain and relaxed. It didn't last. As we lay on the rocky shelf on the far side, I faced the water as he curled up behind me, trying to control my breathing as thoughts surged through my mind, trying not to lose control.

"It is okay," he soothed, caressing my hip and tracing my tattoo.

"No, it isn't. I can't lose control."

"You can. I'm here. I'll keep you safe."

Forcing myself to slow my breathing, I told him about the offer.

"Wow," he spoke behind me, echoing my response of yesterday. "What a fabulous opportunity. For her, and all of us."

"I want her to take it; I do. She was born for this. She is a natural leader. She is fair, takes the time to listen to all perspectives, and makes decisions to benefit all. She is good and kind. How much happier would we all be knowing she was in charge?"

"You would be safe. The girls too. So what is the problem?"

"She will need to move to Clava, or Auckland, won't she? She will take the kids with her."

"She would. You could visit. Is it Sera you are thinking of?"

"She is Cait's sister! How can I not? But it is Illy too. The twins and Alasdair. I have always been part of their life since the day they were born. Why does everyone I love leave me?"

"I haven't left you."

I choked back the lump in my throat. "I will support her in whatever she decides."

"I know you will. It is okay to be sad, though."

"It isn't … selfish?" I whispered in his ear.

Cam's powerful arms rolled me back to face him. "How is it selfish to be sad that you may lose someone important from your life?"

"I have lost so many people. I can't lose her too."

"No matter what she decides, you will never lose her. You know that."

But do I? I pulled back and got my game face on.

"Come on. We need to get back."

In the still pre-dawn light, we crept back into town and onto the *Eurydice*.

"Would you like to get some more sleep?" he asked kindly as I sat on the side of the bed and took off my boots.

"I think so," I said, lying down. The sound of children ended that conversation as Cait popped her head around the door and, seeing us awake, hurled herself between us. Within minutes we had children in the bed, sitting on the end and chattering so loudly I needed to ask them to stop. Thank goodness none of them had noticed we were clothed, and my hair was still damp.

"Where is your Mum?" I asked Seraphine as she lay between us, wedged beside Caitlin.

She shrugged. "I don't know. She was gone when I woke."

Accepting that I would not be getting back to sleep, I followed Cam to the kitchen with several children in tow. Fortunately, he had already stocked the *Eurydice* with supplies from Jenny. All the original uneaten canned and packaged foods, I noted, remembering the foul slop we had been left on Mousa. Maybe Jenny wasn't so apologetic about her daughter being involved.

As soon as he opened the fridge, I revised this opinion. It was stacked like a tetris game with trays of cakes, lasagnas, biscuits, and baked goods.

"Pastries?" Cam grinned at me, remembering my sweet tooth.

"Danish?" I asked hopefully.
"Apple or apricot?"

Illy returned as we were cleaning up the mess associated with ten children eating flaky pastries for breakfast. They had all disappeared downstairs with Isla, avoiding the clean-up. *Thank goodness Taki isn't with us,* I thought. It would have been impossible not to allow her to have one as the others gorged themselves. There was no way those pastries were vegan with all that butter.

"Morning," she chirped. Assuming my ice queen persona, I greeted her.

Cocking her head to one side, she said, "I'm not, you know. Abandoning you."

"Never said you were."

"You are thinking it."

"Have I told you lately how much I fucking hate it when you do that?"

Illy laughed but sobered quickly. "I have a favor to ask."

"Anything."

"Can you take my two with you back to Lewis?"

My mouth dropped. "Why?"

"I am going to visit the team on Auckland Island, just for a few days. Derek will take me."

"Why wouldn't you want to keep your children?" I asked suspiciously.

"I have asked for some meetings, and it is easier if I don't need to worry about them. I would only trust them with you. I can focus on what I need to do and not constantly be wondering where they are."

"You really trust him, *them*, enough?"

"I do." I bristled at that but was cut off. "I know what they did. I was there, remember? I haven't forgotten. But I need to do this."

Cam stood behind me, his arms around my shoulder. "We will do this, for you. But you need to tell Sera and Alasdair."

Illy smiled. "Of course. When are you leaving? There is no reason to delay."

I glanced at Cam. "It will only take us a few hours to refill the water tanks and stock food. We could be gone by early afternoon?"

"I don't see why not. Let me tell Isla."

A thought occurred to me. "How will you get home? The Nexus isn't exactly operational, remember?"

"One of my conditions is that they give me a vessel and enough food, fuel, and water to get home. They agreed. I only need a few days. With the detour, I will be ten days, maybe two weeks, behind you."

"Do you want us to wait for you? We can stay here and all travel home together."

Illy considered that. "No. I think I want some alone time. Time to grieve, consider the offer, really think about what I want to do next."

That I understood. "Consider it done."

CHAPTER 43

"MUUUMM!!!" ILLY'S GIRLS' SQUEALS could be heard in Edinburgh, making me close my eyes as the needles pierced my skull. The electric car she was driving hadn't even stopped before she was dragged out and swamped with children. Cam and I stood back and watched. Once the deluge had stopped, she checked each child in turn. *Looking at Summer and Ally's stomachs,* I noted. Alasdair and Sera were hanging off her as she turned to Cam and me, hugging both of us.

"Let me unpack and settle in. Can we come for dinner? Likely there is nothing at our place."

"There isn't," I agreed. "We have been feeding them all. One more is no problem."

"So?" I asked as I heard her come through the passage between our homes. She watched me as I set the table. Cam lifted the roast out of the oven. The children could still be heard running around outside, hyped up from all the excitement.

"I agreed—with several conditions. They accepted them all."

My heart sank as I laid the cutlery. "You can be rather persuasive. What were your conditions?"

"The most important thing, while I will visit Clava and Auckland at least once per year, I will live here, with my family."

"They agreed to that?" I dropped the fork, turning to face her.

"They did. With the radio network reinstated, I can guide the teams from here."

"What were the other conditions?"

"That I chose my team to help me lead."

"Team?"

"With your consent, I would like you to be in charge of medicine for the Collective."

"*Me*? I have the least experience of anyone."

"You. You are fair, thorough, and will do anything to assist your patient. There are teams of specialists, but they need a lead. I can't imagine anyone better."

"A leadership role? You were born for this, Frey," Cam said, removing the oven mitts.

"And you," Illy turned to Cam. "I want you to lead the food security project for all communities. Checking in with them remotely, assisting them with quantities, variety, companion planting, and all the other processes you have implemented here to make our growing program such a success. You have already done this on several sites, but now it is time to spread your skills more widely. Quite a few communities are struggling to produce enough nutritious food."

Cam nodded. "Of course. Who else?"

"I stopped at Newgrange on my way here. I have asked Tadhg to oversee communications to all communities. He has already said yes and will reactivate the radios. Callie, Magali, and Bridget will also play key roles in my leadership team. I want people I can trust, who are resilient, but fundamentally are honest people."

"What about the Nexus? Will you reactivate it?" I asked.

"No. That will not be reinstated. I think we can all agree that the risks associated with unregulated travel are still too high. It is possible, one day. For now, journeys between communities should be planned and carefully scheduled."

"Are you happy?" I asked cautiously as I sat beside her.

"I am, you know. I really am. I feel like I can make a difference, ensure equality across all communities. Ensure resources are evenly spread. I have lots of ideas." Her eyes twinkled.

"Oh, I am sure you do."

"Did you learn who the other Players were?"

"Some. We worked out who the players were on Auckland and Clava, and they confirmed it was Mike's twins who broke into your home and cut up your photos."

"They aren't here."

"They turned up at Clava but were detained. When I implement my project, they will be released. But I learned why they used Biblical references."

"Why?"

"Well, of all things, it was just for simplicity. They set missions in code. But soon, they realized that the books they had differed in version. So page 15 of a

Harry Potter book in Australia might differ from a book in Orkney."

"That makes sense."

"But the Bible had specific chapter and verse, and that doesn't change based on the version."

"So it was religious?"

"Not at all. They used it as a validation process. Each of the fires, the slaughter of animals, the killings, they were all linked to a biblical reference. It was how they confirmed they had followed through on their mission. Gained status in the group."

"Do you know who the others are across all communities?"

"Not yet. But that is my first project."

EPILOGUE

Four Years Later

THE ALARM SOUNDING MADE me cringe. There were no arrivals on the schedule. Illy had mandated that movement to and from communities was highly regulated and always approved in advance.

"It's the *Belisama!*" I squealed as I watched the camera footage from our office. Cam came racing in from the kitchen, drying his hands, standing behind me, squinting.

"You need glasses!" I teased.

"Maybe I do. But there is no optometrist here, so it will need to wait."

"I hear there is a wedding, and you didn't invite me!" Sorcha's voice called as she descended the valley in her electric vehicle. Di was beaming beside her.

"You cut your hair!" Cam called.

"Too bloody hot in Australia to have long hair. Besides, the kids were so fascinated with it. I thought I would leave it behind as a gift."

"Where is Sam?" I asked as Kendra climbed from the back seat, throwing herself at me.

"Look at you! All grown up."

"Sam is now a father," Sorcha announced proudly, grey streaks framing her face. I had never seen her before with short hair, but it suited her. A blunt bob to suit her blunt personality. "I have two grandchildren. He and his wife, Dewi, had twins a year ago, or I would have returned sooner."

"I am surprised I dragged her away at all," Di beamed, waiting until Kendra and Mei had finished hugging me. "You should see her. Being a granny suits her. She spoils those kids rotten."

Sorcha glowered at Di, who hadn't aged a day. "I told you not to call me that!"

"Granny!" Cam teased. "I can't believe it! How wonderful!"

"I hear Louis is finally getting married. You might also be a grandparent soon!"

"How did you know?" Cam's mouth gaped.

"I have my ways. Who is the lucky lass?"

"Isla and Fraser's middle girl, Iona."

"She is lovely!" Di squealed. "And the others? How are they all?"

"Well, since you left and I work for Illy, Katrin has taken over management of the med center and is more demanding than Sorcha ever was. Ally is a trainee doctor too, and they are constantly at each other, disagreeing on ways to treat patients. Fortunately, Kat is older, but Ally is super smart, and if the two of them actually worked together, I think they would find a way to make humans immortal. But they challenge each other, and their ideas are cutting edge. I suspect Hamish keeps going up to the still to get away from them. Xanthe started training as a vet, but that didn't work out. So she is the headteacher, now that Bridget works for Illy. She is wonderful at it, and the children adore her. Louis still works in agriculture, which freed up Cam for project work."

"And the little ones?"

"We told Sera and Cait that they are full siblings on their tenth birthday last year, and it has bonded them even more. They sleep in the same room every night, alternating between Illy's place and ours. They have beds in both, so we never know where we will find them. They are closer than the twins, which is saying something. Alasdair is fine, as are all of Isla's. Jorja and Bridget's girls have partnered up and moved away to Newgrange."

"How is everyone at Sessrúmnir?" Cam asked.

"They will never really recover from all those years they spent underground, physically, I mean. Mentally they are thriving, and that was more important. Those children born there have recovered better than the older ones, their bodies being more resilient. There are four babies now, and the Punan have taken over everything. Growing crops, raising fish, repairing the dome, running a school. I even trained Sam to replace me as the medico once I realized he would stay. We returned to the storage facility Illy showed us and have managed to build a bigger and more permanent structure with all the spare panels, so they can expand as the time comes. They grow the moss alongside the aquaponics tanks and are quite adept at planting it out in the additional space, rehabilitating the earth.

Sam and some of them have learned to drive so they can source anything they need. They know they are safe, and they are happy."

"How did you know about Louis?"

"Your friend Illy sent word to Auckland and forced a small team to travel, with communications equipment no less, to Sessrúmnir. Now I can keep in touch with Sam and the kids. They aren't isolated anymore."

"You are staying?"

"Of course. This is my home. Though I may need to oust your daughter. I doubt the team will cope with both of us."

"She will put up a fight!" I laughed. "Kat is doing a wonderful job. The team loves her."

"We nearly killed the team Illy sent. We had seen no one in years and were still fearful about Kiewa finding us. Fortunately, we had met one of them on Clava during Di's treatment. When he finished shaking, he told us about all the wonderful initiatives Illy has implemented. Did she really set up a training program and force all the team on Clava and Auckland to teach there?"

"She did. She is thriving," I admitted. "She told them they had a free ride for too long, and it was their turn to give back. She faced a little pushback in the early months. I think they regretted their decision to appoint her as Chief, but now everyone recognizes the gift we have all been given. We live facing the future, not in fear."

"Even those little asswipes who tried to kill our kids?"

"Even them. That was one of her more creative efforts. Illy conducted a full investigation as her first project as Chief and identified them all. She implemented an exchange program where they were transported to other communities, those less well off, and made them work their asses off for twelve months."

Sorcha roared with laughter. "Illy always believed in thought reform through labor. Did it work?"

"Did it ever. Twelve months spent in scorching desert communities, weeding, plowing fields, digging holes to plant trees, and building homes and schools made them all realize how good they had it. We haven't heard a peep since. Illy gave Sophie and Sanjiv a particularly challenging assignment in Africa. Those three that actually committed the murders were permanently relocated."

"Did you know any of them?"

"I didn't. But it was one of Stefan's boys who murdered Ceri on Clava. Let's just say that was a little awkward."

"Wow. So we weren't too far off in our suspicions. Who was it here?"

"Aroha, as we learned from Isla. The others were Mike's twin boys, Evan and Gabriel."

"Seriously?"

"Aroha was the one who poisoned Summer, but Seraphine was the target. We saw Aroha when we dropped Taki off on August Island. We haven't heard from Jamie and Jacinda since, but I think it is time we made contact. The boys were the ones who broke into our home and destroyed my photos, leaving the message on the mirror.

"And you?" Sorcha looked at us. "How are you two? No more silliness?"

"I don't think we have ever been happier," I admitted, slipping my arm around Cam, who was beaming at me. "We have an awesome boss. We work for the benefit of all communities, have enough time to enjoy our family and friends. Our kids are independent but happy in their lives. We are safe. Life is pretty good."

"But having you home completes it." Cam grinned at Sorcha and Di.

Cam and I sat in the front row beside Isla and Fraser as we watched Louis and Iona pledge their lives to each other. Commitment ceremonies here were relaxed, with each couple making a formal statement of intent. Louis gazed at her with such adoration that it made my heart sing. We might be grandparents sooner than I thought.

"Do you remember our first commitment?" Cam whispered when there was a lull in proceedings.

"I do."

"I wouldn't change a thing."

As I watched our son kiss his bride, I was surprised to realize, neither would I.

BOOK CLUB QUESTIONS

1. Did they make the right choice to take the children and run to an isolated community?

2. While on the vessel, they tell the girls they are immune. Should they have told the girls this? Can children comprehend something of this magnitude at six years old?

3. Heuristics is the name given to natural biases in the way people think. It is natural to have bias, and we all have them. What bias do you have? How do you ensure it doesn't impact your everyday interactions?

4. Mental health is a theme that runs throughout the Antipodes series. In this book, Freyja struggles with PTSD after her experiences on Clava and this leads to her making some poor choices. She finally confesses to Cam what happened to her. Should we normalize the conversation of speaking about mental health the way we do about physical health? Or is it a private matter?

5. Freyja admits that seeing Cam with Laetitia destroyed her, seeing him happy with another woman. Would you feel the same or did she overreact as a result of her trauma?

6. While in Kiewa, Sorcha encounters Angie, a heavily pregnant woman who has had thirteen children, and whose husband refuses to have a vasectomy, with no other birth control options available. She encourages Freyja to sterilise the woman. Did Freyja do the right thing?

7. Freyja describes the lifestyle of warriors chosen to go to the afterworld Sessrumnir, as feasting and drinking beer for eternity. Cam surprises her by saying that his priorities would be family and time. What are your life priorities?

8. Several life altering events occurred at the girls' seventh birthday in Kiewa. Which surprised you the most?

9. After Sanjiv tries to kill Caitlin, they learn about The Players, who set missions for each other, including killing the chosen children. But their rationale was that the children were abominations, manufactured "freaks" and not normal. While killing is never justified, are they right in some way?

10. While in India, Ashton finally confesses that he was the architect of the scheme to produce immune children. Was his reasoning sound? Did the scientists have an obligation to produce an immune generation to ensure the survival of the human race?

11. When they travel to Borneo, Freyja feels guilty, saying that it isn't her role to knock the Nexus offline and affect the lives of many. Is she correct?

12. When they discover the twenty-two Punan people living underground, they continue with their plan and relocate them. What other alternatives did they have? What challenges will the Punan face?

13. What changes would you make if you were appointed as Head of the Collective?

AUTHOR BIO

T.S. SIMONS IS AN Australian author of Scottish heritage. Living in the alpine region of Australia, she believes in the values of sustainability and community in a world where we place greater value on possessions than people. The Antipodes series addresses the question—if we gave young people the opportunity to start over, would we replicate the mistakes of the past?

She holds Bachelor and Master's degrees from Monash University and enjoys strong coffee, travelling, mythology, and snow skiing while attempting to live as sustainably as possible. She is owned by two rather bossy standard schnauzers and two rescue cats who co-manage her household.

The Antipodes series includes Project Hemisphere, The Space Between, Infinity, Circle of Protection, and Sessrúmnir. She is now working on a related series, The Latitude Series.